A Prior Engagement

S. L. Scott

A Prior Engagement

Print Edition

Copyright © S.L. Scott, 2013

All Rights Reserved.

Published in the United States of America
ISBN: 978-1-940071-02-2

Cover design by Jada D'Lee
Cover image by Ryan J. Lane

For My Kids

Follow Your Dreams

.

A Personal Message

I've traveled a path—long and winding. Sometimes I had vast views of the ocean and sometimes I couldn't see beyond the trees. You were there with me always, supportive and strong, like-minded and challenging, peaceful and inspirational. I will always remember and cherish you for taking this journey with me.

I give all my love, gratitude, and my forever to my amazing husband and best friend. My kids and my family are everything to me. Thank you for supporting me as I follow my dreams.

Thank you to the lovely fandom community that accepted me with open arms and embraced my stories. You have touched my heart, warmed my soul, and encouraged me.

Not only are the following women talented, but they are also smart, funny, and great friends. Thank you: Becca, Irene, Jada, Jenn, Marni, Marla, Mary, and Susi for all of your hard work on this book, but also for your friendship and support, and for suffering through the endless emails, DM's, IM's, tweets, texts, calls – yeah, you get the picture. Thank you. Special thanks to Wyndy and Sydney—you are wonderful friends.

There are people in your life that make it better just by being in it. These are those people to me: Flavia, Jennifer S., Kerri, Kirsten, Laura, Sonia, and Suzanne. You are all fantastic and I'm fortunate to know you. I treasure that we share so much of our lives like we do, and you make me smile.

"Happy are those who dream dreams
and are ready to pay the price
to make them come true."
~ Leon Joseph Cardinal Suenens

Chapter 1

Forty-five minutes into British Literature, Professor Lang unexpectedly dismissed his students. Everleigh Wright pushed her long brown hair behind her shoulders before piling her belongings back into her bag as a scruffy faced, wrinkled-shirted boy scooted past her. She stood and followed behind him as he headed to the end of the aisle toward the exit.

That scruffy face belonged to William Ryder, who had noticed the attractive brunette the prior week when the professor called on her to debate the issue of novels of the 1900s being over-romanticized because women writers had found a market niche. She said, "Women writing for women is not a niche, not then and not now. Back then, they were being practical. Women authors knew what they wanted to read and weren't finding it in celebrated male authors of the time. When I think romance, I think Austen, not Dickens."

William leaned forward to get a better look at the girl attached to the lovely voice. She was pretty and soft-spoken, but precise in her words, and held a conviction that deserved attention.

After her confident statement, she had captured

William's full attention. But he also knew Austen was an easy answer and he bet if challenged, she could also defend male writers of that era.

When he passed her by, he glanced down, not able to bring himself to speak to her. The atmosphere in the auditorium and prying eyes of the other students was intimidating. He knew she hadn't paid him any attention anyhow, at least none he was aware of. Although, he was well aware the cute girl never spoke to anyone else in class either, and often appeared to be daydreaming in the middle of the lecture class.

As William walked down the stairs of the large auditorium, he glanced back at her one last time before he exited. He knew he wouldn't see her again for two days and wanted a visual to carry with him.

Following the students out of the building, he tossed his bag over his shoulder, deciding to head to his favorite coffee shop.

It was a warm spring day, and he walked to campus today instead of riding his bike like he had all winter when he had to hurry for cover from the cold. While walking the two Manhattan blocks from campus to the locally-owned coffeehouse, Bean There, he let his mind wander back to the girl from class. He wondered what her name was and what she daydreamed about because she often seemed lost in her own thoughts. She likes to wear fitted cardigans and pants, not jeans. Did she always look so put together and proper? Did she ever run around in sneakers and workout clothes like most girls on campus? She made the effort for school, but what did she wear in other facets of her life?

He was smiling as he entered the coffee shop, but felt a little ridiculous as if his thoughts were visible for the world to see.

William ordered his usual—double espresso black

and plain scone. The barista had started preparing it as soon as he opened the door. She set the coffee and scone down on the counter, and asked, "Would you like anything else today, William?" Leaning over the counter a little closer to him, she smiled.

Looking up for the first time since he had entered the small shop, their eyes met, and he said, "No, thank you. How are you today, Tracy?" Because Tracy was always friendly when she served him, he returned the smile and set his money on the counter, leaving the change as her tip.

"I'm really good. Um, so how are you?" She asked in a chipper voice.

"I'm good. I have a lot of reading to do and need a coffee boost. It's gonna be a long day." On that note, he turned and walked toward his regular table, but stopped when he saw the table was occupied. A wave of indignation rolled through him, but dissipated just as fast. The girl from class who had occupied more of his thoughts than he was comfortable admitting, had stolen his table.

William couldn't hide the smile that erupted when he realized the opportunity presenting itself.

"Your table's taken," Tracy said. There was an edge of anxiety to her tone he picked up on. "But there are plenty of other ones, or you could try a seat at the counter today?"

He wasn't deterred, he was hopeful. Before moving toward the table again, he mumbled, "Yeah, sure, another table. Good idea."

After dropping his bag on the table closest to his usual spot, he settled into his chair.

Everleigh was startled by the bag landing loudly on top of the table next to hers. She glanced at the well-worn burgundy backpack and then around the small shop. There

3

were only two other customers in the place and they sat on a couch together near the front window, which meant there were plenty of other tables available. She felt uncomfortable that someone had chosen to sit so close to her.

Looking up at the guy next to her, she was both cautious and intrigued. A straight nose led to a smile under eyes that were closer to navy than sky blue in color. She didn't stare at him long, although she did notice his handsome features hidden under the days-old scruff he was sporting. His hair was unkempt, a lot like his clothes, and was disorderly and wild, which made her wonder if he was too.

She went back to reading the essay on her laptop, trying to ignore the guy who sat uncomfortably close. Picking up where she left off, she began typing again, but found her attention drifting back to him. Sneaking peeks at him out of the corner of her eyes, she noticed his textbook teetering on the edge of the table as he unloaded his laptop. With a quick swoosh, it landed with a bang on the floor between them, causing her to flinch. Her reflexes sent her hand to pick it up just as his did, and their heads hit in the process.

She grabbed her head. "Ouch!"

Without thinking, his hand covered the one she had pressed to her forehead. Angling his head, he said, "I'm sorry. Are you all right?"

She slipped her hand out from under his, which left his against her skin, putting pressure on the spot that hurt the most. Her skin tingled under his touch, and her heart started to race.

His lips parted and he sighed.

"I'm okay. It was an accident." She smiled, returning

4

her hand to her head, but was obstructed by his, which remained.

He was reluctant to remove his, but was unable to justify its place on her any longer without seeming like a weirdo.

"Are you all right?" she asked, and strangely already missed his touch.

When their eyes met for the first time, he was entranced by the deep, oceanic blue of her eyes. "Yes. I am now." He smiled at the way she let a little laugh escape and then he laughed with her.

Feeling comfortable in this odd meeting, she tapped his textbook, and asked, "Are you taking this class?"

"No, I like to read college textbooks for fun."

She didn't get his joke and didn't say anything more, feeling embarrassed for asking in the first place.

"No, I'm kidding. I'm in your class. Professor Lang's class," he said, making up for his bad joke.

"Oh. I... uh... I apologize. I haven't seen you in there." She felt rude for not recognizing him.

He reassured her, not wanting to lose her interest because of some stupid remark he made. "There are over a hundred people in the class. It's okay."

Everleigh opened her mouth to say something, but the words didn't come. She didn't know what to say to that, so she closed her mouth, and pondered his statement a moment longer. Pointing at her laptop, she felt sheepish. "I have a lot of work to do and not much time left to do it in."

William found her reaction fascinating, not quite typical. He didn't usually have trouble talking to girls, most of the time they even initiated the conversation. But this girl was given the perfect opportunity to continue the conversation she had started, and she didn't take it. He began overanalyzing their entire exchange starting with how she flinched when his book fell. Her expression exposed a reaction he didn't quite understand. It was just a book falling, after all, but she flinched. Then she seemed to shift back, and relaxed, enjoying their interaction. After a few minutes, she reverted back, and went to work as if nothing had happened. Maybe she's telling the truth, and he's over-thinking the situation.

As Everleigh pretended to read her laptop screen, she was thinking how nice it would be to have a friend who goes to the same college, even better that they shared a class. She spied on him, and thoughts of a 'study buddy' began to cross her mind. Knowing Tom would never consent to her having a friend he didn't know, she returned her gaze back to her own studies, trying to forget the crazy idea before it developed into a possibility.

They didn't say another word, but every now and then she could feel the weight of his eyes on her and she *liked* it.

Over the next hour, she could feel something building between them, a heavy sensation—a tension of sorts. She didn't have time to explore the feelings because she had to leave. After packing her bag, she stood up and glanced over at him. He was engrossed in highlighting his textbook as she walked around the table. Out of politeness and because she wanted to, she stopped, turned toward her neighbor, and said, "Good-bye." Then she left without giving him an opportunity to say anything in response.

She was so quiet when she spoke that William wondered if he was supposed to hear her pleasantry. Regardless, he knew it was for him and that made him smile... *again*. He glanced up and saw Tracy grinning at him as she did a little wave of acknowledgment. William felt embarrassed he'd been caught smiling because of the girl who just left his side. It was obvious by her friendly gesture that Tracy assumed he was smiling at her. She's cute, but he wasn't drawn to her like the girl he'd bumped heads with. He returned his focus back to his book and finished highlighting the sentence he wanted to memorize later.

Everleigh made her way two blocks up from Bean There and waited on the side street as instructed the evening before. The car pulled up to the curb promptly at four. She opened the door and tucked her body into the sleek, new sports car. Thomas Whitney loved to show off and this car was his new toy. She believed cars in Manhattan were ridiculous, but would never say such a thing to him. "Hi," she said in the tone she used to test the waters of her fiancé's mood.

"How was your day, Everleigh?" Tom's deep brown eyes drank her in with approval.

She was relieved to hear he was in a good mood. "It was educational." She laughed at her own joke. *He didn't.* "We're starting on the Austen era, so I can't complain. You know how much I love her work."

"That's nice. I'm sure you'll do great." He smiled, and patted her on the knee. He was four years older than she was, but often treated her as a child, which she found frustrating and annoying.

But in a turn, his hand slid up her leg and squeezed her thigh, a clear indication of his intentions later that night.

She tensed, undecided how she felt about his gesture at that moment. She should've appreciated that he was touching her gently, but she didn't.

Glancing at him, she noticed his usually meticulous styled hair was in slight disarray and needed a trim. She liked his hair a little longer. The wavy blonde locks made him look younger than his personality made him seem, but she knew to keep such thoughts to herself.

His shirt was a little wrinkled. She only noticed because his tie was loosened at the collar, which was unusual for him.

"How was your day?" she asked curious to why he looked worn out.

Closing his eyes briefly, Tom rolled his neck to the side to release the tension. She knew he carried it in his shoulders. "It was fine." His response was short as was his tone.

He gave her leg another squeeze, and she took a deep breath to counteract the gasp that wanted to escape instead. His touch was all wrong, but she remained still and composed. If she was truthful, it wasn't just this one time. His touch hadn't felt right in a long time. *He* hadn't felt right in a long time. She tamped down those feelings and concentrated on the present. Dwelling on memories of the past wouldn't change her future.

After buckling her seatbelt, she folded her hands in her lap as he pulled into traffic. The distance to her home wasn't far, but with city traffic, it always took longer than it should. As it started to sprinkle on the windshield, Everleigh directed her attention to the people on the sidewalk.

When the drizzle turned to rain, Tom asked, "Aren't you glad you're not out there?"

She nodded to please him. It was easier to agree. She didn't want to start an argument over something he didn't expect a response to in the first place. He often asked

8

questions he wanted her to agree to, not give her opinion.

Trapped inside the car, she wished she were out there with the strangers on the street. She couldn't remember the last time she walked in the rain, or even got caught in it, reminding her of an old song her nanny used to sing. After thoughts of pina coladas crossed her mind, she tried to remember the last time she had walked home from school. Before today, the Town Car was always prompt, picking her up at four o'clock. It was a very manageable walk, but she struggled to remember it.

Although the change in cars was nice, the pressing silence saddened her when she realized how closed-off she had become to the rest of the world. She watched it roll by from the confines of the luxury car, knowing she was allowed to touch it, but not be a part of it. She didn't realize what she was truly choosing when she chose Tom, but four years later it was becoming quite apparent.

The doorman rushed to escort his residents to the protection of the awning that led to the shiny glass and brass doors just as Tom pulled up to the curb. Walter opened the car door and greeted the couple with a smile. "Good afternoon, Miss Wright, Mr. Whitney."

"Good afternoon, Walter. Only a drop off today. Take care of my girl." Tom winked at Everleigh before he leaned over and kissed her on the cheek.

His gentle kiss reminded her of how sweet he could be when he chose to be. His youthfulness was showing. That was the side of him she had fallen in love with, which was also the side of him she thought he'd outgrown. "You're not coming up?"

"I can't, but I'll be back around six-thirty."

She nodded as she stepped out of the car then dashed for the door. Walter raced to keep up, but she got to

9

the door first. She held it open for her doorman, enjoying the reversal of roles.

Tom hit his palm against the steering wheel twice he was so mad. He hated when she acted childish because it was a glaring reminder of how much more he needed to teach her. Angry, he pulled into traffic, realizing he would need to have another discussion with her about her behavior. That was an issue he thought he'd already covered.

A sudden rush of freedom swept over her as she rode the twelve floors up. Once inside, she went straight to her room.

After one loud knock on the door, her sister Audrey barged in, making herself comfortable on the bed. "Hey, Evie, what's going on?"

Her sister lounged across her bed watching Everleigh stand in front of her large bay window.

"It's raining," Everleigh said wistfully, her thoughts still on the inclement weather.

"Yeah, I know. I'm bummed. I really wanted to go out."

Surprised by the whine in her sister's tone, Everleigh turned around, and asked, "Why don't you then?"

"Well." Audrey paused before speaking again as if in debate. "I guess I could—"

"You should. I can go with you." Everleigh grabbed her sister's hand and dragged her toward the elevator.

The doors opened, but Audrey hesitated, stopping her sister from moving forward. "We don't have our coats—"

In her excitement, Everleigh lowered her voice as if to share a secret. "I know."

They rode down together and as soon as the elevator doors reopened, Everleigh ran like she was escaping. In her mind, that was exactly what she was doing even if for only a few minutes. By the time she reached the sidewalk, the last drop of rain hit her hair then the clouds parted to reveal the afternoon sun. Releasing one long exhale of disappointment, she struggled to keep the tears at bay.

"What's going on with you?" With her hands on her hips, Audrey's face showed her concern.

"I... I don't remember the last time I felt rain. I wanted to feel the rain again. That's all."

Since Everleigh was already outside, she made the decision to stay there, and started walking down the street. As the distance grew behind her, Walter stepped outside and asked, "Miss Wright, are you okay?"

Tom had always been very adamant about her being escorted down the streets of Manhattan, even if it was in the well-heeled Upper East Side. She hummed trying to rid her mind of Tom's condescending voice echoing inside her head. She didn't want to over think a simple walk or feel guilty for doing something for herself.

Having heard her parents and Tom's warning about the impropriety of the surrounding area to her posh neighborhood many times, she took a deep breath as a feeling of liberation came over her. Going against their direct wishes, she continued walking the four blocks to the section of Central Park she remembered being closest to her building. Holding her breath in anticipation, she hoped it was the part of the park she remembered from when she was a child.

She gasped when the park came into view. It was

breathtaking. The flowers were starting to emerge from the dead of winter and the trees were showing their newest green leaves. The yellow tulips and the Redbud trees were in full bloom and she could see raindrops falling from the lowest leaves of the Weeping Willow off to the left. This park was the most beautiful place she had ever seen. Amongst the beauty of new life, she found herself wanting the same for herself.

Inhaling her surroundings, she enjoyed the scents of freshly cut grass and the recent rain mingling with the breeze. With hope in her heart, she allowed herself five minutes of bliss in this little piece of heaven before she decided it was time to head back home, but not before promising herself she would return soon.

Two hours later, she was dressed and ready for the night ahead. She plastered on her expected smile and walked out to a gathering of their families. Tom greeted her with a kiss on the cheek while handing her a glass of champagne. "You look beautiful, darling."

She continued to smile, finding pleasure in the knowledge she could still excite him in that way. "Thank you." She kept her tone polite and formal, the way she was raised.

She joined the ladies in their genteel conversations of brunches, ballets, and charities to keep up appearances while sipping her champagne as a distraction from the shallowness of it all.

Dinner conversation at the upscale restaurant was easy. She had mastered this social game and Tom was always happier in these settings, which eased her mind, even if only for a moment. She also knew she made him proud of her in these situations. She was charming, learning early in her upbringing that others loved to talk about themselves. She gave them that opportunity. She also let Tom bask in the praise he received on his choice of partner, though he never used the word partner when speaking to her.

This was a good night and it made her wonder how he would act once they were alone. He was unpredictable and she felt conflicted. She had wanted his appreciation for so long that when he gave it to her, it made her question the negative thoughts she had been having recently.

Chapter 2

William left the coffeehouse an hour after the girl, convinced his fascination in her was well-placed. She was different from the other girls he knew. She was quiet and thoughtful, insightful, and a little quirky. She didn't flirt or question him to see what he had to offer. She had an innocence about her he found enchanting and he liked the way her face lit up over the little things, like the coffee drink she had ordered. Behind her buttoned-up image, she seemed to appreciate simpler things in life like he did.

Maybe it was the short time he spent with her, or the second cup of coffee, but he was feeling energized, so he decided to ride the ferry to Staten Island to visit his family. He hopped onto the dock, grabbed a cab to the house he grew up in, and entered as if he still lived there. After he made a sandwich and watched the news, his brother Dallas sauntered in with his girlfriend Abby in tow.

"Well, I guess that's one way to ruin a mood," Dallas said, signaling toward his brother who was sitting on the couch with his feet propped up on the coffee table.

"Good to see you too." William waved to them over

the back of his head.

"We have thirty minutes until Mom's home. Couldn't you have come for a visit just thirty minutes later?"

William laughed because he had blocked their teenage romp. "I'll keep that in mind next time. Hey, Abby, good to see you."

"Yeah, you too, Will." She took Dallas by the hand and said, "We always have my house."

"Hey! Whatever happened to good old angst, maybe even a little romance?" William sat up to look over his shoulder at the young couple, but a pillow hit him in the face.

Dallas turned to Abby and explained his brother's view on dating. "Remember, he's into old-fashioned courting and stuff like that." Dallas and Abby went upstairs, making a quick getaway.

William knew they were hoping to use up the few minutes of unsupervised time they had left and he let them be.

An hour later, food was on the table and the dinner conversation was lighthearted as his family caught up on their days' activities. He took in each of their faces—mom, dad, and brother— memorizing their smiles and the lively sounds of their interactions. Living in the city, he missed this. There was security here amongst his tight-knit family.

He watched as his dad took his mother's hand above the table and kissed it, quiet appreciation for the dinner, but William suspected it was more than just thanks for the food. William had seen his father do this a million times growing up, but now, as he really opened his eyes to the bond they shared, he noticed his mom's smile showed all of the love she held for his dad, which was the same kind of love that William also hoped to find one day. He wanted a love so strong that it withstood the years, the hardships, and thrived beyond the honeymoon. He wanted what his parents share—laughter, support, and devotion.

After dinner, they watched pre-season baseball before William's dad drove him to catch one of the last ferries back to the city. He was a true New Yorker in every sense and had never felt shame for being from Staten Island. He was proud of his upbringing. The city was his playground though, and he often drew literary inspiration when he walked the darkened streets.

Something he realized once he moved from home is that he would never trade lives with the Park Avenue crowd. He thought it was sad they would never understand New York the way he did. Some had never had a hotdog from a vendor down in Battery Park while watching the Statue of Liberty's lights turn on at sunset. Many have never ridden the ferry over to Staten Island to watch minor league baseball at its finest. In his opinion, they lived on the glossy surface while he lived in the belly. He experienced everything life had to offer here and loved it.

When he entered his second floor studio apartment, he flicked on the small lamp in the corner. It wasn't a great reading lamp, but it would do and was comforting because his parents had bought it for him.

He readied for bed, and then climbed under his cotton sheets, pulling them up to his stomach. He laid on his back, resting his head on his hands and reflected on his day, a nighttime routine. As he lay there, he thought back to the girl at the coffee shop, letting his mind wander to what her story might be. For some reason, his instincts told him there was more to come with her, and he smiled at the hopeful thought before falling asleep.

Uptown, with all the expectations Everleigh's

parents had of raising a well-respected young woman, their rules were lax when it came to her fiancé. They adored Tom and encouraged the relationship before Everleigh had reached dating age. At twenty-two years of age, she spent the night at his place on a regular basis with their approval.

Twenty-seven blocks away from William's small apartment, Tom was tipsy and wooing his girlfriend with kisses he knew she liked, hoping to get her in the mood. Little did he know, Everleigh had already given up the notion of resistance when the first kiss landed on her neck. She never took these moments for granted, giving in with hopes that tomorrow would bring the change she desired.

She disappeared into the bathroom to freshen up and slip into a sheer pink nightie. She chose pink knowing his mood. Tonight did not warrant passionate red and his kisses were stronger than a white negligee would justify. She settled on the pink, which was appropriately in the middle of the two, just as his mood reflected.

Tom liked her lingerie color choice, which allowed him a figurative pat on the back. *Maybe she had learned more than he gave her credit for*, he thought while appreciating her body.

Just like the pink nightie, they made love not passionately and not too gently either, but somewhere between the two before falling asleep.

The next morning, Everleigh was reading the Arts section of the paper. She set it down as soon as Tom walked into the kitchen already showered, shaved, and dressed for work.

He voiced a disappointed grunt before pouring his own coffee. She had gotten caught up reading about a rare book collection on display at the public library downtown and had forgotten to bring his coffee to him, which explained the grunt.

She didn't relax when she stayed at Tom's apartment because she had to try and decipher his mood. She couldn't count on any consistency from day-to-day, which made it emotionally draining to her. "Good morning," she said, then took a quick sip of her coffee while gauging his reaction. "I apologize for not bringing your coffee to you."

"I don't ask much, Everleigh . . ." He let his sentence linger between them unfinished. It carried more in its meaning than he would admit and she felt the guilt weighing her down.

"I won't forget next time."

"I hope not." He skimmed the front page of the New York Times. The paper was wrinkled and she knew how much he hated his paper being wrinkled. "Did you find what you were looking for?" he asked, looking not at her, but at the section of the newspaper in front of her.

She took a deep breath to calm her nerves before responding. "Yes."

Thinking about their previous night, she wanted to bring sweet Tom back—the one that smiled more and the one that kissed her. Everleigh slipped off the bar stool and rubbed his shoulders as she kissed him on the cheek. He made it apparent her touch was not wanted and wriggled out of her reach.

"Don't forget I have poker tonight." He walked toward the door, his tone dismissive, leaving on that reminder.

Leaning forward, she gripped the counter for support, silently berating herself for letting him affect her like he did. She should be used to it by now, but after last night . . . he was an ever-changing tide that she would never be able to predict.

19

Taking another deep breath, she pushed the thought to the back of her mind, exhaling the breath, her anger, her disappointment, and him from her system.

"Have fun," she said right before the door closed.

Even though it was a warm day in late April, Tom's mood had been chilly. Looking out the window, she wanted sunshine, not rain. It was beautiful outside and she wasn't going to let him ruin the day. It was as if the clouds of her heart had cleared and the sun broke through, lighting her from within.

She went into her small corner of his large walk-in closet and pulled down a cotton sundress. She was dressing for sunshine, but also grabbed a cardigan just in case.

The chauffeur rang to let her know he was waiting to take her home and she left Tom's place the way he liked it, tidy as if she hadn't been there at all.

As she ran down the stairs of his building, preferring it to the elevator this morning, she got an idea. *What if she walked today?* Not for exercise, but for pleasure. She considered her options as she neared the doors leading to the waiting car.

Con: She knew Tom would not be happy when the driver reported she walked home instead. She could already hear his lecture in her head: "It's not of society and good breeding to be wandering the streets of New York unaccompanied and aimless in direction." It was his fancy way of saying no to her idea.

Feeling his words heavy on her heart and not able to come up with any 'Pros' to justify her actions to him, she got into the car. But another daring idea started forming and a plan was hatched on the way back. For appearances, she would arrive safely home. No bad reports, no witnesses, and no judgments could be made. She smiled, but quickly tugged her lip between her teeth, stifling the smile of excitement that was dying to reveal itself.

She thanked the driver as Walter held the door wide open for her. Okay, there was one witness she hadn't counted on—*Walter*. She walked into the lobby and waited at his desk for him to re-enter and sit down. "Walter, I was wondering if I could possibly ask a favor of you?" She wasn't above using a little harmless charm to get her way. She couldn't take her bag up to her family's apartment because her mother would be home and would want to spend time together, which would keep her from leaving. She couldn't risk it if she wanted to accomplish her day's mission.

"Yes, ma'am, of course."

"I want to see an exhibit downtown and was hoping I could store my bag behind your desk?"

He didn't question her though it would have been acceptable. "No problem," he replied as he took the overnight bag from her and hid it behind his desk. "It will be here when you return."

"I shouldn't be long." She reached for the door not wanting to bother him with the task, but stopped before she left, and said, "Thank you, Walter."

She rushed into the sunlight of the morning feeling whimsical. She used to be more carefree, but she tended to avoid any thoughts of her girlish dreams of how she envisioned her future. Those memories would make her sad and it was too pretty of a day to be sad.

Feeling energized, fifteen blocks passed under her feet faster than she thought possible and she wasn't the least bit tired. She decided right there on the steps of the public library that she would start walking more. This city had too much to offer to only see it through the tinted glaze

21

of a car window, no matter how nice the car window was.

The library was majestic and still one of her favorite places in all of New York City. She climbed halfway up the stairs before stopping to admire Patience and Fortitude, the marble gargoyle lions that guarded the library's main entrance, before carrying on.

The doors were already open, displaying the information for the rare book collection. She made her way to the Genealogy Room, by far the most beautiful room in the entire library, and stopped to take a deep breath. She could smell the age of the books and the wisdom this place long held. She exhaled, reveling in the release of the tension she carried with her these days.

There weren't many people here to see the exhibit, which allowed Everleigh the chance to examine each book without interference. At one point her heart raced as the connection to her life began feeling too heavy to face on a seemingly nice day. The ugly truth was the books were locked away in the display case, secure from the world, but still on display for everyone to see and inspect. She shifted realizing the books mimicked her own life more than she liked.

Often told how beautiful, poised, and lucky she was, Everleigh would trade it all for a life outside the confines of her fated existence. She would be nothing more than someone's prized wife and only allowed to be a shadow of what she once was. Her heart slowed as she looked up from the books and gulped down any hope that had previously existed this morning when she tried to spread her wings by coming here.

Fifteen minutes later, she had already analyzed the five books in Homer's Iliad in the glass case before she moved to the next lot, not noticing someone next to her until she bumped right into him. Looking up, she apologized, but was surprised by the encounter. "Hello again," she said, keeping her voice respectful of the environment.

William looked at her, his attention to the books forgotten, and he smiled. "Hello again, yourself."

Even with the pause between them lengthening, neither one spoke too soon. They glanced to the books in front of them and then to the ones in front of the other. "After you," he said, swinging his arm in front of his body. William took a step backward allowing her to cross in front of him.

"Why thank you, kind sir." She giggled. Wanting to talk to him, but not sure what to say, she kept her eyes on the books, and whispered, "It's a great collection." Taking another step to her left, further away from him, she continued to view the books and break her connection with him.

His mind went into overdrive trying to come up with any reason to keep her there or to justify him moving along with her, but she knew he'd already seen the books she hadn't and vice versa. He shrugged. "Yeah, it's great."

Without his knowledge, she stole one last peek at him before moving to her left again.

By the time she finished viewing the collection of ancient poems, she looked around to see where he was, but found he had already gone. Leaving the library content in her mission, but confused by her lingering thoughts of him, she was reminded once again that she had no friends with her same interests. She did *have* friends, lots of friends and even more acquaintances. But her friends were of society, had finished their schooling, were married off, and had entered the committee game. They were busy chairing this committee or that committee, registering future children on the most premiere of preschool lists, and planning futures full of private Pilates lessons and cooking classes that would never be utilized beyond the lesson.

Everleigh knew her fate had been mapped out long before she even comprehended she had other options, and sadly, had accepted her reality.

She always felt her English degree would allow her to excuse her escape into books with dreams of one day working in publishing. She dreamed of discovering a hidden gem of a writer who somehow slipped through the fingers of major players in the industry.

But these were dreams she had during the daytime hours. She reserved her nighttime hours for the fantasies of the books she relied on for comfort—knights in shining armor, angst-ridden heroes who found their soul mates and the forbidden love that withstood all else in the end—even death. She never spoke of these dreams to anyone. Especially not Tom, who because of his privileged upbringing, believed his love *was* the ultimate gift.

She rolled her eyes thinking of his arrogance then brushed it off, accepting he would never change. She was resolved to the life she was committed to, like it or not.

She left the library deflated, reminded of her obligations and the promises she made as a teenager. But as she walked out of the Beaux-Arts building, the sun was still shining and it instantly brightened her mood.

She continued down the steps, almost skipping, when she heard someone yell, "Hey!"

She turned to see her classmate from inside the exhibit walking across one of the large platform steps toward her. He stopped two feet in front of her then adjusted down a step to give her the upper vantage point. They looked at each other, not rushing to speak. William, after a second, broke the silence first and asked, "How'd you like it?"

"It?"

"The book collection? How'd you like the collection? Pretty amazing, huh?" He shoved his hands in his jacket pockets, feeling awkward and full of self-doubt.

"Yes. I wish I could have touched them. To feel something that old and fragile and important . . ." Her eyes turned to the sky, letting her sentence trail off, and she smiled. She caught herself and dragged her wandering thoughts back to the present. "It was amazing." She took a step down, putting her closer to William and said, "I guess I'll see you tomorrow in class."

She didn't wait for him to respond since she was in a hurry. She walked down the rest of the stairs, embarrassed she had acted so weird in front of him, and blushed from the humiliation of what he must think of her.

William was in complete and total awe, watching her walk down the sidewalk. The twinkle in her eyes when she spoke of the books made him feel close to her. He had never met someone who felt the same as he did about books and he made a pact to get to know this girl. He had to find out more about this fascinating creature, *starting with her name.*

That night a hundred names crossed his mind, but none of them seemed to fit the beautiful girl. Her beauty wasn't common. She was a classic beauty with her straight nose, defined cheekbones, and slender neck. Tiffany, Pamela, or Christy didn't seem to suit her at all. They were pretty names, but improper for her. After spending way too long on this exercise, he finally fell asleep.

Chapter 3

Everleigh hurried home from the book exhibit in a great mood, even if she had embarrassed herself in front of the handsome guy from school. She smiled, enjoying the brief interaction a bit too much.

As she walked into the lobby of her building, Walter handed her bag back, and gave her a warning, "Mr. Whitney is in a foul mood."

"Thank you," she said. Her stomach flipped once before sinking further into her body. As she rode the elevator up, she felt ill-prepared for the potential confrontation.

She walked into the foyer of her family's apartment and looked around, feeling immediate relief when she discovered he wasn't there. She ran to her room, dropped her bag and shut the door behind her, feeling safe.

She needed a few minutes to gather her wits about her and to freshen up to look presentable again before seeing him. Unfortunately, she wouldn't get those few minutes because to her surprise, Tom was already waiting for her by the window.

She gasped out of fear, startled to find him there. His body language told her he was angry without him saying a word.

"You seem a bit on edge, darling," Tom said. His pace was slow, but calculated as he walked toward her. With every step he took, her heart beat louder in her chest, pounding in her ears.

She gulped, telling a lie. "No, not at all." She was terrified. It was the buildup that frightened her more than the act itself.

"Where were you today?"

"I, uh, I—"

"I, uh, I . . . that doesn't sound like you. You're usually very well-spoken. You're babbling and it's unbecoming. It's a simple question." He stopped in front of her and searched her eyes for the lie he knew was coming. It wasn't like her to lie, but she wasn't acting herself and that worried him.

"I went to see an exhibit on books—"

"Where was the exhibit?" he asked, turning his back to her while crossing his arms over his chest. Tom felt his insides seething and he hated feeling betrayed. So when she responded "Downtown," he lost it. She knew his body language enough to recognize what was coming, and terror caused her to cower against the door.

"Who were you with?" He fisted his hands at his side.

"No one." The words fumbled from her mouth as she pressed harder against the door behind her, shrinking further against it for safety.

He spun around and just as Everleigh thought she

28

might get a chance to beg for forgiveness for breaking an unspoken rule, it was over.

She held her hand against her flaming cheek as he walked around her. Opening the door, he stopped without looking. "Please don't keep us waiting for dinner. It's rude."

He didn't slam the door behind him as he left her room, but it would've felt more appropriate considering what had happened.

She exhaled out of relief because if that was the extent of her punishment this time, she could handle it. A simple slap, *no problem*, she convinced herself. The pain she had become accustomed to, but the daily emotional beating she still had trouble dealing with.

She changed clothes, heeding his request to hurry. After touching up her make-up, she pinned her hair back away from her face the way Tom preferred. The red from the slap faded minutes later, allowing her to join her family for an early evening cocktail.

After the first sip of wine, Everleigh eased back into her role flawlessly. She walked over and gave Tom a proper kiss on his cheek before whispering her apology in his ear. "I'm sorry." As she said those words, she found herself confused to why she should be sorry.

He looked to her, tilting his head, and clarified the situation. "I can't have you traipsing about the city by yourself, Everleigh. It's dangerous. Furthermore, what if someone had seen you downtown wandering the streets? Then I would have to explain that your mind tends to live in the clouds. Frankly, it's embarrassing. You need to be focused on our future. I hope you don't get any more unseemly ideas in that pretty head of yours." He paused as if waiting for something.

As expected, she filled in the blanks. "I apologize for

disobeying."

His hand slid down the graceful curve of her back, coming to rest on her bottom. With a small pat and smile, he said, "Thank you, darling. Let's be more aware of how our actions affect others from now on, shall we?"

"Yes." Hoping to move on from this topic, she asked, "How was your day?"

He smiled down at her knowing all he wanted was her loyalty, which to him also meant obedience, before he would walk down the aisle. This is how she would have to be all the time. He had patience, though it was starting to wear thin. She was worth it in beauty and pedigree and tonight, she proved she was still willing to learn which made him happy.

As an incentive for her, he raised his glass and proposed an autumn wedding date. Her family began celebrating a fall nuptial as Everleigh's stomach churned, magnifying all the doubts she'd been suppressing. She looked down at her wine, swirling it around the inside of the crystal glass a few times, hoping to shake the horrible feelings swirling inside of her.

When she looked up, she caught her sister's gaze. Audrey was the only one not toasting the supposedly happy occasion. Her little sister quirked an eyebrow up and tilted her head in question.

Everleigh put her shoulders back and lifted her chin up with a smile in place. She raised her glass, hoping to throw her sister off. Audrey didn't deserve to be burdened with her problems. Everleigh wanted nothing more than for her sister to have the life that she couldn't—happy and carefree. A seventeen-year-old shouldn't have to worry about her troubles behind closed doors.

When no one was looking, Everleigh rubbed her

temple and shook off the uneasy feeling that was lodging itself into her heart. She played the role of ecstatic fiancée until she crawled into her bed later that night, and cried until she fell asleep, finally able to release her true feelings with every tear cascading down her cheeks.

When William walked into class the next day, he tried to contain the pangs of excitement he felt. He scanned the room, attempting nonchalance, before spotting the girl eight rows up, sitting in the middle of the auditorium. He chose the ninth row and one seat past hers, sliding down and getting comfortable.

He wanted to talk to her, but had trouble finding the words that felt right in the moment.

She tried in earnest to concentrate on her note taking, but sensed someone behind her. She peeked over her left shoulder to find the now familiar boy listening to the professor's lecture while a pen hung from the side of his mouth.

Indulging in her crush, she stared at him, finding him more handsome than she should. He fascinated her and seemed thoughtful with his relaxed expression and the pen resting against his lips. Seeing him made her feel funny inside—in a good way.

She closed her eyes needing to stop herself from staring before she got caught, but when she reopened them, he was looking at her. He grinned, followed by a wink. Her mouth dropped open in shock and she spun back around as her faced flamed red. Sticking her own pen between her teeth, which she never did, she bit down hoping to ease the discomfort of being caught.

The class felt longer to her today. Every second of every minute weighed on her as it passed. Although, she felt a constant nag inside to look back at him, she feared being caught again and knew she wouldn't be able to handle another of those sexy winks. *Sexy?* She shook her head, surprised by her feelings.

She wanted to know his name and she wanted to know if he would be her school friend. No pressure at all. *I don't have any other school friends. Will you please fill that role for me?* She reined in the crazy idea and stood with the other students, realizing Professor Lang must have dismissed them while she was lost in thought.

Gathering her materials, she walked to the end of the row. He was standing there, almost as if he was waiting for her. An awkward smile graced her face then she filed in front of him. By the time she entered the hall, her cheeks were hot again just from his proximity. Uncomfortable in these new emotions, she escaped into the nearest restroom.

She wasted enough time to allow the students from her class to disperse from the hallway. Leaving the security of the bathroom, she exited the Lit building and made her way down the two blocks to Bean There.

Only having visited the coffee shop a few times, she already looked forward to coming after class because she enjoyed the quiet, relaxing ambiance. She also liked that she had seen *him* there before. She ordered her coffee and turned to go to the table she liked best, but to her annoyance, it was already taken.

The girl at the counter made a suggestion. "There are tables in the front by the window."

Everleigh was distracted though when she discovered *he* was the one occupying the table. With confidence, she walked toward him and set her books down on the table next to his as he had done two days earlier.

As she unloaded her laptop onto the small bistro table, *he* leaned toward her and introduced himself. "I'm William. What's your name?" He asked her this as if the world would stop if he didn't know.

Looking up at him, she replied, "I'm Everleigh. It's nice to officially meet you." She pushed her hand forward and he took it between his own, covering hers completely. The gesture was sweet and gentle, just like the boy doing it.

Everleigh looked from their joined hands straight into William's eyes where she saw a spark flicker as his pupils widened, drawing her in. She wanted to say her breath hitched at that moment in reflection, but it didn't. It lurched, swan-diving right off a cliff, then stopped altogether.

In that moment, she knew her life would be changed forever.

Chapter 4

Everleigh, *Everleigh*, E-V-E-R-L-E-I-G-H. Her name was perfect no matter how many times William repeated it. There was not a more fitting, more perfect name than Everleigh, he thought as he smiled at the girl. He was reluctant to release her hand, but did. "Everleigh is a beautiful name." He said her name because he wanted to see how it felt on his tongue, and it did not disappoint.

"Thank you, William," she said, emphasizing his name as if trying it out for the first time. It's not like she hadn't heard the name William before, but she'd never given it much thought until now. Now, it seemed fitting for the thoughtful man sitting next to her.

They sat together smiling, sitting close, but still feeling too distant. The warmth between them radiated, pulling them toward each other. Though their bodies never shifted, their hearts most definitely did.

Everleigh, he inwardly sighed. It might have been outward, too, but he hoped not.

"You can call me Evie if you like." She surprised herself by making this spur of the moment suggestion. Everyone called her Everleigh, except for her sister who

35

called her Evie, so she didn't know why she offered to let him call her that, but it felt right.

"I'd like that very much," he replied, and they both smiled. He didn't know if everyone called her Evie, but her offer felt special to him.

They returned to their individual studies, but couldn't stop from peeking at each other every couple of minutes, observing without the other person noticing. He studied her profile and she focused on his kind eyes.

More time passed before she eventually looked at her watch, and in a sudden shock of horror, she gasped. She bolted from her seat and slammed her laptop closed without turning it off, threw her notebook into her bag, and swung it over her shoulder. She hurried past William as he jumped up, confused by her actions. At the door, she stopped, taking the time to say good-bye, "I'll see you Friday, William."

Surprised by her sudden departure, he remained standing and watched her leave the coffee shop. "Bye, Evie." He rushed his words, but she was already gone and didn't hear him. He noticed Tracy watching him as he dropped back down into his chair. He gave a forced and tight smile, trying not to be concerned by Evie's abrupt exit.

He started reading his book again. Even though his eyes were scanning the pages, the words meant nothing. His entire mind was focused on Evie, not on the text.

Her voice replayed in his head over and over again. The way she said his name was as if they knew each other much more intimately and that made him smile.

Everleigh had too many thoughts going through her mind to formulate an excuse that would defend her tardiness. She still hadn't come up with any legitimate reason by the time she reached the car, so she resolved that the truth would be best and to face the consequences head on.

She lowered down into the spotless sports car, and smiled at Tom. "I'm sorry I'm—"

"Please don't insult me with some poor excuse you conjured up while keeping me waiting on you."

"Oh, I would never—"

He turned his hard glare on her, which made her lose her ability to speak. The fury in his eyes cut through and his disappointment was evident. She shrunk into her seat with complete fear of being trapped inside this car. Even though every bone in her body told her to run, she stayed in spite of her instincts. He put his hand on her leg, recognizing the fear he had created. With a calm and softened tone, he said, "I would appreciate if you don't keep me waiting again, but if you're going to be late, call me and let me know. I was worried."

This change in him surprised and relieved her. She couldn't believe he was going to let it go. Exhaling a long breath, her body relaxed as she buckled her seatbelt.

"I will." She leaned over the console and kissed him on the cheek.

They drove to his place and as they rode the elevator up to the apartment, he took her hand in his. After he unlocked the door, she retreated into the bedroom closet to her small designated section. But unaware of their plans for the evening, she walked into the kitchen where he was mixing a drink, and asked, "Are we staying in or going out tonight?"

"What would you like to do?" He was uncharacteristically leaning against the counter with his sleeves rolled up. He looked exhausted.

She knew what she wanted to do. "I'd like to stay in."

"Then we shall. Maybe we can order Chinese food and watch a movie."

She shook her head in disbelief wondering what had happened to Tom. *Chinese food and a movie?* That sounded nice and not like him to make such a suggestion.

"Does that sound good to you, Everleigh?"

"Yes, that sounds great. I'm going to change clothes for . . . Chinese food and a movie then." She went back into the bedroom, closed the closet doors, and walked over to her one allotted drawer in the dresser. She pulled out a T-shirt and for a split second, she almost opted for a pair of his boxers, but decided that wasn't a wise choice. Instead, she grabbed a pair of terrycloth shorts instead. Unsure of her choice in attire, she was apprehensive when she returned to the kitchen.

Tom stopped to look at her, puckered his lips, and squinted his eyes. "Comfortable?"

"Yes. I thought this would be okay for staying in."

"Yes, well, I guess it will do," he said, eyeing her bare legs. He topped each drink with vermouth then stirred. Handing her a precisely made Manhattan cocktail, he raised his glass for a toast. "To us and a new beginning."

She hadn't been aware that he had thoughts of a new beginning and as she sipped her strong drink, this would overtake all her focus for the evening. Wishful thoughts swirled around her head and hope began to spring from within. Maybe just maybe, he meant it when he said 'a new beginning.' She dreamed of the words that were presented tonight and spent the entire movie lost in the wistfulness that maybe setting an official date had put him back on course for the life she desperately dreamed of having. She smiled, giddy with optimism.

Meanwhile, William walked back to his place dazed. Evie had left an impression on him that felt strong, like a new tattoo or a fresh scar. She had somehow already permanently marked his soul. At home, he settled down at his desk with a bowl o'noodles made in his hotpot. Even though it would be difficult, he needed to focus on his studies and not the pretty girl. Pulling his textbook out, he finished highlighting the rest of the chapter in which he would soon be tested.

Chapter 5

William clocked in at Manhattan Messengers on Thursday morning at ten o'clock and filled his bag with the next two hours' worth of deliveries. He liked his job because it mixed his enjoyment for the outdoors, the excitement of the city, and required no deep thinking; he did enough of that every other day at school.

By the time William made his first delivery of the day, Everleigh was making an egg white omelet with a mixture of chopped up vegetables. She felt healthy and happy today. Tom didn't make love to her last night, but he did hold her during the movie. She preferred that because sometimes she didn't enjoy sex, in fact, most of the time she didn't. None of that mattered to her because the hope she felt for the future this morning was better than sex anyway.

Since Tom was at work, she opened her textbook while eating and started highlighting the stuff that would be most helpful for her upcoming finals in a few weeks. An hour passed before she decided to get ready for the day. She packed her overnight bag with her dirties, locked up, and left his apartment around one. She didn't call for the car because she decided to walk back to her home instead. This time she headed straight home though, with no detours to the park or to the coffee shop that she really wanted to stop by.

"Good afternoon, Miss Wright." The longtime doorman greeted her with a smile.

"Good afternoon, Walter," she said, always polite.

By seven that evening, Evie reemerged from her room after a busy day of studies, dressed for dinner with her family. She didn't bother putting on her rather large engagement ring since she wasn't leaving the house. She wore it when she attended events and parties. She chose not to wear it to school because she wanted to blend in with the other students at the university. She hated drawing attention and the ring with a centered five carat pink diamond and another carat in diamonds on the sides did not blend in with the other students' attire, which was much more casual. Another reason was that both Tom and she worried she might get mugged wearing a bauble like that around the city.

The conversation always seemed to revolve around Tom and she didn't want to talk about him. She wanted to share her passions, and what was going on with her schooling, but instead watched as her sister fidgeted—as usual.

Everleigh didn't get caught up in the wedding planning since she had her finals to worry about, and let her mind drifted the remainder of the meal, eventually settling on William. An unintentional smile spread across her face and it was received with much attention.

"It's nice to see the love that you have for Tom shine through," her mother said, noting her daughter's smile.

"He's from a good family," her father interjected into the conversation, which was rare for him. He made

42

comments like this as if that information held any importance.

Her sister said nothing. The way Audrey looked at her older sister made Everleigh feel guilty. Her sister had an uncanny ability to see through her façade. Everleigh shifted uncomfortably in her chair before correcting her goofy grin into a more poised smile. "Please pass the haricots verts." She hoped that satisfied the onlookers.

* * *

William finished his shift ten hours later. Exhausted, he didn't even bother having a snack when he returned home. After a shower and quick recap through his thoughts, he was asleep.

By eleven the following morning, William entered his first class of the day. He sat down at the desk that seemed to be made for middle school kids and stretched his long legs out in front of him. Setting his notebook down, he grabbed a pen from his bag, preferring to write his notes instead of type.

Everleigh was seated down the hall in the History of Modern European Writers class, an accompaniment to British Literature for English Majors.

By noon, both of their minds floated to the other and for a small flicker in time they felt connected on a more surreal level. Both turned to look out the window, hoping to dissolve the excitement now brewing inside of them as they realized they only had thirty minutes left until they reunited again.

With haste after class, Evie made her way into Professor Lang's class and chose a seat in the general area where she normally sat, eight rows up and in the middle. She tried to seem oblivious to William when he entered the classroom and scanned the auditorium. Attempting to play it cool, she smiled casually when he spotted her. She failed at casual. Her smile was huge, and her cheeks flushed with heat embarrassed as he worked his way up to the eighth row and the middle where one open seat still remained. She had purposely draped her sweater over the chair to insure it remained available for him.

"May I?" William asked her, appearing calm.

"Yes, please do." She picked up her sweater and laid it across her lap.

Both were quiet as they sat there until William finally got the nerve and attempted to start a conversation. "Hi, Evie."

When he said her name, it sounded romantic, and she heard the reverence in his words.

"Hello, William."

They both pulled their notebooks from their bags, avoiding each other for lack of words, but delighted to be there all the same. Evie tapped her pen on her notebook then looked at William again and smiled. *He's very handsome and he smells good*, she quickly assessed. *I bet he has lots of girlfriends.* She sighed. *Smelling and looking like that, he must*, she determined. This upset her, which then confused her because she didn't understand her own feelings.

He sat up and saw her frowning or frustrated, he didn't know her well enough to decipher all of her expressions yet. But one thing he did know is that he would make his best efforts to learn each and every one of them. "How are you today?"

She rearranged her face to smiling again before she responded, "I'm fine, thank you. How are you?"

"I'm great."

Great? He's great. Wow. She couldn't recall responding to such an everyday question with great. She decided to explore further. "How is studying for finals going?"

"Good. You know we have our paper due in another week? I think I've gotten all my research together to start writing. How're you coming along?"

"I've gathered most of my information, but need another trip to the library before I start writing."

"I'm going to the library tomorrow. We can meet up . . . if you like?"

It seemed innocent the way he phrased the proposition, but it warmed her entire being. "Yes, I would."

William had always thought her eyes seemed sad when he watched her in class. But lately her eyes didn't look sad at all. They sparked to life when he asked her to study with him.

Not wanting to draw any attention from their neighbors, he whispered, "One o'clock?"

"All right, I'll see you in the Brit Lit section of the library tomorrow at one."

William also liked the way she repeated every detail of his proposal as if confirming each word in disbelief. He answered with a nod and she returned the favor. Professor Lang turned on the microphone, which meant the students had to pay attention because this lecture would be on the test.

But Evie was too giddy to pay attention. She was distracted by her new friend and glanced at William often. As he took notes, she noticed that he had very nice

45

penmanship; his long fingers grasped the black ink pen in his right hand. She used blue ink, but wouldn't let his small, flawed preference for black ink be a deal breaker.

Her mind ticked through several reasons that might excuse this small infraction. Maybe he grabbed the pen from a huge jar of pens and didn't think about blue or black the way she did, though she still thought it was obvious that notes were meant to be taken in blue ink. Or, maybe he stole it from a waiter at a restaurant because he liked the way it glided across the receipt he had just signed. *Wait a minute! Break what deal?* She was shocked how casually her thoughts regarding him entered her head fifteen seconds earlier.

William looked at her, and again she had that strange flustery-frowny expression on her face. It dashed his hopes a little, and he turned back to the professor.

"I'm going for coffee after class," she whispered.

William perked up, but he wasn't sure if she was asking him to join her for coffee or just letting him know that she's getting coffee. It was a statement, not a question, right? Maybe she was only thinking out loud. No, she was saying that to let him know she wants him there, too. *Yes, I'm sure that's it, yes. She wants me to get coffee with her.* His reply was cryptic at best. "Coffee after class?"

Evie was confused. *Is he backing my statement or agreeing to join me?*

Everyone stood up around them shuffling their stuff back into their bags. William and Evie looked at each other realizing they had been dismissed, once again oblivious to the rest of the world when they were together.

She took a deep breath just as he exhaled as if he had been holding it for minutes. They packed their belongings without speaking to each other and stood at the same time.

46

She gave him a sweet smile and he allowed her to cross in front of him. "After you."

Leading the way out of the auditorium, she walked slowly, so he could catch up. Then they matched their stride to each other.

As he opened the door for her, she unintentionally brushed against him, making both of them smile. When the sunshine of the afternoon hit their faces, William admired Evie when she closed her eyes and smiled toward the sun. She was breathtaking.

When she opened her eyes, she suddenly felt self-conscious. "Sorry," she said, picking up her pace again.

"No need to apologize. You were just enjoying the pretty day. "

"Yes, it is a lovely day. I think the warm weather calls for iced coffee."

William liked her randomness. She was unique and it made him want to try new things, too. "I think I'll join you in that."

"I thought you always had double espresso, black with a scone?" Her cheeks warmed by her admission and hoped he wasn't scared off by her observation.

He wasn't.

He liked that she knew what he drank, although he didn't know what her specialty drink was. He knew she drank coffee, but not how she liked hers—if it was a latte, espresso, macchiato, or straight. Somehow, she knew his usual down to the smallest detail of black, no sugar or cream.

William also realized that those were the most words they had ever exchanged and their time together felt like a

47

real beginning.

They entered Bean There and walked to the counter together. As they perused the menu up on the wall, with an annoyed tone, Tracy asked, "The usual?"

"No, today calls for iced coffee, please." Evie looked to William for reassurance.

"Same for me please," he said, tempted by her selection.

Evie noticed Tracy looking between the two of them a little confused before turning back to blend their drinks. A minute later, two iced coffees were set on the counter with a huff. William and Evie barely noticed the baristas' annoyance because they were too caught up in each other to care.

Evie held two fingers in the air and added to the order. "Two blueberry muffins also, please."

William smiled at her. "I'll buy."

Evie picked up her coffee and muffin, thanked him, and headed for her favorite table. As usual, William left the change for Tracy. He walked over to his second favorite table in the place and set his coffee and muffin down next to Evie, who already had her book open and her highlighter resting in the crease of the spine. "Hope you like muffins," She said.

"I do." His eyebrows went up with enthusiasm. He especially liked having muffins with her.

"After ordering new drinks, I thought it would fun to try something else new, and scones don't scream new start to me, but blueberry muffins do." She laughed and William watched completely enchanted by her.

While pulling his book and pen out, he watched as

she separated the entire top of the muffin from the wrapped base and began eating that portion. He didn't understand her muffin method and tried to dismiss the strange flaw he had discovered as inconsequential.

William carefully peeled the wrapper down from the sides and removed the baked good. He took a bite making sure to include some of the top, bottom, and the bit in the middle. He also couldn't help but wonder if she intended to eat the rest of the defaced muffin. Pointing at her squandered muffin, he asked, "Are you going to eat the bottom part too? That's the best part!"

Reading way too much into his question, she got defensive. "Do you always use black ink?"

There was a moment of silence and staunch glares were exchanged between them before they realized they had reached an impasse. William was willing to set aside his own opinion on the matters at hand, but to his surprise, Evie wasn't.

Taking one last defensive stand, Evie discarded the bottom part of her muffin into a napkin and crumpled it into a disfigured mess.

Disturbed by her waste, William shuddered then picked up his black ink pen and started writing with it in defiance.

She rolled her eyes at the complete abuse of black ink.

William saw the anger flash across her blue eyes as her breathing deepened. Right then, she was, without a doubt, the most beautiful woman he'd ever laid eyes on.

Evie watched him look at her as if she was the most interesting thing in the world. Uncomfortable in the attention and still mad, she pointed to her notebook to end the standoff. "We should get, um . . ." she started to say then blinked, breaking the trance between them. "I should get back to studying."

"Okay." He was awe-struck by her, but when she blinked, he came back to reality and cleared his throat. "Yes, we should get back to, um, to studying." He stuck the end of the pen in his mouth and turned his head back to look at his own notebook while dragging his sweating palms up and down his jean-clad thighs several times. He took one big, deep breath then resumed writing.

Neither one of them could explain the passion they saw in the other's eyes, but both were more than willing to return to these two particular topics of conversation—-at a later date—to find out.

They busied themselves with their own work, but stopped occasionally to discuss a topic that Professor Lang seemed to emphasize for no apparent reason.

A random thought popped into her head, and she realized that William wasn't a boy at all. Yes, she referred to guys and men her age that way sometimes, not in a demeaning manner, but in the same way she called herself a girl. But now, he was different to her. *He was a man.* But again, that didn't fit. That noun seemed too mature for both of them and the "boy" officially in her mind became a "guy," settling the issue once and for all.

She also happened to notice his T-shirt under his unbuttoned flannel shirt clinging to his very fit chest. She took the last drink of her coffee then stood to stretch, needing to clear the dangerous detour her mind had taken.

It felt good not having to always be talking or listening. Evie didn't talk much these days and found the silence comforting, especially between two people becoming friends. She picked up her trash, as well as his, walked across the shop to the bin and dumped the garbage.

Walking back, their eyes met and they both smiled. His smile was honest and meaningful. Hers was warm and sincere. *It's natural to feel joy when hanging out with friends*, she remembered as happiness invaded every inch of her body.

By three-thirty, she started to wrap things up, but stopped to ask, "It's the weekend. Any plans?" This seemed like a normal question for a friend to ask another friend.

"The library tomorrow at one, *remember*?" His heart sped up thinking she'd already forgotten their date.

"Oh, yes. I wrote it in my planner already."

He smirked then stirred the pot by asking, "In pencil or ink?"

"Ink, *blue*, to be exact." She smiled as she said this, but he knew women well enough to know that a grin like that had hidden meaning. That was her chance to drive home a belief of hers—not a rational belief—but a belief all the same. He accepted that retort and allowed her a victory on the subject because the color of ink in her pen was not a deal breaker for him. Maybe the wasted muffin bottom, but definitely not the ink issue.

He stood when she did and they walked out together, but Evie wanted to confirm that she would see him again. "I'll see you tomorrow."

"I'll see you tomorrow, *Evie*."

She waved good-bye and left, feeling as though she was floating. She still couldn't get over how amorously he emphasized her name and deep down hoped that he would say it again tomorrow.

Chapter 6

Everleigh was expected at Tom's for breakfast on Saturday morning. When she arrived, he didn't greet her though she knew he heard her come in. She entered the living room and found him at the kitchen bar working on his laptop, his brow was furrowed, and his body tense. She rubbed his shoulders and tried to keep things light. "Why would you ruin a perfectly good morning with work?"

"This work is what keeps the money rolling in. Keeping you in the lifestyle your parents have generously spoiled you with," he snapped, shrugging out from under her touch.

She stood there shocked and disappointed since he'd been nicer lately. "I guess Tom is back." Her sarcasm was evident as she walked toward the couch.

Tom grabbed her arm, jerking her around to face him. "What does that mean?"

"I meant that lately—"

He glared at her. "You should speak kinder of your fiancé."

"I would if there was something kind to say." As the words left her mouth, she felt stronger, more confident. She yanked her arm back and walked to the couch.

He rushed her, spinning her around and forcing her to sit down. Fear set in and she stuttered out an automatic response. "I . . . I was rude . . ."

Leaning over, a mere inch from her, he was firm in his demand. "You will respect me!" Tom fisted his hands at his sides, his knuckles turning white. "Your sarcasm is unacceptable. This will be your only warning."

She couldn't move. She couldn't breathe. She couldn't think because his words pounded in her ears. And then the oddest thing happened. She focused on two dried rings on the coffee table—two cups—maybe mugs. The watermarks were pale, coffee-colored, and fresh.

Two.

"Do you understand me?" he asked, gritting his teeth as he spoke.

She was at a loss if this was rhetorical or not, so she remained silent, knowing that option was best.

He calmed down, but still had an edge of threat to his tone. "Do you understand me, Everleigh?"

She nodded as she spoke the word, and he turned and left the room. When the bedroom door slammed shut, she gasped for air. Her heart started beating again and she slumped over on the couch and let the tears fall.

She should have left, but was too afraid to face the fury if she did. Ashamed of her weakness to stand strong, she curled up on the couch and stared at the two rings on the table in front of her. Her mind filled with curiosity as to how they got there and how long they had been there. After a few minutes, she closed her eyes, willing everything to go away.

When she awoke a few hours later, she discovered Tom was gone. She gathered her belongings and straightened up as she always did then left. In recent years, she was resolved to the role of Thomas Whitney's wife. But as she made her way to the library, she had doubts. Doubts she typically shoved to the back of her mind knowing she could never be the wife he wanted. Today, a new perspective had started to implant itself into her psyche, allowing her to daydream of different things—like a whole new life.

In this moment, the promises she made when she was seventeen years old didn't matter. In this moment, she felt free.

After picking up a half-shift for extra money this morning, William headed to the library to meet Evie. He didn't have time to shower and felt embarrassed by how dirty he was, but wasn't going to risk being late and miss the chance to see her again.

After a detour into the bathroom to rinse his face and wash his hands, he worked his way to the small British literature section of the library on the fifth floor and found a table for two by a large window in the corner. He spread his stuff out to reserve the table then opened his textbook and started into his highlighting.

Evie walked straight back to the corner and saw William sitting there as if he'd been there for hours. *Maybe he had*, she thought. She moved forward plunking her bag onto the table. "Is this seat taken?"

"Yes, it is. I'm sorry, I'm waiting for someone." When he said this, it confused her. Was he joking or was he waiting for someone else? Maybe he had forgotten about their appointment and didn't want to be disturbed. "Evie,

I'm being sarcastic. Of course, it's saved, for you."

"Some people find sarcasm unacceptable." She paused for impact. "You're lucky I'm not one of those people." She laughed at her own joke and it made him smile. Looking at the book in front of him, she pulled the chair out and asked, "Are you highlighting the entire book?"

He set his marker down and chuckled. "No . . . maybe, I'm not sure. I don't take great notes, but I have a good memory and I highlight what Prof Lang covers in lecture. It fills in the gaps of my horrible notes." He looked down, kind of embarrassed by his confession.

"My notes are very thorough. I write fast. You can borrow them if you like."

"Or we could study together?"

"Yeah, like study buddies," she said with excitement.

He tilted his head and looked at her strange enjoyment over her statement and once again, it gave him hope. He wanted to know all about her and jumped at the opportunity. "Where'd you come from?"

She didn't want to talk about Tom or that she came from his place. "What do you mean?"

"I've been in this major for two years and I just now have a class with you?"

"Oh. Um, I've been here all along."

A small ache formed in his chest when she said this and he looked up to meet her blue eyes, which she hid from him. The second she looked up their eyes met. He thought her eyes were graceful and caring and she indulged in the depth of his eyes.

They broke their gaze by busying themselves with mock obligations of reorganizing her bag and acting as if he'd lost his place. She pointed down to the only sentence not highlighted, and said, "I think you left off here."

He chuckled. "And so I did."

"I'm going to find the book I need. I'll be right back." She said this as if she owed him an explanation for leaving.

He watched her, taking in as much about her as he could before it was considered rude to be staring. She was dressed conservative today in short pants and a buttoned-up sweater. When she turned back to sneak a peek at him, she caught him staring. He retreated back to his highlighting, but smirked to himself.

With a book in hand, she peeked over the pages and snuck another glance at him. He looked rugged and a little tired today. His hair had been in a hat and was sexy in an unkempt kind of way. His clothes needed a good washing and were a wrinkled mess as she had come to expect of him.

She took the book in her hands back to the table and noticed a thin line of dirt across his hairline, becoming even more curious about him. Maybe he was homeless and couldn't shower or wash and iron his clothes or maybe he didn't care.

He stood up to stretch and with the air sweeping toward her, she smelled his sweat mixed with cologne. Homeless people don't usually wear cologne, at least not in Manhattan. The smell was masculine, and for some reason, she found it quite sexy. She giggled at how she had named two different things about him as sexy and both have to do with him not showering. His proximity must be messing with her hormones because she never used to find dirty men sexy.

He sat back down as she tried to find the passage in the library book.

After thirty minutes, she became frustrated by not being able to find a quote she needed for her paper. "Damn it."

William asked, "Can I help?"

"I don't know. I've read *Pride and Prejudice* many times, but I can't remember where the quote I need is."

"What part are you looking for?"

She laughed. "It's silly and kind of obscure. It has something to do with the world confirming her beliefs that merit and schooling doesn't make a person a better man. Oh, I don't know. I . . ." If only he knew how true that was, she thought as an image of Tom occupied her mind.

"'The more I see the world the more I am dissatisfied with it.' That part?" He tilted his head and smiled his charming imperfect smile.

Dumbfounded, she whispered, "Yes."

He continued, the words coming to him slowly, as she took notes. "'Every day confirms my belief in the inconsistency of all human characters, and on the little dependence that can be placed on the appearance of merit and sense.' I think it's around chapter twenty-three or thereabout."

A few minutes later she found the quote. "Chapter twenty-four, you were very close. Do you have the entire book memorized?"

"No, only the quotes that mean something to me." He looked back down, embarrassed in his revelation.

She leaned across the table, closer to him, and

58

continued to whisper. "Why does that quote have meaning to you?"

"It's . . ." he said, hesitating, "... it reminds me that other men may have fancier degrees or more money . . . or even a prettier girlfriend, whatever..." He rolled his eyes, "that I'm still their equal. They're not better than me, just different."

"Why would *you* ever feel less than someone else?" Evie was shocked by his admission.

"I don't come from a fancy zip code and I'm the first in my family who will graduate from college. Guess I'm a little insecure. Kind of dumb, I know. Why'd you want that particular quote anyway?"

"Not dumb at all." She looked down at her hands, and said, "I know firsthand that a fancier zip code does not a better man make." She placed the attention back on him. "I may be speaking out of line, but I can tell you're a good person and I think that is more important than a fancy degree any day."

As she leaned forward, a silver necklace escaped her sweater—a silver cage pendant with a bird flying away on the chain.

"I like your necklace." He was sincere, but felt like she might be hiding a secret from him.

"Thanks," she mumbled, tucking it back under the collar of her sweater.

"What does it mean?"

Suddenly, she wanted him to know more about herself. "You can't cage something meant to be free."

He looked into her eyes, knowing there was something more to her words than she was revealing.

"Even if free only in their heart?"

"Yes, even if only in their heart."

Hoping she'd continue, he asked, "What's with the black ink thing the other day?"

"Enough about me today." She had turned serious from the vulnerability she felt deep inside. "We can have a discussion about ink and its appropriate uses at a later date."

Although, ink seemed to be a touchy subject for her, he found her passion for it fascinating and couldn't wait to discuss it further . . . *at a later date.*

After an hour of intense concentration and the strong smell of wet highlighter invading her senses, Evie felt lightheaded. She slammed her book closed all of the sudden. "I need some air. I think I'm done for the day. What about you?"

"I'm hungry. You wanna grab some pizza?"

She looked at her watch and as much as she wanted to, it would be impossible in regards to time. "I can't today. Thank you, but I need to get going." she said, standing and packing her stuff up, "But, I'll see you on Monday in class."

"Sure, in class. Have a good rest of your weekend."

Before she walked away from him and their little table in the corner, she said, "Hey, thanks for the company today. I got a lot done." They exchanged one last smile before she left.

Everleigh arrived home to find her sister hanging out in the family room. She hurried to her room, shutting the door behind her, needing a few more minutes to get the excitement she felt from her "meet-up" out of her system.

Ten minutes later, Audrey barged into the bedroom uninvited.

Startled, Everleigh said, "I didn't say you could come in."

"Oh lighten up, sis. Where've you been all day?"

"At the library," she said without looking and pulled her notebook from her bag. "I have a paper due Monday."

"That's boring stuff! Nothing exciting?"

"No, why?" Everleigh answered too fast and too defensive to sound natural.

Audrey looked at her sister who was smiling to herself. When Everleigh looked up to meet Audrey's stare, she appeared serious. "What's going on?" Audrey asked, putting her hands on her hips.

"Nothing. I just need to get this done. Can you please leave?"

Audrey tried to get her sister to open up one last time by teasing her. "You seem . . . what's the word I'm looking for? Oh, happy! You seem happy. That's new."

Everleigh threw a pillow at her, not responding to her keen observation, but she did feel happy inside. Happier than she had in a long time and she kind of wanted to bask in the afterglow of her study session with William. Audrey stomped out of the room, shutting the door as she left and Everleigh let her smile reemerge as she began typing her paper.

On Sunday, both William and Everleigh anxiously waited for Monday.

* * *

61

William entered the large auditorium and spotted Evie right away. She still had open seats on either side of her, so he took a deep breath at the end of the row then tried to appear casual as he walked the rest of the way, dropping his bag on the floor next to her.

She looked up and smiled. "Hi."

"Hi." When he sat down, he pulled his notebook out and began digging at the bottom of his bag for a pen.

"I brought this for you."

He looked over and saw her holding a pen between them—a *blue ink pen.*

"Nice. Thanks. You know one day I'll figure out your obsession with pens." He took the pen, stuck it between his teeth, and smirked at her. He figured if he had the answer to this mystery then he would also learn a lot more about what made this girl tick.

After class, they walked to Bean There. They occupied the two respective tables that seemed reserved just for them and laughed, talked, he highlighted, and she studied.

He loved listening to the delicate hum she sometimes made. He didn't think she was even aware she did this. She sneaked glances at his concentrating face, forming an appreciation for the smell of yellow highlighter, and smiled, feeling smug that he was writing in blue ink.

Her self-righteous thought was broken by him asking a simple question. "Where's your favorite place to go in the city?"

"For me, the city lost its luster a long time ago," she said, discouraged.

Surprised by her reaction, he pressed for more

information. "Can I show you that magic still exists?"

Although Evie knew better than to accept offers from guys she barely knew, especially guys she wanted to know better, she felt the need to say yes to him. She *wanted* to say yes to him. *Maybe good still exists in the world, after all*, she thought. Maybe *he* was good. She really hoped he was. She was willing to give him this chance, but more importantly, she needed to give him this chance before all her truths were proven accurate.

"Tomorrow?" she asked, tentative.

"Hmm." He pondered aloud, but remembered his conflict. "I can't tomorrow. I have to work—"

"*Oh*. What do you do?" He had shared another tidbit and she wanted to soak it in.

"I'm a bike messenger, sometimes a foot messenger. It sucks some days and other times I dig it. It changes day-to-day."

This explained a lot. "Did you work on Saturday?" She was worried about asking him this because if he didn't he might've found this question offensive.

"Yes. I should've apologized for my appearance. I didn't have time to shower before meeting you. I probably looked awful."

"No, not awful. Not bad at all," she said, remembering how good he looked.

"I love New York, but the streets are filthy and the dirt and exhaust from the cars gets all over me. Sometimes I wear a mask because I get paranoid about my lungs and stuff."

She noticed he was very clean looking today, his clothes, shirt, hands, and face. "So, when then?"

"What?"

"When do you want to show me the magic of the city?" She was astounded by her own boldness, but she liked being this brave.

"How about after class on Wednesday?"

She pulled a small planner from her bag and skimmed through her week. "Wednesday after class is perfect." She jotted down the rendezvous.

"Blue ink?" William asked, pointing at her pen.

"Always."

She packed her stuff up, and said, "I have to go, but I'll see you Wednesday."

"Bye," he said, but his voice broke, making her smile as she left the coffee shop.

When Everleigh got into Tom's car, he leaned over and kissed her on the cheek. "Good day?"

"Yes," she answered, "very good day." Lost in her thoughts on the ride home, she was thinking about how the day had been better than she could have imagined.

They walked into her home together and he poured a drink while she sat down on the floral settee overlooking the park in the distance. With his back to her, he asked, "Do you want to go out for dinner tonight?"

As she stared at the back of his head, she realized he hadn't really looked at her in a long time, not the real her. "No, I'd like to stay home." She glanced at his profile, seeing his nostrils flair. It wasn't the answer he wanted, but in some sick way, she almost willed him to be mad. His anger was an emotion she understood. It terrified her, but it was predictable. His other moods, these in-between moods were unpredictable, making it difficult for her to keep her own emotions in check.

Against her better judgment, she gave in. "We'll go out if you prefer."

"I do."

And with that, carefree Evie had gone and Tom's Everleigh was back.

Chapter 7

It was a simple ferry ride, but Everleigh hadn't been on one since she was a small child. She loved that William had suggested something unique, something opposite from her normal routine.

They found an empty place against the railing, and William didn't waste time. "Do you work?"

"No."

He noticed she didn't apologize for that fact or seem embarrassed which meant it wasn't necessary for her to have a job. She must come from money.

It was her turn to ask the questions. "What do you like to do for fun?"

"Um . . . I like to read, but I guess you already figured that out from my major. I read at home, parks, bookstores, coffee shops. I enjoy writing, too."

"I read at the park the other day. It was blissful." Her face glowed, remembering her two stolen hours there.

"Sometimes you reveal the most interesting things. You read at the park the other day as if it's the first time you've ever done it. You grew up in Manhattan, but don't seem that familiar with it."

"I know a lot about the city. I've worked with charities and galleries, hospitals, and different leagues here."

"But I have a feeling you live in a bubble of sorts." He saw the light disappear from her eyes so quickly that he adjusted his statement not wanting to hurt her feelings. "I don't mean to be rude. I think the best way to get to know a city is to experience it, not just study, or talk about it."

"Honestly," she said, folding her hands together on the table in front of her. "I would love to experience it more than I have. Today was a good start." She looked into his eyes and maybe it was the bravado from the comfort she was feeling, but she held his stare without blushing and without blinking.

William leaned closer to her ear, and whispered, "I would love to experience it with you and today was a great start." The ferry docked.

Knowing their time was limited, her expression softened and she tilted her head wanting the moment to last.

He gave her the most heart-stopping smile, and asked, "Do you still have some time?"

She licked her lips as a distraction, looking away from his piercing eyes. Peeking at her watch, she calculated the time in her head then sighed. "I need to get going."

William tried not to let his disappointment show, but he had trouble hiding his feelings. She didn't like seeing him sad, but she knew their day together had to end.

Walking to the center of Battery Park, they stopped.

When she turned to face him, he lifted her bag off his shoulder and placed it onto hers. He stood so close and reacting on instinct, her hands went to his chest and stayed there as if they had known each other longer than they had. With both of their hearts racing, she said, "You gave me an amazing day. I wish I could return the favor and give you the same."

"Don't underestimate yourself, Evie. My day was amazing because I got to spend it with you." He brought her small frame to him and hugged her while burying his face into her hair. He inhaled before pulling away to ask, "I have two more places I'd like to show you. One is my favorite café near the university. It's called Pizzeria La Cucina . Have you been there?"

"No, it sounds yummy though. I haven't had pizza in such a long time."

"I live off pizza and theirs is the best."

"And the other place?" She loved he had thought this through.

"The other takes place at night. We can do both."

Although she knew there was nothing right in accepting his proposal, she was convinced there was nothing wrong in it either. People are selfish. *Love is the most selfish emotion one can feel*, she believed. *Love*—is that what she was feeling? No, but traces of it were blooming deep inside her heart already.

Her pause gave William too much time to overthink and his doubts started to get away from him. He wanted to give her everything, show her everything. *I mean, love is the most unselfish emotion one can feel.* Is that what he was doing? Was he trying to show her his love, to give her his *love*?

"Yes."

"What?" he asked, breaking from his inner *love* monologue.

"Yes, we can do that one night. When?"

"How about next Monday?"

She flipped through her calendar in her mind, wanting to make this work. "What time?"

"I work Monday afternoon, but I could meet you at eight?"

"All right, eight then. I'll see you Friday in class." She took a few steps away from him heading east, but stopped and said, "Thanks again . . . for everything."

He waved back to her with a huge smile on his face.

* * *

As she made the final block to her building, she straightened her skirt. She pulled her hair tie out and replaced it with a stiff headband from her bag, trying to look appropriate and presentable.

When William arrived home, he flicked on his small lamp and tossed his bag to the floor. He didn't want to shower because every now and then, he got the faintest whiff of Evie from their embrace and he liked it.

William worked a long shift on Thursday, but still managed to fit some studying in over a hot bowl o'noodles. In the morning, after a quick breakfast of cereal, he left earlier than usual, anxious to get to class.

By his second class, he sat in his chair with his knee bouncing with nervous anticipation until Evie walked into the auditorium. She started up the steps before looking up and their eyes met. She eased down the aisle and sat right next to him. His knee stopped bouncing as his insides calmed.

"Hi," she said, feeling a little sassy.

"Hi. Looking forward to Lang's lecture today?"

"Yes. Most definitely!" she said, sarcasm lacing her tone. "Our finals are in two weeks. Are you ready? Highlighted all you can highlight in that textbook of yours?" She laughed out loud, causing a few of the surrounding students to look over.

"I think I'm finished with the highlighting for now." William laughed as well, looking down at his pen, the pen she had given him.

"We have a lot to cover today and yes, it will be on the final," Professor Lang announced from the front of the large room. William and Evie both focused on him giving their full attention. They angled their bodies forward and prepared to take notes.

After class, Evie whispered, "I can't get coffee today. I'm sorry."

He could tell she was disappointed as much as he was, but he didn't want her sad. "Being a bit presumptuous, aren't you?" William said, but he couldn't keep a straight face long enough to hold his own joke. "I'm giving you a hard time. It's all right."

She chuckled. "I thought I was being rude there for a minute."

He felt bad now. "I'm sorry. I was just joking." He touched her arm briefly in reassurance. "I understand if you can't go." Leaning closer, they walked through the exit doors, and in a very low voice, he said, "Though, I do wish I could see you before next Monday."

He mumbled the last part, but she heard him and she liked that he spoke to her in such a seductive voice. "Me too." She did, too. She continued walking very close to him, and said, "I have some *obligations* this weekend I must tend to. But, I'll be looking forward to Monday."

Her words and smile helped to melt the disappointment he felt.

She angled her head as she tapped his hand with her fingertips. "I'll see you then. Have a nice weekend." She turned and headed east, walking one block up to a waiting car.

William went to Bean There, still feeling a tingle across the top of his hand where her fingers had ghosted across his skin.

When he entered the coffee shop, he saw Tracy was working. "Do they ever give you a day off?" He joked as he approached the counter.

She laughed, flirting, not ready to give up on him, especially not when they could share a laugh like they were. "I like to work and I need the money. Most of us don't have daddy still supporting us." She turned around and started on his coffee.

"Yeah." He managed to reply, but was unsure of what she meant by the comment. He didn't have his dad supporting him, so he figured she must have been making a general statement.

She continued her mini-rant. "Not all of us can be as lucky as your friend. Some of us have to work for living."

Her comment, though said in jest, felt somewhat disrespectful toward Evie and he didn't like that. Evie admitted she didn't work and that was okay with him for some reason.

William found Evie delicate in many ways and felt the need to protect her. *What am I thinking?* He reined in his thoughts, focused back on his coffee, and paid Tracy. "Thanks." Walking to his table, he was upset by the thought of someone, even someone who was nice like Tracy, taking a dig at Evie's expense.

He had also assumed Evie came from money before it was confirmed. It wasn't a hard assumption to ascertain when she told him she grew up in New York, but not just in New York, in Manhattan specifically. Most people can't afford that luxury. He barely scraped by paying for his worn-down pre-war studio apartment. It wasn't his place to judge her in a negative way because her family might have money. He also didn't envy her for it. Everyone has their own set of problems—money just wasn't one of hers. He decided to blow it off and read his book.

Evie walked into Bean There on Saturday afternoon with her designer handbag draped over her shoulder. She had convinced her family she needed to get more studying done in the city and they went to the Hamptons for the weekend without her.

She had lied. She had other things on her mind. Other things like cute, disheveled guys from Brit Lit. She had also left her phone off most of the morning to avoid their calls to join them. They were known to guilt her.

She scanned the coffee shop before approaching the counter.

Pleased by Evie's bad timing, Tracy smiled all smug and said, "He's not here right now."

"*Who?*" Evie feigned innocent.

"We're going to play it like this, are we?" Tracy scoffed. "Okay, what can I get for you then?"

"A decaf mocha latte, *to-go,* please."

The place was empty, so Tracy decided to make small talk with her only customer. "I'm Tracy."

"Hi, I'm Evie."

"Do you go to Hunter College?"

"Yes, I'm an English major."

"Oh, that explains a lot."

"What do you mean?" Evie felt like maybe she should be offended by the barista's tone, but tried to hold off her assumption until she explained.

"You and William. He's also an English major." While Tracy was making the latte, she saw Evie smile at the mention of his name, so she probed further. "You have classes together?"

"Only one."

"He's cute, don't you think?" Tracy placed the coffee on the counter and watched Evie's reaction.

Evie blushed, looked down, and lied. "I hadn't noticed."

Tracy knew that look and there was no way anyone wouldn't notice how attractive William was, but since she didn't want to make things awkward by continuing to talk about him, she dropped the subject.

Evie set her money on the counter. "Thanks, I'll see you soon."

As Evie added a dash more sugar to her hot drink,

Tracy, feeling nice, said, "He was in this morning, but got his coffee to go. He had to work today."

Evie allowed an outward smile this time.

Right then her phone rang. *Tom.* Her happy bubble dissipated as reality sank in. She debated not answering it, but decided it was best to talk to him now. "Hello?"

"Why haven't you been answering your phone?" he asked, not nicely, but a demand.

"I need some space from . . ." She looked at Tracy who smiled back at her. Evie knew she needed to have this conversation in private.

"From what? *From me?*"

She rushed out the door as he yelled into the phone.

All of her strength escaped and she wavered in her stance. "Tom, please listen to me," she pleaded. "I apologize. I have finals and need to study. I've got too much on my mind right now and I don't want to fight with you or anyone else."

"I can be more understanding than you give me credit for. All you have to do is talk to me. I love you, Everleigh."

"I know. I'm sorry."

"You have today to yourself for your studies. I hope that eases some of your worries. I'll see you tomorrow night."

Evie had reviewed her obligations for the week in her planner, and although she didn't want to upset him any further, she needed to remind him of her commitments. "Tom, I have the Latham fundraising meeting tomorrow night."

"I fly out to Chicago for the expansion project on Monday, but I'll be back on Tuesday." She already knew about his trip. She always wrote down his events in her planner. She liked to be prepared. "I'll see you Tuesday then. Let's do lunch and change things up," he said.

"Yeah, let's go crazy and do lunch—" The words left her mouth before she could stop them.

"Everleigh, you know how I feel about sarcasm." His reminder was firm.

She did know how he felt about sarcasm. As long as it was him and not her, he was good with it, but she held that sarcastic thought inside.

"Lunch on Tuesday, Tom."

She hung up and dropped the phone back into her purse.

She was quick to shake the feelings Tom had instilled in her as she strolled along the busy avenue back toward her home, having trained herself to release the anger and fear and focus on the happy. It was the only way she could survive. There was no other option or she would lose everything and everyone that meant anything to her.

It was a beautiful evening and she felt hungry, not having eaten anything since the chef was given the weekend off. She now stood in front of Pizzeria La Cucina and decided she'd grab a pizza to take home with her. She knew William wanted to introduce her to the place, but she decided she'd be more relaxed on Monday if she knew what she was getting into.

When Evie approached, the hostess asked, "Table for one?"

She'd never eaten in a restaurant alone before, but

fought against her nerves, and said, "Yes, table for one." It felt good to make a decision all on her own and so spontaneous. She felt emboldened as she followed the hostess to a table in the front corner against the window.

As Evie read over the topping options, she decided on the Margherita pizza. She also ordered a glass of wine to go with it. After sipping, she smiled, savoring the taste of the rich, red wine as it settled into her body. Sitting back, she relaxed into her chair.

While waiting for her food, she enjoyed the people watching her table by the window afforded. This simple activity was exhilarating and she started to feel like her own person for the first time in a very long time.

It was early for most diners, just gone six o'clock, but a guy in a helmet and sunglasses walked in alarming Evie. His face was covered in dirt, but the hostess didn't appear fazed at all by the man and greeted him. He must be a regular, so Evie turned to look out the window, not giving him anymore of her attention.

William removed his helmet and mask and ran his hands through his hair, lifting the flattened locks. Looking around, he saw Evie sitting there and smiled as he strode toward her with confidence.

When she glanced at the man, she recognized his smile in an instant. She had thought about it often enough and it made her smile in return realizing the fortune of seeing William here tonight. "Hello, what brings you here?"

She wanted to stand and hug him, but instead she sipped her wine for courage and replied, "A trusted friend's recommendation. I hear it's the best pizza in town."

The waitress brought Evie's pizza to the table at the same time the hostess handed William his box. They laughed at the coincidence. "If you're not in a hurry, you can join me." The wine had gone to her head. She was shocked by her behavior, yet didn't feel bad for wanting to spend more time with him.

He looked down at his clothes, feeling dirty from his day on the streets and embarrassed. "I don't think I'm really dressed appropriately for a restaurant. I was getting mine to take home."

"Maybe I can get mine to go . . . and join you?" She really was speaking without thinking now.

William was surprised by the offer. "I'd like that very much."

"It's all settled then." Evie's sense of freedom from her family and Tom was growing stronger with each decision she made on her own.

Chapter 8

They walked out of the restaurant and stopped on the sidewalk. Evie was quiet as she waited for him to direct her, watching as he unlocked the chain around his bike. "Do you want to take a cab and meet me there?"

"No, I'm good walking with you unless you'd rather ride your bike back? Is it far?"

He strapped her bag and then the boxes to his bike and pushed it on foot. "I'd prefer to walk with you, but it's a long walk. You sure you're okay with that?"

They walked the first few blocks content to listen to the bustling noises of the street around them.

Evie started a conversation. "You worked all day?"

"Yes, ten hours." He looked down at his dirty clothes. He wanted the attention off himself, so he asked, "What've you been up to?"

"I studied and ran some errands." She didn't mention stopping into Bean There in hopes of 'running' into him, and steered clear of the fact that she lied to her family to stay in the city alone for the weekend. But they did talk about their favorite authors and libraries they liked to study in.

"Here we are," he announced, pointing at his building.

She looked up and saw the building. It was a bit rundown, but had some charm to the exterior. "Although we live in different parts of the city, it doesn't feel that far from my house."

"Really?"

"Well, it feels closer than I'm sure it is. I don't walk as much as I'd like."

"That's the beauty of New York. It's all these different worlds meshed together. But quite honestly, I can't even afford to walk on the street two blocks from here," he said, joking. He picked his bike up and led her through the building door and halfway up the first set of stairs. He stopped to warn her. "I'm sorry, my place is small and probably not up to your—"

"Don't apologize. I'm glad you trust me enough to bring me here." She gave him a reassuring smile as he led her to his second floor studio. He attached his bike to the railing outside his door, removed her bag and the pizza boxes, and then unlocked the deadbolt, gesturing for her to walk in first. She entered holding her handbag in front of her and stood in the middle of the room. William closed the door and watched her intently. He was in awe of her beauty and the vulnerability she showed almost as if she didn't know what she should be doing or how she should react.

He was overanalyzing his thoughts on Evie because her opinion of him now mattered. And instead of wanting her approval, he now needed it. He liked her too much and it would hurt him if she didn't accept him or his life. He realized he was showing his hand by bringing her to his place and she would either like it or not. He couldn't predict how she would react to his way of life, but took the risk.

"It's nice." She turned to face him and noticed his expression was more tense than usual.

Feeling relieved and accepted, his eyes brightened as he walked closer to her. He took her bag and set it on the floor near a small table in the corner. "Thanks. It's been home for a few years now. If your pizza's cold, there's a microwave. Can I get you something to drink?"

She remained standing in the middle of the room, and asked, "Yes. What do you have?"

"I have water, soda, or beer."

"I'll have what you're having. I don't want to be any trouble, especially since I kind of barged into your night." She hated feeling like a burden.

"I think I'll have a beer with my pizza." He reached into the fridge and pulled a can out, opened it, and handed it to her. "Make yourself at home. If you don't mind, I'd like to take a shower before I eat."

"Yes, yes of course. Go right ahead."

William walked into the bathroom and started the shower. His body was worn from the day and long walk, his muscles aching. He undressed, piling his dirty clothes into the corner then stepped under the warm water and drenched his face. As he cleaned up, his heart raced knowing she was in such close proximity to him. He was standing naked in the shower and thinking about her. His hand wrapped around his erection, but wanting to hurry back to spend time with her, he washed and willed any deeper thoughts of her away.

Evie sat down on the only dining room chair in the room. She went about setting the table with napkins and plastic ware the restaurant had provided. She put her box in front of her and his across the table though there was no chair for him. She looked around thinking maybe he was using it somewhere else, but didn't see one. So she waited by leaning back and sipping her beer before being reminded why she never drank beer. It tasted awful. But feeling like she needed the liquid courage, she drank some more before resting her hands in her lap and looking around the apartment. It was small—really small. She didn't know apartments could legally be this tiny.

William popped the door open, startling Evie. "My clean clothes are out here," he said.

She directed her eyes downward as he rushed into the room covered only in a towel. Wanting to peek, she pressed her forehead on her hand with her elbow resting on the table to try and control herself. He glanced over at her once and then shuffled through the small dresser that supported his hotpot and microwave. Evie was feeling sneaky and curious. Lowering her hand in front of her eyes, using her fingers as protection, she made a shield before she parted her fingers just a smidge, enough to see him.

His body and hair were still wet and her eyes followed a trail of water as it ran down his defined back. His tan skin was beautiful and smooth over his muscular physique. She wanted to touch him, but kept her hand against her forehead and fisted the other one in her lap so she wouldn't. She felt out of sorts as her heart raced, but in a good way, actually, in a great way. Her mouth dropped open as her eyes drank him in.

He turned back to the bathroom and she quickly closed her fingers, holding them together and hoping he didn't see her ogling him.

As he shut the door behind him, he couldn't believe he caught her not-so-sneaky spying eyes on him. She was too cute and this side of her surprised him. It was little revelations like this that made her so fascinating, her free flying bird pendant coming to mind. It's more fitting than he expected by her guarded and very proper appearance.

He walked back in, and smiled. "You waited?"

"I waited for you," she said, referring to her uneaten pizza.

William walked to the fridge, grabbed a beer, and pulled his desk chair over to the small table in the corner. "Would you like me to heat yours up?"

"No. It's fine." She put a napkin under her slice and took a bite. He did the same, but finished his entire slice in five bites while half of hers remained.

He stood and walked to the television. "Do you mind if I turn on some background noise?"

"Not at all, it's your place, after all." She felt awkward as she drank more beer to help clear the pizza from her throat. "I feel like I'm intruding. I mean it is Saturday night, you might have plans or something better to do."

He stopped searching through the channels, and said, "No, no, no. I don't have anything better to do. Wait! That didn't come out right. I want to be here with you." He mumbled the last part, but she still heard him.

"Thanks, and thanks for having me over."

After eating, she finished her beer and vowed to not to drink that stuff again. Yuck!

"Want another beer?"

"Sure, why not?" she responded while wondering who took over her body and when they started liking beer so much? Deep down, as usual by never admitting it to herself, she knew it wasn't about the beer, but being with him *here.*

She stood up, wanting to explore—technically to snoop around. She walked to his desk, which was very organized, and then burst out laughing when she spotted a coffee mug filled with various yellow highlighters.

"What?" he asked with a nervous edge to his tone.

"I'm laughing at your collection of highlighters. You might want to seek help for that. You definitely have a problem." She was teasing him.

"I have a problem? What about your blue and black ink obsession? You want to share that one with me or seek a professional's opinion first?" He laughed.

She stood there and crossed her arms across her chest, feeling defensive. "I have a very justifiable reason for my ink preferences." Distracted by a car's horn, she turned and looked out the window at the lights, traffic, and the people below. She was surprised how much street noise she heard from his apartment. "Do you hear everything here?"

"Pretty much. I could never live in the country. I think the silence would drive me mad." He stood back up and started cleaning the mess by throwing away the trash.

When she looked around again, she noticed his tidiness throughout the space. "You are very neat."

"I try to be clean." He tried to hide the dirty dishes that remained from yesterday by stashing them in the small oven that had broken over a month ago and the landlord kept putting off to fix. "With a place this small, one mess can wreak havoc. It's taken me many years to become better organized."

The bed was the last remaining corner of the room unexplored. She saw an old tattered book on his night table and his bed was neat, made up with his pillow tucked under the blanket and hidden from view. She turned back to the television not sure if she was allowed to sit in this area. An old black and white movie was starting and she said, "I love this movie. I haven't seen it in ages."

"Let's watch it then." He liked her enthusiasm and jumped at the opportunity.

She started to sit on the floor in front of the bed, but William quickly grabbed Evie's arm and pulled her up. "You can sit on the bed if you'd like. It will be more comfortable up here."

The gesture made her smile. "Thanks." Leaning down, she took her shoes off, and scooted until her back rested against the wall. He slid onto the bed next to her, but kept a safe distance between them. During the movie, he watched her, without her knowledge, of course, as she drank from the beer can then looked around to find a place to set it. It was times like these he wished he had a full kitchen and not this make shift kitchenette. He would have rather offered her a clean glass instead of having her drink from a dirty can, but the few he had were dirty, making him feel bad.

He reached over and took the beer from her. "I'll keep it over here." He set it on the little table sort of surprised at how full it was still. She obviously didn't care for the beer. *Wine, yes, I should keep wine on hand, but then that would require me to store wine glasses and where would those go?* He rolled his eyes and focused back on the movie.

Evie's body was relaxed after the carb-loading, beer, and the comfy bed she was now resting on. She glanced over at William and adjusted her body with her hand dipping into the divided space.

He felt her presence as the gap between them tightened and it made him want to touch her hand, to hold it, and maybe if he was so bold, to kiss it. If he followed his heart, he would kiss her on her mouth as he pulled her into his arms and flipped her under his body. A loud gulp sounded from him. She cleared her throat not aware of his sordid thoughts as he settled his attention back on the movie.

Another hour passed before she moved her body forward and stood up. "I should get going. I'm sure you're tired from work and—"

"You don't have to go. We could do something else?" The words rushed from his mouth as he tried to think of a way to keep her there.

She didn't want to go, but knew she should. Evie took a deep breath, slowly releasing it before speaking again. "Thanks, but I do need to get home.

"I'll walk you back. It's getting late."

"No, it's fine. I can catch a cab."

"It's a nice night. I'd like to walk you home, Evie," he said in a lowered, sexier than usual voice, and her body weakened a little with her knees succumbing to the difference in tone.

"Well, since . . . you . . . put it like that." Her words were staggered and a bit breathless. "I'd like that, too." She reached for her bag, but William hurried over and picked it up before she had a chance. "Thank you."

He followed her out the door and locked it before heading down the stairs and out the building's main entrance to the street. Shoving his hands in his pockets, he asked, "Which way?"

"Umm." She thought, trying to figure out her location in the city. "I think it's this way, back closer to the way we came." She looked over at him for confirmation though he didn't have any idea where she lived. When she began walking, she gave him a shy smile when he walked close to her. "So, William Ryder, tell me about yourself."

She scooted even closer to him, their arms now touching, to let a couple pass on her left. His hand automatically pressed against her lower back to direct her to the safety of his side.

"There's a loaded question. What do I want to tell you versus what is the right thing to tell you? Very tricky indeed." He smirked, attempting to keep his eyes forward.

"Wow, this sounds promising." She contemplated the options by rubbing her chin playfully. "Let me decide. Okay, I want you to tell me something you'd tell me if I'd known you longer."

"All right. Let me seeeee." He laughed quietly and shook his head. "I'm definitely not telling you that!" He saw her sincere, happy eyes waiting, *wanting* to be in on his secret. "Okay, I'll share." It didn't take much for him to confess to her. "I like when girls wear skirts," he said, eyeing hers and seeing a blush wash across her face as she caught his meaning. "But, I also like when girls can wear jeans and a T-shirt and feel confident." He knew that was a cop-out answer, but she responded well to his insight, and decided to really open up, hoping he didn't scare her off with his honesty. "Sometimes my local bartender gives me free drinks when I'm too broke to buy one. And, sometimes when I get lonely, I escape into my books."

"I do that," she said softly, cutting in. "Sometimes, I'll be at a party surrounded by friends and family and I feel completely alone, like I blend into the furniture and disappear." She pulled her cardigan tighter to her body and looked at the ground while she walked.

William nudged her with his arm. "I don't know how you could ever blend into a crowd much less the furniture. I think you're the most beautiful girl I've ever seen." He picked up his pace, embarrassed he said that out loud for her to hear.

She stopped in astonishment and her lips parted at the sweetest words she had ever heard.

He realized she wasn't next to him and turned around. She was standing five or more feet behind him on the sidewalk. Smiling, he said, "Come on. Don't make me feel more embarrassed than I already do."

She caught up to him, smiling from ear to ear, laughing and prodding. "So you think I'm beautiful?"

Rolling his eyes, he laughed again. "I knew I shouldn't have said that the second after I said it."

"Isn't the phrase 'the second I said it?' " she asked, cocking her head to the side still enjoying his admission.

"Yes, but I didn't regret it when I said it. I regretted saying it the second I realized I'd said too much."

Evie took his hand without thinking. "It wasn't too much! It was very sweet and I think the nicest thing someone's ever said to me. Thank you for sharing that. Never regret a true emotion." She held onto his hand, realizing how good it felt against hers and continued walking.

Her words struck his heart as he repeated them in his head, 'Never regret a true emotion.' Living by her words and being honest with himself, he knew that was the moment he started falling in love with her.

William's hands were warm and large, a little rough, but his grasp on hers was tender. When they turned the corner to her block and saw the street sign, he hesitated.

"What?" she asked, not sure why he stopped.

He shook his head while closing his eyes as reality sank in.

She dropped his hand in concern, worried about what happened to change his mood so unexpectedly. "What is it, William?"

They moved closer to the nearest building to talk. Once they were out of the pedestrian traffic, he explained. "I was hoping you lived on another street, like one or two down from this one."

Evie didn't understand why he would wish this. The street she grew up on was beautiful compared to most in the city. The large trees sparkled with tiny white lights lining the avenue for five or more blocks. All the doormen looked regal in their uniforms and the sidewalks and street were clean compared to most Manhattan streets. She was baffled by his reaction as if these weren't good things.

He looked over his shoulder then leaned toward her and whispered, "I was hoping you were more middle class, that's all."

"Oh." This, she didn't expect. He didn't like that she came from money, but she wanted to know why. "Um, is this all right?

"I just confessed to you that sometimes I bum drinks because I can't afford them. I . . . I know a million things to do on the cheap in Manhattan out of survival, not just for kicks. I wish I could say I can afford nice restaurants and opera tickets, but I can't. You should know this now." He hated feeling this way. He wished he could give the city to her on a silver platter, but he couldn't and by looking around her street, that's what she's used to.

Uncomfortable, he leaned back against the wall waiting for her to tell him their friendship, whatever this was they were to each other, was over. He expected as much. He didn't know rich people, but he knew they tended to stick to their own kind. He watched as Evie shifted in front of him looking down at her shoes and as she tucked her hair behind her ear in quiet contemplation, he wished she would say something. He also wished he could hold her hand again like they did a few minutes ago before fate deemed it necessary to interfere. Suddenly, he was very aware of all the things he'd wished he had done before this moment, before the realities of their different worlds collided.

Her voice broke into his pity party, and she lifted her chin, and said, "I don't like the opera and you can afford nice restaurants. I like Pizzeria La Cucina and you introduced me to it."

"It's just a pizza place—" he said.

"I don't care about that stuff!" Evie professed more than she was comfortable doing because she didn't want their friendship to end over money. Money seemed to control every other aspect of her life, but it had never played a part in *their* relationship. Little things had led them to where they were, what they were in this moment, and she loved that too much to let it go. "I like you, William. I can't take away my parents—my family's money, but I've done all those things you say you can't afford and I don't need those things. I've enjoyed the time we've spent together."

He stepped forward, pulling her against his chest

and buried his nose into her hair again, something he couldn't get enough of. His strong arms slid around her body and held her close. His first thought was she smelled delectable. His second was that she wanted to spend more time with him despite their differences. Holding her tight, he hoped it showed her how much he wanted to be with her as well.

Enjoying the smell of him, she rested her cheek on his chest. As she wrapped her arms around his body, she worked on the adjectives that best described his smell to her, but the only one she could think of was delicious. She rolled her eyes at her thoughts, knowing she sounded silly, but it was true; maybe delectable worked also, but either way, he smelled really good.

He pulled back, breaking their embrace, but took her hands and clasped them together with his. "Do you still want to slum it with me on Monday?"

"I definitely want to slum it with you on Monday if you won't hold all of this . . ." She pointed behind her. ". . . against me?"

"You can't help that you're rich, so I won't hold it against you." They both laughed, and then he said, "I'm gonna go from here if that's all right. I think you've learned more about me than you should have at this stage in our relationship." He handed her bag back to her and shoved his hands into his pockets as she pulled her sweater closer to her body once again for warmth. "Goodnight, Evie."

"Goodnight, William."

Chapter 9

Sunday afternoon William rode down Park Avenue, one of the wealthiest streets in Manhattan. His mind wasn't on the impressive buildings on either side of the tree-lined street, but on Evie—the pretty girl who lived on it.

His body was weary today and he checked his watch. Another four hours and he could collapse into bed and sleep some more. Last night, he was restless with thoughts of Evie. Memories of the feel of her hand in his, and a few images of her lying in his bed wearing nothing but that freed bird, kept him from deep sleep.

William also got whiffs of her perfume every now and then and his whole body seemed to react to it, keeping him more awake than he liked. He already knew that girl was going to drive him crazy, so he pushed his face into his pillow, accepting that fact and fell asleep.

The morning came too fast, and he was tired as he started his shift. While delivering packages throughout the city, he remembered how he had vowed never to be ashamed of his roots. It was easy to lie in Manhattan because everyone seemed to be from somewhere else, but he was always proud to claim Staten Island as his home and that wasn't going to change now. He would show her his roots and hope she accepted him.

When she walked into Professor Lang's class on Monday, she was giddy and a little goofy, very un-Everleigh like, feeling more Evie these days. She found a seat and started to gnaw anxiously on her pen.

William walked in, squeezing ahead of slower students anxious to find Evie. When he spotted her, he took the stairs by two and shuffled down the row. Sitting down next to her, he leaned over, and said, "I was looking forward to seeing you." His voice was a whisper making sure no one else was listening. "But even more to tonight."

"Me too." She giggled, but kept her voice low.

William saw the chewed pen resting against her bottom lip, and felt the need to remark. "I thought you of all people had more respect for pens than that."

He was staring with a raised eyebrow, which made her remove the pen and look at it. "Oh this? I was nervous . . . or excited, maybe a little anxious." She set the pen down on her notebook and looked at her hands in her lap instead, knotting her fingers together to distract her mind from the pen.

"I hope that's because of me."

Every hair on her neck stood on end and she tried to keep from kissing him right there in the middle of Professor Lang's British Literature for Majors class. She took a shallow breath trying to regain her composure while he leaned back, sliding down in his seat to get comfortable. She didn't say anything because she didn't need to. They both already knew the answer.

Evie didn't take as many notes as usual and William noticed she had random doodles across the pad in between the notes she was taking. His hand wandered over to her pad and he wrote, *a little distracted today?* She was embarrassed and couldn't hide her emotions from him. She felt so immature and frustrated that she shut her notebook and sat back to listen to the professor.

William saw that he either embarrassed or annoyed her. He wasn't trying to do that at all. He thought it was cute she couldn't hide her emotions. He touched her forearm where others couldn't see. "I'm sorry. I'm also a little distracted today." She liked that he reassured her and exposed his feelings to equal hers. When they left the building after class, he asked, "If you still want to meet me tonight, I can meet you at your place?"

Smiling at him, she hit him playfully on the arm. "Of course, I still want to go, but let's meet somewhere else."

He adjusted his bag from sliding off his shoulder then ran his hands through his hair resting them on the crown of his head. He was hoping to be a little more official tonight and meet at her place and go from there. He was now worried she might be embarrassed of him. He struggled to answer her, but rushed out a suggestion anyway. "Um . . . let's meet at Pizzeria La Cucina at eight."

"Yes, that's perfect."

Watching her walk away, he said, "Bye."

Evie spent her afternoon writing an essay she hoped would get her into a summer class that Professor Lang was offering to a small, select group of students. After printing it out and tucking it into her bag to turn in on Wednesday, she showered. The warm humidity had frizzed her hair earlier, and she spent a few extra minutes trying to manage the waves that had appeared. She liked the soft natural waves, but with everyone else's disapproval of the wilder look, she was usually instructed to straighten her hair.

As she was trying to decide what to wear when going out with a new friend, she remembered how William said he liked when girls wore skirts, but equally liked a girl in jeans. He had seen her plenty of times in skirts, so she decided to dress more casual, like he did. She found her most worn out pair of jeans with frayed spots on the legs and cuffs at the bottom—a pair she adored, but kept hidden in the back of her closet. She put a simple white V-neck T-shirt on that hugged her curves and slipped on a pair of white sneakers. They were too bright white for her liking since she'd never worn them before, never having an occasion to before tonight. After some simple make-up, she sprayed her signature scent on and grabbed a short black cardigan because it was still chilly at night.

She almost made her escape undetected, but Audrey saw her and stopped dead in her tracks, stunned by her sister's appearance. "What are you wearing?" She asked, blurting it out.

Feeling self-conscious, Evie crossed her ankles and slid her hands into her front pockets. Sensing how uncomfortable her sister was, she clarified. "I mean you look amazing, Sis. Where are you going?" She was surprised her sister actually looked her age for once, instead of always being perfectly put together.

Appreciating the approval from her younger, and much hipper sister, Evie smiled. "I'm meeting a friend from school. We're going to blow off some steam from all of the studying we've been doing."

Audrey lost interest as soon as school was mentioned, and tuned out the rest. She walked back toward the kitchen and waved over her shoulder. "Have fun and I'm so borrowing your outfit soon. Those jeans are hot." She disappeared into the kitchen, letting the door swing behind her.

Evie left the apartment in a hurry, almost feeling as if she was sneaking out. As soon as the elevator doors opened into the lobby, she ran out. "Hi, Walter. Bye, Walter."

She beat him once again to the door which made both of them laugh. "Have a good time, Miss Wright." Evie noted the smile on his face reflected the one she had, almost as if he knew her secret and was happy for her.

Evie was running later than she'd expected, so she took a cab over to the pizzeria. She gave the driver a large bill for the inexpensive fare, not caring about the money, and rushed into the restaurant without waiting for change. William was already at the bar. She slowed her pace trying to regain control of her breath as she walked over and sat down on the barstool next to him.

Thrilled to see her, always thrilled to see her, he gave her his best smile. "Hey there. Wow, you look great tonight. I haven't seen you wear anything like this before. I like it."

"I thought I would go for casual tonight since I didn't know how to plan accordingly."

"Would you like a drink?"

"No, thank you."

"Do you always know what's ahead, so you can plan accordingly?" He stood up and offered her his hand as assistance, which she graciously accepted.

"Too much."

"Too much?"

"Yes, I always know what I'm doing, what to wear to do it, and what is expected of me at all times. I know too much. I think that's why I'm looking forward to tonight so much." They walked out the door and down the street chatting.

He looked down at his shoes feeling sad for her. "That's disappointing to hear."

"No!" She jumped in front of him making him halt with her hands on his chest. "No, that's not the only reason I was looking forward to tonight, that's only one small part of it." She waited until he smiled again and then they started walking.

As they took two steps down to the subway, she stopped and looked around worried, the inner turmoil building. "What is it?" he asked, concerned.

"I . . . um . . . this is going to sound weird, but I've only been on the subway once when I was seven."

"You're kidding me, right?" He was amazed by this tidbit. If she grew up in Manhattan and had ridden the subway only once in her life, this girl was rich, but not just rich, *stinking rich*. William couldn't help but feel intimidated by her wealth now.

"No, I'm not kidding and I was always told never to ride it at night." She looked nervous.

William took her hand protectively in his and reassured her. "Don't worry. I'll take care of you."

Evie remained close to him as he loaded his MetroCard to cover the fare, went through the stalls, and boarded the train. All the seats were taken, but one, and he offered it to her. She shook her head not wanting to be alone, surrounded by the mass of strangers, so he sat down and pulled her onto his lap. When he wrapped his arms snugly around her, she felt safe.

Three stops later, William led Evie off the train and back to street level. A bit frantic, he turned to her and said,

"We've got to run." Squeezing her hand tight, he pulled her behind him. They ran to the booth and he told the man about their reservation. A bit put out, the man signaled for them to board.

"Another ferry?" she asked as she smiled at William.

"Not just any ferry, but one that will show us how lucky we are to live in New York." The wind had picked up, but they both chose to stay outside the boat cabin and enjoy the lights of the skyline.

"Just so you know, I've been on a night cruise around the harbor before." She knew he thought she hadn't really seen the city, but felt proud to be able to say she had experienced this before.

"I bet not on a ferry."

She laughed under her breath and then shared more. "You're right, only by yacht. I prefer the ferry."

"I think I'd prefer the yacht." William was only half joking.

Because he wanted to and the moment seemed to call for it, William wrapped his arms around her middle and pulled Evie against his chest. She relaxed her back on him. They both liked the feel and the heat from being this close. She smiled, losing herself in the moment of being with someone so wonderful, feeling like a different person, and wanting to blank out her reality. And, although she should have caught the obvious signs of William's attachment to her, she enjoyed being free for the first time in years. She felt like who she wanted to be.

They didn't talk the rest of the hour-long harbor cruise except once when William complimented her. "I like your hair like this. It's pretty." This was the first time she felt confident letting her naturally wavy hair show.

When the ferry docked, they walked hand-in-hand to Little Italy and sat at a sidewalk café. William knew this particular restaurant would charge him more for sitting outside than inside, but it was worth it for the people watching. He had discovered that Evie found this a formidable form of entertainment like he did. They shared a large plate of Alfredo noodles and a bottle of house Chianti. Their conversation flowed as easily as the wine and to their surprise, it felt natural and not forced in any way. When the check came, Evie spoke up, grabbing it from the waiter. "Let me get this, please."

"What kind of guy would I be if I did that?"

"The kind of guy that allows a girl to thank him for all of his generosity. You paid for the subway and the cruise. If you let me get this, I'll let you get the cab ride back."

"No subway then?"

"I think I've had enough excitement tonight."

He leaned forward as the waiter left with her credit card and whispered, "By the way, before you think I'm some knight in shining armor, you should know the cruise is free. You just have to make a reservation. The cruise is courtesy of our tax dollars and the city of New York."

"I had no idea. That's actually really cool." She still didn't feel bad paying for dinner. It even made her feel more independent.

They were quiet again during the taxi ride to her home. As they neared the Upper East Side, William scooted a little closer, trying to be nonchalant. "I had a memorable night with you. I hope you feel the same and we can do it again soon."

She took his hand, pulling it onto her lap, and closed

the small gap between them. Starting to feel tired, she rested her head on his shoulder. "I would love to."

The cab pulled up to the curb in front of her building and Joe the overnight doorman was prompt to open the door. "Good evening, Miss Wright and Mr . . . Oh."

Evie interrupted, "Good evening, Joe." She turned back to face William. "Thank you for an amazing night. I'll never forget it."

"May I have your number?" William asked, feeling timid now.

She smiled as she took his phone from him and added her name and then her number to his contacts list.

It was now or never, he thought. William dragged his sweating palms down his thighs and tried to smile at her though his nerves were getting the better of him. Although he never remembered being this nervous with a girl before, he went for it anyway. Slowly, he leaned toward her, closing his eyes, and kissed her. She didn't pull away which he took as a good sign, so he slid his hand up her bare neck and came to a stop on the side of her jaw. His fingertips disappeared into her silky hair and he pressed his lips a bit firmer against hers.

Evie tilted her head, feeling a rush of emotion fill her heart, and though she wanted to deepen the kiss, neither of them did. They kept it innocent and sweet, perfect for the pace of their relationship.

As they pulled away, she was the last to reopen her eyes. "I'll see you soon," he said in a hushed voice for her ears only.

Without realizing she did it, she closed her eyes and touched her lips unaware of her audience: the cab driver, Joe, and William. When she opened them again, she and

William exchanged one last knowing smile before she got out and ran into the lobby. She dashed upstairs and into her room, locked the door, and melted against it, sliding to the floor. She could still feel the pressure and heat of William's lips, of his kiss on hers. She smiled and giggled, feeling lightheaded and giddy thinking of him and that perfect kiss they shared.

William leaned back, sinking into the back seat as Joe shut the door and the taxi took off into traffic, but he stopped the driver one block up. "I'll get out here." He could barely afford the current fare, so he paid the cabbie and walked the remaining fourteen blocks home to save money, thinking of Evie, and smiling the entire way.

Chapter 10

The next day, Everleigh walked into Rock Center Cafe and approached the hostess stand, "Can you please tell me if Mr. Whitney has arrived?"

The hostess scanned her reservations list, and looked back up. "No, he hasn't."

"Thank you. I'll wait over here." Everleigh turned and went to sit by the window. She felt sick to her stomach thinking of the mess she's created with William. With her mind preoccupied, she dragged the cage pendent back and forth along the chain of the necklace. She just wanted a friend, a study buddy, but she got so much more. William had already become important to her in such a short time that she knew she was in deep. Guilt engulfed her in the last twenty-four hours. Last night, she overstepped propriety. But when she was with William, all of her problems, Tom and her family washed away, and she lived in the moment. She also found she was whom she always wanted to be when she was with him.

Tom walked in and spotted her, greeting her with a kiss on her cheek then pulling her by the hand up to the hostess stand. "Thomas Whitney, table for two at twelve-thirty." Tom was still in business mode. The formality struck her in direct contrast to last night.

The hostess winked at him, disregarding Everleigh altogether, and spoke to Tom. "Follow me."

They were seated in the middle of the restaurant and as Everleigh took her menu in hand, she asked, "How's your day?"

"Our new CFO is paranoid thinking there's going to be a takeover. He's been on a war path, but it's being handled."

She looked over the top of the menu at him. "Sounds worrisome."

"It's nothing for you to be concerned about. We're a profitable company that's very attractive to outside parties. Of course, investors will be looking to buy us out. I take it as a compliment. We're too smart to let a takeover happen though. What looks good for lunch?"

Everleigh felt more like one of his employees instead of his fiancée by the tone he was using. Although typical, it was still disappointing. "I'm thinking the pasta with blackened chicken—"

The waiter walked up to greet them, and Tom said, "I think you should order the grilled fish. It's much lighter."

Embarrassed by his insinuation in front of the waiter, Everleigh sat there inwardly fuming.

"Are you ready to order, sir?" the waiter asked.

"Yes. I'll have the Chicken Pasta Frizole and she'll have the grilled halibut with steamed vegetables. Two iced teas and no breadbasket." Tom handed the menus to the waiter, proud of his choices.

Leaning forward with her hands tucked on her lap, under her breath she accused him. "I can't believe you did that."

"What, the fish? Seriously, Everleigh, that's what has you upset?" Tom chuckled, adjusting his napkin on his lap and scoping out the restaurant clientele to see if he recognized anyone. This is what he did. He liked to be seen. He liked showing off his possessions and Everleigh knew that's exactly what she was to him—a possession.

"Stop telling me what can and can't upset me! That was rude and embarrassing. I wanted the chicken not the fish and you disregarded my desires and ordered what you thought I should eat."

Tom turned back to focus his full attention on her. He was demanding as he gritted his teeth together. "Everleigh, you will not speak to me like this—"

"I will, damn it!" She raised her voice higher than she intended. "You are twenty-six, not sixty. You are not my parent. You can talk to me like a normal person, like your equal."

"I treat you like a child because that is how you act. You've been petulant and irresponsible. You have to earn respect, Everleigh. All you've shown me recently is that you need discipline, and with that, punishment. That's all you've earned."

"I'm already being punished. I live in Hell. It can't get worse than this!" Her eyes welled with tears.

He leaned forward resting one of his hands on the table while the other took her hand in his. After he brought her hand to his mouth, he kissed it. "You don't know what Hell is, but keep this up and you will soon find out."

She yanked her hand away like she had been burned.

"You can't destroy me anymore than you have. I'm nothing when I'm with you!"

"Be careful what you say next. I'm warning you now, Everleigh, the wedding is on the line here. I don't care how many years I've invested in you."

She stood up in protest, but managed to speak in her normal tone. "Invested? I'm not a business acquisition that shows profits and losses. I'm a person. And please don't threaten me with the wedding. That's not a threat. That would be a dream come true." She threw her napkin on the empty plate in front of her and hurried through the crowded restaurant and out the front door.

She ran to her left back into the heart of Manhattan and away from this part of town as fast as she could as crazy thoughts flooded her mind. Hailing a cab, she jumped in as soon as one pulled to the curb to make her escape from Tom. She leaned forward, giving the cabbie directions to the park near her home.

With her thoughts frenzied, she took her phone out and called William on a whim. He didn't answer, but she left a message asking him to join her. She knew she shouldn't have, but she needed the comfort only he could provide.

The sight of this part of the park calmed her anxiety over the fight with Tom. She paid the cab driver and started walking. Just as she found a vacant park bench, she received a text from him:

William: *Five minutes until lunch. I'll bring subs and meet you there.*

Evie: *I'll wait for you.*

The bench was dirty, but she didn't care. Her mind was weighed down with more important issues today. He didn't keep her waiting long, explaining he was close to the area when she called. There was more silence than words in the beginning because he could tell she was troubled and he didn't want to push.

As they ate, she debated whether she should tell him about her first lunch of the day. But she couldn't bring herself to say anything. She enjoyed her time with him and didn't want to ruin it, so she remained quiet on the matter. It was a conversation they needed to have, but she was not ready to risk *this* . . . this . . . what they were sharing right now. She took another bite of her sandwich and said, "This is good."

William still found it amusing and intriguing that she ate such normal foods like it was the first time she had ever eaten them—first the pizza and now the sandwich. Surely, she's had a sub sandwich before. "Do you eat many subs?"

"Not really. I had a nanny who used to take me to a local deli and we would share one. I liked that nanny."

William thought most of her stories about her childhood seemed gloomy though he didn't think she meant them that way.

"Does your mom make dinner?"

"Ha! No, but we found the best French chef two years ago. He is amazing." Her mood brightened as she said this.

William laughed with a full mouth of food, but quickly covered it so as not to be gross before he grabbed his drink to wash it down. After he stopped laughing, he asked, "Have you ever eaten a hotdog from a street cart?"

"No. I was never allowed." Evie's expression turned serious. She looked down at the crumbs left on the sandwich wrapper. "Please don't make fun of me."

"I'm sorry if it came across as teasing. I wasn't making fun of you at all. I'm just surprised by how untainted you are by the real world—"

"Oh, I'm tainted more than you know."

"You say things like that, but never elaborate. And, a lot of time, I see sadness in your eyes. Are you sad, Evie?"

She felt his eyes heavy on her. He was searching for answers she couldn't give him, not yet, at least. "I have things in my life to be sad about, yes. But not when I'm with you." She said this with conviction.

Her little confession surprised him. "You're the most honest person I think I've ever met. Don't ever change." William reached across the bench to touch her hand, but she tucked it to her side.

Feeling the sting of rejection, he wasn't quite sure what went wrong between them in the preceding moments.

Tears filled her eyes again for the second time today, but this time for very different reasons. She knew she hadn't been honest with him and she hated herself for lying. The guilt was consuming her. Just as a tear escaped and rolled down her cheek, she stood and announced, "I have to go." Picking her purse up, she thanked him for lunch before she rushed away.

Evie made it about ten feet before she was grabbed and pulled against his chest. He held her tighter than she had ever been held. She couldn't escape him if she wanted, but she didn't want to, so she stopped trying and relaxed within the safety of his arms, letting him envelop her.

His heart beat strong as she breathed in his scent, a combination of soap and a light sweat, made her a bit lightheaded. She wanted as much of him as she could get right then, but her reality was a dark cloud hanging over her. She took a deep breath as William stroked her hair, gaining her strength to fight all the good in the feelings he brought out in her.

"I'm here if you need a friend, Evie. You can tell me anything."

Pushing against his body, she detached from him, and with her head held down in shame, she replied, "Not this." Then she walked away.

"Evie?" William wanted to run after her. He wanted to convince her that she could trust him. No matter what problems she had, he would help her, but something about their exchange made him think she wasn't ready for that. She needed more time. He hoped deep down that he was doing the right thing by letting her leave, but had a sinking feeling she needed more than a friend—she needed an ally.

Evie kept walking; her heart felt empty and pained at the same time. She couldn't tell him she was engaged. She didn't want to hurt him, but knew someday soon she would have to be honest with him and that made her cry even more.

When she entered the lobby of her building, Walter smiled and greeted her in his usual chipper voice. "Good afternoon, Miss Wright. You have company expecting you upstairs."

She kept a steady pace and didn't look at him for fear of breaking down again. He was a constant in her life since she could remember, always good to her. Walter had always felt like an uncle to her though she never wanted to burden him with the bond.

Feeling sick to her stomach, she said, "I'm sure I do." She kept her sunglasses on, hiding her eyes, as she entered the elevator.

Knowing who was waiting for her on the other side of the front door, Evie stood outside for a full three minutes trying to collect her thoughts and settle her nerves. She took one last deep breath before she opened the door to the apartment.

She was unsure of which Tom would be waiting for her—she prayed for predictable today.

No one was in the foyer, but when she rounded the corner and entered the formal living room, she saw Tom with his back to her. He was holding a crystal glass filled with ice and scotch and was staring out the large window. He didn't appear to realize she had entered the room.

But he had. Tom, without losing focus on the world outside the window, said, "I never get tired of this view. You're a very lucky girl to have grown up here." His tone was ominous and then he tipped the glass back and finished the alcohol in one large gulp.

After the clatter of the ice cubes against the empty crystal glass subsided, she set her purse on the table, careful in her choice of words. "Your apartment also has breathtaking views."

With a slight shake of his head, he looked down at his now empty glass. He turned, his brown eyes piercing her, and asked, "Drink?"

"No, thank you." Evie sat down in a side chair, pressed against the arm and tried to appear calm.

"Hope you don't mind if I do?" It was rhetorical, so she didn't answer. Tom walked over to the liquor tray, dropped two new ice cubes into the glass, and poured the liquor from the decanter up to the middle of the glass. "Scotch is an acquired taste."

She sat there silently, never taking her eyes off him as he paced. She was too afraid to lose sight of him. After taking another long drink, he came and sat in a chair next to her with their knees barely touching. She was having trouble reading him and took a staggered breath, sensing he could see her fear though she attempted to hide it.

He sat up and said, "Your dress got dirty." His finger rubbed the dirty spot near the bottom of her skirt. "If you'd like I can take it to my cleaner. I'm sure he can get the spot off and make it look good as new again." Evie remained frozen, not wanting to reveal that she had been at the park. That was her secret and she had no intention of sharing it.

Tom leaned in even closer and let his free hand run along her cheek. His breath hit her face. "I hope you can forgive my rudeness this afternoon. I was out of line holding the wedding as a threat. I would never let anything . . ." He looked her straight in the eyes. "... Or anyone come between us. You can continue our wedding plans as scheduled." He picked her hand up, bringing it to his mouth. "My sweet Everleigh. My life is only complete with you in it." He kissed her hand, eyeing her the whole time.

Everleigh's mind was racing with unanswered questions: *Did he not hear what I told him today? Was he not listening to me? What am I doing?*

He pulled her in for a kiss. With some resistance, their lips met just as the front door opened. "Oh, we've walked in on the lovebirds, Audrey. Hurry to your room and give them privacy."

Audrey stood there, glancing between Evie and Tom before she decided to leave the room. She felt uneasy as if they had walked in on something not quite right, something maybe even a little dark. But Evie had eyed her as if to tell her to go, so she did.

Paying no mind to Audrey, Tom stood and greeted

Everleigh's mother with two air cheek kisses. "Kitty, you're looking lovely today."

"Tom, that may work on Everleigh, but I've been around the block a time or two to know a fib when I hear it." They both laughed, and he took her bags from her as she settled down on the settee next to her daughter. "Darling, how did your dress get dirty?"

Tom stepped forward to reassure Kitty. "Don't worry. I'm going to take it to my cleaner. He's a miracle worker."

Everleigh stood up abruptly, disgusted watching Tom and her mother play their weird, twisted game of 'all is right in the world.' She picked her purse up off the table and walked around the chair. Tom followed behind and pulled her by the arm, his lips pressed against her ear, and whispered, "Tell me you forgive me, sweetheart."

She nodded automatically, knowing she had no other option. Then as a perfect distraction, her mother pulled out the wedding planning book and Tom rushed to sit next to her on the couch.

Everleigh shut her door and slid down the solid white wood, numb to the world. Reaching up, she locked it before she had any unwanted visitors trying to get in, and technically, everyone was unwanted at that moment. Though she also knew deep down that a lock wouldn't keep the monsters out.

Her phone beeped, bringing her back to the present, and she opened her purse to see who had texted her.

William: *I don't know what happened today. I'm sorry if I said something wrong. I'm here for you if you want to talk.*

Tears barreled over her bottom lids in a rush of

emotion. It was clear to her now. William represented everything she would never have, but her heart still struggled to come to terms with that.

She needed to scare him off. She just witnessed how entangled her family was with Tom and knew how they thought. William would never be accepted and Tom would never let her get away. She was trapped.

Everleigh: *I'm not an honest person. I struggle every day.*

William continued on his bike, picking up speed, needing to burn away his conflicting emotions. He didn't understand her cryptic text. Was she telling him that she lied? None of that mattered because he had already fallen in love with her. He stopped to text her again, wanting to tell her more, needing her to know she's not alone.

William: *We all have struggles. Sometimes it's easier to overcome them together. I'm here for you.*

Chapter 11

William got inside the auditorium at his usual time, but he couldn't find Evie. While trudging up the steps to find a seat, he said a silent prayer that she was just running late. Before he even set his bag down, she came from behind, and said, "Hi."

She was beautiful and in the split second their eyes connected, he could tell there was still hope for them. Although he wanted to say so much more to her, he didn't, knowing now was not the time. "Hi," he replied, keeping it simple, uncomplicated.

They both pulled out their notebooks and pens. His being the pen she gave him, which was his favorite.

Professor Lang started at the top of the hour. William tapped her notebook with his pen and when she turned and looked at him, he whispered, "I'm sorry about yesterday."

"Why are you sorry?" His apology surprised her.

"I felt like things ended on a weird note."

"I should be apologizing to you. I'm sorry for leaving

115

like that. I . . . I . . . just, I can't explain it, but I am sorry."

"No need for apologies, Evie."

After class was dismissed, William hoped she would join him. "Coffee?"

"Yes. I could use some today. I'm need to turn my paper in first."

They worked their way across the aisle and down the steps to Professor Lang. As she handed him the paper, William noticed the professor seemed pleased. Lang pulled William aside to talk in private. Evie turned to look over her shoulder when she overheard the professor tell William that he had been accepted into his summer program. She kept walking to allow them privacy and left through the auditorium doors.

He rejoined her in the hallway and as soon as William and Evie got outside the building, she stopped upset by what she had heard. "Why didn't you tell me you're doing Lang's summer program?"

"I'm doing Lang's summer program." His response was flat and he was confused why she was upset.

"William, he said you're in!"

"And?" He was perplexed by this conversation.

"When did you turn in your paper?" she asked with her hand planted on her hip.

He hesitated, thinking about how he could phrase this best. "I didn't." He settled on honest and direct.

"What do you mean? To be considered for one of the ten spots you have to submit an essay. Lang said he had received forty-five. How have you already been accepted when the deadline is today?"

"He asked me to participate." William shrugged, watching her reaction and hoping she didn't freak out any more than she already had.

"He asked you?" Her voice went up an octave. "As in, he wants you in the program, so he just gave you a spot?"

"Yeah, I guess so. It's also the final credits I need to graduate."

"Okay, but that's still incredible. Maybe I underestimated you."

They started walking again. He looked over and said, "A lot of people do."

She stopped again as reality dawned. "Wait! That means there are forty-five people vying for nine spots." She looked at him, shaking her head. "Those odds aren't good and I need the credits for graduation, too."

They started walking once again.

"You're an intelligent girl, Evie. I don't think you have to worry. Lang can see talent just as much as I can."

"So you're saying you became friends with me because of my intellect?"

He laughed as he opened the door to Bean There. "It was a little more superficial than that."

She smiled, laughing. "You became friends with me because you had insidious plans for me behind your charming façade?"

"You think I'm charming?" A playful smile spread across his face as he teased her.

She hit him on the arm, feeling embarrassed as they ordered their usual drinks. Sprawling their stuff across their two favorite tables, they started going over the notes she had taken and the highlighted portions of his book.

After a few hours of studying, Evie sighed, resigned. "I have to go."

"Why?"

"I just do. I have a commitment." She wanted him to read between the lines, hoping she would never have to say it, but he was trusting in her answer.

Before she had a chance to stand, he took her hand, leaned in and said, "Are we good?"

"More than good." She left the coffee shop with a smile on her face and happiness in her heart.

* * *

Evie, unlike her usual self, had finagled her way out of several dinners with Tom and one society dinner using her finals as an excuse. But by Saturday, she needed a break from all the reading and some fresh air. She wanted to see William, but he had picked up extra shifts and hadn't been able to spend any other time with her. She felt she might be the reason for his lack of funds and took the burden of blame since she had made him pay for the long cab ride they took after dinner. She wanted to connect with him again, and texted him:

Evie*: Hi.*

He responded quickly: *Hi.*

She tried to think of something clever, but nothing came to mind. Finally, she asked what she really wanted to know, hoping it would kick off the conversation: *What are you doing?*

William*: I'm working. Off soon. What are you*

doing?

Evie: *I'm about to go to the park.*

William: *Wait an hour? I can join you.*

And with that tiny texted question she knew she had to see him. She felt happy and typed: *I will.* Her hands shook from nervousness waiting for his response even though she didn't even ask him anything.

Her phone beeped and written on the screen was: *It's a date.*

It's a date. *A date.* Her mind was focused on him alone, leaving her realities behind as her stomach did flips and she jumped to her feet, running into her closet. She had no idea of what to wear to the park in the middle of the afternoon to meet a boy that you like a lot. She settled on a pair of jeans because William was a jeans kind of guy and she so desperately wanted to be a jeans kind of girl. But, jeans baffled Evie in many ways. Her mother had raised her to believe that etiquette deemed jeans were for ranchers or to wear when helping someone move, which they never had. They were not for everyday use and she wouldn't approve of them for a casual walk in the park on a sunny Saturday afternoon in Manhattan. What if someone saw her?

On the other hand, she had worn them once before on the ferry and her sister practically lived in jeans when not doing the family thing. Apparently when it came to her family, it is acceptable for seventeen-year-olds to wear them out of the house, but not anyone above high school age.

With that challenge firmly set in her mind, she slipped on a pair she felt looked quite nice on her and grabbed a green shirt from its hanger. While putting on her metallic flats she pulled her hair back in an untidy ponytail and left the house. Looking at her watch when she entered the lobby, she saw Joe was here today, and smiled at him trying to race him to the door. Unlike Walter, he was overly serious on the job and wasn't amused by her antics.

William showered then pulled out a pair of khaki slacks hanging in his closet. He knew Evie would appreciate that he wasn't wearing jeans and he wanted her to know through this gesture that he wasn't just a jeans and T-shirt kind of guy. He searched through his three clothes stashes: the closet, under the bed, and in the small dresser for his one nice collared shirt, but couldn't find it. He must have left it at his parents' home the last time he exchanged his summer clothes for his winter ones. Frustrated, he grabbed a plain heather grey T-shirt and threw one of his plaid flannel shirts over it. He knew he couldn't tuck these in or he would look ridiculous, so he left them hanging over the top of the pants. He threw on his sneakers doubting his look, but headed over to meet her anyway. When he rode into the park, he smiled at the simplicity and beauty of her choice of favorite places.

As she rounded the corner to the park, she saw William locking his bike to a park bench. She hurried over and hugged him as he stood up. After catching his balance, he wrapped his arms around her not letting this opportunity pass. The smell of her hair mixed with the feel of her body against him almost did him in, but he changed his thoughts to Dachshunds on leashes, burly men smoking cigars, and his aunt's weird obsession with ceramic pigs. That did the trick. Pigs, burly smoking men, and dogs were not sexy in the least.

Evie had seen that strange look of confusion before on William. It made her feel that maybe she had crossed the line with him. But when he smiled at her, taking her hand in his, and asked, "Shall we walk?" all her self-doubts disappeared. They walked all the way to down to the water and then back. There was not a lack of conversational topics and the other person always listened with great interest. Two hours had passed when Evie looked at her watch. "I have to go, William. I have to get back home."

They stood facing each other while holding both their hands together near his chained bike. William didn't want to take his eyes off her because he knew he wouldn't see this beautiful girl for two more days once they parted. But, she needed to go, he reminded himself and they dropped their hands to their respective sides.

Her hands felt empty without his, which triggered a train of thought signaling his importance in her life. She once again swept those feelings under the rug in her mind that it's not her choice to make and to focus on the moment. William started unlocking his bike and Evie decided to be brave and honest. "I think you look great. I really like your pants."

William laughed. "This is my version of dressing up for you." He propped his bike against the park bench then walked back taking her in his arms, and whispered, "You look incredible in jeans." He kissed her on the top of the head then grabbed his bike again. "I'll see you on Monday."

"Okay. Monday." Evie smiled, watching him ride away. It was an uncontrollable, silly kind of smile. She felt light and pretty from his words. She had never heard such a sexy compliment in all her life. With a sudden burst of energy, she started running home filled with excitement. As the world blurred by, she decided right then that she would buy more jeans . . . *and wear them more often.*

Evie had been reading a style magazine and feeling relaxed after arriving home, relaxed enough to kick her feet up on the coffee table just as Tom walked into the room, startling her. He hadn't been announced by security, which usually gave her enough time to prepare for his visits. After a very cut and dried greeting, she stood to go to her room and change clothes. She saw the way he looked at her, judging her attire, though he said nothing. Tom followed her into the bedroom. His tone was demanding when he said, "I don't want to be late, Everleigh, get a move on."

"Late for what?" She snapped back, already feeling beyond irritated by his shortness with her.

"We're meeting with the project manager for the Chicago expansion. He's bringing his wife. Did you forget?"

"Oh, uh . . ." She had forgotten which was very unlike her, but didn't have time to finish her cover up before being interrupted.

"You have a planner for a reason, use it. I can't have you missing important meetings. That would be embarrassing."

"Embarrassing for you or me?" she asked.

"Both! Now get in the shower. You smell like the outdoors." He dismissed her with a wave of his hand and left the room.

She should have known they had plans when he showed up. They didn't 'hang out' that much. It seemed to her they had become stale a long time ago and at this stage, it was a matter of convenience to have a steady date to all of these events they were expected to attend.

Change was coming though. She could feel it on the inside, and in her heart. Fear had kept her here, but could this other emotion blossoming inside overtake that fear? Not tonight, but she liked the feeling of hope that was building at just the thought.

Everleigh rinsed the outdoors off as she had been told and thought back to a conversation her dad had with her the night of her first date with Tom.

"Honey, this is a very important time in your life," he said, standing in front of her window, looking out. He turned to face his eldest daughter as he continued. *"We're good friends with the Whitneys'. You told your mother once that you thought Tom was attractive. This is your chance. You winning is the same as our family winning. You are our star, Everleigh."*

There seemed to be an intensity on his face that wasn't normally present when he spoke to her. But it was there now as he continued. "It's time you start thinking about your future, honey. It seems a lot of young men of proper background are marrying Europeans they meet on holiday. The number of eligible men in your age range is dwindling and Manhattan has a lot of competition. Tom is a catch—a damn good catch. We've known his family and him almost his entire life. He could bring a lot to the Wright family. " He rubbed his chin. "You're an adult now and I need you to think about the future of the Wrights and our place in society. Don't disappoint your mother and me." He walked to the door and opened it, but stopped long enough to say, "Keep that in mind tonight."

At seventeen, I was surprised I was even allowed to go out with a twenty-two year old.

Evie felt sick as the water beat down on her. She grabbed her stomach as if she had a cramp, the guilt her parents burdened her with twisting the hope that now eluded her. She slowly slid down the white tiled wall and gave herself two solid minutes to cry before she stood back up. It may be a burden, but as her father said, it was on her to carry it now for the family. Lifting her chin to regain her composure, she swallowed hard then turned off the shower. Her mindset was back where it needed to be because she would do anything for her family and this was all for them.

In the back of the car on the way to dinner, Everleigh watched Tom as he took a business call. She looked at his eyes and how focused they were. She watched as his hand tapped his leg, reinforcing the authority in his tone. When he glanced over at her and smiled, she saw it held no malice or irritation. It was sincere, genuine in nature, and her return smile was automatic.

She used to love him. She used to be *in love* with him. This engagement was not forced. In the beginning, she had wanted this. She had wanted to be his wife one day, but somewhere between then and now, things had changed. She had changed. As she watched him hang up his call, she knew he had changed, and not for the better. Maybe it was a domino effect. Maybe he was who he was because of whom she was now.

She also believed that she deserved happiness. Determined to regain her teenage dreams of him, she thought she might be able to find that love again. She had to . . . for her family.

Just before midnight, Everleigh walked into her bedroom and saw the jeans she had worn earlier lying on the floor. She pulled them on before she even took her dress off. After slipping her dress off, she hung it back in her closet then pulled the T-shirt she also wore earlier back on. She climbed into bed and in the dark and quiet of her room, she could smell the outdoors and William all around her. And if she concentrated on the image of William at the park today, she could also feel his body against hers. She fell asleep with her arms wrapped around herself, finding comfort in the memories.

This same night, William went to a baseball game with his childhood best friend, Bobby, and his little brother, Dallas. A guy's night out was always a good time, but he found tonight his thoughts were elsewhere. As the game went into extra innings, Dallas noticed William wasn't his usual talkative self. He nudged him and asked, "So, who's the girl?"

"What?" William looked to his right in surprise.

"Who's the girl who has you looking like a jackass with that goofy grin you've been sporting all night?" his brother asked again.

Bobby jumped on this opportunity as it all became clear to him. He loved to taunt and wouldn't miss an opportunity. "Give us the deets, man. We know you've got'em."

"There's a girl," he admitted, turning back to Dallas, "that I like."

"Where'd you meet her?"

"She's in one of my classes." William's response was sharp, trying to end the conversation because his admission made him feel uncomfortable. He wasn't ready to share Evie with them just yet.

Sensing his unease, Dallas made a suggestion. "Bring her home soon. She sounds like someone we should meet."

"Yeah, maybe I will."

Chapter 12

Exam day. William leaned to his left and whispered, "Good luck," just as Evie said it to him. After a shared laugh, they begin the test.

Since she finished before him, she walked down the stairs to hand in her paper.

When William finished, he saw Professor Lang speaking with Evie at his desk. Wanting to give them time to talk, he walked down the stairs, taking his time. He hoped Lang was giving her the news she wanted to hear, which was the same thing he wanted—she's in the summer program. After setting his paper in the tray, he left not realizing she was trailing behind.

As soon as they reached the hallway, Evie asked with hope in her voice, "I've got the whole day, what about you?"

William turned around, happy to have her near, but paused to look her in the eyes and give her his most devilish smile. "When you say the whole day, do mean the entire day or an hour or so and then you have some other commitment to rush off to?"

She didn't even try to fight a laugh. She tilted her head and enjoyed hearing his excitement in the prospect of time together, but clarified for his sake. "The whole day, not night, but day."

He grabbed her by the hand, and greedily announced, "You're all mine then! Come on, let's go."

They hopped on the subway down to Battery Park and she started to question their destination. "The ferry again?" she asked, raising her eyebrows, when they arrived. "You might need to seek help for this obsession with boats after you work out your highlighter addiction."

"I'm taking you home." He smirked, feeling lighthearted while teasing her.

"We were closer to your home when we were at school."

"I'm taking you to Staten Island to meet my family."

If it wasn't attached, Evie swore her chin would have hit the ground, but in his happiness, William leaned down while sliding his hands into her hair and kissed her, calming her developing concerns. Without hesitation, she wrapped her arms around his neck needing this kiss more than she ever thought possible. When their lips parted she leaned her forehead against his shoulder smiling and felt breathless. "That was just..." She didn't finish, but instead sighed with a smile on her face.

William grinned at her, his eyes sparkling as hers looked up with a sense of vulnerability. Holding her close, he kissed the top of her head. He wanted to take away all of her concerns and worries and for her always to feel safe in his arms.

Evie's eyes watered from the joy she felt in her heart and she realized that unconditional love did exist in the world and she had found it. He loved her for her. Her family's name and money didn't matter. Tears slipped down her cheek, but she wiped them away before William was the wiser.

When the ferry blew its horn, he grabbed her hand and said, "Let's run for it." They ran just as the bridge was pulling back from shore. They made it onboard and he promptly wrapped his arms around her again, loving the way her body fit with his. He hadn't had a girlfriend in a couple of years, not wanting one because he wasn't meeting the right girls. But with her, he wanted all of that and more. He couldn't resist sharing a secret with her, so he leaned down close to her ear. "I never knew true happiness until now."

He placed three consecutive kisses on her neck, making her knees weak. She gripped the railing a little tighter to help support her faltering weight.

Being sentimental, William wanted to tell her he loved her and be with her forever, but he knew it was too soon and that would scare her. Instead, he held her with one protective arm around her waist and entwined their fingers.

When they reached the Staten Island dock, they walked toward a main road. Evie was unfamiliar with the island and was curious. "Do we need a cab?" She held her hand across her stomach as butterflies threatened to escape. She couldn't believe she was going to meet his family. She hadn't had enough time to come to terms that this was real and going to happen.

"Yeah, come with me and stay close."

Although that statement should have worried her, her stomach settled when she saw how comfortable he was in his hometown surroundings. William pointed out the different sights of his childhood neighborhood as they took the short cab ride. She found it interesting that she had always thought he seemed so in his element in Manhattan as well. It was then that she realized he was just happy in life and that transcended to wherever he was physically. No wonder she always enjoyed being with him.

After they arrived and he paid the ten-dollar cab fare, he said, "My parents bought this house the year they married twenty-five years ago."

"That's incredible. I can't wait to see inside." The house was older, but she could tell that they took care of it. She wanted to know everything about him, and that he trusted her enough to bring her here spoke volumes to her heart.

"My family's not home yet, but they will be soon. Get ready."

"Get ready? Is that a warning?"

He laughed and took her inside the living room without explaining further, setting their backpacks near the door. She stood there not wanting to intrude, waiting for him to lead the way. Evie noticed the living room was cozy and the furniture looked well lived in. She liked that it looked like homes she had seen on television—not perfect, but real.

William walked into the kitchen, inviting her to come with him. The kitchen was of decent size and there was a table placed near the window with just enough room between the counter and table to walk to the back door. "Soda?" he asked, bending over with his head hidden behind the open fridge door.

Her eyes widened at the site of his backside and smiled enjoying the view. "Yes, please." She giggled while looking around the room where she saw a large family portrait hanging on the opposite wall. "You were a cute kid."

"Hey, I'm not that old now." He handed her a glass of cola and they went back into the living room.

"Well, you're pretty cute now, too."

He laughed.

"I want to see your old room, will you show me?" She wanted to see William's history, his life. She wanted to see everything he was willing to share with her.

"It's embarrassing because they haven't changed it since I left. I think they still want me home," he said, climbing the stairs.

"Or they want you to stay seventeen and under their thumb forever."

Leading her out of his small childhood bedroom, he said, "I don't think my parents want me seventeen again. I got into a lot of trouble." He laughed at the memories, but she didn't respond. Noticing her hesitation at the door, he told her, "You can snoop. I don't mind."

"You know I want to." She was giddy as she walked around the room looking at random knick-knacks, trophies, awards, and books. "Wow! Your bookcase here is even bigger than the one at your place in the city."

"I keep my favorites with me, but I can't part with these either. One day I dream of having a library inside my home."

"You should come to my house and see ours. It's an entire wall of the informal living room. I've helped acquire a lot of the collection."

This was the first time Evie ever invited William into her life, and he immediately accepted. "I'd like that." He kissed her to show how he felt and as they stood there, they got lost in each other, momentarily forgetting where they were. They swayed out of weakness for each other, but he moved back, pulling her with him until his legs bumped into the bed. William sat down and she moved against him, their mouths meeting in the middle. She wanted to live in this kiss, this world, *his* world, and decided that when she was with him she would be wholly his and would selfishly take these few precious moments of happiness.

He pulled her down onto the bed and rolled over next to her. William knew Evie wanted him. He could read it in her body language, but he would never risk losing her by doing something stupid in a fleeting moment of rampant hormones. He had to remember that his mind was stronger than his body. Taking a deep breath, he inhaled her soft perfume and her Evie-ness deep into his lungs. He closed his eyes and pressed his body against hers, struggling not to attack her, trying to remember to be polite.

Evie had never felt so out of control before. Her body ruled her mind and she didn't want this feeling to ever end. She knew right then that she could never let this man go. She couldn't get enough of his kisses, enough of his body pressed against hers, or enough of him. She grabbed his shirt and pulled him down on top of her as her mouth attacked his with a sexual desperation she had never known.

Just as she felt his passion for her against her thigh, she heard, "Whoa! Dude, what are you fifteen?" His brother joked as he passed by the open door to the bedroom.

Evie and William bolted up, alarmed from being caught. She tried to catch her breath and get back into her right mind as she straightened her shirt, skirt, and her hair.

William stood up, hoping he wouldn't have any obvious signs of how she made him feel. He glanced down at the front of his pants then toward the door, and yelled, "Get the hell out, you perv," and kicked the door shut. Knowing he couldn't hide his infatuation with her, he ignored his erection and willed it away. He turned back around, reaching his hand out for her to take, and pulled her to her feet. With eyes reflecting what he considered a missed opportunity, his voice was husky. "I can die a happy man now, Evie." He straightened a section of her gone-crazy-from-the-bed-session-hair then caressed her lips against his for one last sweet kiss. They held hands and went back downstairs to the kitchen.

William laughed when he saw his brother chowing down on a bag of chips. "This is my younger brother Dallas. He's a pretty good guy when he's not pestering me." William brought her hand to his lips, kissed it then introduced her with pride. "Dallas, this is Evie Wright."

"It's very nice to meet you." Evie admired how handsome Dallas was and thought of her little sister. Audrey was totally boy crazy and would go nuts over this one.

Dallas stuck his hand out with a smile on his face. "Nice to finally meet you."

Dallas using the word *finally* wasn't lost on her, but with Audrey on her mind, she turned back to William letting Dallas finish his chips and asked, "Did you know I have a younger sister? She's seventeen." William liked that she seemed comfortable enough in his home to share more information about herself.

They turned toward the back door when it opened. His Mom raced to William, hugging him in delight. "I didn't know you were coming home tonight. I would've planned a proper meal. We're just having what's in the fridge." She looked at Evie surprised to see this pretty girl standing in her kitchen. She was used to both her sons dating pretty girls, but she didn't expect to see one today and certainly not one she had never met or heard of before. After a quick introduction, Evie became the center of Angie Ryder's attention. "How did you and my son meet? Do you go to school together? What's your major? Where are you from?"

William cut in, stopping his mom's barrage of questions, and answered for Evie, "School. Yes. English. The city. That's enough of the interrogation for now." He laughed and everyone else followed suit.

"I'm sorry, Evie. I just got excited to meet someone who is obviously special to William. He doesn't bring dates home."

"That's because I don't go on many dates."

His mother rolled her eyes and turned back to Evie. "Will you stay for dinner?"

Evie smiled at the kind gesture. His family was open, and so opposite of her own that she wanted to say yes, but couldn't. "Thank you for the invitation, but unfortunately, I have a prior engagement."

"Maybe another time then," Angie responded, smiling. "I'm going to start dinner. You kids hanging out for a little while?"

"Yes." William pulled a barstool out for Evie then sat next to her.

Dallas walked to the fridge, and Evie asked William's mom, "Dallas is a unique name. Is there a story behind it?"

"William was named after my father, but Dallas, well, my youngest was named after the city we once visited."

Evie looked at all the happy faces and could feel the

134

love they shared for each other. "So he's named him after the city?"

"No, they named me after the city I was conceived in. How gross is that?" Dallas butted in, "The city where my parents got it on." He laughed. "Anyway, lucky me with the weird name. I think I got my ass kicked every day of my sixth grade year. Staten Island guys don't take to a runt with a name like Dallas . . . yeah, I would've kicked my ass, too."

"You're so tall though," she said.

William chuckled. "Now he is, but back then . . . man, I got tired of fighting."

"You fought for him?"

"Sure, he's my brother."

Evie smiled at his response that seemed ordinary to him, but she knew loyalty like that is what made his family extraordinary.

Chapter 13

Word traveled fast in the neighborhood William grew up in and before he could go undetected with Evie, Bobby was walking in the back door as if he lived there.

Bobby had practically grown up at the Ryder home and was treated as such, volunteering to stay for dinner as soon as he walked in. But over the hour he sat there joking with the Ryder clan, he also observed . . . even stared, surprised to see how close his best friend and this new girl in his life had become.

William was more serious than Bobby expected. And, as much as he wanted to be happy for his buddy, he sort of felt left out since William had stayed mum about her. She was very pretty and his friend was a goner.

But it wasn't one-sided. By watching Evie, Bobby could tell she was as far gone as William. He also noticed how different she was from the other girls William had dated. She was well-mannered and soft spoken, classy, and everything about her seemed to be put together with thought and care. She was different from the outspoken girls they grew up with, which made Bobby wonder just how serious they were.

William looked at his watch, knowing she said she only had the day. He felt he was pushing his luck by staying any longer, although she seemed to be having a good time. He also knew she was too polite to interrupt the Ryder banter to leave, so he did the honors. "I need to get this girl back to the city," he said, standing up and pulling her chair out for her. He gave a round of hugs and then Angie hugged Evie, inviting her back.

As they rushed from the cab to the ferry, William said, "Sorry, it's later than I thought."

"No, please, don't be. I had such a good time. I enjoyed your family very much." As they settled back onto the boat, he turned on the railing to face her, his expression turned serious as he traced her lifeline on the soft skin of her palm. "It meant a lot to me that you met my family. I know it's a bit early in our relationship, but I'm glad you did. And, I'm glad you got to see my roots. You survived. I was worried that being the center of their attention might scare you off."

She shook her head. "No, not at all. They were lovely."

"Forewarning though, my mom may try to adopt you."

Evie leaned her head onto William's shoulder feeling accepted here. She wished she could always feel like this. "Forewarning, I might accept." She looked up at him. "I liked getting to know you better." She felt their knees brushing together and looked down. "I liked being in . . . I mean seeing your bedroom." Evie wanted to slap herself for the slip up. She had enjoyed being in his bedroom very much, but that was too forward to say.

He pulled her chin up to look at him, leaning in to where their lips almost met, and whispered, "I liked you in my bedroom, too." He kissed her with passion.

When they docked, Evie looked at her watch and realized she needed to get home. She hadn't left messages for anyone and knew she would be missed. William watched her reaction to the time and after shoving his hands in his pockets, felt like he was still being kept out on a part of her life. "Why do you have to go? Why is it you're always rushing away from me?"

Evie found his wording the exact opposite of what she wanted to do and it upset her that he took it personally. "I don't rush away from you. I, well, like I've told you, I have commitments, obligations that have to be dealt with. They're not always fun, but I've committed myself to see them through." She walked ahead of him so he couldn't see her face or the shame she felt.

William was confused and he wanted answers. He took her by the arm and made her face him. "Why do you speak in ways like I'm supposed to understand, but don't?" He dropped his hand and with his eyebrows pulled together, pleaded. "Am I missing something deeper in your words or is it as simple as what you say?"

She looked over his right shoulder, avoiding his eyes. Evie had always loved the way William looked at her. He saw her the way she wanted to be, but right now, he was seeing her reality and it was unsettling. "I need to go, William. I would like for you to ride with me in a taxi, I'll pay."

Something changed in her and he saw the transformation happen before his eyes. She was not his Evie right now. He hit on something she didn't want to talk about and he could tell it scared her. Heck, it scared him, too. Maybe today was all wrong. Maybe he'd been reading her all wrong. She looked at him with hope in her eyes, still waiting.

"No, I'll take the subway," he said. He hated hurting

her feelings, but right now he needed time to think and if she wasn't going to give him any answers then he needed time to process that as well.

Her face fell and the glimmer of hope she had disappeared. Her voice was low and the rejection stung. "I'm sorry. I have to go. I'm so sorry."

She felt the tears coming as she turned away from him and started walking, but he ran and blocked her path. "Wait, it can't end like this. Classes are over. When will I see you next?"

He saw the sadness deep into her eyes as she tried to cover it by putting on a happier expression. "I got into Lang's summer program. I meant to tell you earlier."

"I knew you'd get in. Now I'll get to see you in the program."

"Five days a week for five weeks. You think you can handle seeing that much of me?" She tried for a joke because she didn't want this day to end on a bad note.

"If I had my way, I'd wake up to you every day of the week."

Evie's breath staggered at his proclamation—*his way*. She raised an eyebrow, stunned he could talk to her like they'd known each other for years and like he was in love. His sweet words always made her feel good, like anything was possible. Feeling confident from his statement and a bit sassy, she said, "How 'bout we try out the five days first and work our way toward the seven and see how that goes?"

He liked that she was admitting she wanted more, just at a slower pace. Although it was crazy to feel this strongly for her, William already knew in his heart he would wait forever for this girl. He stepped closer and was relieved when she remained in place, anticipating. Leaning down, he touched her bottom lip. "Evie, I've never felt like this about anyone. I can wait. I'm willing to wait for you if that's what it takes."

William was a poet, a romantic, and a gentleman. Evie knew in that second, through her woozy clouded mind, she could not have him wait forever. She knew she had to be with this man no matter what the cost to herself. In her romance-induced fog, she got on her tiptoes and kissed him. She couldn't be mad he wanted to know more about her. When they were together, they lived in that very moment and that was all that mattered.

She pulled away from him and ran for a cab, ducking inside then waving good-bye.

In that kiss, he forgave her for all of her other commitments, he forgave her for her prior engagements, and he forgave her for not spilling all of her secrets. He believed half the fun of dating was finding out these things in their due course.

Walter approached the cab and opened the door for her when she arrived home. She looked at the meter and down to her left and more frantically to her right then to the floor. It dawned on her that William still had her bag. She smiled at the doorman. "I seem to have left my bag somewhere. Can you cover my fare for me please and I will repay you as soon as I get upstairs?"

Walter was happy to cover the thirty-dollar cab ride for Evie. He knew she was good for it. As they took the elevator up, he started questioning where she was coming from in the city to rack up such a big fare. He gently probed, curious. "Good day so far?"

"Lovely."

"Doing a little dining downtown?"

141

"I was at the park."

Central Park was too close for that high-dollar fare, so he thought she had probably been somewhere she wasn't supposed to be and let the subject drop.

Everleigh flew into the apartment, coming to a skidding stop when she saw Tom and her mother sitting in the living room discussing wedding plans. Tom stood, greeting her with a kiss. She was hesitant and looked down which did not bode well with him. Sticking her finger into the air to halt him, she rushed back to her bedroom. She pulled a hundred dollar bill out of a clutch she used the previous week.

She was hurrying back to the front door when Tom stopped her. "Where are you going, Everleigh?"

"I didn't have money to pay the cab fare. Walter paid it for me. I'm going to repay him and then I'll be right back." Everleigh left him standing in their foyer with his hands on his hips and a confused expression.

Walter had held the elevator open for her. She handed him the large bill and smiled. "Thank you. You were a life-saver." She saw his baffled look toward the bill. "Keep it. Thanks again."

"Thank you, Miss Wright, but that's not necessary."

"Please call me Evie."

"Thank you, Evie." He paused as she walked to her front door. "That was a large fare. Did you have fun at the park?"

She turned around with her hand on the doorknob, and smiled. A hint of blush covered her cheeks. "Yes, I did. Thank you for asking."

Tom had questions and Everleigh explained the best

she could during his cross-examination regarding her day. She kept things vague.

He found her in character for her recent untrustworthy behavior. That didn't mean he understood the changes he was seeing in her and it confused him more to what brought them on. He started contemplating drastic measures to get her back on board with the way he thought she should be by the time they married in October.

William had watched Evie run for the safety of the taxi and speed away. By the time he realized he still had her bag slung over his shoulder, she was out of sight. He knew he couldn't call her since her phone was in the bag he was currently holding. But he did know where she lived because even though he never escorted her to the building, she had pointed in the general direction of that corner the night he walked her home. He headed for the subway and as he descended the stairs into the tunnel, he had made a decision. He chose to return her bag, rationalizing she would need her wallet, phone, and the bag in general. It was the right thing to do.

He exited the subway one block up from Park Avenue and even though he had ridden his bike down the street many times for work, he had never walked down the pretty street, never having a reason to before. Evie was right about the avenue. It was one of the most beautiful in the city and at night seemed magical with the tiny white lights in the trees and the doormen all standing in their starched uniforms. But, William didn't kid himself with the façade of the wealth that lined this street. He knew behind every door everyone had problems—just different ones than he had. He walked up to the building he hoped was hers and approached the doorman who was sitting behind his desk.

"I'm sorry, sir. I was caught up in the baseball game on TV. How can I help you?" Walter asked, standing out of respect for the visitor.

William smiled at the man as he explained the situation. "I have a friend's bag I need to return. She left it by accident today." William smiled while taking the bag off his shoulder. "Evie Wright? I hope this is her building."

Walter recognized the backpack right away. "Yes, Sir, it is. I can get that to her if you want to leave it with me?"

He was relieved to know she would have her stuff tonight and not have to worry. "I'm William, what's your name?"

"Walter, Sir." Walter gave a firm, but friendly handshake.

"Please don't call me sir."

"Ok . . . William." Walter set the bag behind the desk, his curiosity piquing, and he asked, "So, how do you know Miss Wright?"

"We go to school together. Who's winning?" William leaned over the top of the desk to get a look at the small television hidden from the lobby's view.

Walter looked the young man over, noticing his casual but well-worn clothes and his backpack slung over his shoulder. His bag looked like it had seen a few years. Walter smiled, connecting the dots of the evening between Evie and William. "We're down in the sixth. Where do you live, William? Who's your doorman? I know most of them in the city."

"You know, Walter, I don't have a doorman. I live in an old walk-up about eighteen or so blocks from here."

Walter had liked William immediately, but now he really liked him. "Starving student, huh?"

"Something like that. Actually, exactly like that." They shared a laugh, bonding over baseball and honesty.

Walter rushed and opened the door for a tenant and when she was on the elevator, he turned back to William and said, "Miss Wright's a wonderful girl." He tried to sound relaxed like it was everyday conversation, but for some reason he wanted more information. He didn't tend to stick his nose in resident's business, but when it came to Evie, he hoped for her to live a better life than the one she was living and this new man might be the key to that.

William knew it was a statement, but still felt the need to address it. "She's a great girl." He felt his cheeks heat, but he didn't know why, so he looked down at his sneakers as a distraction.

Walter knew in that instant that William *was* the reason for her better, happier moods of late and he could tell he sincerely liked her. He wasn't going to ruin it with the mention of moody abusive fiancés. He figured that was a situation for them to talk to each other about in private.

William smiled. "I should get going. Thanks for getting the bag back to her and it was nice to meet you."

"Likewise," Walter said, rushing past him to hold the door open. "I should get back to work."

William nodded and shook Walter's hand as he walked out. "Yes, and the game."

They shared a laugh as William left.

Everleigh felt a wave of relief at ten-thirty when Tom announced he needed a good night's rest and was heading home. She felt almost giddy entering her room and locking her door, now having the time she needed to process her day, her feelings, and her thoughts of William.

As Tom walked through the lobby, Walter held the door open for him. Seeing the doorman reminded Tom he had to cover Everleigh's fare tonight. Finding that odd, he acted as casual and friendly as he could and as if the thought just occurred to him, he asked, "Everleigh mentioned you paid her fare this evening. Thank you for taking care of her. By the way, do you recall how much her fare was by chance?" Tom stood there pondering this while eyeing Walter.

Walter knew this thought had not just occurred to Mr. Whitney and was never casual with him. He was up to something for sure, so he covered for Evie. "I think it was around ten dollars."

"All right. She took care of you?"

"Yes, sir. But I was happy to help."

He nodded once more. "Have a nice night, Walter." For some reason, Tom did not feel as satisfied as he thought he would. Everleigh had stayed close according to Walter, but she came home with nothing, no shopping bags, no purse, not even her book bag. He felt his frustration growing, but decided he would not address the issue tonight. He had been working on a business deal that was becoming a royal pain in the ass and it was wearing his patience down. He wanted to go home and go to bed. Well, he really wanted to have sex and release some of the tension he was carrying around with him, but seeing Everleigh tonight, he knew that wasn't going to happen.

She was distant and fearful, but also somewhat confrontational and irrational. Tom almost didn't recognize the girl he fell in love with. He knew she was in there and he was willing to move forward with her knowing that she just needed reminders of what they once shared. Basically, she needed to be handled even if that meant manipulated.

Walter waited for Tom to leave before ringing the

Wright residence. Audrey answered, telling Walter she would let Evie know about the bag. Within five minutes, Evie bounded into the lobby and straight for Walter's desk. She leaned over and saw the bag tucked behind his chair. As he handed it to her, she eagerly waited for him to say something, anything, that would let her know he knew what was going on or give a clue that he was still oblivious to her escapades. She needed to know if she was going to be busted or if her secret was safe.

"That's a heavy bag, Miss . . . I mean, Evie. It's good to have friends who will carry that for you when exploring the park."

He wasn't asking her a specific question, but she wanted to know about William's visit. "Yes, it is." Her smile sank as she realized he wasn't going to give her the information she desired, and she turned back toward the elevators.

Walter wanted to make her happy again. He had daughters and knew how they wanted everyone to feed into their schoolgirl notions. "William seems like a real upstanding kind of guy."

Evie stopped, and spun on her heels to face him. After closing the distance between them, she leaned against the desk. "Yes, he is. It was very nice of him to bring this by tonight."

"Yeah, he mentioned where he lived and your building is not really on the way home for him."

Her face was lit up talking about William, even if in veiled conversation. "No, it's not," she admitted. "Did he leave a message for me by chance?"

"No." Walter looked around to make sure no one but she could hear him then lowered his voice to a whisper. "But he looked disappointed not to be able to see you

147

again." She remained smiling at him, but confusion also flashed across her eyes. "I didn't ring because I knew you wouldn't want to be disturbed while Mr. Whitney was visiting." He gave her an I'm-in-the-know-about-that-guy look.

She realized Walter knew more about Tom than she cared to discuss, but more important was that she realized how he covered for her tonight. Tom went home none the wiser and that was a good thing. "Walter," she rested her hand on his and said, "Thank you for everything."

"You're very welcome. Please feel free to ask me if you need any assistance in the future."

"Thank you. I'll keep that in mind. Goodnight."

She returned to her bedroom and pulled her textbooks out of her bag, retiring them to her bookcase before clearing out the bag in preparation for her new books for Lang's summer course. She also pulled her purse and phone out, setting them on her desk. As she removed her pen case from the backpack, she saw a piece of paper crammed inside. After unlatching the case, she pulled the paper out. The words were written in black ink: *"Better to be without logic than without feeling."* She recognized the famous quote from Charlotte Bronte's *The Professor*.

Her eyes scanned further down, and she read: *"Dearest Evie, you have left me bewildered and with immense emotion. Love, William."* She had caused him to lose his logic as he had done to her. She was surprised by his beautiful note and it made her feel like anything was possible.

Her days had been overflowing with thoughts of him, but she had no idea he had immense emotions for her as well. She didn't know he was feeling the same until he made that simple declaration. Her heart swelled just thinking about him taking the time to write the note, *in black ink*, and putting it in her case. Holding the note over her heart, she swooned, flopping down on her bed.

Lying there, she realized their plight. She didn't know when she started thinking this way, but she did know how to describe their relationship. Deep in her heart, she knew it was 'us against them' and she was willing to fight the battle. To be by William's side gave her strength and she would use that strength when the time came. Everything changed for Everleigh this night.

She wanted to talk to him, to kiss him, to be with him, but she knew tonight she couldn't, so she did all she thought she could—she texted him: *Thank You.*

He responded quickly, ending the anxiety building within her: *You're Welcome.*

She wanted to say one last thing to him so he understood she had immense emotions for him also, and she texted: *You had my heart when I saw the black ink. Sweet Dreams.*

William understood now. It had occurred to him while he was writing his note in his usual blue ink. Blue didn't seem to give the words enough meaning. Blue ink was not expressing the depth of the feelings he wanted to share with her. He dug out the old black pen he had stolen from work last week and rewrote the note. As he read it back to himself, he understood the importance of the black ink. It was for contracts and serious documents, or for letters with meaning. Black ink was for love letters, poems, and works of written art. William would never interchange blue and black ink again. Evie gave him a newfound respect for not just written declarations, but also for the instrument that allowed those confessions of the heart to be professed through the purest form of art and poetry.

He texted her one last time for the night: *Sweet dreams, my beautiful Evie.*

After the final text, he set his phone down and flipped off the television so he could lay with his thoughts. He performed his regular nighttime routine then fell into bed swimming in immense emotions for the girl who made him feel true love for the first time.

Chapter 14

Due to other obligations, William and Evie didn't get to see each other until the following Monday—the first day of Professor Lang's Summer Program. The ten students chosen gathered in the English Department's second floor lounge and waited for the Professor to arrive. Evie leaned on a short bookcase overlooking the quad and started to think about the discussion she had with Tom and her parents in East Hampton over the weekend.

Tom stood with his back to her, gazing out at the ocean. "I don't understand why you've chosen to make a commitment without regarding what your family's needs are this summer."

"I'm not going to be rushing between home and the Hamptons all summer." She looked at Tom, putting her foot down. "I haven't taken any summer courses before so I could be here for the family and for you. If I take this seminar then I can graduate. So this summer, school is my priority."

He turned to face her, drink in hand. "Your top priority should be spending time with me, with your family, seeing your friends. Balancing business and social responsibility."

"I won't be missed if I don't attend any parties." She got up from the chair and walked right past him onto the vast green, manicured lawn toward the ocean. "I think I'm going to use this summer to focus on me, since it's apparent this is the last time I'll ever get to." On that brazen note, she dashed toward the water, not looking back until she reached the beach. Suddenly, she felt more Evie than Everleigh and relished the freedom she felt. She was strong, and she liked it.

Kicking her shoes off, she walked across the sand until she stood at the water's edge, and thought of William. Away from his presence, guilt settled into her heart, twisting in pain. She was leading him on and she knew that now.

Their story would be short-lived, at best. He would reject her once she told him she was engaged and she would deserve that. Her heart ached while her eyes watered over the pain she knew was coming. He would hate her, but not more than she hated herself for lying to him.

William rubbed her arm, bringing her attention back to the lounge where the students were waiting. "Lang's here."

The Professor entered the room, commanding their attention. "Ladies and Gentleman, let's lay the ground rules. This is not an orthodox program and you are my guinea pigs." He laughed, rubbing his hands together in an evil fashion. "Now for the good stuff. I need you in pairs. I'll dole out assignments and both team members are responsible for the work done, or the work not done. You will share a grade and hold each other accountable. I need one person reporting the team's progress to me once a week."

Evie glanced at William, hope building when their eyes met.

The professor continued talking. "We have an opportunity to analyze a set of rare books by Thomas Kyd and Wilkie Collins. I will give you each a selection of short stories in which you will help determine the authenticity of the works. This is groundbreaking research, people. As much as I know you love the romantics, this can be a great discovery in literature if we can determine the rightful authors." He held the books up wearing white gloves then set them back down on his desk. "The pages have been copied for us and you will use those photocopies as your reference. Choose your partner and tell me your author preference."

William and Evie immediately turned to each other. William spoke first. "Will you be my partner?"

"You didn't have to ask."

"I wanted to. Kyd or Collins? You choose." He smiled, realizing how much time he was going to get to spend with her.

"I'm not into detective stories. My vote is for Kyd. We'll also have *The Spanish Tragedy* as a reference to compare to."

"Good idea." He looked at her, pointed to himself, and asked, "Do you want me to be the team liaison, or would you like to do it?"

Evie slid down into a leather chair, getting comfortable. "You can do it."

After chatting with the professor, he returned holding a small stack of papers and sat down on the arm of her chair. "Basically, we have three weeks to complete the research, turning the paper in on the fourth week. We also have to be here on Fridays for a weekly check-in and go over our findings for the week. It looks to me like we'll be spending most of our time at the library."

"Great! I think we should consider doing a day trip to Philadelphia. Their main library has a great historical novel and play collection, including British authors."

"We'll definitely have to work that in, then. I've never been," he said, impressed by her knowledge. "You want to go over to Bean There and start looking over these two short stories?"

"Coffee sounds perfect."

They grabbed their bags and walked the few short blocks to the coffee house.

William ordered their usual then went to sit down at *their* tables. She had pushed them together, making him smile.

With both laptops out, they started doing the basic legwork online to confirm or eliminate these stories as an original Thomas Kyd work. Nothing showed up online which excited them both equally. William pointed to her laptop screen, and said, "This makes it a true mystery to be solved."

"We're embarking on something big here," she said with a glint in her eyes.

His heart leapt. "The stories or us?"

She couldn't stop the feelings bubbling up, forgetting all about what she should and what she really wanted to say to him. Instead, she spoke from the heart. "Both."

William analyzed the shape of her pink lips as she formed the word, and he repeated, "Both."

"William . . . William?" she said, bumping him with her elbow.

He snapped out of it, startled. "Oh! Yes?"

She tapped the papers tucked under her computer and demanded in a playful tone, "Focus!"

"I'm focused . . . now." Smirking at her, he poked her lightheartedly in the ribs, making her giggle.

A few hours later, they packed their bags, knowing they had overstayed the time the cost of their coffee warranted.

William's phone rang when they got outside. "It's my brother. Do you mind waiting a moment?"

Evie signaled for him to answer it as they stood on the busy sidewalk.

"Dallas, hey, what's up?" William listened to him explain how Abby had broken up with him for a guy who went to Boston College. Dallas was upset and rambling.

"Uh huh." He interjected when Dallas stopped for air. William doled out reassurances. "Abby was nice and I know you liked her, maybe even loved. She was the first girl you were with, but this is how things work." He lowered his voice. "Most people don't end up with the person they lose their virginity to. I know you don't want to hear this from your older and much wiser brother, but I'm happy to oblige since you called me. There will be others, Dallas, trust me, and yes, you will have sex again." William was trying to comfort his brother without downplaying his brothers' feelings.

When he looked up, he saw Evie watching him. Keeping his eyes on her, he tried to wrap up the call. "You will find who you're meant to be with." William sat on a chair outside the coffee shop and finished his dating pep talk. "Abby was your first, not your last. Come on, dude, the girls are crazy about you. Enjoy being single for a while."

Evie turned toward the busy street seeming to be lost in thought again.

"Give yourself a few days and the world will be golden again, Dallas, and come to the city. We'll go out. You're out of school and you can stay at my place for a few days." The brothers said their good-byes and hung up.

William stood and joined Evie a few feet away. She smiled, but he could tell it was just for show. Her eyes gave her away. "Are you all right?"

"Do you really believe that?" Evie asked skeptically.

"What?"

"That no one ends up with the person they lose their virginity to?" She tilted her head and looked at him while she waited for his answer.

"I, uh . . ." He thought it was interesting she picked up on *that* part of the conversation. "Can I ask you something personal?"

She looked down to the ground, but then fixed her posture with her arms crossed in front of her body and looked back up. "Yes, you may."

"Are you a virgin?" William was direct.

Evie's face immediately turned red with embarrassment.

Not meaning to make her feel self-conscious, he grabbed her and pulled her against him.

She always felt protected in his arms, and
156

whispered, "No."

He smiled that she trusted him enough to share that kind of intimate detail. Lowering his head so he could see her, he said, "See, that proves my point."

Her eyes closed and she inhaled his scent as the realization that he was right set in. One thing she knew for sure was that Tom was not her true love.

William felt victorious and on an Evie high, he leaned down and kissed her on the forehead. Stepping back, he said, "I have to go to work. Will you meet me tomorrow?"

"Tomorrow is too far away, but yes, I'll wait until tomorrow."

Tilting her chin up, he kissed her on the mouth. With his lips still pressed against hers, he whispered, "Good-bye, my love."

She stood stunned to the spot, as he turned and left. Her insides were in complete disarray at the word "love" being given so freely to her. Love had always come with a price . . . until now.

He glanced over his shoulder, and laughed at how cute it was that he could affect her so. She was always so controlled and yet there she was left reeling from a simple kiss. He liked that. A lot.

Lightheaded and happy, she took a cab to her favorite little park. Lying back on the small hillside, she enjoyed the feel of the cool grass beneath her, and the sunshine warming her skin all the while love swelled inside. Was William worth throwing everything away—her family, the comfort of money—and starting life over with him? She was starting to believe he was.

Chapter 15

Evie and William spent the next two weeks using their detective skills to uncover the true author of the two short stories. They had one week left and their campus library offered no substantial clues. William decided to throw out the road trip idea she once suggested. He looked at her sprawled out on the floor of his small studio surrounded by papers, and said, "I think our last hope is the Philly library."

Considering the idea, she kept her eyes on the Kyd writing samples. "I can do Monday."

"I can also do Monday."

Evie sat up, crossing her legs, and rested her chin on her hands in front of her. She was careful with her words, hoping she wouldn't offend him. "How about I buy the train tickets and you buy lunch."

He knew what she was doing and as much as he wanted to pay for everything, he also knew the tickets to Philadelphia would strain his budget. "All right. Thank you." She made it easy for him to accept the offer and he appreciated that.

The first couple of weeks of summer were easy for Everleigh. Tom and her family had been in the Hamptons most of that time since Tom's associates were basing their work from there also. But Tom insisted on Everleigh joining them again this weekend, and out of obligation, she did. He hired a car to drive her and when she arrived, she could admit she was pleased to be there once again. She loved this house, the ocean, and always felt closest to her family here.

Tom's family home was fifteen minutes away, which she also liked. He wasn't staying at hers during the summer, so she had some privacy part of the time. As she carried her stuff down the upstairs hallway, she saw Audrey across the hall in her room listening to her MP3 player and reading a magazine.

Evie dropped her bags, stood in the doorway, and knocked loudly. "Miss me, little sis?"

Audrey's head popped up and she smiled taking an ear bud out, "Actually, yes. It's been kind of boring this summer. Are you here for the weekend?"

"I head back Sunday afternoon."

She turned to go to her room, but Audrey quickly asked, "Do you think you might want to hang out this weekend, maybe go to a party or two together?"

Evie smiled. "Sure."

Two hours later, Everleigh was lying by the pool with Audrey when Tom arrived. She heard him before she saw him.

"There's my favorite girl," he said, coming through the back door of the house. As both girls turned and looked at him, Everleigh felt her heart race, but didn't know why — *fear, love, or just plain confusion?* She watched him from

160

behind her large sunglasses and could still see traces of the attractive man he was—his sandy blond hair even lighter from summer and his brown eyes happy, more carefree than usual. He seemed different to her and she hoped he was sincere this time.

Audrey slammed her magazine on the ground capturing Everleigh's attention and stood up. "I'm going inside."

Lowering her sunglasses from the top of her head, Audrey walked past Tom as if he didn't exist. He smirked at her and felt the need to comment. "Oh, to be opinionated, moody, and to know everything. I'd almost forgotten what it was like to be a teenager."

Audrey ignored him and continued inside.

Tom took the abandoned chair next to Everleigh and smiled. "It's good to see you." Picking her hand up, he ran his thumb over the large engagement ring on her left finger, feeling pride as he admired it. "I missed you, Everleigh." Leaning forward, he kissed her on the lips.

She didn't respond, as she knew she should. "It's nice to be here for the weekend."

He pulled her forward by both hands, hugging her tight. "Everleigh, my darling. My Everleigh. I love you so much that it hurts sometimes. Your rejection hurts me." His voice was kind and sounded loving, but pained.

She had never heard him talk like this. This was her chance and she took the opportunity to be honest. "You've hurt me. I don't feel whole because of what—"

"I'm sorry. I'm sorry. I have no excuse." He gripped her tighter as if she would disappear if he didn't. He often worried she would leave him and the thought was unbearable.

She had never heard him apologize and closed her eyes letting his words sink in.

"I love you so much. I don't want to lose you. I can't . . ." His voice trembled on the last words as they trailed off, and his hands trailed down her bikini-clad body. They stopped on her hips and he nudged her head with his, exposing her neck and resting his forehead on her shoulder. He was apologetic and appeared defeated.

Her hands had been strategically placed on his ribs to keep him at a distance, but with him openly showing his feelings, she slid them around to his back and embraced him.

Tom smiled as he lifted his head up and kissed her. She was responsive to his kindness and the love he was showing her, having her tender Tom back. He pulled away, though, and then took her left hand into his right. "Come with me." He led her to the pool house, around the billiards table, and into the bedroom.

Evie's body and mind were starting a small battle in her heart with each step she took. Her heart was winning. She couldn't do this, she shouldn't do this, but her mind moved her forward and into his arms. That was the logical thing to do. The thing she had done so many times before that there was a small sense of comfort in the habit, even if it was a bad habit.

As they sat there on the bed, he took her sunglasses off and his eyes smoldered. A look that used to send tingles down her spine in desire, now only confused her conflicting soul.

When he stood up, he lifted his shirt over his head then took his pants off revealing his boxers. Everleigh took a deep breath, willing herself to relax.

Tom crawled back onto the bed and she stiffened,

paralyzed by her thoughts. She couldn't do this. She couldn't do this to William. She didn't love Tom, but he was being everything she used to love about him—kind and sweet—attentive, gentle. Maybe, maybe she should. Maybe he could be everything she needed again.

Evie closed her eyes trying to figure out what she needed to do versus what she wanted to do. She felt his lips on her chest as he kissed his way up toward her neck. Could she do this anymore? Could she shut her eyes and let sweet, kind, attentive, and gentle Tom make love to her?

She snuck a peek at him, but clamped her eyes shut tight. Maybe she should pretend this was William? Even after all the years she had invested her heart, mind, and soul into Tom, she couldn't stop thinking about William.

Her heart raced and her breathing became shallow, quickening unnaturally. She opened her mouth and gasped for air.

"Are you okay, Everleigh?"

Her eyes flashed open and she bolted upright to a sitting position.

Startled, Tom leaned back. "What's going on? Are you okay?"

"No. No," she said, shaking her head, her hand hovering over her heart. She couldn't do this. With reminders of the responsibilities to her family and commitments she made years earlier swarming her thoughts, William stood out above all else. She stood abruptly. "I'm feeling lightheaded. I think it's from being in the sun too long. I should eat something."

With a look of concern, Tom stood and started to getting dressed. "I'll take you to lunch then."

While sitting at Dan's Grill, her favorite restaurant in Montauk, Everleigh stared out at the water lost in her thoughts. She felt twisted inside and disgusted with herself. *What am I doing?*

The couple sat quietly together drinking Cape Cods on the outside deck of the restaurant. Her mind wandered back to her current predicament and when she turned to look at Tom, and he said, "I think you're pushing yourself too hard. You're so close to getting your degree and all of this work is catching up with you."

Underneath any faux concern he showed, his smug expression gave him away. He was gloating. He knew she was stressed and although some of it had been school and her final exams, he didn't know the other half, the part that made her life better, happier. So as she sat there trying to figure out what twisted game Tom was playing with her, it finally occurred to her. He was nice to gain her trust again, to trick her into sleeping with him even.

She gave him a confused look that turned to irritation as she figured him out. "You did that on purpose, didn't you?"

His hand reached over to rest on top of hers and he feigned innocent. "What on purpose, darling?"

"You conned me. You acted like that to get on my good side." She spewed these accusations without thinking.

He looked injured as if her words had hurt him, and calm, he looked too calm. "I didn't know I was on your bad side."

"I thought you meant it by the pool. The way you were acting. You were being what I want you to be—"

He sat back, removing his hand from hers and crossed his arms over his chest. "It's not hard to figure out

164

what a girl is going to respond to. It's ridiculously simple in fact."

"I thought—"

"I know what you thought and you should continue to think that. That was me back there. I know you think I'm a monster, but that was the real me back there. I was happy to see you." He leaned forward, his voice sharp. "To be with you again. I missed you and needed to . . . we need to reconnect. It's been too long. A man has needs, Everleigh. A husband has needs and I expect to have mine met." He sat up straighter as the food was brought to the table. "So don't be melodramatic about it. It wasn't a charade. I love you whether you choose to believe it or not."

Not knowing what to think, she sat there mulling over the truths and lies. "Well, you don't have to lie to me—"

"Don't I, Everleigh?" His hand slammed down on the table making the silverware clang. "We haven't had sex in over a month and you act like I'm taking advantage of you. I see how you react to me. Something's going on with you and I want to know what it is, damn it."

She shook her head in disbelief. "I don't even know what's going on anymore. You're driving me insane. Maybe I'm the fool after all. If you acted more like you did this afternoon then maybe I would want to have sex with you."

She stood up, throwing her napkin down next to her seafood salad.

His tone was direct, bordering on menacing. "Sit down and let's finish this. This is the most interesting conversation we've had in years."

"Well, what does that tell you?" She walked away leaving him alone with his lunch. Rushing into the ladies room, she leaned against the counter, and cried out of anger and frustration. She felt the walls of her former idyllic life caving in around her, feeling as if she was fighting for her life.

After a few minutes of solitude, her waitress walked in. The girl stopped, letting the door close behind her and a soft smile appeared. "The seafood salad isn't that bad, is it?"

Everleigh laughed, needing the release of the tension that had built up. "No, it's quite good. My favorite thing on the menu."

The waitress handed her a tissue. "Your fiancé sent me in to make sure you were okay."

"As much as I can be, considering the mess I've made of my life."

"Is it all that bad?"

"Worse actually."

The waitress hopped up on the counter, sitting next to Everleigh in front of the mirror. "My mom had a quote on our fridge when I was growing up. I read it every day. 'Happy are those who dream dreams and are ready to pay the price to make them come true.'" She looked down at her dangling feet, contemplating the words herself.

Everleigh looked at her and asked, "Who wrote that?"

"I can't remember off the top of my head, but it's good, isn't it?"

Everleigh nodded and closed her eyes, replaying every word silently in her head as gospel, feeding her soul. The waitress was right, but she already knew this by the little smile on her face. Everleigh smiled, too, and said,

166

"You should've been a psychologist or a bartender, you know. How'd you know that would mean so much to me?"

"It always meant a lot to me. I'm glad it does to you as well." She hopped off the counter and walked to the door, and took the knob in hand. "I'm studying psychology in school by the way, so good guess. I'll tell him you'll be out in a minute." She opened the door and walked out.

When Everleigh sat down, she took a long sip of her drink, her eyes locking on his. "I think we need to talk, Tom."

He looked at his watch. "As much as I would love to dig deeper into our deteriorating relationship, I have an appointment in ten minutes." He stood up, placing his crumpled napkin on the table. "You were gone so long I took care of the check and called Audrey. She'll pick you up. I'll see you at the club tonight." He leaned over and kissed her on the cheek. "By the way, I really was happy to see you today."

Evie took a deep, cleansing, fresh-ocean air breath before walking to the parking lot. She spotted Audrey waiting in her dad's Jaguar and climbed in.

Unaware of the war raging inside of her sister, Audrey asked, "How was lunch?"

Evie laughed. It was a sarcastic, caustic laugh. "Eventful." But she didn't want to ruin her time with her sister, so she tried to think of something the two of them could do together, something to take her mind off the lunch she just endured. "Hey, how about doing some shopping?"

The suggestion made Audrey happy and she accepted then drove to their favorite East Hampton boutiques. As Evie lingered at a table stacked with jeans, Audrey flipped through the shirts on the hangers behind her. "Sometimes you seem withdrawn, and sometimes you are lit from within with happiness."

Evie wasn't sure how to respond or if she should at all. She remained quiet, flipping through the rack of clothes.

Audrey trying a different approach to get her sister to open up, said, "You know, if you need someone to talk to, you can always talk to me. I know we don't always relate, but I want you to be happy more often. I like when you're happy. Are you happy, Evie?"

Evie considered her kind words and nodded while looking down. She was desperate to talk to someone she could trust. Right then she realized just how much her sister had matured and decided to open up. "Sometimes I am happy, but my happiness isn't a factor that comes into play."

"What makes you happy and why isn't it a factor? I know school does, but what else?"

"I have a responsibility to our family, to our—"

"I know what's expected of you, Evie. I know all of that, but the last couple of months I've seen a change in you, a change for the better." Audrey stood in front of Evie and asked her pointblank. "If you didn't have to worry about the family, money, anything, all of it, what would you do?"

She felt uncomfortable, so Evie did what she always did, she blew off the seriousness and redirected. "Oh, come on, it's not that dramatic" She touched Audrey's shoulder, saw the worry on her sister's face, and tried to ease it. "I'm happy, okay? Don't worry about me." She turned away and pulled a blouse off the rack to try on.

Audrey was not satisfied by the blow-off and it set her mind spinning, knowing she'd have to discover Evie's secret on her own. Step one: Return to Manhattan soon to investigate the situation further. But for now, she'd let it slide.

* * *

William was in the city working. He cycled through his day embracing the easiness of his Saturday shift. He thought about Evie while trying to avoid being hit by cars. Their relationship was developing slowly, but it was deep and laced with important shared moments, and he felt bonded in a way he didn't expect.

He wondered if this trip to Philly would be a good time to make it *official* and establish what their relationship was. He felt he needed to tread lightly around his deepening feelings for her because he didn't want to push her faster than she was willing to go— emotionally or physically—at this stage.

As much as he wanted to tell her everything he felt for her, he decided it best to play it by ear on this trip and let things play out naturally.

After shopping and thinking about the quote the waitress told her, Evie purchased two train tickets to Philadelphia. The rest of the afternoon was a relief because Tom was in meetings all day, and she got to enjoy her freedom to think about William as she pleased. She wasn't aware of the eyes that were following her. She bent down to smell a red flower along the large fence on the right side of the house, and it tickled her lip. She smiled in delight at the memory of William's lips against her own, soft, but with purpose.

"Right there! That's exactly what I'm talking about." Audrey busted her. "What's that giddy, silly smile on your face for? I know a flower didn't do that to you." Audrey placed her hands on her hips, standing a few feet behind Evie.

169

"I love the garden this time of year, Audrey." Evie couldn't look Audrey in the eyes or she'd give herself away by giggling in girly delight. "I don't get this obsession with my happiness."

"Because you're acting weird." Audrey came closer to smell the flower for herself. "I love a pretty flower as much as the next girl, but come on, it's just a flower." She looked at her sister who was avoiding eye contact at all costs, and asked, "Are you in love?"

Evie laughed at the question, but answered with honesty. "Of course I am. That's nothing new, Detective Wright."

Audrey huffed in annoyance and turned on her heel to head back to the house, knowing Evie wasn't going to give her any information.

"I am most definitely in love," Evie whispered, loving the sound of saying it aloud as she touched her lips once more.

Audrey started walking backward and pointed an accusing finger at her sister. "I'm on to you, Evie. I will find out your dirty little secret." Audrey was laughing which made Evie smile even more, kind of hoping she would.

Chapter 16

Evie awoke on Sunday renewed from her short visit in the Hamptons, but anxious to return to the city and to William.

Dallas showed up at William's apartment at ten in the morning bearing bagels. As they ate, he informed his older brother of his plans. "I got a catering gig here in the city. The pay is good, but some of the events will be later than the ferry runs. Cool to crash here those nights?"

"Yeah, of course." William looked over at his brother sitting at the desk. "You doing okay since the break-up?"

"Yeah, you're right. There are other girls out there. I mean, I can admit I was pretty into Abby, but whatever." He spun around in the chair to face William who was lounging on the bed. "I have a date on Wednesday with a girl from school. What about you and Evie?"

"Progressing, but it's slow."

"So it's okay at your age to take it slow?"

"Dude, I'm twenty-two. I'm not Dad's age or anything." William lay back on the bed. "She's worth the wait. I know that sounds strange, but I feel different about her. I don't feel the need to rush anything. It's like we have all the time in the world."

Dallas went back to Staten Island around noon and William decided it was time to take care of a few things. He cleaned his apartment, which didn't take long, he bought a few things from the corner market, and then packed his bag for tomorrow's journey.

Without anything to distract her, Evie decided to text William: *Hi.*

She felt like an introductory text was appropriate when in actuality she just wanted to text him more than once.

He didn't keep her waiting: *Hi there. How are you?*

She wasn't sure what she should text, and stuck to etiquette: *Good. How are you?*

Great. What are you doing today?

She was relieved he was leading the conversation and relaxed: *Lazy Sunday, you know how it is.*

Lazy Sundays lead to Amazing Mondays. He wondered if she would pick up on his desperation to see her again. He hoped not.

Smiles Yes, they do. I have the tickets. Meet me at the train station at 7 a.m.?

Yes. I'll bring coffee.

Platform 8. I can't wait.

William typed: *15 hours until I see you . . .*

But then he deleted it thinking it might come across as too forward. Instead, he texted: *I can't wait to see you again.*

Everleigh smiled and typed. *I can't wait either. See you in the morning.*

William sent one last message to her: *Goodnight. Sweet dreams.*

Both Evie and William spent their night anticipating tomorrow's planned journey to Philadelphia and the time they would get to spend together.

Walking to the platform ten minutes before seven in the morning, William saw Evie sitting on a bench ahead. She stood when she saw him, her face lighting up. William liked that her happiness showed in her eyes, and he smiled, handing her a cup of coffee." Are you ready for our quest for truth?"

"I'm most definitely ready for our adventure."

They walked several train cars until they found an empty cabin with only a few passengers, and settled into seats next to each other, setting their stuff onto the table in front of them. "I'm very sleepy today. I didn't sleep well last night," Evie said, slumping over the table.

"Why didn't you sleep well?"

A slight pink colored her cheeks. "I was a little nervous . . . and excited about today."

"I was, too." He reassured her that her feelings weren't one sided. "If you'd like, you can lean your head on me and rest."

Yawning, she held her coffee up. "Thank you, but I think this is all I need right now, but I might take you up on that nap on our ride home."

William liked sleepy Evie. He realized that she didn't

hide behind her words as much. So during the train ride, he found out she had never been to an amusement park, an IHOP, or to Staten Island before she met him. William couldn't get over how sheltered her life seemed. She was an oddity to him, a beautiful one, but an oddity all the same. She had traveled the world, but not her own city.

An hour and half later, they exited the train and hopped in a cab over to the city's largest library, which was situated downtown. They approached the front information desk and promptly directed to a particular section of the library.

When they finally got a hold of the comparison manuscripts, their disappointment was palpable and they slumped. There were many similarities to Thomas Kyd's work, but had as many markers to the contrary. Once again, their findings were inconclusive. William flopped into a nearby chair and watched as Evie perused the surrounding bookshelves. She seemed fascinated by the old spines as she dragged her finger across them.

Thoughts of his true feelings surfaced and he knew he was in love with her. A smile spread across his face, enlightening his feelings through his eyes and his whole expression.

When Evie came to the end of the row, she looked out the window. Even though he was near, she imagined William's face in her mind. Closing her eyes, a feeling of warmth passed through her and she found her fingers gracing her lips again. When she turned around to look at him, all those cozy feelings of love disappeared instantly. She now spied a girl who had made herself comfortable on the arm of the chair in which he rested. William was smiling at her and seemed happy in their exchange.

Possessiveness took hold of her and Evie stood more upright, wanting to let the girl know through her body language that William was hers. But he wasn't hers and the jealousy rushing through her veins wasn't a fair emotion. She had made a decision not to tell him before, but she started rethinking her position altogether.

When Evie walked closer, she saw the girl set her hand on William's shoulder in a blatant act of flirtation. Evie stopped in her tracks, knowing she had no rights or claims over him. Rights and claims was what she so desperately wanted to have with William and she decided she was ready to pay the price for happiness with him.

His eyes met hers and his brow furrowed in confusion. Turning back to the girl perched at his side, he realized what the situation must look like. With a quick shuffle right out from the girl's friendly gesture, he stood. "This is my gir . . ." He stopped, catching himself indulging, wanting to call Evie what he already considered her. He thought Evie might not appreciate that shared with a stranger when they hadn't even discussed it privately. "This is Evie," he said, walking to stand next to her. He took Evie's hand and turned back to the girl who was now standing, surprise on her face. "Jenny was telling me about early Kyd works located in the main Boston library. She did a little research for us and set up an appointment for Wednesday to see them." As William pulled Evie forward with him, she suddenly felt silly for her unfounded jealousy.

"I should get back to the information desk." The girl's tone was clipped as she walked away.

Evie should be ashamed by her behavior, but couldn't bring herself to be because William was still holding her hand.

He turned, putting his free hand around her waist and leaned down, and hugged her. Moving into his caress, she let her mind focus on his warm breath against her neck. Closing her eyes, she felt her whole body stir in response and she wrapped her arm under his, hooking it up and around his shoulder. William moved his head to the right, running his nose along the shell of her ear. Her knees began to buckle under the intimacy, but his grip tightened.

He whispered, "I'm yours, love. You don't ever have to worry. I lo . . . I care about you." She inhaled every word he spoke and rubbed her cheek tenderly against his jaw.

William stepped back, keeping a grip on her hand and picked up their bags. He led her out of the historical building, but stopped on the steps out front. "I . . . uh, I," he started to say as he dropped the bags down and rested his free hand on the back of his neck. "I think you should know I really like you, if you can't tell already." He laughed and looked away. "I sound childish."

Shoving his hands into his pockets for a tangible support, he tried to focus back on her by looking straight into her curious eyes. They made him feel better, stronger as he spoke. "I'm falling for you, Evie. I hope I'm not speaking out of place here. I saw what happened in there and wanted you, well, thought you should know how much I care about you. You don't have to worry. I'm not interested in anyone else."

While he was giving his heart to her, Evie's joy from his words was crushed when she realized she couldn't say the same things back. She could tell him, yes, but knew she would never be able to reciprocate fully until other things were handled. She would have to deal with things with speed and care, although she would still have to tell William the truth. He deserved the truth. But she didn't want to ruin this moment, especially not for him. She cared too much about him to do that.

When he stopped, he didn't wait for her to say anything in return. "I want you to know that."

Dreaming of his kisses since the last one, she closed

176

her eyes, wrapped her arms around him, and kissed him. Their lips parted, gentle and slow, and they deepened their connection. As their bodies pressed closer, their heartbeats sped up. When their lips separated with reluctance, both Evie and William felt the loss as cold swept across their mouths.

They didn't have to speak to make the moment more perfect than it was because it was as close to perfection than either had ever felt. William looked down at their bags and she watched his face and movements. The connection they had was different than either had experienced before, and strong, and meant to be. He picked up their bags, and with a sweet smile, asked, "Lunch?"

She nodded still too caught up in the moment to say anything. With her hand in his, he led her down the wide cement steps to the sidewalk below. When they found a sandwich shop, he turned to her, eyed her once, and said, "Have you ever had a Philly cheesesteak?" He had a feeling she hadn't.

"I haven't. I'd like to try one though," she replied.

A few minutes later and with sandwiches in hand, they sat down on a picnic bench jus outside the shop. She smiled, and picked at the bread. "This looks good."

"They're amazing." William took a large bite and moaned in pleasure.

Following his cue, she picked it up, mimicking his hold on the sloppy sandwich, closed her eyes, and took a small bite. As she was chewing, she opened her eyes to see him grinning at her and for the first time in her life, she felt it was acceptable to talk with her mouth full. "This is soooo good." She finished chewing. "Like really good."

William was still smirking when he stood up and leaned over to kiss her on the mouth even though it was full of another bite. He didn't care because he found her sexy relaxed and happy like this.

She kissed him, not caring about how she looked or propriety. She did what she felt and she felt like kissing him twice, so she did.

After lunch, they did a little sightseeing, stopped for frozen custard then headed for the train station. As the train barreled back to Manhattan, Evie turned to William. She felt shy, but wanted a photo of him. "May I take a picture of you?" She knew once again she was crossing a line, but she felt selfish and wanted something just for her.

He chuckled at her formality. "Yes, if you want."

She took a picture of him looking at her the way she most liked to see him, *in like of her*. His darkened eyes said everything they both knew it was too soon to say and she hoped to hold onto that look forever with the photo.

When the photo loaded onto the screen, she stared at it. She was soft spoken, but he heard her. "You look sexy like this."

The right side of his mouth lifted into a smile, a bit confident, a tad cocky. He pulled his phone out and flipped through the options. William stopped and smiled at his display. "I think you look really sexy like this." He turned the phone around for her to see and her mouth dropped open.

"When did you take that?" She tried to act mad, but she thought the picture was funny.

"I like the way you're about to lick the ice cream, tongue out all greedy-like." He laughed again when her fist hit his arm. "Okay, okay. I shouldn't have taken it without you knowing, but I really do think you're pretty damn sexy eating ice cream. That right there is what fantasies are made of," he said, pointing at the picture.

"Ewww! Stop it right now. No doing anything dirty while looking at that picture," she demanded, trying to grab the phone.

He held it out of her reach and continued the joke. "I don't need this picture. It's burned into my brain." He felt her playfully hit his arm again. Grabbing her hand, he eyed her. "No worries. I only have chaste thoughts about you." He tried to sound convincing by saying that with a straight face.

But her expression changed. "Well, that's disappointing."

Putting his arm around her, he squeezed her into his side and laughed. His grin got even bigger when she relaxed into him for the remainder of the ride back to New York.

Evie found William so comfortable to be around that thirty minutes later, she was asleep. He kissed the top of her head and rested his own against hers. Her breathing was even and calm. She slept peacefully the remaining hour. When the train came to a stop, he kissed her once more on the head then gently nudged her awake while whispering, "Evie, we're home. We're back in Manhattan."

When she opened her eyes, she popped up, her surroundings unfamiliar, but calmed when she saw William. She looked at him, feeling embarrassed. "I fell asleep. I'm sorry. I didn't mean to fall asleep on you."

He talked softly to calm her down. "It's okay. I liked holding you. Are you all right?"

She tried to settle her racing heart as she came to her senses. "Yeah, I'm fine. I guess we should go."

They exited the train station and knew they were

going in different directions, so they stood on the sidewalk first, both feeling awkward and neither wanting to say good-bye. William decided to take a chance. "Do you want to come over or go do something?"

"Yeah, but I told my sister we would hang out tonight. I'm sorry."

"Oh, okay. Well, I guess I'll see you tomorrow then?"

"Uh-huh." She turned to walk away, but turned back and flew into his arms, which he opened to embrace her fully. "Thank you for today. I had such a good time." Her cheek was pressed against his chest and she closed her eyes, wanting this to last forever.

William kissed her head. "So did I." He kissed her once more on the forehead and they went their separate ways.

While Evie took a cab home, William walked to save the money.

Chapter 17

Evie had a charity brunch the next day that she had committed to months earlier though she had no interest in going. Because it was for charity, she put on a pretty dress, her pearl necklace, and earrings, slipped on her engagement ring, and left for the event.

She had a good time despite feeling anxious to meet William later in the afternoon. He had texted asking her to meet him at Bean There at 2 p.m. She drank her mimosa and purchased several purses from the fundraiser before slipping out, she hoped undetected.

William and Evie arrived at Bean There at 2:00 p.m. to form their game plan for the trip to the main Boston library the next day. He had complimented her on how beautiful she looked and felt underdressed in comparison.

Tracy served their usual coffee, pausing a moment to watch the couple up close. "School work or social visit today?" she asked.

"Both," William said followed by a smile in Evie's direction.

"You're all dressed up and your ring." The barista

smiled, though Evie felt no warmth behind it. "Wow. Just wow!"

"Thank you." Evie's response was polite, but short and her tone left no opening for further discussion as she glanced at William who was carrying their coffees to the table. She needed to talk to him. Maybe tomorrow on their trip, she could. For now, she just wanted to enjoy this feeling they were sharing.

Guilt started to shroud her thoughts as William bumped his chair up against Evie's and pointed to her laptop. "Boston is over three hours by train."

"Everything is due on Friday. I think this is our only hope if we're going to figure this out before the deadline."

"Let's buy tickets." Evie searched the train schedule and zeroed in on the early commuter times. "How about six? Can you meet at six or too early?"

William tapped her on her scrunched up nose, and said, "We can sleep on the train. Six is good. We'll get to the library by ten."

"If we catch the four o'clock train back we can be back home by eight?"

"Sounds good."

She logged onto the purchase tickets page and then offered, "I'll buy the tickets and you buy lunch?"

He saw the price glaring back at him on the screen and agreed. "Deal." Disappointed he couldn't contribute more, he leaned in and whispered, "Thank you... again."

His breath on her neck, made her own catch and she closed her eyes. Remembering the feel of his lips, she knew she couldn't resist him. She didn't want to resist him anymore either, and opened her eyes. "You're welcome, but actually, I'm kind of doing this for selfish reasons."

"Oh?"

"It guarantees more time with you all to myself."

"Well, I thought as much Miss Wright, but I didn't want to embarrass you by pointing it out." He smiled at her while moving closer. Her heart beat faster and she reached down and took his hand, their fingers folding together.

Sharing a small smile, their eyes met and held the gaze of the other before she looked away, returning her attention to their research. He kissed her on the cheek before focusing back on the work they needed to get done.

A few hours later, Evie walked into the lobby feeling on top of the world. She went to her room and sat down at the window seat, watching life below and reliving every moment of her day with William. In a spontaneous moment, she decided to go to her special place around the corner and texted William to join her. Minutes, hours, days didn't seem to be enough time with him.

She left the building, waving to Walter and walked to the park.

What she didn't know is that Audrey had enlisted Walter in an undercover, covert operation. Audrey wanted her sister to be happy and knew the doorman, who had always treated them well, also cared. With too much time on her hands and a wild imagination, Audrey set up a sting operation. Walter dialed Audrey to let her know Everleigh, aka Lark, had flown the coop.

Audrey, aka Blue Jay, was on the hunt tracking Lark's every move. To her surprise though, she was following her to a park near their home. Annoyed by the lack of excitement and boringness of her older sister's adventure, she felt disappointed. But as she rounded the corner, she stopped in her tracks, jumping back behind the building for cover. She blinked repeatedly, not believing her eyes.

William rode his bike into the nearly deserted section of the park and spotted Evie right away. "Hi, pretty girl. You know New York City parks around dark aren't the safest place to be or didn't your daddy ever warn you about that?"

Evie turned and smiled. "No, I was never warned because I never went out alone growing up. Sheltered life, remember?" she said, shrugging.

"Well, I don't want you hanging out here alone after dark, Evie. Okay?" William protectively leaned forward as he scanned the park.

"Yes, sir." She was playing with him, but she really did like his caring nature.

"You look beautiful tonight." William took her hand and kissed the top of it. He immediately noticed the ring she was wearing again today. She was dressed more casually, and it stood out. "Wow! I hope that's not real or you really might have been in danger out here."

Evie laughed, but it was awkward. Having him this close to something that represented a whole other life, another world, something she would end soon to be with the man who was now kissing the palm of her hand, unnerved her.

Sitting on a park bench, they chatted about everything and nothing, content being near each other as the sun set.

They strolled along, holding hands, as the streetlamps flickered on, lighting the path. Ducking under a large Oak, William pulled her to the trunk. He wanted to kiss her—long and deep. He wanted to connect with her and take their relationship to the next level. He wanted her, he wanted everything with her.

When he leaned back on the tree trunk, she leaned forward against him, chest to chest, her body against his. They looked at each other, the step they were about to take feeling forbidden, but both willing participants.

He pulled her in for a passionate kiss. It was gentle, almost delicate at first. But when his hands slid over her shoulders and up her neck to cup her face, she gave into everything she desired. Grabbing his shoulders, she lifted higher up on her feet, kissing him with just as much passion.

Their kiss became eager and then with her hands on his chest she stopped it. They immediately looked away from each other knowing if they weren't careful this could turn inappropriate for a public place.

She glanced down before looking back at him. "You make me forget myself. You make me forget all my problems."

"And that's a bad thing?" His lids were heavier than before. He was drowsy with love for this girl.

"It's a great thing, but they're problems that can't be easily solved."

"You want to share them with me? I'm happy to—"

"No, I can't, not yet." Evie looked away again, upset at herself that she let their feelings develop to this point. "It's not something you can help me with."

William snuggled around her, still protecting her under the tree in the park which was cemented as his new favorite place in the world.

Audrey went back to the apartment and while she was lost in her own thoughts of what she had witnessed, Walter asked, "Any luck, Blue Jay?"

She did a half nod mixed with a small shake, which confused Walter. "You lost Lark?"

The funny nickname brought her back to the present and she smiled while leaning on his desk. "No, I found her, but I also might have found out more than I maybe wanted to know." She let out a sigh, not sure what to make of this new information. Suddenly, she felt like she was carrying her sister's burden. "How can something that makes her so happy be a burden?"

Walter responded with logic. "It can't."

Audrey looked at his kind eyes and perked up. "You're right. You are absolutely right." She moved to the elevators, and said, "Thanks, Walter. Have a good night."

"Good night, Blue Jay."

William wanted to walk Evie home, but she stopped at the corner, tugging him by the belt loops into the shadows close to the stone wall. He leaned forward, pinning her there. She loved this feeling and kissed his mouth, which she found ready to meet hers. They spent minutes like this, occasionally feeling the need for air.

Walter had gotten some fresh air, standing under the awning when he spotted the young couple. He backed toward the door then went inside to give them privacy.

Evie gave William three quick kisses on his nose, mouth, and chin then said, "I should go in."

William's hands tightened on her hips as if he could hold her there. Leaning his forehead against hers, he closed his eyes, and savored the moment. "I don't want you to."

186

"I don't want to either, but I have to."

"One day, I hope you let me in here." He tapped her head softly, and said, "And let me help you with all of those unsolvable problems. One day, I don't want us to have to say goodnight on the sidewalk. One day."

"One day." She murmured with her lips pressed to his neck. "But for now, goodnight, William Ryder."

"Goodnight, Evie Wright, until the morrow."

She slipped out of his grasp and went inside, smiling at Walter as she walked to the elevator.

William passed the entrance and gave a polite nod to Walter.

Walter gestured back with a wave, realizing what Audrey had seen. He felt sick thinking about the harsh repercussions Everleigh would endure because of this illicit affair once her monster of a fiancé found out. One thing he was positive of was that Tom Whitney would not find out from him. He would protect her if he could.

Chapter 18

Four-thirty came too soon. Evie was tired and in a haze as she got dressed, pulling on fitted cotton capris and a blouse, slipping her ballet-style flats on, and putting on her jewelry, including her ring, without any thought to the matter.

Before the train left the station, William produced two travel pillows and adjusted one around Evie's neck for comfort. They had opted not to have any coffee this morning, wanting to sleep instead. Snuggling the best they could while sitting side-by-side, they closed their eyes. Boston greeted them with heavy rain and Evie pulled her umbrella out of her backpack. "We can share."

William took the umbrella, holding it more over her than himself as they rushed the four blocks to the McKim building which housed rare and historical books.

"That wasn't so bad," she said as they wiped their feet at the library's entrance.

He took hold of her hand. "But this is better."

As they approached the large information desk in the main city library, both of their stomachs filled with butterflies. Evie placed her hand on her belly, and asked, "Why am I nervous?"

Taking a deep breath first, William slowly released it along with his nerves before answering. "I feel like this is the defining moment on this project." He took her hand in his, and with confidence led her to the counter to speak to the clerk. "We have a ten-thirty appointment in the Rare Books Department."

Three hours later, they had a definitive answer for the Kyd stories. One was authentic and the other falsified. They exhaled their relief and both relaxed, sinking into their chairs. Evie giggled. "It feels good, right?"

William chuckled. "So good." Leaning his head back, he closed his eyes. "I can't wait to present our findings on Friday."

"Well, we have just the minor detail of finishing the report for that to happen first."

"Very minor, my dear, very minor detail indeed." He popped his head up with eyes open then said, "Let's go celebrate." He stood up, pulling his jacket back on and throwing their work into the shared backpack he was carrying today. When they ran out the front doors of the library, they got drenched, though they were too happy to care.

They ran to a nearby diner and fell into a booth by the window. After ordering two sodas and burgers, Evie looked across the table into William's eyes, feeling wistful. "No one's ever made me feel as vulnerable as you do."

William's expression softened to hold her gaze even though confusion shot across his face. "I don't want you to feel vulnerable. I want you to feel safe when we're together." His saddened tone seeped through his words, hurting her heart.

She was quick in correcting what she meant by standing and sliding in next to him in the booth, taking his hand in hers and kissing his knuckles. "No, you misunderstood what I was saying. I feel exposed in a good way. Being with you." Pausing, she looked away from him to the tabletop, and said, "I can be me." She fumbled through her words. "I'm not used to feeling like myself. I'm numb to life most of the time, most every day, but with you . . . I feel alive. You make me want to be present in my own life again. You make me excited for the future." She mustered the courage to look at him and he reversed their hands so he was now holding hers. "You like the real me and you make *me* like the real me." She leaned over and kissed him on the lips just because she wanted to.

During their kiss, he had a thousand things running through his mind, but at the forefront was that she had shared a secret of hers. "You feel vulnerable because it's a new feeling for you?"

"Exactly." She smiled because he got her.

"This," he said, waving his hand between them, "is all new for me."

She rested her head onto his shoulder, and whispered, "I like you, too." She wanted to tell him she loved him and her heart will be forever missing once they part, but she settled with *I like you, too.* They left the diner as a couple 'in like,' instead of a couple of friends.

With less than an hour left before their train back to Manhattan, they headed to the station and waited on a bench and people watched.

They both slept on the train back to Manhattan and awoke when their arrival was announced. Drowsy, they made their way off and out to the taxi stand. They held hands, neither wanting to break the connection, but knowing it was time to part.

"So?" William asked more like a question.

She let out a little yawn. "So . . . I'm not ready to leave yet."

William's heart almost leapt out of his chest with her simple declaration that she wanted to spend more time with him even after spending fifteen hours together. Broke, he offered what he could. "I can make you a bowl of high-sodium, fattening noodles."

His smile was endearing and she knew he was teasing, but how could she ever refuse? Feeling shy and a little silly, she tilted her head, leaning it against his shoulder. "That sounds delicious."

Rubbing her back, he laughed. "I know this great place. C'mon, beautiful."

As soon as he walked into his apartment, he turned on the small lamp in the corner and dug out two shirts and two flannel sleep pants from his dresser. He watched her all perfect, a little mussed from the adventure—her clothes wrinkled and a bit dirty—and wondered who he had to thank for bringing her into his life.

Handing her a set of clothes, he offered the use of the bathroom first. Right before the door closed, she poked her head out and asked, "Do you mind if I take a shower?"

"Not at all," he replied, too fast. An image of her naked was already racing through his mind.

While she showered, he changed his clothes, getting more comfortable. At one point, he thought he heard a soft moan from the bathroom that shot right to his pelvis. Desperate, he tried to quiet the crazy thoughts bouncing around his head in case she felt the need to make another amazing sound again. But instead, the water cut off and he ran and jumped on the bed, trying to look casual and hoping she didn't hear the loud springs screeching in protest as he landed with a thud.

As William sat with his back against the wall, he ran his hands through his hair pulling and tugging at the roots. *I've got to get control of myself.* He imagined getting slapped across the face to shake him out of the state he frenzied himself into when he heard the door open. Evie walked out in his T-shirt, and what appeared to be nothing else. The shirt hit mid-thigh on her and William gulped loudly, not sounding casual at all. "Do you mind if I use your hairbrush?"

"No," he answered, three octaves too high for a twenty-two year old man, but was quick to lower his voice, even if unnaturally. "No." Once again, he tried to sound older than a twelve-year-old prepubescent boy hoping to see a naked girl for the first time.

She continued smiling, but narrowed her eyes in confusion.

He was unraveling before her eyes and he worried she would start worrying for her safety if he didn't rein in the crazy.

"Thanks." She turned on her heel, feeling awkward, and went back into the bathroom. Evie returned two minutes later with the flannel pants on and William released a huge sigh of relief.

She furrowed her brow still confused when he offered her noodles. She didn't see that he had much of a setup for making her homemade pasta. Following him to the hotpot, she watched as he started making dinner. "You're a very confident cook," she said matter of fact.

"Um, adding hot water to a Styrofoam bowl full of dehydrated noodles and veggies isn't cooking."

"It's more than I can do. I'm impressed."

"Well," he said, waggling his eyebrows, "wait until this oven gets fixed. I'll make you a real meal then."

"I look forward to it. Though I'll happily admit, I'm looking forward to this meal just as much."

After eating, they settled down and started on their final report. They found they had worked well as a team during this entire project and it wasn't lost on either of them that they worked well as a couple, too.

A small yawn betrayed Evie as she looked at the clock to discover it was past midnight.

"Guess it's pretty late, huh?" he asked, scooting down from the desk next to her on the floor and making his boldest move yet. "I'd like you to stay tonight."

Evie only hesitated a few seconds before asking, "You wouldn't mind?"

"I would love for you to stay with me." He shut down his computer and she turned hers off. She pushed her stuff closer to the wall and out of the way as he straightened his small corner desk.

She wanted to stay. She wanted to stay with him as long as she could and was willing to take the risk. "I can sleep on the floor."

"No, no." He shook his head. "I would never make you sleep on the floor. You can have the bed." He moved to the bed and dug a bag out from under the metal frame. "I have an extra blanket and pillow down here—"

Her instant reaction surprised both of them. "No! Please. William, I . . ." Calming, she said, "We can share."

He stopped and looked up to her, unsure of what he

S. L. Scott

should do. He knew what he really wanted to do, but could he be that close and just sleep instead? He was willing to take the chance to find out. "Are you sure?"

"Yes, very sure."

"Okay, would you like to brush your teeth with me? I have a spare toothbrush you can have."

"Yes, I really need to. The major downside about surprise sleepovers is you aren't prepared."

Evie had realized in the shower that she was wearing her ring. It had been early when she dressed that morning and it was next to the small diamond studs she put on. At four-thirty in the morning, her brain wasn't awake and she slipped it on not thinking about her day ahead.

Her heart ached looking at it and she wondered if she should tell William tonight. She felt he might be, no, she knew he would be upset, but also knew he would give her a chance to explain everything. He was that kind of person and hoped he would see how much she cared for him. After today, she couldn't imagine a life with Tom. This life was too good. She would end her engagement no matter the consequences the next time she saw Tom. William was worth any repercussion. She took the ring off and tucked it into the inside pocket of her purse.

Following William into the bathroom, she watched as he pulled a new toothbrush from his small cabinet. As they brushed their teeth together, the intimacy of the act was felt inside her heart.

Ready for bed, she stood in the main room while he flipped the covers back. "You first, so you don't fall off the edge."

William switched the light off and eased under the sheet and blanket.

195

They lay there, their breath intermingling in the darkness, facing each other in the dark until their eyes adjusted.

She could feel the bed dip even more, causing her to fall forward a bit until William's body stopped her. His hand rubbed her shoulder and his lips found her mouth, and he kissed her in appreciation.

With a heavy heart, Evie hated ruining this for herself, but especially hated ruining this for him. "William?" she whispered between them, her words not having to travel far.

"Thank you for staying," he said, stroking the hair off her face. There was enough moonlight to see her pretty features in the dim light. "We don't have to do anything. I just . . . I just want to hold you in the quiet of the night."

After those words, she couldn't do this to him, not now, but promised herself she would tell him everything in the morning. She didn't want their bubble to burst and news of dreaded and abusive fiancés would most definitely burst it. She rolled over. "Spoon me." It was a quiet request shared between them.

As soon as she turned, William moved closer to her until his chest was against her back and wrapped his arm around her waist. His face rested with her hair on the same pillow, allowing him to breathe her in. Evie's breathing changed pace, which made his speed up racing to catch up.

Turning around quick, she found his lips with hers. She didn't care about anything in the world except what she was feeling right then, and how he made her feel.

He kissed her, remembering all the times he dreamed of her being there and now it was real. She moved even closer and he adjusted his hand on her lower back, supporting her closeness. They stopped kissing to both take

196

a breath before she took to kissing his jaw, his chin, and briefly inhaling all that was William. She had wanted to do this for so long that lust was sure to win out if she wasn't careful.

He leaned over her until she was on her back, kissing her mouth and enjoying the connection. They swam in the kiss as it became needier. But even with William losing his focus, he stopped to take another breath and a moment of clarity hit him. His eyes dilated, taking her beauty in. She took heavy, but shallow breaths as he rubbed his hand along her cheek and said, "I can't kiss you anymore tonight." Then he added, "I won't be able to stop myself if I do. I find you so sexy and you being this close while wearing my clothes, well, I'll just say that I want to be sensitive to your needs when we do . . . when we're together for the first time, but I can't promise that right now." He watched her mouth turn up in a smile that reached her eyes and sparkled with understanding. Leaning down, he kissed her on the lips, lingering a moment longer on her forehead. "Sweet dreams, beautiful."

He flopped onto his back in the tiny bed with his shoulder half hanging off.

She reached over and kissed him on the cheek. "I still want you to spoon me." With a quick roll away from him, she awaited his touch. He didn't disappoint and rolled onto his side, tucking his knees behind hers, resting his chest against her back, and snuggling into her with his arm around her waist.

Chapter 19

Evie woke before William and stiffened at the feel of his hand underneath her shirt, resting dangerously close, but just below her left breast. She smiled, not minding it there at all. She giggled, enjoying how comfortable she felt in his arms—safe and sexy—for the first time in her life. She attempted a turn, but the large warm body resting against her and the dead weight of his arm kept her in place. "William," she whispered in amusement. "William?"

He stirred, causing his nose to disappear into her hair, which hung over her shoulder. His hand grazed the bottom of her breast and his eyes popped open, alert and very aware of where his hand was located. She laughed and he smiled at the beautiful sound, smell, and sight of the woman next to him.

"Are we pretending your hand is not under my shirt?" she teased.

His hand was still, but his voice was lighthearted. "Technically, it's my shirt."

"Well, in that case, did you know your hand is under your shirt touching my boob?"

He played the innocent. "What?"

"Your hand is touching my boob," she repeated for his comprehension.

"I just wanted to hear you say boob again." He laughed, and she spun around to face him while smirking.

"Boob! Boob! Boob!" She laughed at the silliness of the word.

His hand was still under her shirt, but now on her back. He caressed her shoulder blades and spine and explored, rubbing lightly up and down. "Good morning," he said, still smiling.

"Good morning, Mr. Ryder," she replied, appreciating the heat of his hand on her skin. "I need to use the bathroom."

He was reluctant, but withdrew his hand, and she immediately felt its absence from her body, the cold setting in as William slid out of bed allowing her to slip out. He lay down, covering himself back up and she kissed his nose. As she walked to the bathroom feeling sassy, she said, "And don't think I didn't notice you copped a feel when I rolled over, Mr. Ryder."

He burst out laughing, knowing he was that bad. He was officially fourteen again.

They both took turns getting dressed in the bathroom. Evie had decided to wear his T-shirt since hers felt dirty from traveling the day before.

It was drizzling once again as they walked hand-in-hand to the coffee shop. Evie took a deep breath, relishing the feel, as she looked up at the overcast sky. "I love the rain." William always found these little comments surprising, but liking how much she appreciated such simple pleasures.

They walked into Bean There at seven-fifteen in the morning. The professional crowd was getting their caffeine fix, but William and Evie didn't mind the wait.

Tracy smiled at William just as he smiled at Evie, leaning on the counter. "Good morning." Tracy glanced at their joined hands then between the two of them. "You're meeting here early."

"It's a great morning," Evie replied, unable to remove the delirious, happy grin from her face.

William chuckled, feeling as happy as Evie. They were a couple and he loved that he didn't have to hide the fact. "We came together."

"Oh. Um, all right. Coffee?" Tracy asked.

Evie looked at Tracy surprised by her tone. She seemed shaken, as if they had said something to offend her. She went ahead and ordered to steer into a safer topic. "I'll have a mocha latte with skim milk."

William added his order. "Double espresso black with two blueberry muffins." Being gentle, he took Evie's fingers pulling her to him and kissed her on the cheek. "I'll get this." Evie nodded and walked over to their favorite table.

As Tracy set the blueberry muffins next to the freshly made coffees, she leaned across the counter. "You two, huh?"

He smiled, the spark in his eyes acknowledging the answer before he responded. "Yes."

Tracy could see it written all over his face. He was in love. Keeping her voice low, she looked over his shoulder at Evie then back to him. "But then why does she still wear the ring?"

Thrown by the question, he became curious. "What do you mean?"

Tracy's expression quirked, and she explained without hesitation. "Her engagement ring? She's not wearing the ring today, so I assume she's not engaged anymore."

He looked at her before glancing over his shoulder confused by what Tracy was talking about, more importantly, what she was inferring.

When he turned back, Tracy gave a sympathetic smile, and started to cover for her slip. "I just figured you wouldn't be with her if she was still engaged. I mean, I don't know you well, but you never seemed like the affair type of guy."

He felt relief when it dawned on him which ring Tracy was referring to. The large fashion ring was justified in his mind. He chuckled then explained, "It's an heirloom, I think. It's only a ring she wears sometimes when she dresses up."

Tracy lowered her voice to a whisper so only he could hear. "That's an engagement ring, William. Do you really not know?"

By the size and color of the ring, he never questioned it. He'd even joked about it. Because she wore it on her left ring finger didn't mean it *had* to be an engagement ring, did it? He felt sick to his stomach, the relief he was feeling seconds earlier dissipated. William set the money down on the counter wanting to end this conversation. He grabbed the coffees and muffins then walked over and set them down on their table.

Evie took a quick sip as William remained standing,

staring at her. "What is it?" she asked, feeling the change in the atmosphere between them.

He grabbed her by the left hand, feeling the small indentation on her ring finger with his thumb. "Get your stuff." She was confused, but did as he requested. She was used to taking orders, even if it was now from William. He pulled her by the hand and back outside to the cloudy day. Evie stumbled to keep up, purse in hand, knowing something had happened to upset him. He stopped at the farthest table from the door away from the windows of the shop. "Are you engaged?"

Evie's world shifted as the first piece of her happiness crumbled around her. The question felt like an unexpected slap across the face. Her stomach knotted and she stuttered trying to come to terms that they were about to have a huge fight, a fight that had the possibility of ending their relationship. "I . . . I . . . uh—"

"It's a simple yes or no kind of answer here, Evie, but I'm taking by that response, it's a yes." He dropped her hand like he had touched fire and ran his fingers through his hair out of frustration and anger. "How can you be here with me this morning, be with me last night if you're marrying someone else?"

She put her hands on his chest, but he backed away not wanting her touch, needing space between them. "I, yes, I am technically engaged, but I don't want to be. My heart isn't his—"

"Technically? That's a romantic way to describe your engagement and a very loose interpretation of the word 'engaged.'"

When he started to walk away, she rushed behind him, pleading, "Yes, maybe. Okay, yes. It's a loose interpretation within the truth." She took a breath, choking up as tears filled her eyes. "William, please listen to me. It was a commitment I made a long time ago. I don't love him. I don't! I want to end it, but it's complicated. It's an obligation that seems—"

"Wow! Unbelievable!" William shook his head and stopped to stare at the person in front of him, now unfamiliar to what he knew of her even a mere ten minutes earlier. Everything he thought he knew about her was wrong and distorted and his heart ached feeling played. He looked her straight in the eyes. "An obligation? It's obvious to me now that we are two very different people. I would hate for my fiancée to ever consider me an obligation or an unwanted commitment." He started walking again, but stopped. With his back to her, he said, "To be clear, I don't want to see you anymore." With that painful declaration, he started to leave.

The rain picked up, coming down harder than before and soaking her hair and clothes. It didn't matter though. Nothing mattered, but William. She rushed behind him, trying to explain, but careful not to touch him. She couldn't handle him pulling away again. "Yes, an obligation, William. In my world, I was committed to him by the time I was ten. The ring came at seventeen."

He stopped, but still refused to face her. He adjusted the backpack on his shoulders and listened because although his heart was breaking, he hoped she would have a justifiable reason for lying about this, for cheating on him and her fiancé. Evie's words were fumbling from her mouth, desperate to salvage their relationship. "It's a social hierarchy. Our families agreed upon our bond before I had a say in the matter."

Fuming, William spun on his heels and looked at her. She stood, drenched like him, but beautiful and pained, and crying, still wearing his T-shirt. "That's ridiculous! You have a say in the matter—"

"You're right. At seventeen, I was in love and accepted the ring, and made the commitment to marry him, but I was tricked. I was foolish and young, too young, to make such life-altering decisions."

His pain and anger were battling inside his head. William couldn't look at her any longer. He wanted to, but if he did, he knew he'd go to her, comfort her, and protect her. Right now, he needed clarity and he couldn't find it being this close, and took a step back, away from her. "I was falling in love with you," he confessed, his words barely heard above the passing traffic and over the pouring rain. "I had already fallen."

"I've fallen in love with you, too. You're everything I want—kind and generous, patient, and supportive. Please, I'm asking you to understand, to liste—"

"I can't be with you!" He dug deep within and found the strength to look up. "I'm the one who was tricked here, lied to. You aren't a woman I can want or have, so this discussion is over." William shoved his hands into his pockets and left her standing a block away from Bean There in the rain.

Evie's mind went blank except for one thought. *I hate the rain.* She remained standing there watching him walk away from her in the opposite direction. He never looked back, not even a glance, with his head dropped down and his shoulders slumped forward.

By the time William arrived home, he wanted to punch something. He felt deceived, hurt, and didn't understand how to deal with these emotions. Hiding a detail that major from him was lying and he hated when people lied. He didn't care about the daily little fibs everyone told to make their lives easier. Those don't matter, but he hated the big ones and this was a doozie. He took a hot shower, hoping this mess and the pain would wash away with the dirty rain. It didn't. It lingered around him, on him, consuming him until he broke down, slamming his fists against the shower wall until he cried out in anger, frustration, and loss.

Evie approached her building with caution. In her current state of mind, she detested this place. It represented everything she hated in life. She didn't want to be here. She wanted to be at William's where she felt safe and cared for and loved. But this place also represented everything she had tried to hold onto by doing what was considered the right thing. She loved her family, so she made her way to the doors to confront her turmoil.

Walter opened the door, allowing her entrance. "Morning."

His greeting was somber and she wondered if he had just had his heart ripped out, too.

He could tell something was wrong, very wrong. She looked a mess to him and it wasn't because of the odd outfit or because she was soaking wet. Something in her face, her eyes, told him that she was in pain.

"Morning, Walter."

But before she reached the elevators, he called to her. "Evie?"

Evie was numbing with every step she took, but stopped upon hearing her name. She turned around, trying to smile though she didn't know if she succeeded or not. "Yes, Walter?"

"Mr. Whitney is waiting for you upstairs."

Those seven words made her heart stop then drop into the pit of her stomach, and she gulped. She turned back around and pushed the button calling the lift to the first floor.

"He's very upset," he said. "He arrived late last night. He's been waiting for you."

"I'm sure he has." This was not good, but facing Tom couldn't be worse than losing William.

He walked closer. "I don't think you should go up there. I think you should go to a friend's place, go get coffee, go to the park, go anywhere, but up there."

"Walter, one thing I've learned is it doesn't get better with time. It will be worse tomorrow if I don't face him now."

Walter followed her, putting his hand on her forearm right before she stepped onto the elevator. His words were rushed, but sincere. "If you need anything, anything at all, please call me."

She nodded, not knowing what truly awaited her upstairs.

Walter remained standing there, distressed by her false bravery. She smiled at him in fake reassurance, hating for people to worry over her, just as the doors closed.

Walter never did understand how rich people turned a blind eye to the atrocities of their own behavior. She now knew he would be there if she needed help, so he went back to his desk, sat down, and worried in silence.

Chapter 20

Walter hadn't had any assurances regarding Evie for four days when she appeared, walking off the elevator and out the front door with the slightest of greeting in the form of a nod. And though he was finally seeing her in the flesh, that she was alive and safe, he realized when she nodded, that the corner of her mouth was a little swollen and bruised. Her large, dark sunglasses didn't reveal her thoughts, but as she crossed in front of him exiting through the door he held open for her, he saw the discoloration circling the outside of her eye. He turned his gaze to his shoes out of respect, and she left without a word spoken between them.

During the past four days, William had become an utter mess. He couldn't get the girl with ink obsessions who wore a bird flying free necklace off his mind. Besides spending three nights in a row at his local bar bumming drinks from friends to numb his thoughts, he went to class and turned in their report on Friday despite Evie's absence. And since he wasn't sleeping much at night, he spent a lot of the day catching up on it. When he wasn't trying to sleep away the pain, he was working long hours, picking up shifts, and pushing his physical limits on his bike, being reckless from lack of care.

Almost a week later, he was leaving the student lounge in the literature building when a small girl interrupted his slow downfall. "Hi, you're William, right? Can I talk to you?"

He stopped to look at her concerned face. Removing one of the ear buds to his mp3 player, he looked at her, but didn't say anything.

"I'm Audrey, Audrey Wright, Evie's sister. My friend Walter told me your name." William took a step forward, away from her, and Audrey started talking faster. "I understand this seems strange. I don't even know if you knew she had a sister, but I need to talk to you. I need your help."

With the last sentence spoken, William halted his stride and turned back to her. "I knew she had a sister," he said indignant. He studied her face more carefully this time. "I see the resemblance in your eyes."

She smiled and a slight blush spread across her cheeks. William could see they shared that familiar trait as well. "Audrey, I'm not trying to be mean, but I can't help her. I assume you know what happened between us or you wouldn't be here now—in her place."

"She doesn't know I'm here. I'm not even supposed to know about you—"

"Because I was a fling or an affair or something insignificant to her?"

"No. No, you weren't. I mean you're not insignificant. She cares a lot about you. She's just committed to another."

William started walking again. "I don't want to hear about her obligation or commitment. I've heard enough about it, that's for sure."

Audrey grabbed his arm, turning him back to her. "Please. She needs help and you're the only one who can save her now."

"Save her? I can't do shit for her. If she doesn't want to be engaged to this guy then maybe she should break it off! End it like a normal person would."

"It's not like that. It's not that easy. She's caught up in what's expected from her family, him, his family, their friends, geez, all of Manhattan it seems. She loses everything if she ends it. Honestly, he'd probably kill her first anyway." She mumbled the last part and her eyes faded from his view. She looked back up to him, showing defeat. "Arranged marriages are alive and well. You're in her class, so you study these books about societal influences and commitments arranged between people for security, for gain, for power. It's something like that and she was young, my age, and a union was formed. For her, it was love, or so she thought. But for him, it was two powerful families uniting as one for a higher standing."

William stood at the door before opening it and looked at this young girl with such big things to say. "What about you, then? What are you seventeen, eighteen?"

"Seventeen."

"You said she was your age, and yet I don't see a ring on your finger?"

"It's different for me. The firstborn has the obligation to the family. She secured the family fortune, giving me an easy ride."

He pushed the door open and walked outside with Audrey trailing behind. "I thought that ring was just another ring like the girls wear for fashion, not an engagement ring. That thing was so big I never thought twice about it being real or fake. I assumed it was a fake or maybe an heirloom since you guys are from money."

"It's five carats in exchange for power and ownership. It's an unfair exchange in a sane person's view, but it's his claim on her for the world to see."

"He marked what was his with a ring that any other fool would've recognized as a woman taken, except me." He removed the other ear bud and finished. "I feel like an idiot for not knowing, but it doesn't take the sting away that she never told me either." Then he became curious about something else. "If she didn't talk about me, then how do you know about me?"

Audrey scurried to keep up. "She changed and I noticed—a change for the better. I tried to pry info out of her, but she was tight-lipped. So, I followed her one day. I saw her meeting a man in the park. I'd never seen him before and couldn't tell how well she knew him because they were only talking at first. But then, I saw him take her hand and they walked together. I couldn't believe what I was seeing. My sister, my sister Evie, was having an affair. I was shocked by her rebellion. But what surprised me even more was seeing her smiling, so carefree. I hadn't seen her happy in a long time. I also saw her do something I never expected." William hung on every word as Audrey described the lovers meeting. "She went under a tree and kissed him. I heard them laugh. I heard my sister burst out in uncensored laugh. She isn't a frivolous person, but there she was in public, laughing for the world to see." Audrey locked eyes with William and could see the love he held for Evie. "When I saw how you treated her with such kindness, holding her like you did, I knew you were the one who could save her." She took a long, deep breath, as if exhausted.

William gulped. "I didn't know our dates were secretive. They weren't to me. I was openly showing her how much I cared and she was hiding her feelings for me from the world. It's not right. I can't save a girl who doesn't want to be saved."

"Oh, but she does!" Audrey was desperate, and demanding. "She didn't hide her feelings that day from the world. She was there, expressing how she felt for you. She doesn't know how to help herself out of this mess."

"Break it off. Be willing to lose everything. Do what you have to do!" William was mad. "What do you want me to do?"

"I thought you could talk to her or something, secretly, of course."

"Of course, secretly, how else would it be?" he replied with sarcasm.

Audrey's gaze dropped to the ground and sadness returned before she spoke. "I thought you'd understand. Maybe I'm not explaining this the way I should, but I did the best I could. I'm sorry for wasting your time." She turned without so much as a good-bye and walked away.

William took a deep breath to calm down. He exhaled. "Why hasn't she been to class?"

"She'll be back soon. She needs some time to . . . she just needs some time."

"Well, you should tell her Professor Lang has been going over our reports, so she should come back to class."

"I'll tell her."

He could tell he made Audrey feel bad, but really, what did she expect him to do? The change had to take place on Evie's side, not his. *Evie.* William still loved that name, maybe the girl still too—*definitely the girl.* He started to consider Audrey's proposition. He started considering talking to her again, even if only *secretly, of course.*

On Tuesday, before any thought-out plan was hatched by William, Evie took a seat eight rows up and in the middle of the auditorium for Professor Lang's monthly literature lecture series on good versus evil in the classics. She was relieved it was not the normal summer program of ten students. All students were welcome to attend, making it easier for her to blend into the crowd better. She sank down in her seat just as she spotted William running up the stairs past her row. She was relieved he hadn't seen her because she wasn't ready to face him, and he was very clear the last time they saw each other that he didn't want to see her.

William scooted down row ten to the middle and sat. He threw his bag in the seat next to his and sank lower into the theater-style chair. Professor Lang was ten minutes into his personal theories on why every story needs a villain and a hero when he stopped, walked a few feet forward, and made a request. "Miss Wright, please remove your sunglasses during my lecture."

William bolted upright in his chair to see Evie sitting two rows down from him. He hadn't thought to look for her because they weren't required to attend today's lecture. He leaned forward, watching her remove her sunglasses from her face. Her movements were slow, hesitant. William looked back to the Professor whose mouth dropped open. He cleared his throat and recomposed himself. "You may wear them today."

To anyone else in the room, this was an odd thing to say. But for Evie, it drew unwanted attention and she could feel her face burning red. She hid behind her hands for a moment until everyone started listening to Professor Lang again, putting the glasses back on.

William couldn't stop staring at her. He had a side

view of her face and by the time the red disappeared from her cheeks, William could clearly see brown, blue, and yellowish coloring on the outside of her eye and more bruising near her mouth. In that instant, he connected the Professor's comments, the odd coloring on her face, her absence from class, and the unexpected visit her sister had paid him.

His heart hurt thinking if he would have listened to Audrey maybe this could have been prevented. Then he felt a surge of adrenaline as his anger grew, realizing somebody did this to her. He stood up, threw his bag over his shoulder, and hopped over the two rows and across the aisle to her. As gentle as he could and yet still get her attention, he took her by the elbow helping her up. Evie was startled, but didn't want to make a scene and acquiesced to William's nonverbal request.

William grabbed her bag and they exited the auditorium. Standing in the corridor outside the lecture hall, they stopped, looking at each other in silence. A moment passed and she turned and walked outside the building, heading for home, but William ran after her. "Please. Please stop. Let me see your face."

Evie didn't know what to think or feel anymore. She had lost her stubbornness and was too weak to argue these days. So she turned back around and lifted her sunglasses, resting them on top of her head as if daring him to see her reality.

William's mouth opened and his heart ached for her. He wanted to heal her wounds with his touch and soothe her pain with kisses, but he knew he couldn't.

His expression reminded Evie of her shameful appearance and the slow healing bruises that were scattered across her skin. She reached for the protection of her sunglasses again, hoping to hide from the world, but his hand grabbed her wrist to stop her. She flinched, and shut her eyes tight, an instinct of hers to protect herself from years of escalating abuse.

His grip loosened, and released her. "Don't be scared. I would never hurt you, Evie."

"You hurt me worse than this already. This is superficial physical stuff. You broke my heart, William."

"I found out you were, are engaged! My heart is broken, too."

"I know. I know I don't have a right to blame you, but I . . . I imagined a different outcome." She looked down, shaking her head at her own stupidity, her own naiveté.

William's mind was reeling, but he pushed his own pain aside, and was able to see her pain clearly right then. She was lashing out after years of abuse. Though she hurt him with her words, he knew she didn't mean it. He reached his hand out, and in that gesture offered her what she needed most—a friend and ally. "Come with me. Please," he said, keeping his voice calm and hoping she would trust him to be there the way he should have been days before.

The silent pause stretched between them then she nodded, slowly taking his hand, and together they took a cab to his apartment. Silence continued to fill the space on the ride to his apartment.

Once inside, she dumped her bag on the floor and walked to the window. With her arms wrapped protectively around her, she stared outside.

She turned around and as his eyes examined her bruising, he asked, "Will you tell me what happened?"

"Do you really want to know because honestly, I

don't know if we're even friends right now?" She was defensive.

Even though he expected and even respected her defensiveness, he ventured to tell her the truth about how he felt. "We're more than friends. You know that. Please talk to me."

With his kind words easing the tension between them, she headed straight for the bed. Her shoes dropped to the floor and she sat there so small and perfect waiting for him to say something, anything. She hadn't thought not to make herself at home in his place, it just felt natural to do so. William watched her slip onto his bed and smiled to himself at her level of comfort here. Kneeling down in front of her, he took her hands, encouraging her. "You can tell me anything, Evie."

She restrained herself for many reasons, but mainly because she didn't want William to feel responsible and she knew he would, but she would also never lie to him again, and told him what happened. "I went home after our fight and he was waiting for me."

"Your fiancé?" He choked on the words, not liking the taste of the word when referring to Evie's obligation.

Opening her eyes, she looked right into his concerned ones. "Yes. My family is still in the Hamptons and he was also supposed to be there, but he came back early, to surprise me, and ended up waiting all night for me to come home. When I didn't, he got mad." She paused with heavy tears in her eyes. "Do you really want to hear this?"

Though stunned, William nodded, not sure if he'd be able to handle it.

"His expression was blank at first, controlled. But I saw the anger take over." She blinked her eyes twice, willing the tears and memories away. "I only felt the first hit. I don't think I was conscious for the rest. I can't remember anything after that."

William got on the bed and wrapped his arms around her.

Her voice broke when she said, "I woke up on the bathroom floor. There was some blood on the marble and on my face. My head felt like it was going to explode from the pain. It was hard to move. I felt weak, my body a bit limp."

He held her tighter, unable to reason how someone could hurt her. Here was the prettiest, most perfect girl William had ever seen telling him how a man took that beauty and smashed it with his own hands. William thought he might be sick if he heard anymore. That monster destroyed her spirit. He could see the light dimming in her eyes, the hopelessness, the pain and loss she has suffered. He vowed right then that he would try his damnedest to save her. "How can I help? What can I do? Let me help you, Evie."

"You're helping me more than you know."

He stroked the back of her head, and said, "We should call the cops."

"There's no point. Money and power can buy anything, including the police."

William wanted to believe that good still existed by justice being served. "Don't give up. We can try. Together. We'll do this together."

She looked up at him. "I'm not giving up. I'm facing reality. I don't want to drag this out into the public. All I want to do is forget it ever happened. Help me forget, William. Take away all of the bad and make it good.

Please."

Doing anything for her meant doing what she needed, and right now she needed to forget that evil was real.

She slumped against him and her small voice cut into his thoughts when she asked, "Do you mind if I take a nap here? I know that's a lot to ask, but I've not slept in what seems like days."

Although he was mad and felt twisted inside, William tried to calm himself as he stood up, releasing her. "Consider this your home now. You can't go back there. You're not going back, not alone at least."

Evie didn't want to talk anymore. Her body was failing her as a result of the emotional burden she'd been carrying for the last week. She stretched out on the bed, putting her head on his pillow. She could smell William's scent and that made her smile, which still hurt a bit to do.

"Sleep. I'll keep you safe." He leaned down and kissed the bruise on her temple, the one on her cheekbone, and then the one on the corner of her mouth—soft and gentle—loving. He was surprised how fast she fell asleep and knew it was because she felt safe for the first time in a week, or maybe longer.

Chapter 21

While Evie slept, William paced his apartment wanting to destroy this so called *fiancé*—not a man, a monster. Frustrated by the helplessness he felt made his body tense and his hands fist. He was lost in his emotions until a small whimper from the bed broke through his thoughts. Stopping, he looked at her as another soft cry escaped her. She was shaking and her face was scrunched in fear.

William had fantasized about Evie choosing to spend her nights with him, but those fantasies were of her getting peaceful sleep or making love and not sleeping at all. They never included fear or crying. Yet, here she was afraid as she slept in *his* bed and that pissed him off as much as it broke his heart.

He kicked off his shoes and did the one thing he hoped would comfort her and help her sleep. He curled up next to her, wrapping his arm around her waist and held her.

Four hours later, she woke up feeling rested. She felt William's warm breath against her neck and the weight of his arm around her. His hand covered hers, his touch light, but sweet. Turning her head, she looked around the tiny apartment to see the time, three o'clock. William's words lingered in her mind, *consider this your home now.* She liked her new home and was relieved in the knowledge that *he* would never find her here.

William stirred, slowly waking up. He leaned forward putting a light kiss on the back of her neck then whispered, "Did you get some rest?"

She rolled over to face him and smiled. "The best sleep since I slept here last."

"I haven't slept well since then, either."

"Thank you."

"For what?"

"For being good to me when I hurt you." It was too painful to look at him, guilt consumed her.

This whole situation was messed up and he felt they had suffered enough. It hurt knowing she lied about something so important, but he understood why she did it. She had no choice. So every time she spoke of obligations and commitments that was her way of speaking of *him* and the burdens she carried. He hated that she was weighed down in sadness. But he hated it more that she was beaten emotionally and physically to keep her 'obligated' and 'committed.'

He wanted to forgive her based on selfish reasons as well. This past week had been hard, more than hard, horrible. William missed her a lot.

She whispered, "Did you mean what you said about me staying here?"

"Every word of it." His voice firm in his conviction.

"Then I need to get to my bank." Evie sat up and

slipped out of bed. She put her shoes back on, and asked, "Will you come with me?"

"Yes, but why do you need to go to the bank?"

She grabbed her purse out of her backpack as she explained. "Because if they find out I've left, they'll freeze my account and I won't have any money which means I'll have to go back."

"You don't have to rely on your parents."

"I need money, William, and I have a monthly allowance. I'll take what I think we can use. I can't have you paying for everything."

"Why do you want money from people who condone this?" he asked, signaling to her face and the bruising. "Fuck them and their money!"

She went to him to calm the fire raging inside of him. "They don't know he did this. They are oblivious to him as much as everyone else is. He's got everyone fooled."

"Not me, and he's going to pay for what he's done to you."

* * *

Thirty minutes later, Evie and William walked straight up to the available teller at the bank, handing her two bank cards and her ID. "I need eight-thousand from this account please."

The teller smiled, checking the ID then the card. "Yes, Miss Wright."

William stood frozen in shock, and then stuttered, "Eh-eight-thousand dollars?"

Evie gasped at the realization. "You're right, that's

223

not enough. Make it ten please and I'll have five off the other."

"Large or small bills?" the teller asked.

"Large is fine. I don't have a large purse today," Evie said nonchalantly as William's stomach turned inside out. He was dumbfounded by the normalcy of her getting fifteen-thousand dollars out just because she wanted it. It was insane she had access to that kind of money and he struggled to wrap his head around it.

As they were leaving, the security guard stepped forward, eyeing William. Evie smiled while taking William by the hand. The guard stepped aside with a nod of acknowledgment, letting them leave without a word.

Evie stopped once they were on the street. "We need to get out of this area now. I'll need to buy some clothes. Where can I go that's near your place?"

"You don't want to get your clothes from your house?"

"I can't go back there. I don't want to ever go back."

"Okay. There's a Gap kind of near my apartment. I can take you there." William had gotten over the initial shock of the bank experience, but was curious. "What do you need all that money for and how do you even have access to it?"

"I'm supposed to ask my parent's permission if I want to spend over eight thousand, but I felt it was an emergency, so I got ten. And the other money was from T... from his account. I can get up to five out on that card." Her smile was devilish. "I need clothes and money to live off, don't I?"

He shook his head in disbelief. "Will they call the

224

cops on you?"

"No. As I said, I'm allowed to get it. I didn't steal it. Anyway, they probably won't even notice it's gone, but they will cut me off as soon as they find out I've left. I did what I had to do."

"Your Dad won't notice ten thousand dollars gone from his account?"

She stopped in the middle of the sidewalk once more, and asked, "Do you want the truth or do you want me to make you feel better?"

"The truth."

"No, he won't notice. I get an allowance and I'm allowed to spend up to eight without his permission. He won't notice ten either though."

They start walking again, but William's mind was racing with questions. "What would you need to spend eight thousand dollars on in a month if you live at home and don't have a car?"

"Shopping, gifts, I don't know. You're making me feel weird. Does this offend you?"

Money talk made him antsy and he ran his palms down the front of his shirt. "The money doesn't offend me, but spending that kind of money on clothes or whatever meaningless crap you're buying does."

She lowered her voice, getting a bit irritated, feeling judged. "There are many things I owe you apologies for, but how I was raised is not one of them."

William stopped and immediately cupped her face. "You're right. I'm sorry. I know those pants you're wearing in this year's shade of blue were worth every penny." His sarcasm was dripping then he kissed her on the nose.

Evie should have been mad over his comment. But she wasn't. Instead she laughed, allowing him to laugh and showing she could also joke. "Stop it, or I won't share my money. And I really want to share with you."

They stopped by a drugstore, the Gap, and a food market on their way home. When they arrived back at William's, Evie set her purchases in the corner by the little dining table and yawned. "I'm exhausted."

William booted up his laptop and sat down at his desk. He glanced over at her, feeling tired. "I am, too."

They ordered pizza, watched reruns, and then readied themselves for bed. He gave her a large T-shirt of his and let her have the bathroom first. As she pulled the shirt over her head, she caught a glimpse of her face, which she had forgotten about all afternoon until now. The bruises were starting to fade, but it would still take a few more days for them to go away altogether.

The internal bruises would take much longer. But today, William allowed her to forget for a while. She brushed her teeth and set her brush down parallel to his in the cabinet. When she walked out, he had turned down the bed and gestured to it. "If you want to sleep in it alone, I'll understand."

She climbed in, pulling the covers up as he took his turn in the bathroom. When William came back out, Evie flipped the covers open for him as an invitation. He turned off the small lamp and eased in next to her. "I wouldn't want it any other way," she said, stroking some stray strands of hair out of his eye and kissing him.

He set his hand on her side, but she flinched reminding him of how damaged she was still and anger swelled inside of him again. *Fucking bastard. Who beats a woman anyway?*

One thing William knew was that he would not take advantage of the situation no matter how much he wanted to be with her. As their lips parted, Evie rolled over and he molded his body against hers.

In the early hours, William awoke. He was careful to stay still because he didn't want to wake her knowing she needed the rest and to heal. He was appreciating everything about the girl he held in his arms—her scent, the feel of her body, even the gentle, peaceful breath he could hear escaping her mouth.

Forty-five minutes passed before William determined he wasn't going to be able to fall asleep again. He slid out of bed and tiptoed to his desk. He switched on his small book lamp, keeping the light isolated to the desk, so he didn't disturb her, and started reading over his paper, which was due in class by Friday. As he was editing the last page, in the quietest tone he heard Evie say, "Come back to me." William's head bolted up and looked over to the sleepy-eyed angel lying in his bed.

"I want you to hold me, William. Come back to bed."

This was a request he could never deny her or himself. He turned off the light and climbed back in next to her. As they looked at each other through the dim light from the streetlamp outside the window, he breathed in just as Evie exhaled, and said the first thing that came to his mind. "You make me feel parts of my soul I didn't know existed."

With her eyes drowsy and half-open, she warmed inside, and shared her feelings. "When you're with me, my heart only beats for you."

"Every breath I breathe is given new life. All because of you, beautiful Evie."

"You make every breath worth taking, my sweet
227

William." Evie leaned forward and kissed William gentle and slow. Maybe it's the words they shared or the time of day or just the close proximity, but she wanted more with him, she wanted everything with him. She pressed her back into the mattress and encouraged him on top of her.

They kissed.

William was lost in the softness of her lips and the sweetness of her breath as he maneuvered himself above her. Their lips didn't part as their bodies became more acquainted. They both wanted more, but it wasn't the right time. They had just reunited. She needed to recover, if that was even possible, and he would prove his dedication to her first.

When they parted, they both relaxed back onto the bed and snuggled, eventually falling asleep again in the beauty of the early morning.

Evie woke up several hours later and looked over her shoulder to see William sleeping. She lay there thinking of their intense kisses during the night and as her fingers touched her lips, it was as if she could still feel the heat from their bond. She arose from the twin bed and walked to the window. Lifting one of the individual blinds up, she peeked out at the day. It was blue skies and beautiful, which made her sigh in a good way. Evie sat at his desk and watched him, leaning on her arm for support.

She analyzed the features of his face as she went through all that she knew about him. He was kind, which by far was the most attractive quality about him. He was also so handsome that he made her heart quicken. William was strong, strong physically, but also emotionally.

He opened his eyes and smiled at her. "Shall I compare thee to a summer's day?"

"Shakespeare in the morning? You're relentless,

William Ryder!" She giggled as she knelt on the floor in front of him and kissed his forehead. "Good morning."

"Good morning. Why are you up so early?"

"I need to get to school and work on my paper. I haven't started it yet."

"If you'd like, I can go with you and finish mine." She nodded, wanting to be with him as much as possible. Staring into his lovely eyes, she could see a future, *their* future, and forever behind the happy blue of his irises and that made her smile.

Hand-in-hand, they walked into the student lounge and settled at a table across from each other. Though Evie tried to concentrate on her assignment, she was finding it difficult. She would sneak peeks at William—sometimes he caught her and sometimes he didn't.

She wanted to touch him, wanted to talk to him and kiss him, but she tried once again to focus on her laptop. After another few minutes, she gave up and gave in. She slammed her hand down on the table, grabbing his attention and a cocked eyebrow from him. She stood up, walked over to his side of the table, and slipped onto his lap, kissing him hard. She kissed him how she wanted to be kissed, with a firmness and possessiveness, love and passion.

Sitting up, she took his baseball cap off his head, running her fingers through his flattened hair, and making it stand upright from the roots again. He looked a mess and utterly irresistible. Evie loved that they could be relaxed in their appearance. She reveled in it and appreciated a few days' stubble on him and his wrinkled clothes.

She rested her other hand on his bicep, all casual and appreciative of its strength, while William's hand rested on her thigh, rubbing it up and down. He liked that she had initiated the kiss and started feeling a stronger urge down lower. Just as William was about to lift her off so she wouldn't feel his body's reaction, they both heard a throat clearing. "Um Hum!"

They were surprised and startled to see Professor Lang clearing his throat to get their attention. Evie stood up, turning red, and greeted the professor. "Hello, sir. We were just working—"

"Miss Wright, I'm glad I've run into you. We need to speak about your absences. Do you have time now?" He asked this while his eyes shifted between William and Evie.

"Um, yes. Yes, sir."

"Would you feel more comfortable meeting in private?" He glanced at William again.

Evie looked to William feeling confident. "No. I'm fine with William being here."

"Let's sit." Lang gestured to the chairs at the table. After they settled themselves, he took a moment before he spoke. "Are you all right?

"Yes." She was the one to clear her throat this time after her voice wavered.

"You missed three days. In summer school, that's the equivalent to almost two weeks' worth of work. Do you want to talk about the reasons for your absence?"

Her voice was low and a bit shaky. "I guess you can see by my face that something happened."

"Were you in an accident?" Professor Lang asked, showing concern.

"No. Someone did this to me. Someone I know." She felt ashamed just like she had this entire past week as if she was to blame for the beating. William watched them and listened, but stayed silent, trying to support her by letting her confide what she wanted to reveal. Though he could admit he felt anger filling his chest again as she spoke of what she went through at the hands of that bastard.

She dropped her head into to her hands to shield her face from her sympathetic teacher, overcome in the moment.

William reached across the table and held her hand in his, hoping to comfort her. Looking up, she realized she's not alone in this anymore.

The Professor stood up, his face gave way to his relief to see the young couple's bond. "You can't miss any more classes, Miss Wright, or I'll have no choice but to fail you or give you an incomplete. I'm sorry to hear you have gone through something traumatic and," he said, lowering his voice, "I'm here for you if you need help and I'm sure Mr. Ryder is doing all he can to help also. He's a good man there, but please come to me if I can be of any assistance. I'm happy to help you in any way I can."

She looked up, but didn't meet his eyes, she couldn't. She was embarrassed. "Thank you, sir, and I understand. Thank you for giving me this second chance."

He patted her on the shoulder and added, "You're one of my brightest. You've earned your second chance. I'm very pleased with yours and Mr. Ryder's research on the Kyd stories. I think you'll both be pleased with your grade."

William stood up. "I think we should head over to his office for today's assignments, don't you? You heard the man. No more missing class." He winked at her and his smile comforted her.

She knew without a doubt she was in love and the amazing man before her loved her just as much.

Chapter 22

Four days later, Evie and William were teasing each other while leaving the lecture hall. She took his arm, entwining hers around it, and pulled him close enough for her to rest her head on his shoulder. They continued to laugh and settled into a feeling of contentment accompanied by deliriously happy smiles. They were walking down the hall when her stomach growled, and she asked, "You hungry? Want to go to lunch?"

William leaned down kissing the top of her head just as she stopped in her tracks. Her smile disappeared as well as the security of her new world. The force of her pulling him back a step jolted his body to a stop. He looked at her and saw the fear on her face, the color had drained from her cheeks. Worried, he asked, "What?" Alarmed by her expression, his heart began to race. Something was wrong. He could feel it. Grabbing her by the arms, he tried to bring her attention back to him. "What is it, Evie?"

"It's uh . . . it's uh . . ." she muttered, still not looking at him. He followed her gaze and saw some people on the other side of the glass doors. He didn't understand her abrupt change in demeanor until his eyes landed on Audrey standing next to a taller, older man and a woman. "It's my parents."

She swayed, off balance, but his hands steadied her. Her eyes searched William's for answers.

Shaking his head, he was at a loss for any answers that would help. "What do you want to do?"

"I don't know. What should we do?" Her eyes blurred with tears as she scanned his face, desperate for him to guide her. "Please tell me what I should do here."

He opened and closed his mouth several times before he finally spoke. He struggled to remain calm, not wanting to upset her any more than she already was. "I'll stay with you if you want to talk to them." Taking her hand in his again, he gave a little squeeze to show his support.

She nodded. "Yeah, I should talk to them." Her voice was detached and cold, unlike what he knew her to sound like normally.

Evie walked forward holding William's hand so tight that her knuckles whitened under the pressure. They exited the doors as a united front, and she saw her father straighten his shoulders, the others reacting much different in regards to her escort. A soft smile graced her mother's face allowing Evie to approach without fear. Kitty Wright looked the young man over, her eyes landing on their bound hands. Looking William straight in the eyes, she smiled at him though it stopped on her lips.

Richard Wright, Evie's father, noticed the joined hands between William and his daughter first. His annoyance with the relationship was instantaneous and he was ready for the battle ahead. His smile was firm, but not a trusting one toward the young couple.

Audrey stood at his side beaming at seeing the

couple together. She didn't know what had become of her sister and hoped she was with William, but now she had it confirmed, she was thrilled.

Evie's dad took a step toward William. "May we have a word with our daughter in private?"

Evie had found his ultra-civility not trustworthy and questioned in her mind why he was asking William for privacy instead of talking to her directly.

William kept his eyes focused forward trying to figure these people out. He disliked them for letting their daughter be with an abuser, but other than that, he couldn't get a good read on them. They were all wealth and etiquette, but fake, stiff in appearance. He looked at Evie and in a lowered voice asked for her opinion. "Do you want to talk with them alone?"

She released his hand and faced him square on, resting her palms flat on his chest. "I'll be fine. This will only take a minute." She smiled to reassure him. "Then we'll go to lunch, okay?"

"Okay, I'll wait over here." He kissed her on the temple and left them alone, reaching the closest bench and sitting down to watch the exchange.

Evie took her time breaking the distance between William and herself. Her hesitant steps were noted by all three of her family members standing in front of her. As soon as she approached, Audrey hugged her tight. Evie smiled and hugged her back just as tight. "I missed you, little sis."

She hugged her mom next and then embraced her dad trying to gauge his mood. He spoke first. "Everleigh, sweetheart, we've been worried about you. We didn't know where you went or if you were all right."

"I'm okay."

"Why did you leave?" her mom asked, oblivious to the reality of her daughter's situation.

Her wounds had all but healed and the remaining discoloration of her cheekbone had been covered by make-up that morning. Evie couldn't believe they were this clueless. "You don't know? Really?"

Her dad spoke in haste for the family, his voice stern. "Listen young lady, we've been through hell and back worried sick about you. Poor Tom has been throwing up at the thought that something bad had happened—"

"Something bad did happen, Dad!"

William hadn't heard any of their discussion until her dad raised his voice and Evie tried to match his tone. He realized through their exchange that they didn't know what her fiancé, *the monster,* had done to her and that made William angry. He released their bags from his shoulder, letting them drop onto the bench next to him and clenched his fists. He could already feel his face reddening with rage and looked down at his feet to try to keep his temper in check.

But Evie yelled, "I'm not going back to Tom!" Snapping back into protection mode, William stood up, ready to come to her aid. That's when he noticed a policeman hanging back about fifteen yards, but this cop seemed out of place. Something about his body language was off then they caught eyes, and he found no support behind the man's hardened glare. William stepped forward and he saw the cop react by moving in five or so feet.

A scuffle with the family grabbed William's attention again, and he saw Evie's dad holding her by the arm and he could hear her pleas. "Please, no. I won't go with him. Please don't do this." She looked over her shoulder at him.

"William!"

William saw a man, in his twenties, in a suit in front of her. Even though he had never seen *him* before he knew, *he* knew he was the monster. Her dad was leading his innocent lamb to the slaughterhouse. While Evie was crying and resisting, *that smug bastard* was smiling.

William ran at the same time as Tom and when their fists collided against the other's body they both stumbled backward. William landed one on his jaw, and Tom had landed his punch into William's stomach. William didn't hesitate, and threw an upper cut that connected with Tom's jaw again. "You bastard!"

The cop and another policeman he hadn't noticed prior, grabbed William's arms, restraining him, and threw him to the ground, his chest slamming against the concrete. A foot pushed against William's shoulder blades while the other cop held William's wrists in restraint. He was cuffed, but they couldn't stop William's mouth. "I will kill you for hurting her!"

Tom laughed while standing in front of him then kicked him in the ribs.

Freeing herself, Evie started running to William, but her dad caught her arm again and kept her on track for the waiting car. Tears streamed down her face as she cried to the cops. "Stop hurting him! Please don't hurt him! Help him!"

Tom took possession of her other arm and with blood trailing from the corner of his mouth, he smiled, his face contorted in wicked amusement, his voice threatening. "They're with me, sweetheart. I pay their salary." He laughed as William watched him plant a bloody kiss on Evie's cheek.

Evie moved her head as far away as she could, but

Tom still managed to make contact.

"He hits your daughter how can you—Ow!" William shouted in pain as the cops pushed harder against his shoulders. But through his own tears he could see Tom, standing next to Evie's father talking to her just out of his hearing range. His eyes blurred momentarily, but when they came into focus, he saw Audrey and the look of horror on her face watching the scene play out.

Closing his eyes again, he tried to get his breathing under control, but was struggling. That's when he heard a small familiar voice to his left. "Please don't fight them, William. They'll hurt you." Audrey was crying and her words were colored in sorrow.

He couldn't look at her again, certain she betrayed her sister and him by leading them to Evie's safe haven. The cops pulled William to his feet, twisting his arms and making him yelp in pain as he searched for Evie.

Evie gave up her fight and walked, still restrained but under control, to the open car door. She looked back once before sliding in, the star-crossed couple locked eyes one final time, the pain evident for both.

"Don't do this, Evie! Don't get in that car! I can't help if you get—Ouch!" The cops pulled him back, inflicting more pain than necessary to shut him up.

The first cop sighed loudly. "Listen man, don't make this harder than it has to be. Just play nice and let the girl go. You're fighting a losing battle here."

Looking over his shoulder at the officer, William got the message. As Evie got into the car and her father shut the door behind her, he realized he had been set up, ambushed. They were here to take Evie back all along and the cops were here to arrest him because they knew he would put up a fight. With adrenaline coursing through his veins, the realization thickened in his blood, weighing heavy on his heart. He turned, bloodied face, to one of the officers. "I'm fucked, aren't I?"

"Before you even knew it."

Tom took the opportunity to come back to William and taunt him while patting one of the cops on the back. "Good work, gentleman. I'll sleep better knowing the streets will be a little safer tonight." Turning to William while dabbing his cheek with a tissue, he tried to clean the blood off his face. Tom signaled with a nod to his car and then looked straight into William's eyes. "I came to reclaim my property. Don't mess with my possessions or next time you'll pay the consequences of your actions. I don't play fair, and I won't play nice. For a Neanderthal like you, that means stay away from Everleigh." He turned on his heel and left.

William was defiant. "You're a fucking monster. She doesn't love you. She hates you!"

Tom stopped and looked back at him. "She'll have that ring back on her finger by her own accord by tonight. You just better worry about what's going to happen to you if I find out you went anywhere near her with your di—"

"I don't have to threaten women like you do," William shouted, but realized Tom would hurt her again if he thought they had had sex. "We didn't have sex, you asshole!" He had to say anything he could to protect her and if he couldn't physically do that, he would make sure to clarify it verbally. William didn't care if he had lied to Tom, but this time he didn't have to. They hadn't made love yet.

Tom smirked before responding. "I knew she loved me." He walked to the car, got in, and William watched as it drove away.

William looked around and saw her family had

already left and as one officer walked him to the car, the other grabbed the bags left behind on the bench. The officer pushed his head down, making him duck down into the cruiser. "I don't know if you banged that girl or not, but you saying you didn't was the smartest thing you did today. Boy, I'd hate to see what he'd do if he thought you had."

"I wasn't worried about me. He beat the shit out of her a week ago and you let him get her alone again to repeat the abuse." William looked around the back of the car at the close confines of the dirty car, a car where criminals and crooked cops sat. He couldn't believe he'd managed to avoid being arrested his entire life despite some of the crazy stuff he did growing up and now here he was, sitting in the back of a police car going to jail for falling in love.

William tried to reach Bobby, but the call went to voicemail. He refused to call his parents and couldn't afford a lawyer. He was embarrassed for being charged with assault and disorderly conduct and didn't want them to know until he handled the situation. He also didn't want to involve them in this mess, so he sat in jail overnight.

Early in the morning, his name was called and when he walked to the cell door, the guard told him the charges had been dropped. As he entered the station lobby, he saw an unwelcome familiar face, Professor Lang. Standing with a small sympathetic smile, the professor greeted William with a handshake. "How are you holding up, Mr. Ryder?"

"What are you doing here?" William asked, hating his professor even knowing he was arrested, much less bailing him out.

"I came to bail you out a few hours ago, but they said they were still waiting on paperwork. The charges were dropped in the meantime and thus the bail wasn't necessary. You look a little ragged, which is understandable." He turned and started for the door and William followed. "Can I buy you breakfast or coffee?"

William stopped once they got out on the sidewalk and began to question him. "Why are you here?"

"Let's discuss this over coffee, William."

They started walking side-by-side, no words exchanged. A few blocks up from the station the Professor pointed to a coffee shop. "Let's try there."

But William stopped. "If I'm being honest, I could use something stronger after the last twenty-four hours I've had."

The Professor looked around and pointed across the street. "Then, let's go there."

This was New York and you can find whatever you need at any hour in this city. They walked into a dark bar where the front door was wedged open and sat down on two barstools. Looking around, William was surprised to find they weren't alone in the bar. Desperation and disappointment was more common in the city than he once imagined. The bartender approached. "What can I get you?"

The Professor ordered first. "Two drafts."

William added, "And two shots of whiskey."

The bartender turned, getting their drinks and when he set them down he told them how much they owed and that they close in half an hour so to drink up.

The Professor set a twenty on the bar as he watched William gulp his beer. "Wow! I don't think I've drank this late or . . . early since I was your age. I hope you don't do this often."

William nodded, laughing under his breath. "No, I don't normally get arrested and I don't usually drink at this hour." He looked at his most prestigious and respected professor sitting next to him in this dingy bar and laughed again. Full of sarcasm, he said, "Maybe I should see if this works better for me, though." He picked up his whiskey shot and pushed the other toward Lang. They clinked their shot glasses together then downed the liquor in one heated gulp. Both did a little headshake to ease the taste of the hard liquor. "I didn't see this coming."

"Being arrested or drinking at five-thirty in the morning with your professor?"

"Either. I'd prefer to be drinking with you under different circumstances," William said, his voice steady, but detached. William's mind was all over the place and thoughts that occurred to him in jail surfaced. "I'm thinking I might need a change of scenery, maybe California for my master's degree."

Lang sat up surprised by this seemingly random comment. "Okay, let me know how I can help."

"Thank you." William eyed him while taking another sip, then continued. "I respect you and yet I've somehow dragged you into this mess. How'd you know I was in jail, and why are you here?"

"I witnessed the tail end of the incident yesterday. I thought you got the short end of the stick from what I saw." Lang took another sip of his beer then said, "I don't know what's going on in Miss Wright's life or what yesterday was about, but I couldn't let my brightest student sit in jail for aiding someone who needed help."

Staring ahead at the neon beer sign reflecting in the mirror behind the bar, William said, "He hits her, you know."

"I don't know who he is."

William paused not sure if he should be speaking with his professor so candidly, but needed to talk to someone he trusted, and he trusted Lang. "He's her fiancé. They're engaged, were engaged, hell, I dunno anymore." William felt revulsion of the word fiancé in his mouth when he spoke it.

"Well, that changes things, doesn't it?"

"That doesn't change anything! You saw what he did to her last week. He should be the one locked up right now."

"What do the police say?"

William sighed. "We should have reported it. She didn't want to—"

"Victims often don't. Is this something you feel you can report? I'll go with you, if you want."

"I don't want to betray Evie. Everyone else in her life has. I won't do that to her."

"That's understandable," Lang said. "I'm not sure if it's right, but it's a tricky situation."

"She needs allies, and I need her in my life."

"Love, relationships . . ." Lang stopped to think of what he wanted to say before he continued. ". . . They're very complicated and tend to bring out the best and worst in people. Miss Wright seemed quite enamored with you, but she had this fiancé already?"

William ran his finger down the condensation collecting on the pint glass and then finished the beer. "She's been with... she's had *that* commitment since she was seventeen." He looked over at the professor. "But, she was in love with me. She is in love with me." He rested his head in his hands. "I'm in love with her and she left with him yesterday, the one who beats her, the one who hurts her and doesn't appreciate the person she is. I don't want to believe she left of her own free will, but I have nothing else to go on."

"Affairs of the heart are tricky. I wouldn't have seen that twist, but I also have to say that I agree she didn't look like she left willingly. It looked to me like she was being coaxed into leaving by that man and her fiancé."

"That other man was her father. I didn't hear what they told her, but I know they coerced her somehow. She wouldn't have gone with them otherwise. I'm trying to believe she wouldn't have left me by her own choosing."

The professor stood, drank the remainder of his beer, and patted William on the back. "These kinds of entanglements are wrenching. Everything you studied in the classics tells you the outcome is in your favor, but we live in a modern world where sometimes forces greater than ourselves, greater than love, win out. Do what's in your heart, son. For one shall never have failed if tried and true to thy self."

"Bronte?"

"No. Lang." The professor walked to the door with William following behind. They shook hands on the street and William thanked him for trying to bail him out, the drinks, company, and his wisdom. The professor started to leave but stopped. "I cancelled class today. Make sure you're there tomorrow ready to focus on your studies, Mr. Ryder."

"Yes, sir, and thanks again."

William headed home and showered before doing anything else. He scrubbed harder than he needed, trying to erase the memory of the jail and the incident away. Afterward, he had a granola bar and downed a large glass of water before taking his broken heart to bed. He prayed that sleep would come quick considering he hadn't slept at all in lock-up. His prayer was answered.

Everleigh spent the night in utter fear at Tom's apartment or what she now considered a jail in the sky. The first few hours there, she remained shocked her parents would hand her over to him as if nothing had happened. After a while, her reasoning kicked in and she realized they didn't know. They were still oblivious to the real situation and fell for the lies he told.

But what broke her heart was that they wouldn't listen to her. They chose to believe him when Tom told them she was being hysterical and melodramatic. They didn't know Tom was blackmailing her into staying, that he'd drop the assault charges against William if she went to his place on her own accord. She was left no choice. She didn't want to be the cause of William's arrest, and did what she was told, for William.

Tom had offered her a muscle relaxer, which she took along with a shot of vodka when she arrived at his apartment earlier. She wanted to be numb. She wanted her thoughts separated from her body. She wanted to black out, and at different points in the night, she wanted to die. William was her saving grace, the life preserver she held onto even if only metaphorically speaking.

Tom was smart to leave her alone. He said she needed simmering down time. He didn't know the half of it. He had no comprehension of the hate she held for him and scoffed that he thought time would set things right between them.

She cried—weak, a little drunk, and drugged for hours. He came into the room several times in the night to check on her and seemed worried that she might be worse off than first assessed. Delirium had set in and she laughed at him—maybe it was the relaxer making her laugh in the face of evil.

Finally passing out, she woke up once around three in the morning, seeing the skyscrapers out the windows and realizing where she was. She lifted her head, which felt heavy, her thoughts foggy, and looked at the door across the room. There was a sliver of light coming in at the bottom and she knew then she was indeed still at Tom' place.

Everleigh approached the doors with fear coursing through her, making her hands shake, as she silently tiptoed across the room. She didn't know why she was quiet other than the moment seemed to call for it. When she tried the door, she found it locked. Fear turned to anger as she shook the handle hard. Walking to the window, she stared into the bleakness of the dark for several minutes before climbing back into bed, hoping it would rest her chaotic mind. It didn't, and she turned back to the nightstand and finished her water. She felt drowsy once again and fell asleep ten minutes later.

Chapter 23

Tom, just outside the bedroom door, had not found the same peace. As he looked at her phone in his hand, he heard her try the doorknob to no avail and was now at a crossroads with her. He didn't know where either path would lead, and for the first time in their relationship, he felt like he might lose her. The feeling was very unsettling to his pride and his heart. He couldn't let that happen. He slipped the SIM card out of her phone and hid the device in a console table drawer. He would need to replace it, and wiping out all the missed calls, the next day.

He unlocked the door and left for work early the next morning. On the way to work, he came to the outcome that would best serve his purpose—if she wasn't going to give William up, then he needed to make *him* give up on *her*.

By ten in the morning, he received the information he needed to continue with his plan and he made the call without hesitation. After a few hours of work, he enjoyed a leisurely lunch with a friend down at one of the fancier restaurants in the area.

When Tom returned, entering his office, he spotted the courier he had specifically requested sitting across the lobby. A large column blocked the guy's view, and he didn't see Tom as he walked toward the receptionist's desk. She looked up from her tabloid then jumped to cover her break-time obsession by draping her arm over the paparazzi photos of the latest hot, young star. She cleared her throat, trying to recover from her shock of seeing her boss in front of her. "Mr. Whitney, the messenger is here for a pick-up, but I didn't see a package going out. Do you have one in your office?"

Tom glanced back at the man seated and felt a rush of anger flow over him. Possessiveness and jealousy hit his heart, making it beat faster and harder in his chest when he answered, "Um, yes, but I'll handle this. Give me twenty minutes then send him into my office."

The receptionist gave him an odd look of confusion, but nodded, happy in the fact that he didn't say anything about her reading a magazine while at work.

Tom pushed off the tall desk and made his way down the hall toward his office. He stared out at his amazing Manhattan view, reaffirming how great he was when Everleigh's backpack caught his eye. The police had given him the bag the day he got her back, the day her *friend* was arrested. He laughed at how well that played out in his favor.

Leaning down, he dug through the bag looking for clues to her betrayal with the messenger boy. He tossed it to the side, irritated. It held nothing but school related stuff, which frustrated him in his quest for more details about their relationship.

He wasted time making a few phone calls and returning e-mails before he sat back down in his custom made Italian leather chair and propped his feet up on his solid mahogany desk as if waiting for something to happen. He didn't have to wait long once he called the front desk and told her to go ahead and send the messenger back.

William was too caught up in his own misery to notice Tom saunter into the lobby. If he'd been paying any attention, he would've had enough warning to know what he was walking into.

He wasn't sleeping much and was now a walking zombie. He tried to play the free puzzle app on his phone, but focusing was impossible with his heart broken and from the utter fatigue. He was hurt and that pain was eating away at his soul piece by piece, driving him to distraction.

He stopped his knee from bouncing by slamming his hand down on top of it. As the minutes ticked slowly by, his agitation grew. He sat in the well-appointed lobby of the downtown high-rise not even tempted by the free coffee and snacks like he usually was when he was working.

Flipping through his phone photos, he landed on the one of Evie he'd taken. William felt his heart begin to ache, but he stared anyway, trying to reason that she must be tied up. She must be so busy, that she didn't have time to call or text him.

His pain was being replaced with rage. He stood up, not giving two cares about some random suit's package, no matter how much he needed this job, and was about to head for the exit when the receptionist told him he could go to Mr. Whitney's office to retrieve it.

William decided to do his job since he was already here. He walked down the long corridor, the weight of his hurt weighing heavy on his thoughts. He still couldn't come up with anything that would explain what really happened that day and why Evie chose *the monster* over him. William felt a twinge of pain in his heart thinking about the memories of being with her and then it twisted at the reality of her betrayal.

"Of course, it's the corner office," he mumbled under his breath while clutching his bag tight to his side. *Only a jackass with a corner office would believe he's important enough to make me wait twenty minutes. Like I don't have anything better to do, jackass!* These thoughts continued as he entered the office without knocking.

"Mr. Ryder, do come in," Tom said. His voice was too threatening to sound welcoming as he stood up.

William froze in his tracks, shocked that he was in *this* jackass's office. But his shock gave way to anger again and he rushed him. Diving over the desk, William tackled him to the floor, both of them rolling and slamming against the floor-to-ceiling window. He got in one good punch before Tom pushed him off by hitting him back in self-defense.

Tom yelled the only thing he knew would stop this attack. "I want to talk about Everleigh!"

William's heart was pounding from the rage inside, but when *he* said *her* name out loud, it felt like it had exploded in his chest. He grabbed Tom, dragged him by his lapels, and slammed him against the large wood bureau. It took all of William's self-control to not beat the shit out of him. "Don't you ever say her name, you fucker, you girl beating fucker," he yelled through gritted teeth.

Tom managed to put his hands up in surrender, and although he enjoyed provoking and hurting William, he was still a coward, and smart enough to know he would lose if they continued as they were. Tom was going in for the kill, not the fight. "I know what I've done is wrong, okay. I just wanted to give you an update."

Tom sounded sincere and even though William didn't want to trust him, he knew he had to. He was desperate to find out anything when it came to Evie's well-being. Taking a deep breath, he tried to calm himself and get the information he most desired. "Where is she, you prick?"

"Back up to the door over there and I'll tell you." Tom directed William by pointing across the room, putting his own safety first.

William released Tom's suit, shoving him back into the window for good measure before crossing the room. Wanting the information about Evie, he was willing to play Tom's game to get it. Turning around, he positioned himself across the room with his arms crossed and his jaw tense before he demanded. "Tell me now!"

Two beefy security guards walked in and seized each of his arms without a fight. William didn't struggle because he was concentrating so hard on Tom who was currently stalling in front of him.

Knowing he had backup now—unwavering and heartless—Tom mocked William with his words. "She's in my bed right now." His eyes darkened, leaving no trace of sincerity in them as he continued. "And she's already put my ring back on her finger. She's fantastic when she's feisty. She was like that when I met her. But, like a wild stallion, she'll be broken. She was before and she will be once again. She's mine and if you ever go near her again, I'll make sure you aren't released next time. Take the other night as a warning, Mr. Ryder, and leave my fiancée alone."

William's body reflexively lunged forward, but the two large guards gave him no leeway and he was jerked backward, against his will, and dragged out of the office. William did what any man in his position would do, he fought back and struggled, but to no avail. He yelled every curse word that came to mind, but it made no difference to Tom who stood there smug and protected behind his desk. Tom smiled, crossed his arms over his chest, and raised his chin proud in his victory.

William was thrown onto the sidewalk in front of the building with no care to the passing pedestrians. He didn't even care when a guy stepped over him as he hit the pavement, because in that exact moment of impact, it became clear he had been set up again by Tom. He pushed himself up off the ground and walked to the building's brick wall, kicking it as hard as he could.

The asshole baited me and I fell for it. He's trying to get me to screw myself and I almost did. He can forget that because I won't give up on Evie!

Evie woke up at two in the afternoon, groggy with a fuzzy mind. She sat up rubbing her face and then saw it, her chance. With the door cracked open, she lunged for it, opening it all the way and peeking out before taking a step into the corridor. There were no sounds of anyone around, but realizing she was in her pajamas, she went back into the bedroom and got dressed in a haphazard fashion. Rushing toward the front door, her pace was stealthy.

"Good afternoon, Miss Wright," Tom's housekeeper said with a smile.

Startled from being caught in her escape, Evie jumped. "Hi, Barbara, I've got to go."

"Would you like something to eat first?"

"No, I have to go. I'm sorry. Thank you." Her words were rushed as she backed out the front door then turned and ran. She didn't remember even taking a breath until she was a block away from Tom's building.

Evie slowed her pace and exhaled a deep sigh of relief. She had just walked another block in the direction of William's apartment when a car pulled up next to her— *his shiny sports car*—to be exact. The window rolled down as she continued walking, ignoring the car the best she could, but the tears gave her away, and she started running.

252

"Everleigh, I'll drive you home," Tom said as soon as she stopped another block down for a breath, his tone was controlled.

The word home had new meaning to her these days. She turned to Tom with spite. "You'll drive me to William's?" She had no intention of getting in that car, but she used the only weapon she had in her arsenal to hurt him.

"No, I'll drive you home."

"That is my home now."

Tom looked down at the steering wheel before speaking, as if choosing his words carefully. When he looked back up, his expression broke her heart, not for *him*, but because she could tell what was coming. She knew right then that he had done something to William.

His smug smirk reinforced that thought. "He came by the office today, Everleigh."

Her heart skipped a beat at the mention of his name. "Why?"

"He doesn't want to deal with *all of this*. I hate being the one to tell you, but he put the burden on me to hurt you. He's a coward for not telling you in person." Tom paused for effect then held her backpack up. "He dropped this off and said he didn't want to see you again."

She glanced at the backpack. William had been holding it for her when this all started a few days earlier. It didn't make sense for Tom to have it unless he was telling the truth, but William wouldn't give up on her like that. *Would he?* Tom held the evidence in his hands that William just might. Why else would he give it to Tom and not her? Her heart splintered into a million pieces realizing he chose to give it to Tom because he didn't want to see her—not

253

even to say good-bye.

"Yeah, he said he'd had enough. I'm really sorry, sweetie."

Her heart sank as she stood on the empty sidewalk staring into the distance ahead.

"Everleigh?"

She looked back to him, and as much as she wanted to walk away, she had nowhere to go. With a broken heart, she walked to the car, losing all dignity, pride, and hope. As she slid into the soft leather seat, she quietly requested, "Home, please."

As he drove her to her parent's apartment, Tom was smart enough to leave her with her thoughts, letting William's betrayal sink in, even if false. That was torture enough for one day.

Once she entered her childhood bedroom, she dropped down on the edge of her bed, disheartened as she stared at the soft pink wall in front of her. She hadn't noticed the change in light or the sun setting. She didn't see the day disappear into night through the large window. She sat there, lost in thought of a future that would never be.

Her sister entered her room with a tray of food and a glass of water just after nine that night. Audrey set the tray down on the desk and knelt at her feet.

Everleigh stirred, looking down at Audrey below her. "What are you doing?"

"I came to talk with you. Are you all right?" Audrey asked.

Everleigh looked confused for a minute noticing the dark city through the window. "It's night time."

"Yeah, are you hungry? I brought some of your favorites." Audrey hopped up, carried the tray to the bed, and as Everleigh looked over the food, the faintest of smiles crossed her lips. Audrey then held a soda with a straw up for Everleigh to take and she did.

"What's today?"

"It's Wednesday." Audrey realized her sister was not in a good state of mind.

"I was supposed to be in class today." Everleigh started making statements that were strange and incoherent. "He doesn't want me." Standing up, she walked to the window to look out. "Kyd wrote the one paper. We found proof in Boston."

"Boston?" Audrey didn't understand what Evie was going on about and became alarmed at her weird comments.

"I want a bowl o'noodles." Everleigh turned to Audrey and said, "You can't hear the street noise up here."

"I know. That's why we live on this floor."

"It's too quiet for me to sleep here."

Audrey walked to her sister. "Do you want me to get Henri to make you noodles?"

Everleigh smiled, knowing she didn't want the fancy version. The fifty-nine cent version was what she was craving. "No, no thank you. I think I'm going to shower. Do you know the last time I showered?" Audrey shook her head and Everleigh replied, "I don't either. Isn't that strange?"

"Are you going to be all right?"

She stopped in the doorway. "I don't know, Audrey. I

really messed things up." She walked into the bathroom, started the shower, and then shut the door. Steam surrounded her inside the shower and reality struck her hard. She may never get to be with William again, but he would forever own her heart.

Chapter 24

After storming out of work earlier in the day, William went to see Bobby at the construction site where he worked, a new high-rise in lower Manhattan. He watched the men laboring with their tools and large cranes for over an hour before Bobby clocked out at five and walked over giving William a hand up. "You look like shit, my friend."

"I feel like it," William replied, feeling worse than that on the inside.

"I'll buy you a beer and you can tell me about it."

The childhood friends walked to the closest bar and ordered food and beer. William retold the story and then added the latest episode in Tom's office.

"You've got a war on your hands, brother. Are you willing to fight it for her?"

"Forever, but it seems she's not willing to fight for me."

"Do you trust what that ass says?"

"I don't know what to think. She hasn't returned my calls. I think she's made her choice."

"I don't know. It just seems like . . . like something's not right. I saw how that chick looked at you. She seemed pretty into you."

William rested his head in his hands. "It probably sounds like cheesy bullshit, but she changed my insides. I'm different because of her and this pain is excruciating. It sucks. I don't feel like me without her."

Bobby wanted to crack a joke, but knew better. William didn't want cheering up. William needed someone to listen, so Bobby did. They left several hours later—a little drunker and a lot more numb—just the way William wanted to be. He had developed a bad habit of checking his phone every couple of minutes to make sure it was on and still working and continued to on the long walk back to his place.

After his usual nighttime shower and quick snack, he checked all his forms of communication: His phone, his e-mail, even his online friends' account, which he rarely did. Nothing. He didn't understand why she hadn't called, come by, anything. He felt like he had shown her his heart, given her his love, and supported her, and yet she hadn't even called to see if he was all right. He lay in bed and his eyes filled with tears, but he refused to let them fall.

Once he managed to suppress the tears and the pain in his heart, he tried to sleep. He missed the warmth of her body next to him, her voice, her touch, and her smile. As he rubbed his nose into the pillow, he discovered it still smelled of her. He would never be able to wash these sheets if this was all that was left of her, all he would ever have from her again.

Evie lay in her bed tossing and turning. There was too much room, she thought. This bed was too big. She sat up frustrated, realizing there was still no outside noise or any noise at all in this room. *How am I supposed to sleep in these conditions?* Walking to the window seat, dragging her pillow and her blanket, she curled up on the two-by-five foot cushioned seat. She could hear a faint siren in the distance when she pressed her ear against the cold glass. She fell asleep on the cramped seat in the room that before a week ago was the epitome of comfort to her. Now, it just gave her a hollow feeling and was a poor substitute for a place to sleep.

William arrived a few minutes early for Lang's class on Friday. The professor spoke as William was settling into a leather recliner in the student lounge where the summer class met. "Good morning, Mr. Ryder. I appreciate your attendance knowing you've had a difficult week."

William looked over at him giving him the respect he deserved, but remained silent.

"We're starting a project that should occupy a lot of our time for the remainder of the week left in class. I'm assuming you don't mind taking on a larger task right now. It might ease the mind of other worries."

"I think that's a good idea. I look forward to the assignment." Today was the first day he started to feel his words again. *Day four without Evie is going to be the turning point*, he thought. He could cry and dwell on the loss all day long again, but his heart begged for a reprieve and his head refocused as Lang doled out the assignments.

When William walked out into the first day of a sunny July, he gave in to his logical side by laying down an ultimatum. *I will allow myself to call her one more time and then that's it.* The only way back to each other is down a two-way street. He dialed the number and waited. When her voicemail came on, he closed his eyes and took in every word she spoke. Then it beeped, and he left his message. "Evie, this is my last message, my love. Thirty messages a day is where I have to draw the line." He laughed at how stupid he felt for revealing that he knew he had called her a lot. "I miss you. I don't know what they've done to you and I'm worried. Please call me. If you chose him, then please call me and let me know that you're okay. I have this bad feeling in my gut. I don't really understand what happened the other day and can't remember the days since, but I know they've been empty without you in them. Please call me. I love you, Evie."

When he hung up, William dropped onto the bench holding his head between his hands. Suddenly, he realized he had been to her building, he knew where she lived. He had to try once more, hoping he'd at least get to talk to Walter. He might find an ally in the friendly doorman.

He rode his bike over, not bothering to lock it as Walter greeted him at the door. "You've got to help me. Is she here? Is she okay, alive? Please, Walter, help me." William was pleading, feeling as if he was on the verge of a breakdown.

Walter stepped outside, letting the door close behind him, and said, "She came home yesterday. I don't know where she was before then. I can assume she was at his place. He drove up yesterday, mid-day, and she got out and went straight upstairs. Neither of them acknowledged me. She didn't look happy. I haven't seen her since, but he's up there right—"

William knew he could trust Walter, so he went ahead and asked what he really wanted to know. "Did he hit her? Did he hurt her again?"

"I don't think so. There was nothing obvious."

William found comfort in Walter's words, but that Tom had driven her home and let her go up unescorted, sounded as if she was operating of her own free will. That was unexpected and even more disappointing. His heart hurt that she hadn't called him or come back when she had the chance. "Thanks, Walter." He turned to leave, but turned back and said, "Take care of her."

"I thought that was your job?"

"I did, too, for a short time." They shook hands and William got back on his bike and rode home.

Everleigh had spent hours in the family library going through books in the large bookcases and reorganizing them, doing anything she could to keep her mind occupied. When she returned to her bedroom, she saw her phone on her vanity charging. Tom said he hadn't seen it, so she assumed it was lost in the scuffle that day. She should have questioned how it got there, but she didn't want to waste time. She picked it up and immediately checked for missed calls and messages of any sort. But when she found none, it reinforced what Tom had told her. William didn't want her.

Needing a shower, she let the warm water cover her as she braced her body against the cold tile. '*He didn't want her*' messed with her thoughts and perspective. Ten minutes passed before she realized she hadn't even washed her hair. She hurried through the process, not bothering with the repeat step.

Spending the next hour getting dressed in her pristinely pressed, classic-styled clothes, she felt uncomfortable in the familiarity of the action. She was disappointed that she was exactly where she had been months earlier—like William had never come into her life—like he hadn't changed her inside, or captured her heart.

She was looking for the shoes that matched her outfit in her large walk-in closet when Tom appeared in the door. "Hi," he said, trying to sound sweet.

Leaning against the wall for support, she looked at him with no reply. He lowered his eyes and took a deep breath before speaking. "I know I screwed up, but I'm asking you, no, I'm begging you, Everleigh, to give me another chance at making this right between us." He stepped closer to her and kissed her on the cheek. She flinched, but he remained calm.

When he took her shaking hands in his, she raised her head to look him straight in the eyes. "I will never love you. I will only love him."

He dropped her hands and she trembled in front of him waiting for the first hit, but it didn't come. Instead, with fisted hands, he said, "You will be a good fiancée to me. You will marry me in the fall. You will play the role as you have for years, keeping mine and your name respectable—"

"No, I won't! I don't care—"

"You will or Mr. Ryder won't see graduation. I'll make sure that diploma never gets handed out. Then, I'll make sure there isn't a company or person willing to hire that piece of shit in the entire state of New York. I will ruin him. I have an entire file on his family, friends, classes, his work, his hobbies. I know where he drinks, his grocer, and his landlord. They're at my disposal now. I will ruin everything he has worked for if you so much as smile at him again. Do you understand, Everleigh?"

The tears that had formed in her eyes spilled down her cheeks as she remained silent, listening to the future laid out before her. He finished by saying, "This will be the last time you act like this. You will answer me the first time I ask you a question, you will give the appearance of what I expect of you, and you will be my wife. I've spent too many years invested in us for it to end like this. So, I'm asking you again, do you understand everything I told you and expect of you?"

She nodded, turning away from him and looking at her bare feet. "Yes."

He turned abruptly and left her alone in the closet. Once she knew he was gone, she slid down the wall, and wrapped her arms around her knees and cried.

Ten minutes. Ten minutes to cry. Ten minutes to process his threat. Ten minutes to mourn the loss of her dreams. Ten minutes to say good-bye to William in silence. She stood up, went into the bathroom to touch up her make-up, put her shoes on, and walked into the formal living room to see her parents and Tom having a hushed conversation over cocktails.

They stopped, and all looked surprised to see her. She took a deep breath, lifted her chin up, and said, "I'm ready." The four of them went to dinner at an exclusive French restaurant. This was the night she started playing the role that was expected of her, all for the love of William.

Chapter 25

A week later, Professor Lang approached William who was studying in the lounge. There was an uncomfortable silence between them and William knew it was because Evie never returned to school.

The professor sat next to him, and said, "I've wanted to talk to you. You have one week until you're finished." He patted him on the back. "You've done well. You always make me see things in a new way. You're a very promising writer which brings me to my next topic, the fall semester. I was wondering if you'd consider being an assistant. I teach three classes. It doesn't pay much, but it's good experience and I could use someone as solid as you by my side."

William was stunned by the offer and more than flattered. "I'd be a fool not to take it." He shook hands with him. "I'm honored. Thank you, sir."

"I'm pleased you're eager. I think we'll make a good team and the position will give you solid experience for your resume." He looked down, his demeanor changed. As if to compose himself, he looked back up and said, "I thought you should also know that Miss Wright dropped my class last Tuesday." William didn't respond, but the pain on his face was evident. "And I talked with a counselor on campus. I can file a report of what I've seen, but I wanted to talk to you about it first."

William stared straight ahead, feeling numb. "She wouldn't want that." There was a finality to his statement although he delivered it flat and direct. The thought of Evie made his heart clench. He turned to look the professor in the eyes. "She definitely wouldn't want that."

"I'll take that into consideration. As for her courses, I was relieved to receive the notice because I was going to have to fail her. I didn't get details regarding the reason, but I did leave her a message. She hasn't returned my call. The good news is she'll receive a W for withdrawing instead of an F. Have you heard from her?"

William blinked, easing the burn from his eyes then replied, "No. We haven't spoken. Uh, she's . . . I guess she's made her choice." He leaned over, picking his bag up off the floor and ran his free hand over his temple to soothe the tension. "I guess I should be going. I still have a paper to turn in this Friday to earn that B.A."

"I signed the paperwork on Tuesday afternoon. I appreciate your efforts and look forward to receiving a complete analysis still, but for the record, you've graduated. Congratulations." He reached his hand forward once more to shake hands, and William gladly accepted.

"Thank you again, sir." William turned and hurried out, desperate for fresh air. As soon as he was outside, he gasped like a fish that had escaped its tank. It should have been a moment of celebration, but it wasn't. It felt all wrong. He still felt all wrong without her.

Evie dropping Lang's class cemented her choice, and William wasn't it. He leaned his arm against the wall for support, this fact sinking in. Pushing off, he unlocked his bike from the rack, and rode with a vengeance, trying to lose himself and his heart along the way.

Everleigh woke up to another morning of sunshine and the smell of breakfast wafting into her room. Like any depressed soul, she covered her head with her blankets and wished her day away. All she wanted to do was sleep. She had grown tired over the last week and lost motivation to perform basic daily functions like showering or brushing her hair. But, she knew she would have to leave the safe confines of the soft pink room today. Since the last formal dinner, everyone had left her alone and she wallowed in her misery, considering herself lucky to have the time to herself. Her luck had run out though. In less than one hour, she had a wedding gown fitting to show her family and future mother-in-law, and knew she couldn't keep them waiting. It was chosen by the mothers without her involvement. The wedding was moving forward with her participation or without.

She threw on fitted jeans and a T-shirt that she had worn in high school during her more rebellious days. A pair of high-top sneakers were dragged from the back of the closet, also vintage from high school, and slipped them on. She scrambled into the bathroom and brushed her teeth— the one bit of maintenance she hadn't scrapped. She skipped the large ring and instead put on her usual depressed face, sighed, and then left for the salon.

She arrived late and after everyone else. As Everleigh was taken to the large salon with cream-colored sofas, she noticed all of the fashionable women were wearing pastel dresses, fitting colors for a happy wedding planning activity such as the big reveal of the bride's dress. She heard a collective gasp and a "oh my" when she joined the party. Her mother stood as did Audrey, her face was one of disbelief and Audrey's of pure you-go-girl pride. Kitty Wright eyed her then asked, "Dear? Did you get assaulted on the way here? Is everything okay?"

Everleigh was confused by the question before realizing it must be in reference to her appearance. "I'm fine, Mother."

Tom's mother stood to kiss each of Everleigh's cheeks. "Are you having a pre-wedding insanity moment? I hear they are quite common."

"I didn't dress like this to make a point. I threw on some clothes and came over. That's all, nothing more!" Everleigh snapped at the group. She turned to the sales lady and rolled her eyes. "Where's the damn dress? Let's get this over with."

The group of ladies consisting of her mother, sister, Tom's mother, and three bridesmaids, all distant relations of hers or Tom's, went silent. She reappeared five minutes later and the group remained silent, but out of awe this time.

Everleigh stepped onto the platform in front of the mirror and smoothed the skirt down over her hips then stood in shock at her reflection. The salesperson had twisted her hair up with a delicate diamond comb and was now standing in the corner taking in her work. The group was stunned by her beauty.

Everleigh couldn't stop from commenting. "The dress, the hair, it's perfect."

The two mothers smiled at each other, clasping hands in pride of their work and in her beauty. Standing in front of the tri-fold mirror, she noted how much she felt like those books on exhibit, once more feeling like she was only something to be looked upon instead of someone with feelings and a mind of her own. The smiles dropped from everyone's faces when Everleigh said, "If only it was to the perfect man."

With an audible huff, Tom's mother turned on her

expensive heels, and as she walked out, said, "I never!"

Closing her eyes, she didn't care about her. She didn't care about any of this and lost herself in an image of William and how her skin felt when he touched her and how her lips tingled after kissing him. She would not have her happily ever after. She now knew her true prince did not want the burden of her any longer and she anchored her shoulders into a hunch.

Audrey, watching her sister's breakdown, rushed to her side and lifted her chin. "Open your eyes, Evie. Look at me." As her big sister focused on her, she took her by the hand and led her back into the dressing room. With the door shut behind them, Audrey hugged her. "Don't sell your soul to the devil. Find him. Find him and fight for him. I'm sure he's fighting for you."

In the weakest of voices, Evie said, "He told Tom he didn't want to fight for me. William hates me, Audrey. He never even called."

"Have you called him?"

"I can't," she said, tears falling down her cheeks. "He told Tom that I, this mess, was a burden. I don't want to trouble him anymore. I love him too much for that."

"First off, why would you believe anything Tom has to say?"

"William went to his office to talk to him. I called and asked his assistant. She confirmed he had been there. But that doesn't change the fact that he hasn't spoken or called me. He's done with me and my messed up life. He needs a chance to live his own life without the complications I bring."

Audrey stood there shocked by this revelation and then took her sister into her arms again, comforting her as she cried.

When Everleigh finished the fitting and dried her tears, she took a silent vow to move forward without William. The one thing necessary to help her move on and find closure was to see him one last time, even if from a distance. She didn't want the last image she would ever have of him being restrained by the police. So she left the dress salon alone even after her mother begged her to have tea with her down the street. She caught a cab and went to the first place she thought he might be at this time of day, his work.

Standing in front of the small open garage door of the bustling business, she watched the chaotic cyclists riding in and out on their missions. Feeling brave, she walked straight to the counter where a girl was shouting out assignments. "We're not hiring," she said without looking at Everleigh.

"I'm looking for William Ryder. Is he working—"

"He's off today. He's off all week."

Evie thanked her before she turned and left. Her feet seemed to have a destination of their own as she walked in the direction of William's apartment. Fifteen minutes later, she stood outside his building. Taking a deep breath, she pulled the door open and disappeared inside.

She knocked and stood there waiting, her emotions a jumbled mess. Another knock. She needed to see him just one more time then she prayed he'd be out of her system and they both could move on.

Disappointment shrouded her heart and her thoughts clouded over when no one answered. She heard no movement inside the apartment either. She left, more heartbroken than she had started that day and headed home. Hoping to resolve her feelings in a different way, she detoured to the park she loved. That had become *their* park and was filled with the memories of more carefree times. She was kidding herself though. Those memories had their own set of problems woven into them, but none of that mattered because William had loved her then.

William had ended his bike ride at the little park Evie used as her escape. He locked his bike to the bench and lay on the small grassy hill. With his earbuds blaring, he was listening to songs that ended up depressing him even more. He couldn't help but picture the times he held her and touched her, kissed her and talked with her. He wondered if these seared images would ever stop haunting him, reminding him of his loss. He lay there with his eyes closed, praying for anything to erase or replace these visions of her, when a shadow blocked the sun that was warming his body. His eyes snapped open, and he was blinded by the sun's rays behind the woman's head—his earthbound angel.

She backed up, allowing the sun to touch his skin again, and the woman lay down between the space of his arm that was stretched out and his chest. William tried to get control of his aching and racing heart as Evie settled her head on his shoulder not saying a word.

Lost in this bliss, he pulled her close by wrapping his arm around her, loving the feeling of her against him again. They stayed together this way for a few minutes before anyone spoke. Then he took the liberty. "Why did you choose him? I know you can feel how right we are?"

She didn't want to answer, but needed to say something to her love. "There's no time for questions or answers." Her tone broke his heart. He knew right then there wasn't a battle to fight anymore. She had already given up hope, given up on them.

"This is good-bye, isn't it?"

"Yes," she answered the only question she knew deep down she had to. She had to keep control of her emotions and stay strong and steady with him, *for him*. He had worked too hard to have her ruin his life. Tom was clear with his intention for destruction if she returned to William. Even with that weighing on her mind, she also knew Tom would not disapprove of her ending it in person. It made it all more real.

"You didn't return any of my calls." His tone held a slight irritation in it.

"What calls?" She sat up and he did the same, but she knew it didn't matter if he had called. The reality that Tom held all the cards sank in. "I've got to go."

They both stood and as he looked deep into her eyes he saw the love he'd always known. She was lying to him to make it easier for one of them, maybe for both of them. "I just wanted to make sure you're doing okay and to tell you good-bye." She turned to start the long walk away from him, a walk she never thought she would have to make.

"I have one final request," he said, refusing to accept this as the end.

She turned back, not able to face him as she waited for him to finish.

"One last kiss, my love." He walked closer and she didn't voice a denial. Her eyes gave her approval for the request and he took her face in his hands, tilted her mouth toward his, and brought their lips together.

The kiss deepened and they lost themselves one last time in each other. As they parted, William looked down at the beautiful girl in front of him with her eyes still closed and knew what they had between them was more real than ever and definitely not over. He smirked with a new conviction as she looked back at him, searching his face in bewilderment.

"Good-bye." She didn't look back as she walked away. All she could think of was how her body sold her out. She cursed each disloyal part, starting with her traitorous lips and tongue, hands, and heart. They all fought valiantly over her logical brain and won the battle. She hated that she would remember every element of that kiss for the rest of her life and never again feel the passion they shared.

But for William, it confirmed the thoughts he had started to bury deep down inside. And on that very spot where he still stood, he was re-committed to having a relationship with the beautiful girl because he knew she still loved him, too. So he started on a plan of his own.

Chapter 26

Audrey was easy enough to locate with Walter's help. William caught up with her one day in the local coffee shop closest to Evie's building. Audrey turned around with her fresh brew in hand and saw William sitting there waiting for her. At first, she appeared nervous, but he smiled at her and when it reached his eyes, she knew he had come around to help her sister. She joined him at the tiny table and as she removed her sunglasses, he leaned toward her. "I need your help."

"Anything," she said. "I should have helped. I didn't know how. I'm sorry, so sorry, I didn't."

"It's not your fault and I don't blame you. But I want her back and I think she wants to be with me, too." He laid out his plan for her and then asked about Evie and how she's doing.

"She's been nicer to me. I don't mean to infer she wasn't before, but we get along better now. She's built a fortress around her heart though."

"Your parents should know what he's done to her."

"I tried before. They don't believe me against him.

He's manipulative. He has them believing I'm just a stupid teenager."

"Why do they like him so much?" He asked, confused by the allegiance her parents have shown Tom Whitney.

Audrey shook her head seeming to wonder the same thing before she finally spoke. "They've known his family a long time. They're very close with his parents and he's a good actor. Oh, I don't know." She looked down at the coffee in her hands and stopped talking like she was going into a forbidden topic.

William was guessing, but felt like he got a pretty good idea during their brief love affair. "He knows how to put on a charade. He says what they want to hear and does what they approve of. They aren't aware of the monster he is underneath his polished surface."

Audrey's eyes lifted up and met William's. "Yes. He's a suck-up."

William laughed at the term, but "suck-up" was very fitting also. "I have to warn you, Audrey, my plan is a bit conniving."

"Ooh, I love it even more. Go on."

"I think it's going to be a two-stage process. He's got something on her, or I'm thinking he's using something to keep her going through with this . . ." William looked out the window and never finished his sentence.

"He's blackmailing her somehow, but how can I help with that? Tom hates me. He barely tolerates me and I'm her sister. He won't talk to me. He's also keeping her on a short leash. She can't make a move without him there or calling her."

"We're not going to bother with him. I'm going straight for her heart."

As they plotted and planned, William realized he had found his strongest ally in Evie's sister. And with Audrey's birthday coming up next week, he found the perfect excuse to get her out from under the monster's watchful eye. But waiting a week to see her, to talk with her again, would prove the hardest part of the plan by far. He missed Evie and hated that he couldn't just walk in and take her away from her prison.

He and Audrey exchanged phone numbers and throughout the week they kept each other posted through text messages. William filled the hours working during the day and dreaming of Evie at night. His dreams were filled with him touching her body . . . everywhere. That was something he regretted not doing when he had the chance, but in his heart he knew it was better that they hadn't.

When Everleigh came back to Tom, he had become more patient with his future bride. He tried to break her by trying his "method" of discipline before, but that drove her away. And upon her return he had even tried sleeping pills in her water to keep her calm during her transition back into his world and back into her proper place. But he didn't want to keep her unconscious to be with him. He wanted her smart wit and cleverness back for the world to see. Settling on the most basic of threats to convince her of the right choice to make, he threatened the one she loved the most.

He was surprised over the course of the last ten days how well his plan had worked. Everleigh even allowed him to hold her hand at a party once, seeming as if she was falling back in line with his expectations. Socially, she was gracious, funny, and would carry a conversation, so Tom felt he could relax in his efforts with her. He started to believe that maybe she did want this life; maybe she did want him for real this time.

They walked the two blocks back to her home and as they approached her building, he stopped and pulled her to him. "I want you to come over tonight."

Everleigh looked at him and thought carefully before answering. She knew he wasn't asking. He never asked for her opinion. He wanted to get off, but she couldn't stomach the thought. "Not tonight. I need more time." She looked down at her feet, avoiding his eyes, but made no apologies.

She looked back up at him so earnest and sweet that he knew she would be ready soon and it would be real. He believed she would want to be there instead of him demanding her to be. "Okay. I'll give you more time." He kissed her at the door and said his good-bye.

As Everleigh rode the elevator up, she knew she wouldn't be able to stall much longer, but she couldn't be with that monster, at least not voluntarily. She hoped being married to him would give her the strength to fulfill her wifely duties a bit easier. Many women had married for purpose over love. She knew she wasn't the first. Some even developed feelings of love over time, but that would feel like a betrayal to what she and William once were.

Climbing into bed, she remembered how close she and William had come to being together completely. It was her one true regret of her time with him. They both thought they should take it slow because they had forever. They were fools because their forever was never meant to be. Her soul felt rundown and she had lost her will to fight. Her fighting spirit had left with William. One thing she was positive of is that her staying with Tom gave William the opportunity to pursue his dreams just as he was before she crashed his world. She eventually fell asleep on a tear-soaked pillow.

The next day, Everleigh buried herself in the

required phone calls necessary to make the Latham Fundraiser a success. She had taken on more tasks to stay busy since she dropped her summer class, and to keep her mind from wandering back to her true love.

By five o'clock, Audrey came into her room holding a bag and a large shoe box. "It's my birthday, so I get to dress you for tonight."

Evie lowered her chin and gave her a questioning look. "I'm not even allowed to dress myself now?"

"You betcha. This isn't an uppity uptown soiree. We're going to watch a band downtown." She strode over to the bed unloading the clothes and boots from the box and smiled at her sister. "Remember, it's my eighteenth birthday, sis. You have to wear this for me. What the birthday girl says goes."

Evie held the skimpy cut-off jean skirt up and shook her head in disapproval. Audrey gave her a look that left her no option. "Okay, I'll wear it, but only because it's your day."

As they rode through Manhattan, Audrey started chatting about her friends who would be meeting them at the club tonight and Evie tugged at her skirt, uncomfortable with showing this much skin.

Evie was more than happy to celebrate her baby sister's birthday and had been looking forward to the night all week. It also bothered Tom that she was going out without him which made her enjoy the night even more.

Exiting the cab, Evie followed close behind Audrey. Her little sister fist-bumped the doorman and he let them in without waiting or carding either. That concerned Evie, and she wondered how much partying her sister was doing without her knowledge. But tonight was about her birthday fun and she wasn't going to be the one to ruin it, so she followed her straight up to the bar. Audrey ordered two shots of tequila and set one of them in front of Evie. Society kids were frequenting the bar scene and stealing drinks at fancy cocktails parties at an early age, so Evie downed it in one go and skipped the accessory lime.

Audrey laughed. "Impressive. I didn't even know if you'd done a shot before." She signaled for two more and Audrey excused herself to seek out her friends, taking her shot with her.

Evie turned around with the full shot in hand while leaning against the edge of the bar. That's when she heard her name, but from an unfamiliar voice. "Evie?"

She turned to see a very large guy smiling at her as he approached. She recognized him, but wasn't quite sure from where. But it came to her when he introduced himself. "It's Bobby, I'm William's best friend. I met you at his parent's house on Staten Island."

"Yes, that's right. Bobby, how are you?"

"I'm great." He smiled. Her first thought was that was how William would answer that question too. "Weird running into you here. You slumming it downtown?"

"I'm here with my sister. It's her birthday and she loves this place. I've never been here before, but I like it so far."

"Doing shots?" he asked, pointing at her waiting glass.

"Uh, yeah." She started to feel embarrassed holding the tequila shot.

"Can I join you?"

Evie nodded and scooted a bit to her left to let him squeeze up to the bar. Once he was served, they shot the drinks together after a quick clink of the glasses. "Tequila, huh? What's the story?"

She laughed because she handled the alcohol a little smoother than him. "No story."

"In Mexico, they sip their tequila." He looked her in the eyes as he spoke, but she looked away. "I'm sorry. Is this awkward or too weird hanging out?"

Her face softened, and she tilted her head smiling back at him. "No. I'm glad to see you again. I really didn't have a chance to get to know you, but if William . . ." She looked down and then signaled the bartender for another round. "Well, you must be a good person if you two are friends."

"From what he said, I know you are, too." He paused then added, "He misses you."

She couldn't look at him for fear of falling apart, so she took her glass and tapped it against his and drank the shot. "I wish he didn't."

"I don't know why the two of you aren't together. I'm sure it's some fucked up situation that seems impossible, but ultimately I want my friend happy. He deserves it and you happen to be what makes him the happiest. I can also tell how much you like him. You might even love him or some craziness like that, so don't let some rich wanker mess up something so right—"

"I'm not with William because I love him. Don't let him waste his life waiting on something that can never be." She pointed to his full waiting shot.

He drank the liquor slower than the first, but fast enough not to be outdone by this girl. Changing the topic, they spent the next hour laughing about New York, people in the club, and nothing in particular. At one point, Bobby looked over at Evie. "You can hold your liquor and that makes you a cool chick in my book."

She laughed out loud, feeling free and light tonight. "I was even better when I was a teen. I was a bit wilder then. I'm going to the restroom. I'll be right back."

Audrey worked her way over to Bobby, introducing herself, after she spied her sister leaving. They visited for a minute before the real show started, and they weren't referring to the band playing on stage. They leaned their backs against the bar and watched William make his way toward the bathroom. As Evie walked out of the darkened hall, he grabbed her, pressing his lips to her forehead. Her surprise morphed into calm. Her heart was racing, her mind suddenly numb, but her body operated on its own. She snuggled to his chest nuzzling her nose against his neck. Her hands instinctively went to his shoulders, sliding up and landing in his hair. Her fingers pulling gently as her body moved against him with an audible sigh.

He wrapped his arms around Evie settling his hands on her ribs and then slid them down to her hips, burying his face into her hair. For fear of losing her again, he inhaled her while he held her. He heard the faintest, sweetest voice near the base of his earlobe. "I wish we would have made love. I still dream of you touching me . . . your hands on me . . . everywhere."

He knew she'd been drinking and would've never admitted that if she was sober, but it didn't matter. He loved hearing the truth from her and he was turned on by this girl, the girl he was in love with, moving against him clouding all rationale. She was all he thought about. "I dream of you, too." He could feel her soft lips against his jaw and down his neck and was losing this battle not to grab her and take her away with him forever.

"Hey guys."

His eyes flashed up to see Audrey smiling at him. It couldn't be time already. He was desperate to absorb every second he was able to hold Evie like this. He tilted his head, resting his cheek against hers and said, "We can be together."

With that statement, she pulled her head back to look him in the eyes. "We can't—"

"We can."

"We can't and shouldn't. Trust me on this and do what's good for you?"

"You are good for me." He kissed her forehead. "By the way, you look incredible tonight."

Suddenly, she felt her shoulder being grabbed, and was spun around. William held onto her waist as Audrey demanded, "We've got to go. He's here."

Evie's eyes followed Audrey's stare and she saw Tom standing by the bar. She didn't know why he was there and hoped it wasn't to check up on her, but it was obvious that was exactly why he was there.

She turned to William who said, "He doesn't matter. I love you, Evie. Stay with me. I'll protect you."

Hearing him say that intermingled with the memories of Tom's threats to ruin William's career broke her heart. She shouldn't have gotten so close to William. She shouldn't have let him hold her in that most intimate embrace. And she definitely shouldn't have listened to him. His words were dangerous and reckless. She let her emotions get away from her. She knew he didn't know what he was saying, or even realize the direct consequences of his actions tonight. To protect him once again, she backed away with no smile to be found. She closed off the thoughts behind her eyes and reiterated what she had already said.

"We can't be together. Go find happiness somewhere else because it's not here. It's not with me." She escaped through an opening in the crowd before he could talk her into staying, before he could make her believe happily ever after does exist.

Audrey looked at William, and warned, "Don't let him see you, okay? It will be bad for her if he does."

William grabbed her arm, threatening. "Take care of her, Audrey. I mean it."

"I will."

He repeated. "I mean it! Take care of her. Don't let him hurt her and don't let her hurt herself anymore. She deserves happiness and to be safe."

She nodded and walked away. His heart sank as he watched Evie in the distance leave the bar with that bastard.

"Get in the car, Everleigh." Tom's tone left no room for negotiation.

Everleigh started to cry as she ducked into the back of the cab. Her shoulders shook as her quiet sobs overtook her body.

Tom started to climb in behind her, but stopped and looked back at Audrey. "You dressed her like a whore and got her drunk." Everleigh looked up and saw him shake his head in disgust. "She won't be going out with you again. It's time you grew up, Audrey. Get in the car."

"You can't tell me what to do, Tom," Audrey argued.

"You're right, but I can tell her," he said, referring to his drunken fiancée in the cab.

With that threat, Audrey got in the cab, and looked

at her sister. Everleigh raised her chin with pride and wiped the tears from her cheek with the back of her arm. Not another word was shared on the ride home.

Bobby placed his hand down firm on William's shoulder as if to hold him back even though he wasn't moving. "Your plan worked."

William's stance relaxed, and he smiled. "She looked amazing, Bobby. To hold her like that again . . . she wants to be with me. I can tell."

"You're right. She's the one for you, man. I hope you know what you're doing though because that guy didn't seem like he messes around. So what's next?"

"I'm thinking a grand gesture is in order." He turned to his friend, sticking his hand out. Bobby shook it. "Thanks for hanging out with her and getting her drunk."

"Why'd you want her drunk anyway? Isn't that like taking two steps back? She might not even remember this tomorrow."

"She'll remember. Even if she closes her mind, she'll remember me in here." William tapped his chest over his heart. "And, she wouldn't be receptive to seeing me if she wasn't drinking, so Audrey said it was needed. She was right, too." He smiled at what a wuss he must sound like to his friend and shook his head in disbelief that tonight's plan worked. He now *knew* she loved him. "If she had seen me while sober, she'd convince herself it was wrong to talk with me. This way, she let down her guard and went with her feelings instead." William knew it was kind of cheating to remind her of her true emotions this way, but Audrey had convinced him that was the only way for Evie to admit what she really felt. The words didn't back what her body language confirmed, her real feelings. She wanted to be with him just as much, but something was holding her back. William didn't know why she was putting on this charade, but knew Tom definitely had something to do with it. And if Tom was willing to play unfair, William was willing to play dirty as well if it meant being with Evie.

The alcohol had kicked in and was coursing through Everleigh's system. Tom walked the girls through the lobby holding Everleigh by the arm, which was proving more difficult than it should. "Another late shift, Walter?" he asked as the doorman rushed to push the elevator button for them.

"Yes, Sir. Have to do a few overnights for Joe each month."

Audrey startled everyone when she announced, "I'll take her from here."

"I'll take her." Tom was giving no leeway on the issue as he spoke to Audrey.

"I'll put her right to bed. Thanks for helping me get her to the elevator. You can go home now." Audrey stood her ground and tugged on Evie's arm.

Everleigh was half aware of the strange conversation happening around her. She lifted her head up to see Tom turn a lighter shade of red, but he plastered a fake smile on top and relented. "Very well." He leaned in, kissing her on the cheek. "Sleep well." He moved closer to whisper in her ear. "I'm looking forward to when we can be alone again. I miss making love to you."

As she watched him saunter across the lobby, she found relief in the fact she would not be sharing a bed with him tonight. She had held him off the last two months and didn't plan on changing that until after the wedding if she could help it, but she knew he could be demanding and dreaded the day her telling him no wouldn't work any longer.

"Making love!" The loud snort following her statement was aimed at his back.

Tom stopped with his back to her then started walking again, pushing the door open and leaving.

Everleigh continued to giggle. "You wish, Tom." Her tone remained harsh and hateful, no humor found at all.

Tom stopped once again before the brass door shut and looked over his right shoulder at Walter standing there shifting and anxious. "Make sure she stays home tonight. She's been drinking."

Upstairs, Audrey helped Evie slip her boots off and noticed that beyond just drunk, she was sad. "You doing okay there, sis?"

Evie looked up then flopped back onto her bed. "Am I awake?"

"Yes."

Evie moved toward her pillow and tucked her legs under the covers. Audrey disappeared for a minute and returned with aspirin and a glass of water. "Take these. Hopefully, you won't feel as bad in the morning."

Evie obliged her sister, and then continued to drink the entire glass of water. As Audrey went to refill her glass in the bathroom, Evie lifted up on her elbows, and asked, "Was he real? Did you see him tonight?"

After setting the glass on her nightstand, Audrey lay down on the bed next to her. "He was real. He still loves you."

"I still love him."

"You should be with him then, don't you think?"

Evie fell back down on the pillow, closing her eyes and touching her ribs where William had held her. She could feel his hands holding her tight to keep her from leaving, but she left him there because no matter how much she drank or they loved each other, it wouldn't change their fate. "It's complicated—"

"Only because you make it that way. Are you worried about Mom and Dad?"

She opened her eyes and looked at her little sister who only wanted her to be happy. She smiled. "No, not anymore. I can live without their money if I had to. I know that now. They don't want to hear my side of things, so I've given up on their approval. I'm worried about him, about William. He and his family have worked too hard to get where they are. I would never risk being the cause of crushing his dreams."

"As if you could. You are a part of those dreams. He wants to be with you, and you're worried about what exactly? You make no sense. If you love each other—"

"It's not enough. Love is a childish emotion best spent when dreaming of fairy tales. My fairy tale doesn't come with the happy ending," she said as tears spilled from her eyes, dropping onto her pillow. "He'll love again. I have no doubt." She wiped her face and laughed. "It's silly I'm crying. I've made my choice and it's best for everyone."

"Except you. How can you toss your feelings aside when—"

"There was nothing casual about the decision I've been forced to make. I love him and will do anything that benefits him so he can be happy. By giving him up, I'm showing how much I love him." Evie took a deep breath then yawned. She rolled over half out of aggravation and half out of sleepiness. "I'm going to bed, Audrey. Good night and happy birthday."

Audrey wandered toward the door, but before she left, Everleigh sat up and said, "I don't know if you had anything to do with tonight, but if you did, thank you."

Evie rolled back onto her side, and Audrey flipped the light switch off. "Goodnight."

As soon as her sister had left, Evie dragged her pillow and blanket over to the window seat and curled up. She needed a backdrop of life beyond the confines of the bedroom. It was the only place she found any comfort in this huge apartment she used to call home.

Chapter 27

"Everleigh? Wake up."

She woke with a start and immediately cowered in the corner against the pane of the window. Her eyes met Tom's, and she asked, "What are you doing here?"

"I wanted to check on you after last night. You were drunk—"

"I'm fine." She cut him off, holding the blanket up to her chin.

"I can see that. I brought you a hot oolong tea."

She looked at him as if he was insane. Well, she knew he was insane, but she still seemed surprised by his actions. "Why?"

"What do you mean why?" He handed her the cup.

She didn't take it and looked at the drink in disgust. "I don't like oolong tea."

"Oh, I didn't know."

"Of course, you didn't know. You don't know me at

all."

"Everleigh, I'm trying here."

Everleigh looked out the window, relaxing against the wall. "Don't try on my account. You've doomed me to a life worse than death. Tea does not make it all better." She couldn't look at him as she spoke. She was too upset.

"We can have a good life if you give us a chance, sweetheart."

Fury raged inside as she whipped her head around in confrontation. "I don't have much of a choice, do I?" She got up and brushed past him, going into her bathroom and locking the door. Everleigh was pushing every one of his buttons and didn't care.

Tom scoffed out loud. "You're being irrational and immature. I'll come back when you've calmed yourself."

She rolled her eyes. "Take your time. It's gonna be a while."

Determined to make his grandest gesture of love, William continued talking with Audrey about the next stage of his plan over the following weeks. But a complete stroke of luck shone down on him when Dallas asked to stay with him the following week for a job he booked. Without hesitation, William said yes to his brother staying, but had not thought anything more about it until his brother mentioned the name of the event—The Latham Fundraiser.

William had heard that name before, but was having trouble placing it until the following Wednesday while working. William skid his bike to a stop in the middle of a crowded street when it dawned on him. Audrey had mentioned this event to him. It was the same event Evie was helping to organize. This was information he could work with. This event would be the perfect place to make his pronouncement of love. This event would be where Evie would make her final decision, one way or another. It was a risk he was willing to take though, for her. He tried not to dwell on the potential rejection because if she didn't choose him, he didn't know where to go from there.

William called Audrey and got her thinking about their options while he tried to get his mind back on his job.

She called him back thirty minutes later just as he was riding back into the messenger garage and told him he could go as her date. When he walked to the large assignments desk, he looked down the schedule posted for the following week and told Audrey to hold. "Is this schedule final because I need that Saturday off?" He looked at the girl doling out deliveries and pick-ups.

She scoffed at his question like it was ridiculous. "That's it all right. You work it out yourself if you need to change shifts."

He put the phone back to his ear. "I work 'til nine that night."

Audrey sighed, thinking it would be better if he could arrive with her, but she said, "That should be fine. The party will go until eleven or twelve. Listen, I've gotta run, but I'll do some digging to figure this out."

He smiled at her enthusiasm. "Hey, Audrey, thanks for helping me."

"Don't thank me yet, cowboy. But when you two get back together, you both can take me out for drinks."

"How about dinner, my under-aged friend, but seriously, thanks."

Everleigh rejected Tom's niceties, including the roses he sent to her earlier in the week wishing her luck with the fundraiser. She knew the monster lurked beneath the surface and would rear up again. It was only a matter of time.

Within days, the flowers had wilted and the note attached was in blue ink, which further cemented her hatred for him. But the kicker for Evie was that he always seemed to be hanging around lately. She ended his visits with excuses of finishing her commitments for the event. It worked well and she breathed easier once he was gone.

Audrey made sure to be around, casually, of course, when Everleigh was working on the fundraiser and gathered intel for her partner-in-crime. It seemed to all be coming together. But Everleigh had started acting strange closer to the weekend. She seemed confused and to be questioning herself, sometimes even aloud. Audrey interrupted one such moment. "Got something on your mind there, sis?"

Everleigh stopped pacing and found her sister sitting on the sofa. "Oh, I didn't see you. What?"

"You seem to have something on your mind. You want to talk about it?"

"I, er, don't know what you're referring to," she responded, twisting her fingers through her hair then laughed. "I guess I do." She took Audrey by the hand, signaling her to be quiet as they sneaked back to her room, shutting the door and locking it. "I don't know if I can do it."

"Do what, the fundraiser?"

"No, the marriage." She sat down on the window seat and watched her sister as she took the seat next to her with her mouth gaping open.

"Then don't, Evie."

Evie's teeth tugged at the inside of her cheek as her brow furrowed. "If I tell you something, promise me you won't tell anyone."

"I promise. Does it have to do with William?"

She nodded. "The reason I can't be with him is that Tom said he would keep him from graduating and denounce him to everyone in New York. He wouldn't be able to get a job anywhere."

"I knew it!" Audrey exclaimed, pointing her finger at Evie. "I knew Tom was blackmailing you somehow. That is the lowest of low. He's horrible."

"But, the last few days . . ." Evie looked down at her leg propped up in front of her. "The last few months, I can't get William out of my system. I've tried so hard and just when I feel I can go through with this marriage, I slip again. I dream of him at night. I daydream about him. I'm always reminding myself that he can take care of himself. Tom doesn't know everyone in this city, but then I think, but his family and friends do. I often wonder if my love for him could take the guilt away if I'm responsible for ruining his life." She looked out the dark window and answered her own inquiry. "No, it can't. It's easier for me to marry Tom than to feel responsible for hurting William, for taking his dreams away from him just because I love him selfishly. I couldn't live with that."

Audrey rested her hand on Evie's leg and asked, "Are you venting or asking my opinion?"

"I'm venting," she said without hesitation.

Audrey walked toward the door, stopped, and turned around. "You know I have to give my opinion though, don't you?"

Evie smiled and nodded again as Audrey continued.

"William can take care of himself, and I doubt your love for him was ever selfish. Stop making decisions for him and just . . . just be with him. Don't ruin your life over something you'll regret the rest of it. And stop wasting your days away on a jerk that never deserved you to begin with." Audrey rushed out of the room before Evie could argue with her.

Evie leaned against the wall in her little alcove and stared at the traffic twelve stories below, letting her mind wander back to William for the hundredth time today. "Can I really be with him? Will he love me or hate me if he ever found out I could've helped him instead of hindering him?" This was something she had to take into serious consideration, but for tonight, she could only guess.

Chapter 28

William's shift on Saturday was grueling. He never found anyone to cover for him and on top of that, two guys called in sick. He grabbed a sandwich and started eating while perched atop his bike. The thought of the night ahead made him feel sick, so he took one more bite then threw the rest away, unable to finish it. The next five hours were as busy as the first part of his day, but he trudged on trying to focus on the process of picking up and delivering packages.

Everleigh, Audrey, and their mom Kitty returned from the salon by six in the evening. Since their make-up and hair was done, they slipped on their evening gowns and shoes they had spent weeks shopping for to wear to The Latham Fundraiser tonight.

They met in the formal living room at six-thirty where Richard Wright and Tom awaited. Tom's mouth hung open when Everleigh entered the room in a sea blue creation that sparkled and was more than flattering to her figure. But she became self-conscious and uncomfortable under his wanting gaze. She began to question if she should wear something else, something he didn't like so much, but there was no time to change now.

She went and stood by his side as expected and he put his hand around her waist. Leaning in, he kissed her on the cheek, telling her how beautiful she looked. Although her stomach rolled under his touch, she smiled politely.

Dinner at the fundraiser was served at seven-fifteen, and plates were cleared by eight o'clock. Everleigh had managed to avoid Tom the following hour after dinner, using her active role in the event as a solid excuse to leave his side. After he tracked her down, he managed to convince her of one dance, but they were interrupted by his work associates, ending the dance early. She was grateful for the distraction.

She wandered around checking the dessert table, having it replenished, making sure people were having a good time, and sometimes escaping to a dark corner for a moment to breathe, to think, to disappear.

In the dark recesses of the ballroom, Everleigh looked around at what her life had become. It was nothing she cared about. Tom was across the room chatting with his company's Human Resources Manager. She watched from the shadows of the far exit doors as he brushed his fingers across her hand, checking to make sure no one noticed. Everleigh did. So did the woman. She leaned forward straightening his bow tie. The act looked too intimate and they looked too familiar with each other while doing it.

Two watermarks on the coffee table of his immaculately kept home. No sex in months, which she really couldn't complain about, and whispering at the bar in the corner. Things added up. Tom was cheating, but why? Why would he want her when he had that other woman?

She stared as minutes passed before the two separated with a quick embrace made to look innocent, but his hand patted the woman's ass, and Everleigh saw it all clearly now. But what stuck out the most is that she didn't care. She wasn't angry and didn't feel betrayed. She found relief and took her last helpless breath, refusing to live her life like this. She didn't need the money. William had taught her that. It was tainted anyway. If her parents couldn't see her pain or refused to then she would leave them behind for good. Tom wasn't even a factor now. The hate she felt for him would last her a lifetime. She'd be a happy woman if she never saw him again. But Audrey . . .

Audrey had disappeared after dinner, and Evie felt somewhat lost without her support tonight. She sought her out after making a few announcements and was surprised to find her talking to a waiter outside the ballroom doors. "Hey, I've been lookin—" Evie stopped mid-sentence when she saw Dallas. She stood there momentarily confused, a range of emotions crossing her mind, including the feeling she had just interrupted them.

"Hi, Evie, it's good to see you again," the young man said, smiling at her.

"Hi, what are you doing here?" Her heart sped up at the sight of William's brother.

Audrey brought Dallas closer, shrinking the distance between them, and said, "He's working the fundraiser. What a coincidence, huh?"

Everleigh wondered how Audrey even knew him, but struggled for words. Seeing him reminded her once again of what she was missing, her fairytale ending. Gripping her stomach, tears formed in her eyes. Both Audrey and Dallas watched her, both their faces falling into sympathetic expressions.

Dallas reached out and touched her arm. "He loves you just as much."

One tear escaped, but she swiftly swiped it away with the back of her hand. Everleigh pointed over her shoulder.

"I should get back. I'm one of the hostesses tonight." She turned and hurried back into the party. As the door closed behind her, she found the nearest wall for support and collapsed against it. Standing on wobbly legs seemed too much, so she walked to the nearest table and sat down, trying not to look crazy. She played her hostess role well and started visiting with a couple still lingering in their chairs across the table from her, hoping to get her mind off the pain she felt inside.

Tom had been watching Everleigh from the moment she returned to the ballroom out of breath and distraught. He was curious by her strange behavior, but was caught in the middle of an impromptu business meeting. He was stuck, so he watched her over the shoulder of his associate, not really listening to the man in front of him, but catching words such as: Limits, takeovers, and dissolution. These were words of complete unimportance to Tom as he watched his fiancée.

Everleigh slowly recovered and as she walked back toward the other hostesses, Tom saw Audrey and a waiter walking into the ballroom. The young waiter looked familiar, but at the same time, not quite. *Audrey was slumming it tonight*, and wondered if that was what upset Everleigh moments earlier. He would deal with Audrey tomorrow. She needed to learn that her actions were embarrassing not only to her family, but his reputation. Turning his attention back to the man in front of him, he continued discussing the volatile stock market and the board meeting coming up the following week.

After another twenty minutes, Tom had had enough of the lavish party and found Everleigh who was talking with Audrey and another hostess. He took her by the arm and said, "Let's go, now." He followed it up with a kiss on her hand to ease the demand.

Audrey shouted, "No!" Her outburst came as a

surprise to all of them.

They both looked at her as Everleigh tried to figure out her sister's bizarre plea, but couldn't, so she asked, "What's wrong?"

"I . . . I just thought as a hostess you're supposed to stay until the end." She babbled on, hoping to hit on a good enough reason for her stay. "You know the better music starts in an hour. I thought we could dance and have some fun tonight."

"Have you been drinking again, Audrey?" Tom's insult was biting.

"No, I haven't. I just want to spend time with my sister."

Everleigh felt her sister's request was sweet. "We'll stay a while longer. Don't worry."

Tom turned her toward him with a tight squeeze to her upper arm. Gritting his teeth, he spoke. "Everleigh, I'm ready to go. We haven't been together in months." He glanced at Audrey quickly then snarled. "Tonight, I need you, and I won't take no for an answer."

"I'm not ready." There was an edge to her tone she hoped hid her fear. Turning their backs to Audrey, she whispered. "I saw you."

He glared at her. "Saw me what?"

"I saw you with that woman by the bar."

Waving to a friend who greeted them, he had a smile on his face, keeping up appearances as he leaned in. "It doesn't matter what you think you saw, darling. What you need to keep in mind is the fate of your boyfriend."

She hated Tom, but loved William too much to risk

everything now. Everleigh put a reassuring hand on his arm even though it made her cringe on the inside. "A few more minutes please." In her mind, she knew she'd never be with him again, but she didn't want to cause a scene in front of everyone. "I put a lot of hard work into this event and I want to enjoy it a little longer."

Her tone was so sweet that Tom relaxed his stance and smiled at her. "Okay, but only another thirty then go to my place."

She nodded and turned back to her sister who no longer stood behind her. Scanning across the crowded room, she didn't see her.

While Everleigh handled Tom, Audrey had run off to find Dallas at the waiter's station just off the ballroom. She was running so fast he had to catch her in his arms to stop her. "What, what is it?"

"He has to get here," she said almost out of breath. "They're leaving soon. Where's William?"

Dallas called his brother. "When are you getting here? They're leaving soon."

William responded, "I have another thirty left of my shift, but I'll cut out early. Can you stall them?"

"Can you stall them?" Dallas looked at Audrey.

Audrey was speaking so fast that her words mashed together and became one, "Ialreadyhave.Weonlyhaveafewminutes."

"She's tried to stall," Dallas said, speaking back into the phone.

"Have her try harder! I can't show up looking like this. I'm a mess. I need to shower and get ready."

"She's tried, William." Dallas watched Audrey shift anxiously in front of him with a worried expression on her face.

Audrey stomped her foot. "He has to come now. Tell him to get here as fast as he can. I'll find him a jacket to throw on."

William overheard Audrey talking to Dallas, but he needed to go. "Man, let me call you back in a minute. I need to deal with work."

"He hung up on me. He has to figure out how to get out of work," Dallas explained. His eyes checked her out not caring how obvious he was. Easily distracted, he smirked. "Let's talk about—"

She cocked one eyebrow up then whacked him on the arm.

"What was that for, rich girl?" Dallas rubbed his arm. "You used knuckles."

"Control your ogling eyes, waiter boy."

She put him in his place, making him laugh. His phone buzzed in his hand and he read the text: *Be there in ten.*

Tom insisted on sitting at the table with Everleigh and her parents to discuss more wedding plans. She rested her head in her hands, propped up by her elbows, out of sheer boredom.

At least ten minutes had passed and she was getting irritated as she looked for Audrey. She thought they were going to dance and have some fun and knew time was ticking away. She downed the rest of her champagne, and then finished Tom's glass just because it was there and he wasn't drinking it.

In a flurry of lavender chiffon, Audrey appeared, surprising her dad and hugging him from behind as a diversion. Everleigh was about to say something, but Audrey winked at her then shook her head. Everleigh was puzzled as she watched her sister slip their father's jacket off the back of the chair and rush away.

William rode his bike through the streets with no regard for lights or stop signs, cars, or pedestrians. His insides were on fire with determination. This was it. This was do or die, make or break time, now or never.

He rode up the back alley of the hotel, and hopped off. Walking his bike in through the open kitchen entrance, he parked it in front of the staff lockers and ran to the elevators. As soon as the doors opened on the sixteenth floor, Audrey and Dallas greeted him with wide grins. By their expressions, he knew he had made it in time.

Dallas rushed him to the bathroom where William scrubbed his face with the soap from the dispenser, and dried it with paper towels. He tossed his flannel shirt to his brother and tried to straighten his black T-shirt and pants. Black wore better as a messenger in NYC because the dirt didn't show. As soon as William ran out, Audrey grabbed him. "Wait, I got you a jacket so you'll blend in."

He looked at the black tux jacket and smiled. Other than prom, he had never worn one before. As he slipped it over his shoulders, he asked, "Do I want to know where you got this?"

"No, and I need it back soon." She giggled.

"Thanks, Audrey." He smiled at Evie's very helpful and impressively devious little sister.

She straightened the jacket on him. "All black. Very sexy. Go get'em, tiger. I'll cue the band leader." And she was gone.

Dallas shook William's hand and patted his shoulder. "You can do this. She still loves you. Break a leg and make us proud."

"Thanks for all your help." Pride ran through William as he looked at his brother as a grown man for the first time instead of his little brother. "You have a great head on your shoulders."

"A chip off the old dad and big brother block," Dallas replied with his own pride.

They walked to the ballroom doors, but William stopped to tease. "Little sis is cute, huh?"

"Just worry about the big sis. I got the younger one all taken care of." Dallas laughed just as William entered the large party.

William walked into the room and saw Audrey near the stage signaling in Evie's direction. That's when he saw her, *his Evie*, and stopped for a brief moment to take her in. She was breathtaking. She looked bored, but still breathtaking and he liked that she was bored with *him* next to her.

William weaved his way through the endless sea of tables and right behind her before anyone else noticed him. He took her hand in his and in one swift swoop, spun her around, pulling her to her feet. "Let's dance, Beautiful."

Too stunned to work out her own reaction, she followed her heart and his lead. William took her to the safest and most public place he could think of, the center of the dance floor. She was in his arms and their first step corresponded with the very first note of a Frank Sinatra song.

Evie stared into William's eyes, afraid if she blinked, he would disappear. "How are you here?"

305

William was tired of wasting time and knew he would be dragged out by security any minute, so he went for it, declaring his love to her. "I'm madly in love with you. I need you and want us together forever. I can't live without you. I know you still love me. Our kiss in the park and the look in your eyes right now give you away."

Tears swelled in her eyes and she looked away, dropping her gaze. Watching their feet swaying together, her voice was heavy with emotion. "William, it's for your own good. I can't be with you."

"I'm not letting you make decisions for us all by yourself anymore and you can't change my mind . . . ever, my love. I will never stop loving you and I will never stop fighting for you. He can have me arrested on trumped up charges again, but the second I'm released I will be back begging you to be with me."

Evie looked up at him then over her shoulder and saw Tom having a heated argument with her father, who was holding him in place. She made brief eye contact with *him* and that seemed to be the final straw. "Everleigh!" Jerking his arm from Richard's grip, he marched over to a group of his friends—he was rallying the troops.

When she turned back to William, his face held all the love and passion she never dreamed could be for her and she couldn't take her eyes off him again. She was lost in his world, wanting and hoping to stay there, to live inside their bubble forever. But a small crowd being herded away from them caught her attention, and she saw Audrey and the other dancers moving off the dance floor.

"Come away with me, Evie. Please. I promise to love and respect you, care for you, and cherish every day we spend together." William glanced over her shoulder, seeing the chaos in the distance beginning to build. He spun her around as they continued to dance. Pulling her closer, protecting her in his arms, he looked into her eyes. "Baby, I love you with all my soul. Please come with me. We've got about ten seconds before I get taken down by." He looked around one last time before meeting her eyes again. "Hate to rush your decision, but—"

"Yes."

"Yes?" He couldn't hide his surprise.

An audible sigh was heard louder than the ending of the song. This wasn't about pleasing the crowd though. This was about winning the heart of the girl of his dreams, but the crowd's support was nice.

"We need to go," she said, seeing Tom working through the tables toward her. Gripping his hand tighter, she started running, William right there with her, matching her pace.

Tom screamed over the last note of the song. "Everleigh! Stop right now!"

Evie didn't turn back. She wouldn't. She had to move forward with William. There was no turning back now. This was it. William was it. Her future and the life she was always meant to lead would begin now. She had no regrets as she ran away right in front of her family, her friends, and her fiancé.

William let the borrowed jacket slide down his arms as they ran. He shoved the doors open to the lobby where both Audrey and Dallas were waiting for them. William tossed the jacket back to Audrey at the same time Dallas directed them. "Take the stairs up to the roof. We'll lead them down. Give them a few minutes then sneak out through the kitchen."

William was jerked to a halt as Evie came to a complete stop. When he turned back, he searched her face for any doubts she might be having.

Dallas slammed the doors shut and leaned against it with all of his weight.

"This," she said, "I need to get this shackle off my finger." She was confident in her decision as she slipped the ring off and handed it to Audrey, once and forever. "Donate this to the women's shelter anonymously. Don't let Tom see you. It's worth a fortune and should raise a lot of money for the charity."

Audrey's eyes lit up in delight. "It will be my pleasure to get rid of this thing. Now go."

"I love you," Evie said as the couple ran for the stairwell.

William shouted to Dallas when he opened the door into the stairwell. "Stall and distract!"

"I've got this, bro. Go!"

As soon as William and Evie were safely up one flight of stairs, William stopped and asked, "Need a lift?" He pointed at the very high-heeled and sexy shoes she was wearing.

"Hold my hand, and let's go for it. Only two more flights," she said. Reaching the rooftop, they rushed behind a large air conditioning unit that blocked them from view of the doorway.

Both of them panted heavily, trying to catch their breath. Facing each other and then smiling, they laughed. It felt good to laugh, so carefree and their souls bonded together again.

Evie wrapped her arms around his neck. "I love you, William Ryder. I never want to be away from you again."

"You'll never have to be."

She leaned back, needing to look at his face, still feeling this was too surreal to be happening. "I was doing it for you. Always for you. I'm afraid of what he'd do—"

"He can't touch us, my love."

"He said he'd keep you from graduating and he'd ruin your reputation in New York so you can't find a job. I had to stay with him. You've worked too hard to have me destroy it. I couldn't live with myself if he hurt you in any way."

"You were willing to marry a psycho to help me?" He cupped her face. "Evie, beautiful Evie, you can't ruin my future. You only make my future brighter. You should have never even considered ruining yours over some false sense of saving me."

"It wasn't false—"

His hands slid down her neck and stopped on her shoulders where he grasped her gently. "Evie! Listen to me. I've already graduated. My degree was signed two weeks ago by Professor Lang. I'm done with school. And I have a job lined up already. So stop worrying about me and let's figure out how to get off this roof." They walked to the edge and looked over the short barrier wall down to the sidewalk. They could see people rushing back and forth below and they turned and smiled at each other.

But then they heard *him* and that wiped the grins right off their face.

"Everleigh? Everleigh!"

Tom.

She moved away from the edge, afraid he might see her. Her hands started to shake, and William could see the fear start to overwhelm her.

With one last glance down, he saw Tom searching frantically for Evie. William backed away and faced her straight on, grabbing her arms, and making her look at him. "He can't hurt me and I won't let him hurt you. I promise. We're going to be okay. I'll take care of you."

Echoes of Tom's calls for her return filled the air and they embraced. Exhaling, she closed her eyes before looking back up into William's, her voice just a whisper. "I love you. He can't hurt us. He can't hurt us." It was as if Evie was reminding herself instead of repeating the last part for William.

"I love you, and no, he can't hurt us." William watched her, waiting for his words to sink in.

Her expression softened in relief and she took a deep breath, and slowly exhaled. "Never again."

William smiled. "Never again."

She nodded as he pulled her to his chest again.

It became eerily quiet, the standard city noises replacing the calls for Evie and it alarmed William for a second, knowing Tom and his gang would start searching the hotel. "I think we should go now. We'll take the elevator because I'm thinking they'll try the stairwell this time."

Evie stopped him right before he walked into the stairwell that would lead them to the bank of elevators on the top floor. "Are you sure I'm worth the trouble?"

William squeezed her hand and flashed his most charming, irresistible smile. "All this trouble and more, baby. C'mon, let's go home."

Evie loved the sound of the word "home" when William said it. It conjured up thoughts of safety and love, happiness, and passion. Hope.

Chapter 29

Evie entered William's apartment unsure of how she would feel. He shut the door, but remained near it watching her, letting her take her time.

She smiled, feeling calm which was a feeling she had come to appreciate since she hadn't felt it since the last time she was here. "I missed this place," she said, glancing at him behind her. As she got more comfortable by stealing one of his T-shirts out of the small dresser, he let out a long pent-up breath, finally relaxing.

The plan had worked. His plan to win her back, the love of his existence, worked and she was here with him.

Kicking off her shoes, she then went into the bathroom. Her stuff, the stuff she bought from a drugstore the last time she had escaped, was still here—almost like it was waiting for her. She brushed her teeth and went back into the main room holding her evening dress in her hand while wearing just his T-shirt. She took a hanger from the closet and hung it up by hooking it onto the door frame. It would never fit inside of his tiny closet. "My stuff is still here. You kept it just how I left it."

He sat at the desk and she joined him, feeling at

home on his lap, and running her fingers through his hair.

"I hoped you'd be back," he said with sincerity, wrapping his arms around her hips and resting his head on her shoulder.

She kissed the top of his head, catching sight of the cup of highlighters, which made her laugh. "I really did miss this place." He stood, letting his body slide up the front of hers as she added, "I missed you most of all."

They kissed, both knowing it would be more than kissing this time.

William pulled back, his breathing heavy, wanting Evie so much, but he knew he had to stop. "I need a shower. I worked eleven hours today."

She wrapped her arms around his middle and held him. "I like your smell. You smell so . . . manly." He wasn't doused in expensive colognes, and she wasn't going to hide her feelings anymore and with him, she didn't have to. They had made their decision to be with each other and nothing would change her mind now. "I think you smell," she said, lowering her voice to a whisper, "sexy."

He smiled because he knew she was probably blushing. He didn't want to embarrass her though, but also didn't want to be with her when he was this dirty. "I smell sweaty and gross. Make yourself at home. I'll only be a few minutes." He walked into the bathroom leaving her there, leaving her smiling like the girl in love that she was.

When he returned to the living room, freshly showered and wearing only a pair of boxers, the television was on and Evie was curled up on the bed. She sat up, patted the space next to her, and smiled. "I could sleep forever. It's so comfortable. It may sound weird, but I missed this bed."

William laughed because she kept naming everything she missed about his place and him, but it also made him feel good inside.

She had clicked the television off, and he had left the tiny lamp in the corner on for a soft glow.

She was now sprawled across his bed, owning it, relishing the feel of it. "You came for me tonight. You fought for me."

He cocked his head to the side. "Yes, anything for you."

He didn't bother with a shirt and they both slid under the covers, resting their heads on the pillow together. Their smiles morphed into a more intense connection.

Evie looked down, running her hand languidly across his bare chest and her lips parted allowing her to take a deeper breath. William took the opportunity and moved closer wanting more contact, wanting to feel her body fully against his. They kissed, reacquainting themselves in a gentle way. After a while, he leaned over, moving more on top of her. His hand dragged her shirt up and his fingertips traced over her stomach. He wanted to take things slow and appreciate her entire body, but he also wanted her so much that he struggled to find a balance between respectful and pleasing for them both. He slid his finger down the outside of one thigh before sliding up the inside of her other, touching her smooth skin. Her breath caught as she succumbed to her own feelings and to pleasure for the first time in years.

"William," she said more breathy than she liked, slightly embarrassed, but releasing that feeling because it felt so good. *His hands on her felt so good.*

They continued kissing, deepening it even more as his hips shifted, pressing harder against her leg and showing her how she made him feel, how she worked him up.

William's mind was focused. Nothing in the world existed except Evie right then. His mind was filled with her, his ears tuned into her small, alluring moans, his body loving her touch against his, and the smell of her skin with a hint of wildflowers enveloping him. There was a hint of mint and champagne on her breath as he breathed her in, and when he opened his eyes to make sure she was really there, he lost himself even more into the bliss of Evie beneath him.

"Evie." He moaned into her mouth as they both shifted. Pulling back enough to see her face, he looked into her eyes. "Are you sure about this?"

"Mm-hmm. I want to be with you. So much."

She had said she wanted to be with him, but he still wanted to be careful. He knew the monster never had been.

She sat up and took her shirt off then reached for her panties, slowly pulling them down. Evie's heart raced, hoping he liked her body, her shape, *all of her*.

William's breath shortened as he watched her remove her clothes for him, showing him how much she also wanted this.

He showed her by taking off his boxer shorts and climbing back into bed. As she looked him over, her hand slid down from his shoulder to his chest, lower to his stomach, and then stopped. Her eyes were on his erection and then her fingertips. She was being so careful he barely felt her touch as she dragged the tips down and around him making him twitch.

William sat up. "Lay down." She did, but wrapped her hand around his hardness and began to move slowly.

"God, that feels good."

Evie wanted to please him. His pleasure meant everything to her. She leaned closer to his ear as he lay next to her with his eyes closed, and said, "Tell me if I'm doing it wrong."

William's eyes popped open and he shook his head in disbelief. "Wrong? Baby, it feels so right." She smiled and tightened her grip, moving a little faster. "But you've got to slow down or this will be over too fast and I want to make you feel good, too." It was a half plea on his part.

She looked at him, her eyes meeting his. They didn't need any more words. They moved where their bodies wanted until William was positioned between her legs.

With his arms straight, he was above her, admiring every line and curve of her body. She was more stunning than his mind had imagined before. And as his eyes made their way from hers down to her breasts and lower, he saw she had stopped breathing. He whispered, "It's all right. We're not in a hurry. I'll go slow."

She nodded and then a small smile played on her lips because she was about to make love to the man of her dreams. But she sensed a hesitancy just as his body touched her down there.

He pushed back up. "I need to get a condom. They're in the bathroom."

Evie felt like she had to say something to justify her hesitation. "I don't want you to, but..." She closed her eyes feeling ashamed. Tom made her feel that way. Being with Tom made her ashamed she ever allowed him to touch her in the first place. "We should . . ." She couldn't finish, the words lumped in her throat. She turned her head not able to face him, wanting to hide her dishonorable tears from him.

William refused to let her feel guilty. She had nothing to be ashamed of, and it ripped his heart out to see her feeling like she betrayed him in some way. Resting his body on hers, he touched her cheeks with his hands. "Evie, look at me." He waited for her to look before he continued. "I love you. We're together now. The past doesn't matter. No one else matters. No apologies are needed. No shame is allowed. The past is in the past. Right here, right now is all that matters. Okay?"

She nodded. The tears that had already fallen were the only ones that would be shed between them.

William kissed her then went to the bathroom to retrieve the condoms.

Evie steeled herself in the short time he was gone. *He was right, damn it!* She did nothing wrong and the past was in the past.

When he returned, he climbed back under the covers and they kissed. She kept kissing him while she got on top of him, positioning him right where she wanted to feel him. They both moaned into each other's mouth and his hands held onto her waist keeping her where she was as she started rocking.

He was solid beneath her mini gyrations and she pulled back from his mouth, taking the condom in her hands. William watched with rapt attention as she rolled it down his length. "I want you on top," she whispered, looking down at him.

They rolled together, his fingers making their way up the inside of her thigh. He paused to press his forehead to hers before proceeding. Feeling her chest heavy against his, he took a deliberate and necessary breath, but she still gasped when he touched her so intimately.

William was surprised to feel how ready she was for

him. He debated if any more foreplay was even wanted on either part.

"William?" She said his name as a question, but it was clear they both had already decided.

He positioned himself once again between her legs and pushed gently, not going any further . . . yet. Evie's hands found his shoulders and she wiggled, causing him to enter her. Taking her cue, he pushed forward, her warmth enveloping him. William dropped his head to the pillow beneath hers, and he moaned in pleasure. "Mmmm, Baby."

Her lips found his jaw and worked her way to the soft skin around his ear. She kissed and licked and nipped at him, loving the feel of him as he reached her depths over and again.

William stopped moving, enjoying her sensations, but needing a moment to get back in control.

Noticing his face flickering between pleasure and pain, she asked, "Are you all right?"

Leaning up, he kissed her. "I'm better than all right. I'm perfect," he said, his eyes hooded with desire.

"I need you to move then." She tried to restrain the begging in her tone, but she was ready for more.

She felt him take a long breath and exhale before he began deep, slow strokes. Yes, that was what she needed and what she wanted.

Their staggered breaths became pants, which became moans turning quickly into wanton gasps as he moved, giving her what she craved, and he dreamed about. Each motion pushed them closer to their bliss. Just when she thought she couldn't handle much more of the intensity from their connection, his fingers slid between her legs, touching her how she needed it most, and she jolted in response. He slowed his pace, focusing his attention on her.

It didn't take long. She was flooded with long desired yearnings for him that her body gave into, making his own desires release. He was right there with her, chanting her name and praising her body as he did.

An hour later, they lay naked and snuggled together on the twin bed. Evie was relaxed, feeling happier than she could remember feeling in years. That was until fear gripped her as she remembered something Tom had said to her once about "having information." Her heart started racing, and she panicked. "He knows where you live!"

William lazily opened his eyes. "Doesn't matter. Let him come here. He'll never touch you again. If I have my way, he'll never talk to you again either." She was surprised at how calm the words were spoken, but laced with hatred. She hoped it would never come to that either. "Besides, if he was coming over tonight, he'd be here already." He rubbed down her hair and across her chin, stopping on her shoulder. "Sleep, my sweet girl."

She *was* his—heart and soul—and she loved this knowledge. He made her feel smart and pretty, hopeful and sexy all at once and ridiculously happy.

Chapter 30

Evie woke up when her stomach growled. Opening her eyes, she found William also waking up. "Hungry?" he asked with a small smile.

"Yes, I guess I am."

"Let's get some breakfast." He moved closer and gave her a sweet, chaste, worried-he-had-morning-breath kiss. William rolled out of bed, naked, and grabbed a pair of jeans, sliding them on without boxers.

She sighed happy and then disappointment set in when he pulled a shirt over his head and further, hiding his body from her.

He smiled when he caught her appreciating him. "You're pretty damn sexy, too, you know?" He arched his eyebrow up and winked at her.

She laughed and got up, not embarrassed at all being naked in front of him. She had never felt more beautiful and confident than she did with him. But she realized she only had her dress from last night to wear. He saw her expression change and wanted her happy again. "The clothes you bought last time you were here are over there in the corner. I'll give you the dresser if you want."

"I don't want to intrude."

"Intrude? I'm hoping you're staying and not just visiting."

"Being here makes me happy." She looked at the clock on the desk, and was shocked. "It's two in the afternoon already? I haven't slept that late in . . . in . . . in years. We must've been tired. Can we even get breakfast now?"

"First off, I haven't slept that well since the last time you were here. Secondly, our..." he cleared his throat, and said, "...activities last night might've compounded the exhaustion. And thirdly, it's Sunday in New York City, of course we can still get breakfast."

They were happy spending their day together, pushing down any thoughts of the people they left behind last night. Although they found it odd that Tom had not shown up, they kept thoughts of her ex to themselves not wanting to ruin the day.

They ate at a local diner then spent the afternoon both reading in the park. They also made out in the park. Since they'd been intimate, it was hard for them to keep their hands off each other, but they were hoping no one noticed.

They made love again Sunday night, a little quicker, a little harder, and a lot more frenzied than the night before. They had become ravenous for each other, so repeated the act in the wee hours of the morning once again. Who needed food when they had each other?

But when Monday rolled around, they had to figure out what they were "officially" doing.

"I'm moving in here," Evie stated, matter-of-fact.

"I hope so. I thought that was already decided." William looked up from the teaching assistant's handbook he had been given by Lang.

"I'm just making sure you're still on board with the idea."

"I want you here with me, Evie." He could sense she wanted to say more, and waited for her to continue in her own time.

"I need to get my stuff from my parent's home."

"You know I still have all of your money. I didn't spend any of it."

She got up from the bed where she had been lounging and smiled while situating herself on his lap. "You could've if you needed it. I hope you know that. I haven't even thought of the money."

"It's yours and yours alone to do with as you please." William didn't ever want money to be an issue between them.

When she stood up, she made an announcement. "Let's go get my stuff."

An hour later, they approached her family's apartment building. They chose to walk and enjoy the weather, which was something she hadn't gotten to do much in recent months. Walter saw them through the glass before they reached the door and raced to hold it open. He shook William's hand and patted him on the back as he passed.

"Yeah, I'm pretty pleased myself," William said, enjoying the support.

Once upstairs, William got nervous standing outside her front door. Walter had told them no one was home, but Evie didn't have a key on her, so they had to wait for someone to answer. Other than the money he saw her get from the bank, William had lived happily oblivious to Evie's wealth, but right then he realized that blissful ignorance was a safer place to be mentally.

A small woman in a maid's uniform answered and greeted Evie then took leave of them. William followed her into the massive apartment and gawked at the views and sheer size of the place.

Sensing his discomfort, Evie took the lead and pulled him by the hand into her bedroom. She shut the door, making sure to lock it, and got to work getting her suitcases out.

He remained standing where she left him in the pale pink room. After scanning the room, he joined her near the closet, leaning against the doorframe and laughing. "My whole apartment fits into your bedroom two times."

She turned to face him, resting her hand on his cheek. "Let's not do the comparison thing. You are all that matters to me."

William was quick to calm, knowing she was all that mattered to him as well. He went and sat on her window seat, waiting for her to gather her stuff. Thoughts of how much she was giving up to be with him hit him full force. Her whole world—a large pink bedroom, a huge walk-in closet, a maid, a chef, amazing city views and more—she was giving it all up to be with him.

He knew she was going into their future together with her eyes wide open and that made him feel invincible.

They took a cab home since she brought two suitcases and two medium-sized boxes from her previous life on the Upper East Side with her. The rest she could live without. She was just excited to start her new life with William. He cleared a space in the corner of the dining area, and together they decided they would work the stuff to its final destination a little at a time.

The new couple was excited to talk about his new job with Professor Lang over a steamy, hot bowl o'noodles that night. They laughed together and spoke about things they looked forward to.

"I'm excited about your graduation dinner," Evie said, tucking her legs under her on the bed.

"I'm excited about graduating." William dropped his head to the pillow and closed his eyes, releasing a sigh of relief.

"I'm proud of you."

He rolled his head to the side and opened his eyes. He could see how much she meant her words. "I'm more proud of you. You've gone through so much and yet, you're still selfless."

"Stop one-upping me." She teased, poking his ribs.

"Here's a one up to one up all one ups." He grabbed her hand and kissed it, pulled her down until she was lying next to him, and cupped her cheek. "I'm proud of you, proud of everything you do, you will do, and who you are, but mainly, I'm the most proud of your inner strength, and I'm in love with you wholly and unconditionally."

She looked away from him, never having anyone say such amazing things to her like that before. Wiping a tear away, she whispers, "Thank you."

They let the depth of the shared words linger between them, the weight of heavier topics needing to be discussed taking over.

He hated the thought of her having to work, but they both agreed it was necessary, especially since his income wouldn't be much more of an increase over his current job. "It sucks, but I can barely pay my bills, Evie."

He wouldn't be able to support two people on it, which normally would hurt his pride, but she was so supportive he felt proud to have the job opportunity.

"It doesn't matter. We'll make it work. I really don't mind," she said, shrugging. "I kind of look forward to it. It'll be a new adventure."

"I'm sorry, but I promise it won't always be like this. Money won't always be so tight."

She rolled over and straddled his lap while wrapping her hands around his neck. One kiss. Two kisses. "I love you, nothing else matters."

Over the next four days, Evie didn't contact her parents. She had spoken to Audrey who said she talked with them, but they were still "trying" to understand what was going on. Audrey told Evie she couldn't hide what Tom had done to her any longer and she would tell them soon. They hadn't listened to Evie when she tried to tell them the same day William was arrested, and didn't think they would listen to Audrey either, but wished her sister luck. Luck was something Evie didn't feel was on her side. She was focusing on more proven methods of destiny, like action.

The rest of William's week was dedicated to working for Manhattan Messengers, and Evie meeting with Lang. She re-enrolled in school under Lang's guidance and encouragement.

As the week went on, she still hadn't heard from

Tom or her parents, which made her nervous. It weighed on her daily, but she tried to hide that when she was around William.

She also went out looking for a job. Although, it seemed like an unlikely place to go, she marched straight into Bean There and applied for one. There was something about the place that called to her, and she felt like that would be a job she could do, especially since she spent so much time in there anyway.

Tracy gave her the courtesy of interviewing her though she gave her a hard time, her expressions showing empathy for her situation. Tracy may have been the one to broach the subject of Evie's engagement with William, but Evie was to blame for not telling him in the first place. She owned up to her lies and decisions.

After a short chat about her past experience which was none and then to personal business to see if they could even work together, Tracy hired her. "I'm going to give you a chance because . . . well, I'm not really sure why. Maybe it's because I've realized everyone has problems and I like the way you're handling yours."

"Thank you. You won't regret it," Evie said, shaking her hand then grabbing her into a hug because she was so excited.

"You can start when school starts. Business picks up then."

"Thank you again." Everleigh jogged out of the shop, anxious to get home to William and share the news, but stopped a few blocks down. She needed to catch her breath before continuing when she was startled, her hand covering her heart as Tom stepped out in front of her from an empty storefront's doorway. "Don't come near me!"

His hands went out in front of him, attempting to

calm her. "Everleigh, I just want to talk to you."

Her body started shaking, fear overwhelming her.

"Sweetheart, I need you. You've had your fun. Come home with me now. I'm better. I'll be better, I promise." Thomas Whitney was begging. He stepped forward, and she stepped back.

"I'm not going back there. I don't care what you do to me. I won't go. I'll fight this time." Her voice betrayed her words. She squeezed her eyes closed trying to gain physical strength just in case she needed it.

"I love you, Everleigh. My life is nothing without you. I can't think. I can't work." His hands went to his hair and he was falling apart in front of her eyes. "I'll lose everything if you leave me."

"I've already left," she stated, feeling stronger. "I don't care if—"

"I won't lose you and I won't lose my company!" His words were baffling. *What did she have to do with his company?* He continued talking, turning back into the possessive, overbearing Tom she knew. "I want you to come with me. I'm asking you. I'm being a gentleman about this. You've embarrassed me, and I think I've been reasonable. You need to be reasonable, too. You can't live like this. What will people think? What will they say? Don't throw everything I care about away on an affair. I'll forgive you. It will take some work on your part to convince me of your re-commitment, but I'm willing to try. Our wedding date is still secure with the deposits we put down. We can move past this."

Evie stood there flabbergasted. "You're insane!"

He slapped her across the face, making her stumble to the side. Through gritted teeth he threatened her. "I said

I'm willing to try and forgive you. Don't turn this ugly. This is your only warning."

She grabbed her face and turned to walk away. She didn't have to listen to him anymore. She wouldn't. She refused to give into him any longer. He would have to kill her first.

He grabbed her arm and twisted it as he pulled her into the doorway. When she started to scream for help, he slapped his other hand over her mouth and whispered in her ear. "You've got one day to return to my apartment. You do not have your parent's home as an option any longer." He pushed her hard against the brick of the building and walked off.

Beyond being stunned by his threat, it amazed her that several people had walked by and no one offered to help her. Was this the reality of the world she lived in?

Tears filled her eyes and streamed down her face as his words sank in. What she hated most was that he didn't tell her what would happen if she didn't. He was unpredictable. Unpredictable meant dangerous. Her hand covered her cheek again. It was still heated from the slap, and she started back to William's feeling that maybe it wasn't going to be her home after all.

Chapter 31

When Evie arrived back at William's apartment, he wasn't home. She splashed cold water over her face and patted it dry with a towel, hoping to erase all traces of Tom in her expression and from her skin. Fortunately, her face had cooled and the slap mark faded.

When she walked out of the bathroom, William was walking in the front door. He smiled at her. "I love coming home to you." She smiled, but it was small compared to the ones he'd grown accustomed to. There was something noticeably different in her eyes, an obvious sadness. "What is it? What's wrong, baby?"

She went to him, both of them wrapping their arms around each other in a full embrace. Tilting her head down, she leaned her cheek against his chest, needing the security his arms offered. "Nothing," she replied, needing more time to process what happened, time to figure out if Tom would follow through with his threat even though deep down she knew he would. It would be best to be honest with William about what happened despite her fears. "That's not true. There is something." His arms rubbed her back as she confessed, "I saw Tom."

His body tensed around her, but he loosened to look her in the eyes. "What happened?"

She didn't want to tell him he hit her, knowing he would go after Tom. That was the last thing she wanted William to do. If he did go after him, he would end up in jail with assault charges against him. Wanting to protect him however she could, she wouldn't put him at risk again. She wanted to keep William as far from Tom as possible.

"Evie, tell me right now." William was demanding. He was also sick to his stomach by the thought of that bastard anywhere near her.

She gulped before she spoke, needing to phrase it the right way. Backing away, she sat on the corner of the bed. He stood where she left him, but crossed his arms over his chest while staring at her, worry eating away inside. "He said he wants me back."

"No shit!" He raised his voice, stressed.

Evie was stunned by his harsh remark. She stood up and walked to the window giving him more space. He needed time and space from her, at least that's how she felt.

"I'm sorry," he said, his voice lower, concerned he upset her as he watched her move away. "I didn't mean—"

"I understand. He worries me, too."

"Please, Evie, tell me what he said to you."

"He said I have one day to be back at his apartment or else."

"Or else what?"

She shrugged, knowing she didn't have the answers they both wanted. "I don't know. He didn't say."

"You're not going back." William looked at the wall closest to him in thought. "You're not going back." He repeated this more for himself than her. "I don't care what he said or what he does. He can come after me. I can handle him, but I don't want you alone anymore. Tomorrow, I want you to come to work with me. You can get a jump on some of your school work."

"William, I won't hide and I would never go back." She rushed to him, placing her hands on his chest. "Never. He would have to take me kicking, screaming, and fighting the whole way because he would never get me willingly."

They locked eyes as she said this, the assumption not far from the truth. William needed to reassure her. He refused to let that monster dictate how they would live their lives by keeping them in fear.

He took her by the arms and though it hurt her from being twisted earlier by Tom, she wouldn't flinch from William's touch as he reassured her. "He will not hurt us. You don't ever have to go back there. Don't ever go back, Evie."

"I won't. I will never leave you."

As he hugged her, she could feel his heart pounding though he tried to sound calm. "I'll figure something out. I need you to be safe. Please be careful. Okay? Promise me you'll be careful and you'll fight if you have to."

"I promise," she said, tears slipping from her eyes. "I promise."

William kissed the top of her head and took a deep breath to calm down. He would spend all night thinking about beautiful Evie and he would try his damnedest to protect her always.

* * *

It was official—William had earned his Bachelor of Arts degree. Even though he had walked with the May class, he now held his diploma and his family wanted to celebrate because they were proud of his accomplishments. Evie and William, his family and best friend, along with Audrey as Dallas' date all celebrated over lasagna at the Ryder residence with a champagne toast and dessert. The Wright sisters felt welcomed and as Evie helped William's mom in the kitchen, his mom stopped twice to hug her. Thanking her for coming over and being there for her son.

This is how family was supposed to be Evie thought more than once that day. She also teased her sister for falling for the Ryder charms.

With only one week before school started back up, William walked Evie to the library then he went to work in Lang's office. They would meet again for lunch most days. They made dinner together in the evenings, and love at night.

The last day in August, school started. Evie stayed tucked against William's side as they went to the university. He walked her to a lecture being held at the library that morning and left his class a few minutes early to meet her before she came out. They danced around the subject of *the monster*, not wanting to give *him* a second more of their time. She attended William's next class, sitting in the back row and studying her own school work.

She enjoyed watching him, but found him distracting. She also noticed he was a big distraction to several of the other female students in the class. She tried not to get upset over his extra attention, but she couldn't help it. She glared at the girls, trying to burn holes into the back of their heads.

Once she even caught William chuckling off to the side of the auditorium after he caught her. While the students worked on developing a theory Lang had proposed, he made his way to the top of the room and slipped Evie a note.

They touched hands as he dropped it on her desk then returned back down to the front and took his seat off to the side. She opened it and smiled when she read it.

No one else. Only you. You're my heart and I'm in love with you, xoxoxo.

She swooned a little as she slumped down in her seat, holding the note to her chest. Glancing up, her eyes met his and they both smiled. He had fallen in crush with her early on in their relationship when they were "just friends." But over the course of getting to know her, he had fallen in love with her. He knew this was the woman he was not only supposed to be with, but would marry one day. She was love in the truest form.

Every night they sat in silence as if waiting for the world to come to an end. It didn't. Nothing happened the first day. They did the same thing the next day and again the following. They didn't know if they should be relieved or nervous. Friday, without a discussion, they went to school together and spent the day within each other's line of sight. Once again, nothing happened.

In bed, William kissed her and brought up the much dreaded topic. "We've got to live life like we always do. If we don't live our lives, he wins."

"I agree," she said, rolling onto her side and snuggling against him.

"Do you think he'll do anything?"

"I don't know. My gut says yes and my head says no. I don't know anymore. I know he considers me his property and he doesn't share his toys."

"Maybe he finally realizes that you don't love him and he's moving on."

She knew he wouldn't move on that easily. He didn't give up, ever, but she hated worrying William more.

The next Monday, Evie started her new job, and by the end of the day she was promoted to barista. Yeah, she would still be mopping the floors and cleaning off tables, but now she also knew how to work the complicated professional coffee machine as well.

By the second week of school, her schedule was class three times a week and working five. She hadn't found her groove yet and yawned when she sat down to lunch with William at a table in front of Bean There. He'd raced over from campus to visit during her break.

"How is your day, my love?" This was always the first thing he asked because he cared about her, but also because he still felt guilty she had to work.

"Great." She sometimes told fibs to make sure he was happy and wouldn't see how tired she really was from being on her feet all day. The stress of Tom's threat also weighed on her, but she tried to hide that from him altogether. She reasoned it was perfectly acceptable for her to work and for the first time in a long time she felt useful. This may be a far cry from her previous life, but she wouldn't trade this life for anything.

"How is your day?" she asked, resting her hand on his leg.

"I have a bunch of students who think they know everything about classic literature." They both laughed at his sarcasm, knowing that was them last semester.

"Give them a chance, maybe you'll learn something." She nudged him with her elbow.

He leaned in and kissed her. "I love you."

"I know you do, but do you know how much I love you?"

"No, please remind me."

Evie looked around, got up and sat on his lap, wrapping her arms around his neck. "I love you endlessly. I love you forever. I love you with all my heart. I love you, William."

They embraced on the sidewalk right there in public outside the little coffee shop where they fell in love. Life was perfect.

During the afternoon, Tracy wiped down the counter and tried to sound nonchalant. "How are you doing with all this change?" Evie looked at her surprised. Tracy blushed for sounding so soft-hearted. "I'm just curious. I know you haven't worked before and I'm sorry."

"Sorry for what?" Evie stopped with the mop in hand.

"For ruining things for you."

Evie smiled. She had felt Tracy was a good person deep down and now she had proven it by apologizing. "You didn't ruin anything. I did. I should have told him. I was caught up. I appreciate it though. I'm fine now and I never minded working hard. I was busy volunteering with a few charities I supported and hope one day I can get back to that in the future, but for now, I need to concentrate on school and paying bills." Paying bills sounded foreign to Evie when she said it. Her life had changed so much over the last couple of weeks, and yet she knew it was all for the better.

When Evie got home, William was already there. She

liked how affectionate he was, greeting her with a hug. "Good day?" he asked, his nose buried in her hair.

She smiled, nuzzling back. "Better now."

They ate dinner, snuggled, and talked before falling asleep all wrapped up in each other.

Chapter 32

William arrived home just after four in the afternoon. Evie wasn't due back for hours, so he pulled out his papers to grade when someone knocked on the door.

When he answered it, he was met with a very unhappy Richard Wright. "Mr. Ryder." His greeting was formal.

William took a breath. "Mr. Wright, come in," he said, waving his arm like he was gesturing to royalty to enter his small abode. The sarcastic gesture was not lost on Richard. "Your daughter is not home as you can see."

Richard critiqued the small studio apartment then turned to William. "I'm here to see you. I'm well aware that Everleigh is working." His tone was clipped and the words stung of distaste.

William took another deep breath then sighed as he exhaled. He didn't like the surprise visit although he couldn't think of a time that would be better. "I expected you sooner. It's been over a month since she left."

"I was waiting to see how this," he said, referencing the apartment, "this played out—"

"You were waiting to see if she would leave me and come home to you."

"Yes, I expected her home by now. She's been raised in a very privileged lifestyle, including having money at her disposal." A little stab toward William, but he could handle it and listened as Richard continued. "She's never been concerned about necessities, but now, now by looking at this place and discovering she has to work to survive, it makes me question why she's still here. You're not able to provide for my daughter. Her own life is now full of challenges and obstacles. The exact things I've worked hard to insure her life wouldn't have. And yet . . . and yet, here you are, bringing her down to live in rubble, Mr. Ryder."

"She's happy here. I know it's hard for you to understand, but she likes it here."

"She likes having a bed that doubles as a couch?" he asked, picking up a bowl o'noodles container. "She likes eating garbage for dinner. She was raised on the cooking of French-trained chefs and maids and shopping. The girl is going through a phase. You are a phase, Mr. Ryder. She'll soon realize how much she misses her old life and what luxuries that life provides."

William walked to the dining area, picked up a bottle of whiskey and two plastic cups, and poured two shots. He handed one to Richard then sipped his before speaking. "Let me ask you this. When she remembers how she woke up all alone and covered in blood on her bathroom floor, do you think she misses that life?"

"Mr. Ryder, you're out of line—"

"Oh, you don't want to answer that one? How about you ask yourself this, then? Do you hate your daughter so much, that even after knowing the truth, you continued to encourage her to go back to a man that had beaten her for years right under your own roof, right under your own

340

nose?"

"I wouldn't allow her to be with Tom Whitney again even if she begged me. I didn't know about that until recently. But, she'll miss—"

"She'll miss what? Because from where I'm standing, you're as bad as him. You buried your head in the Hamptons' sand to avoid the reality that you were trading your daughter for a bigger piece of the pie." William downed the rest of his whiskey and slammed the cup on the table not looking at Evie's father. His rage was starting to get away from him, and he never wanted to be the cause of Evie losing her family. He would not be the one to cause her any more pain than she had already endured.

"It's easy to stand in your shoes when there's nothing to lose, Mr. Ryder. I love my wife and would never want anything bad to happen to her either. I suppose you feel strongly for my daughter, but will she always feel as strongly about you when you are struggling to get by? How will you support her?"

"I will do everything I can for her, but she wants independence as well. She wants to work after graduation. She wants to do a lot of stuff with her life, and I'll be there supporting her instead of suppressing her." He looked her father straight in the eyes and lowered his voice, deep and confident. "I'll take whatever part of her life she's willing to share with me because I love her that much. And if . . . if she decides she needs or wants her old life and to move back in with you, I'll support her decision on that, too. But until that day, I will cherish every second I get the honor of spending with her." William smirked. "I have to warn you, though. I'm not going away anytime soon. I'd like her to be on good terms with your family. I think family's important, but your fate rests in Evie's hands, not mine."

"That's a good point you've brought up. Family. Your

parents have been married twenty-six years. Your dad has had the same blue-collar job for the entire time. Yes, he's moved up in the ranks, but his pay is still measly—"

"He makes a good living, and he has a family that loves and respects him. Don't drag my family into this." It pissed William off that he had dug up information on his family.

"I want to make sure if Evie chooses . . ." He stopped to signal around the room again, "...this, that she'll be taken care of."

"She's my top priority. I can't guarantee her millions, or that I'll be rich at all, but I can guarantee her she will never feel a lack of love from me and after that bastard is dealt with, she'll never live in fear again." William took a defensive stance and crossed his arms, standing and waiting for what Richard would throw at him next.

Something turned in that instant. The tone of the conversation changed. Richard Wright's expression changed almost as if he believed William.

Opening his wallet, Richard pulled two one-hundred dollar bills out and set them on the desk. "My daughter apparently loves you, my other daughter raves you're a good person, my wife misses her daughter, and she wants us to make amends. So I'm here. William, I hope it's all right if I call you that?" He offered his hand. As William hesitantly shook it, Richard added, "I needed to see her living arrangements with my own eyes. I'm not thrilled with this set up, but my daughter seems to be and I care about her despite what you choose to believe." He took a breath as regret colored his expression. "I don't apologize for my actions or decisions. I never have, which is why I've been successful, but I didn't believe my daughters. I took Mr. Whitney's word over my own children and not only did they have to pay the price, especially Everleigh, but now I am.

342

I've lost her trust." Richard gulped. "So to repair my relationship with her, I will apologize to her and I want you to know that Mr. Whitney won't come near her again."

"How can you promise that? I've been by her side as much as possible and I can't promise that. She lives in fear of him. He threatened to take her if she didn't come back."

"I'm handling Mr. Whitney. That's all you need to know."

Richard Wright's words sounded so final, that for a brief second an image of that bastard with cement blocks being dumped into the Hudson came to William's mind.

"Please stay true to your word and take care of Everleigh." Richard pointed to the money on the desk. "And take her out for a decent meal."

William nodded and opened the door for him. Her father stopped just outside the door. "Everleigh knows where to find me if she ever needs, well, if she ever needs anything. Thank you for your time."

* * *

Lying on the bed holding a plastic cup on his chest, William watched as Evie came through the front door an hour later. Their eyes met, and she instantly knew something was wrong. He didn't greet her as he normally did or even say hello, so she set her purse down and noticed the whiskey bottle on the floor next to the bed. She couldn't gauge his mood and his silence made her nervous. She walked to the bed and sat down next to him. Holding the cup to her nose to verify its contents, she asked. "Are we celebrating?"

He took the cup from her and emptied the remaining drops into his mouth. Looking around the room, she searched for clues, hesitant to ask straight out what was wrong. She saw two one-hundred dollar bills on the desk, which was odd and stood out. Directing her eyes to his face, she pushed the hair off his forehead. "You want to talk about it?"

"I need to know if something bad happens—"

"We'll handle it together."

"If something happens to me, you won't go back to him. I could never rest in peace if you went back to him. I'm sorry I can't give you more and I don't have a bigger apartment with a proper sized bed in it, and you have to eat apples instead of tartlets and other fancy French foods."

Evie's mouth dropped open as she realized the base of all of William's fears. *Rest in peace? Back to Tom?* "I would never go back to him, ever, William. I don't need anything else. Only you. I love this twin bed and now wonder how I slept in a queen all alone for so many years. This place is my home. It's what I picture when I think of the word home. And, did you ever think that maybe I like noodles and fruit?"

"I don't want to be a phase. I don't want to be a novelty."

She stopped breathing while he spoke, but through her own pain she could clearly see his. With a need and no thought behind hit, she straddled his lap, wrapping her arms around his neck and leaning her forehead against his. She whispered, "Where did this come from?" She sighed. "I love you, William. You are not a phase. You are my life. Don't ever cheapen my feelings for you."

He took her face in his hands and kissed her. Their eyes watered as their lips parted. "I will love you, forever, Evie. I will do my best to make our life together happy."

"I know you will," she said without hesitation. They kissed again. "I will too," she quickly added, but then rested her head on his chest, so he couldn't see her face.

"I know it's hard for you sometimes, maybe all the time to open up, but I need you to open up for me." He stroked her cheek with his hand. "I need to know what you're thinking, how you feel."

When she lifted her head, a tear slid down her cheek. "I've been locked inside myself for years. I don't mean to keep anything from you. I try to show you when the words don't come. I don't want to lose you. I'm scared I will."

"You won't lose me. Trust me, Evie. Please trust me."

"I do, or I wouldn't be here. I'm here because I want to be, because I want to be with you." Feeling the weight of the scales of her heart tipping to the side of love, she chose to love him openly and freely, to trust him and to not keep anymore secrets. She kissed his lips, soft and gentle, a promise to trust in him and their love. "So why are you drinking?"

Now it was William's turn to look away, his gaze distant. "Your dad showed up."

She sat upright, still straddling him, but staring down at him.

He sat up with his hands on her hips as if she would fly away at what he had to say. "He stopped by to talk to me. You know, 'a protective father making sure his eldest daughter is being looked after properly' kind of check-up."

"He called you a phase, didn't he?" She gulped, glancing over at the money.

"He was surprised you hadn't moved back home yet, if that's what you mean."

"I am home. As long as I'm with you, I'm home. Don't—"

345

"He knows you're working."

"Don't let him ever make you doubt what we have together—"

"I don't."

"Ever, William! Don't let them taint us. Don't let them ruin us."

He cocked an eyebrow up at her and smirked. He loved when she got feisty and it reassured his soul to witness her strength and passion about them. To spite all odds against them, he had no more doubts. "I won't. Never."

Like every night they fell asleep together, they were wrapped up in each other—solid in love and content in happiness.

The next morning after saying good-bye, they went their separate directions—William went to the university and Evie went to work her shift at Bean There. At two o'clock, the bell chimed on the coffee shop door causing Evie to look up to see her mother walking through the doorway. Her parents had been on her mind ever since William mentioned them last night, but she didn't expect a visit. She smiled, deep down happy to see her.

Her mother looked so excited to see Everleigh, but nervous to approach.

Tracy could see the resemblance and felt the instant awkwardness between them. "Take fifteen if you want."

Evie took off her apron and went to her mom, glad she was there, and took her by the hand to lead her to a table outside.

"Hello, I've missed you," Kitty Wright said in a soft and loving tone as they sat down.

Although Evie was glad to see her, the pain she held inside bubbled to the surface. "I want to tell you I've missed you, but you weren't involved in my life enough before to be missed."

Kitty could see the anger in her daughter's eyes. "Everleigh, I came to apologize to you."

"I don't need your apology." She leaned across the table and looked her straight in the eyes. "You don't get to choose when we make up or even if we do. I do. That's my choice. I make my decisions now."

The pain of Everleigh's tone flashed across her mother's face. She looked down at her purse in her lap and then back up. "I deserve everything you're saying to me and worse. I . . . I didn't know and I know that's not an excu—"

"No, it's not. I tried to tell you and Dad, and I was dismissed as if I was insignificant to you. I pleaded to you that day on campus to listen to me."

"We weren't disregarding you. We were caught up in—"

"Honestly, Mother, I don't give a damn what you were caught in."

Her mother stood up. "Maybe I shouldn't have come. Audrey warned me you might be hostile."

"Hostile? This is hostile? I'm sorry if you're uncomfortable hearing the truth. That truth is my reality and I was uncomfortable living it. This was my life that you, Dad, and Tom were destroying. You all made me believe I owed you something, like my happiness wasn't worth as much as money or your happiness."

Kitty sat back down, listening to her daughter. When Evie looked at her for answers, her mom said, "Audrey told us everything Tom did to you. We don't deserve your trust or your forgiveness, although, I'd be lying if I said I didn't want it."

Evie wasn't open-minded to her parents, it felt too soon for that, but she wasn't closed-hearted either. She dropped her head into her hands and closed her eyes. After a long, deep breath she exhaled, and looked up. "I don't know if I can forgive you for what you put me through. You hurt me when you took his side over mine."

Her mother reached across the table and placed her hand on top of Evie's. "I understand. We failed you in many ways. I'm sorry. If I knew . . ." Kitty started crying. She couldn't face her daughter, her shame overwhelming her delicate features. "I'm so sorry, Everleigh." She stood up abruptly and dabbed at the corner of her eyes with her knuckles. Her daughter had been through hell and no amount of apologies would change that. "I'll do whatever it takes to have you in my life again and I'll be a better mother because you deserve one. You were always a beautiful light in my eyes that we somehow managed to dim by surrounding you with darkness. I'm truly sorry. I should go. I know your break is almost over."

Evie stood up not knowing what to do, or think, or say. The feelings and words she had wanted to share with her mother for so long came rushing out. "I'm in love with William. One day, I'm going to marry him. He makes me that happy."

An inkling of hope bloomed, and Kitty smiled, trying to be there for her daughter now. "Tell me more about him. Tell me about your William."

Evie looked out at the street then back again. "I love him. I know he's the one I'm supposed to be with."

"Would you consider bringing him to dinner? Maybe Sunday. We would like to get to know him better."

Evie looked at the sincerity in her mother's eyes, and replied, "I'll ask him."

Her mother glanced at her watch, looking disappointed. "Your fifteen minutes is up, but I need you to know our home is always your home and you're both welcome there anytime, Everleigh."

Evie was sad they didn't get to discuss more due to the time restraints. "Thank you." She grabbed her mother and pulled her into a tight embrace. "We'll be there for dinner. Thank you."

Kitty Wright cried, but spoke through her tears. "I apologize we didn't help you when you needed us. I'm so very sorry, Everleigh."

They hugged one more time while professing their apologies and love for each other. When Evie returned to work, she smiled, feeling like she finally had the support she always craved from her family.

Chapter 33

Evie and William walked hand-in-hand into the lobby of her parents building fifteen minutes earlier than they were expected for dinner.

Walter smiled while holding the door wide open for the young couple. "It's a pleasure to see you both again."

"Thank you," she said, feeling sentimental in his presence. She released William and grabbed the doorman into a tight hug. "Thank you so much."

"I'm just an old softie." He embraced her back. "Don't get me started."

She let him go and laughed as a tear slipped down her cheek. William handed her a tissue he took from the table in the lobby. With an arm around her shoulders, he said, "She's been a bit emotional all day. It's a big deal for us to be here."

"William, I'm glad to see you again and not sneaking around like before, walking in escorting Miss Wright the proper way." Walter was teasing William, but the message was clear.

The two men shook hands, and William said, "She's right. We have a lot to thank you for. You're a good man, Walter."

"No thanks necessary." Walter pushed the elevator button for them and smiled. "You take care of her, all right?"

"It'll be my pleasure."

Four minutes later, William was starting to sweat as they stood outside the Wright's residence. He gulped and ran his hand through his hair.

"It's all good now. No worries. Okay, baby," Evie whispered while squeezing his hand in reassurance.

The door opened, and it was Evie's father. Her mouth dropped open in surprise as he greeted them warmly, shaking William's hands, and hugging his daughter. "You answered the door?" she asked as he held her.

"I was excited to see you." When they separated, he looked Evie over. "You look well. Life is good?"

Evie hadn't seen her father like this in years. He was smiling and actually looked younger to her with his happy expression.

Evie turned, her guard not down all the way and took William by the hand again, pulling him to her. "Life is very good. Thank you."

"Well, come in. Come in." Richard stepped to the side to let them enter the apartment. "I don't know what's keeping your mother. Maybe you can check on her. William and I can have a drink and a chat."

Evie looked at William, silently checking to make sure he would be all right. He nodded and she kissed him on the lips then disappeared down the hall, leaving the two men alone.

Richard walked over to the antique cherry buffet table by the window and turned over two crystal glasses. He held up a decanter. "Whiskey, right?"

"Nothing too fancy. The Tennessee kind is good with me."

Richard chuckled under his breath as he poured the two drinks. William may not have much money, but he had pride and that was currently on full display. Richard handed him a glass and said a toast. "To Everleigh."

"To Evie." William challenged with a smile.

Richard grinned while looking at his drink then looked back up at the young man in front of him. "Tell me how she's really doing, please."

"Her life has changed a lot, but she's happy."

"She looks happy. I can see it in her eyes. It's as if there's life back in them. It's nice to see the change."

William took another swig of his drink, choosing not to say anything and let Richard lead the conversation.

"It's ironic that as a parent you think you're doing things the best you can. Come to find out that you suck as a parent. This whole situation has been a real eye-opener." Richard sat down in one of the wingback chairs, his face taking on a more somber expression. "I can already tell you're a better man than I ever was. What you've done for my daughter, for my family, it's more than most would do. I didn't even know she had a friend at school and come to find out her deceiving us and Tom would be the very thing that saved her life."

"She would have left him on her own. She was going

to. Evie's stronger than you give her credit for. She survived."

"Yes, I'm slowly finding out more details of what she was living through because of us. I thought that union would solidify our family and get the Wright name the respect it deserves. I put a heavy burden on her at a young age, but I was blinded by so many things at the expense of Everleigh." He huffed as if he was annoyed. "I'm trying to say thank you and apologize. I'm not good with either, I guess."

William leaned forward, resting his forearms on his knees. "I appreciate that, but as I said last week, you owe her the apologies, not me."

Richard sat back and finished his drink. "Tom is going to be arrested. My contact will call me with the details."

William lowered his hand just before taking a drink. "What?"

"I made a large purchase a few weeks ago. I bought the company right out from under him. My accountants found some discrepancies in the books after the buyout." Richard's voice was low, but firm and tinged with anger.

William stared at him, waiting for more.

"There was a board meeting four weeks ago and the members were not happy with his leadership. Because of Tom's lack of attention to the details, the company was threatened by a takeover. I'm convinced the timing of it is not a coincidence. The fundraiser was just days earlier. From my understanding though, he hadn't taken an active role for a while."

"It must have been hard for him to squeeze work in when he was so busy trying to destroy lives," William said, sarcastically.

"I wish I could say it was sweet revenge, but it's bittersweet. It's another example of how much he was fixated on my daughter in such a negative way. I'm going to make it up to her. I promise I will."

Evie and her mother walked into the living room holding hands and smiling. William stood up to greet them. Evie kissed him on the cheek, not afraid to hide her affections for him then joined her father. William sat on the couch just as Audrey entered the room. She made a beeline for William, sitting down next to him on the couch. "Hi, it's been a while. How are you?" he asked.

"Your brother has me all twisty-turny inside. He really has no right to be that cute. It's damn near impossible to even look at him, much less talk to him. He's too distracting in all the right ways with those great eyes and—"

"Yeah, I get it. No need to go into detail."

They laughed.

Flopping back dramatically on the couch, she said, "We've decided to go to your alma mater next year."

"Oh, really?"

"Yeah, Dallas said he still wanted to get your advice to make sure it's the right choice, but I think he just wants your approval." She laughed.

"He's got it. He's a good guy."

"The best. From what I've seen, he takes after his big brother." She smiled at William as she stood up. "Well, not that it matters, but I approve of you for my sis."

He stood up and squeezed her shoulder. "Thanks,"

he said, "That means a lot to me."

"What you did for my family means a lot to me."

He thought she was great for his brother. They were sharing a laugh when Kitty approached. "Hello, William."

"Hello, Mrs. Wright."

"Kitty, please."

"All right."

"Will you join me at the window? I'd like to have a quick chat."

"Yes, ma'am." His stomach turned as he joined her across the room, wondering what she wanted to talk about.

Audrey left the room as her father came in and led Evie out.

Kitty stared forward, her eyes fixed in the distance. With an abrupt nod down, she got choked up. "I want to thank you, but my words will never be enough."

As much as William wanted to help her out, he also knew she needed to say these things, not for him, but for her, so he remained quiet.

"Everleigh was a lively child. Vivacious and beautiful. Why did I not notice the life being sucked out of her?" She turned to look at William, tears in her eyes, shame on her face. "I've apologized to Everleigh, but she'll never understand the depth of the guilt I'll carry for sitting by while my daughter was abused by someone I thought was good for her."

"He deceived all of you. He was lying to you. You can't blame yourself for being manipulated."

"But all else I can. You saw what we didn't. You did what we should have been doing. As much as I will spend my life apologizing to Everleigh, I'll spend the same amount of time being grateful to you. Thank you for everything you did for her. Thank you for taking care of her when we didn't and for loving her." A small smile appeared. "She told me she loves you. She blurted it out like she couldn't contain the emotion. It was wonderful to see this vivacious side of her again."

"She's a remarkable woman."

"And you're a remarkable man. Thank you, William."

"You're welcome. Kitty, I think everyone can heal from this. I believe Evie will heal and that's the most important thing to me. "

"She's lucky to have you."

"I'm the lucky one."

They continued chatting, changing topics to the family photos on the bookshelves.

Richard led Evie into the dining room, and in his own distinct way, he apologized to her. It was roundabout and he got off track several times, but he finally ended up where he should and said the words she knew he struggled to say. "I'm sorry for not being the father you deserved."

She wasn't prepared for all the emotions overwhelming her and this was almost too much. Her happiness overcame her, and she broke down. Her father took her in his arms and held her, comforted her, and loved her. For the first time since she was seventeen, she was whole again.

Kitty had surprised her family with a home-cooked

357

meal. She had never cooked an entire meal and was quite proud of her creation. It was tuna casserole. The family didn't even know what that was, but William was excited. He loved tuna casserole. After a few unsavory bites, the group looked at their plates and set their forks politely down. No one wanted to tell her it was not any good. They gave her polite compliments instead.

William didn't even know it was possible to screw up tuna casserole, but he kept that thought to himself.

Kitty stood up, tossed her napkin over her plate, and announced, "We're going out."

Evie and William took them to Pizzeria La Cucina where they all enjoyed pizza, salad, and wine along with laughter and great conversation. At one point, Evie sat back and watched her boyfriend tell her parents about playing football in high school. Her parents seemed engaged and quite enamored with him. She understood why, of course. William was charming and handsome, intelligent and witty. She fell in love with him long before she ever admitted it. She leaned back in her chair and realized everyone fell in love with William, but he loved *her* unconditionally, and that made her feel all warm inside.

William glanced over to Evie then ran his palm down her thigh until he found her hand and grasped it possessively in his own.

Richard was in the middle of a story about his days on the rowing team at Yale when he received a call and excused himself. He walked outside and stood in front of the large window as he discussed something that appeared to be business to everyone at the table, except William. William knew the call was about Tom and he wrapped his arm around Evie's shoulders bringing her close and kissing her on the head.

Their good-byes were said with heavy emotion and

Evie's heart was full of love when she hugged her mother. As the women hugged, William shook Richard's hand, leaned in, and whispered, "I'd like to be there."

No further explanation was needed. Like William, Richard also planned to be there, front and center, for Tom's arrest. "I'll call you."

With a nod, a bond had been formed. They were now on the same team, working together to right Thomas Whitney's wrongs.

Chapter 34

Friday morning, William and Evie had just arrived on campus when his phone rang. He looked down surprised to be getting a call so early in the day. When he saw who it was, he stopped walking, and answered immediately. "Hello?" With his eyes on Evie, he listened to her father give the details of Tom's fate. "I'll be there. I agree it's best if she's not there."

Evie was puzzled and searched his face for clues to the call, but none of it made any sense to her.

"Thank you. I'll see you then," William said before hanging up. "We need to talk."

Her chest filled with concern as he took her by the elbow and led her to a secluded part of the sidewalk. She went because she trusted him, but every siren was sounding in her head. "What is it? What's happening?"

"Tom's gonna be arrested today."

"What? Why?" she asked, confused.

"Your dad would like to talk to you about that, but I want to be there. I need to see justice being served."

She closed her eyes, and shook her head. "I don't want you near him. He's dangerous."

"I told your father I'd be there and I need to see this through. Do you know how many times I've wanted to hurt him, the feelings of rage he's responsible for—"

She placed her hands on his chest, stepped closer, and lowered her voice. "But you didn't act on that rage. You're not like him."

"He hurt you..." His words caught in his throat as his anger swelled. William cleared his throat and wrapped his arms around her. "I need to be there so I don't take matters into my own hands. I need to watch him fall from glory. I need to make sure he knows he'll never come near you again."

"He needs to know I'm yours, William. All yours forever more." She lifted up on her tiptoes and kissed him. She understood he could be the kind man she fell in love with and still have that tough, protective side to him. What she loved more was that he could control himself, and never cause her to be afraid. With him, she knew she was safe.

"I don't want you there, Evie." His voice was stern, leaving no option.

She agreed. "I don't want to see him again, but I do have a morbid curiosity. I can't let that jeopardize his arrest. Whatever my father has on him, it must be serious. I need you to promise me you'll stay away from him."

"I'll just be there as a witness."

* * *

Across town and hours later, Tom was on a distressing call. "What do you mean I can't access the money?" He raised his voice as his fist slammed down on his desk. "Everleigh Wright is my fiancée. We share everything." He listened as the incompetent banker rattled on about policy, but interrupted because he was too impatient for the man's excuses. "It's my money! She doesn't make the decisions on it, I do. Get your supervisor out of his meeting because my fiancée and I are coming down there to settle this matter once and for all."

He slammed the phone down as he stared at the photo of him and his fiancée from three years ago. Everleigh was smiling in the picture, and he remembered it being genuine back then, not fake like the smiles he'd gotten used to seeing from her. He ran his finger over the glass above her cheek then picked the solid silver frame up and threw it as hard as he could against the far wall.

Time slowed as it flew through the air and shattered on impact.

The relief he hoped he would feel didn't come. Instead, his heart raced as it pounded in his chest. The broken frame didn't change the fact that she chose a kid from Staten Island over him. He hadn't come to terms with the implications this insult would bring when people found out. He'd become good at lying to everyone over the last month.

Everleigh stayed home because she's not feeling well.

Everleigh wished she could have been here tonight, but she has an exam in the morning she needed to study for.

Everleigh went to the Hamptons for the weekend.

Lie after lie, his anger grew during their time apart, but his name being taken off the account was the end for him. She would be his again. His money would be his again, or there would be hell to pay. They would be rich, and married, and together. Life would be how it was always meant to be. He took three short, stilted breaths, and headed for the door, not caring if he stepped on glass from the broken frame along the way.

When he entered the lobby, the receptionist called to him. "Mr. Whitney, the board is waiting for you in the large conference room."

"Damn it," he mumbled. He'd forgotten about the meeting today. He huffed his displeasure and stalked his way down the hall already planning his excuse to leave early.

He opened the door with impatience and stepped into the room. All six members of the board were already seated, and his seat at the head of the table was empty, left for him as expected. He started to close the door when he saw the others: The two police officers, on his personal payroll, and Richard Wright.

Tom slipped into character so easily that he almost laughed out loud at his acting talents. "Richard!" he said with a huge smile on his face. He walked toward him to shake his hand. "Good to see you." *Richard is my ticket to Everleigh. What a stroke of luck today.*

Richard didn't accept his offered hand. He stuck his hands in his pockets instead, and said, "I think you should sit, Tom."

Tom's fake smile faltered, but he agreed. "All right. Are you here on business since you're in my board meeting?"

The door closed just as Tom sat at the head of the table on the opposite side of the room. That's when their eyes met. William stared right back at him. "What the hell is he doing here?" Tom stood, hands planted on the table in front of him. His eyes darted to the police officers which made no sense for them to be in this meeting, the same two officers he paid to back him up two months earlier. "Arrest him for trespassing on private property," he demanded, pointing at William.

Richard leaned with his hands planted on the other side of the table. "Actually, you're the one being arrested." He stood straight up, strong and firm. "You have embezzled money from the company that your family built, you've set it up for a corporate takeover, the government is looking into your taxes, and you assaulted my daughter on numerous occasions."

"Prove it, Richard."

"I don't have to. Your sloppy cover-up is proof enough."

Not caring about Richard or the company any longer, his anger flared as he stared at the man who was his undoing. He wouldn't go down without a fight, especially not to some punk kid from one of the boroughs. William didn't waver under his direct glare and that irked Tom inside, so he yelled at him. "I'm Thomas Whitney. Who are you? You're nobody, and you'll never be anybody important in this world. This is the big leagues now. Did you come to play?"

"I won't play your sick games. I don't have to because the one thing, the only thing that will ever matter to me is that I'm Evie's somebody."

"Everleigh!" Tom shouted. "Her name is Everleigh!"

William didn't react to his words.

Tom watched as he crossed his arms over his chest and smirked—smug and satisfied. *How dare he! How dare he look down on me!*

All notions of right and wrong, charades, and cares left Tom as he leapt onto the table and ran across the top. Lunging at William, he swung as hard as he could. He would take him down. He would be the one to pay. Tom's body slammed into William and they hit the corner wall, falling into a heap. Both men fought to get the upper hand.

William kneed him then threw an upper cut that sent Tom to the floor gasping for air as he balled up to protect himself. The officers jumped into action, yanking his arms behind his back and handcuffing him before rolling him onto his stomach, and pressing a foot between his shoulder blades to still him.

He found some satisfaction in the fact he'd caused William some pain, but his own pain, both physical and emotional he felt right then far outweighed his joy. This couldn't be his ending. No way. "Get these cuffs off of me, you idiots. You work for me."

The burly officer smiled, and said, "We actually work for the City of New York and it's a good day when we get to arrest the real bad guy."

"Bad guy? I'm Thomas Whitney. Look at the name on the wall. Whitney Industries! Whitney, you asshole! You've arrested the wrong guy."

Richard squatted down next to Tom. "It's a division of The Wright Corporation now. Your role in the company has been dissolved. Your family no longer owns any part of this company thanks to you."

The first cop sighed loudly. "Listen man, don't make this harder than it has to be. Just play nice and let the company go. You're fighting a losing battle here."

Looking over his shoulder at the officer, Tom got the message. With his cheek against the expensive Berber carpet he'd chosen just six months prior, Tom watched

Everleigh's father help William up, offering him a tissue for the blood on his face. That's when he realized he had been set up, ambushed.

William sauntered closer, standing above him. "Good work, gentleman. I'll sleep better knowing the streets are safer tonight." Then he bent down, and whispered, "Don't ever come near Everleigh or myself, or anyone in our family again. I'm warning you. I won't play fair, and I won't play nice next time."

It was all becoming clear—he'd lost. He had lost everything: His money, his company, and Everleigh.

He watched William walk out of the room, followed by Richard, and the board members, two of whom stepped over him to get out of the room in a hurry.

"I'm fucked, aren't I?" Tom asked, needing someone on his side.

"Royally," was the only reply the officer gave him before he started reading him his rights. "You have the right to remain silent..."

* * *

The following Sunday, Evie and William walked into the Wright home, welcomed with open arms for a dinner that was becoming tradition.

William waited for Richard to speak, knowing he knew more of the logistics of the situation. "Tom was arrested. He's in custody downtown."

"Why was he arrested?" Kitty asked, shocked.

Richard Wright paused, worried his family might think him weak for seeking revenge, but he needed to repair his relationship with Everleigh, and that meant telling her the truth. "I'm not proud of much these days and you might think less of me for doing this, but I'll admit I found some pleasure in it. I bought Tom's company."

"You what?" Evie felt sick to her stomach. "How could you do that? How could you," she said, standing up. She threw her napkin onto the table. "How could you attach us to his family, to him, like that?"

Tears filled her eyes as William stood up and started to rub her back to comfort her. "Evie, you've got to hear him out. It's not what you're thinking."

Richard also stood up, his face falling as he watched his daughter's hurt and disappointed face.

She stared at him needing more, pleading with her eyes to correct her assumption.

"I bought it to take him down. That's what I'm not proud of. I bought it to get revenge on him. I bought it in a moment of weakness on his part, maybe on mine, too."

"Tell her about the books," William added.

Evie sat back down with the two men doing the same.

Richard continued. "I had my accountants go over the books with a fine-toothed comb. They discovered he was embezzling money right out from under the company's nose."

"His family has money. You know this. You're friends with his parents." Evie's tears had stopped as questions flooded her thoughts. "How is that possible?"

"I guess he didn't tell his parents he needed help. It's a white-collar crime, but this morning he had his bail revoked because he's on suicide watch. They want to make sure he stands trial. There are some issues with taxes and the government won't drop the case."

Evie knew she shouldn't, but she did care—just a little. She remembered the good in him, the good times they had together before he changed, before she changed. She took a sip of her wine and then said, "I'm feeling tired. This was a lot of fun and meant more to me than you know." She looked at her parents. "Thank you for supporting me and William."

"Are you okay?" Kitty asked her.

"Yeah, it's a lot to take in. I understand the sentiment behind what you did and I can't say I'm upset over that. I want him to pay in every way possible, but killing himself . . . I just can't believe it's come to this."

The dinner was cut short, no one in the mood for socializing. They said their good-byes and William held her hand when they left. He let her have time to process the events of the night as they headed home. He walked beside her in the warm night air, but let her think.

Several times she looked at him and they caught eyes. They smiled. Their relationship was easy, trusting, and blissful. Evie swung their hands between them, and said, "I don't care about him in that way."

"I know you don't."

"I'm in shock. I can't believe he'd kill himself."

"He won't."

"How do you know?"

"He loves himself too much for that. He's trying to garner sympathy." William was positive of that.

Evie stopped and tugged him to her. "I'm sorry."

"I know you don't care about him. It's that you care about people in general. Someone's hurt and you don't

369

want anyone to be in pain. You tried to make everyone else happy at the expense of your own happiness. You've got a big heart and I know it's not that you have feelings for Tom. It's that you wouldn't want anyone to hurt."

"You're amazing, you know that?"

"The bruises and stuff have healed, Evie, but you still have a lot to resolve, emotionally."

She was quiet in thought again.

William didn't want the night to end thinking about Tom. *He* didn't deserve their attention. "C'mon on, pretty girl, I have plans for you and that big 'ole heart of yours."

She smiled at the insinuation. "My heart, huh?"

"Well, maybe not your heart in the physical sense other than making it race, but definitely this area covering your heart." He pointed straight at her chest, circling his finger in the air.

She stopped shocked by his sexual boldness, but she loved hearing him talk like this. "My boobs?"

"Evie, you have incredible boobs and I still love that you call them boobs." He pulled her along again until they were walking. "And yes, I'm going to do lots of dirty things with and to them."

"Breast is way too formal of a term." She giggled. "I love you, you know?"

"Yeah, I know." That comment from him warranted a whack on the arm. "Okay, okay, I love you too, baby." He laughed, making her laugh as well.

Chapter 35

Evie and William arrived home a little after eight-thirty at night. She felt like she had another pound of burden lifted from her shoulders with each step she took. Several times she looked down at William's hand that held hers as they walked, still somewhat in disbelief this was it. They were now free from the monster and the past. They could now move on together and live their lives.

As they rounded the corner to the apartment, Evie took off racing. William was right behind her laughing as he watched all her worries disappear. It was beautiful the way her skirt blew behind her and her hair flowed in the breeze. She was beautiful. He grabbed her by the waist right before they reached the front door of their building and spun her around, catching her before she lost her balance.

They laughed and panted, trying to catch their breath. *Freedom*. This is what freedom felt like. It had been many years since Evie felt freedom: Freedom from *him*, freedom from the constraints of social standards and expectations, freedom to love, freedom to live and breathe and be who she was meant to be. Freedom was wonderful.

She stood on her tiptoes and grabbed William by the

face and kissed him—hard. She smiled, blushing, and said, "I want you to make love to me."

William didn't wait. He grabbed her by the hand and pulled her in through the main door, up the flight of stairs, and once he unlocked the door, inside the apartment.

They didn't bother with lamps or lights of any sort. The light from the street was enough for them to see each other and their surroundings.

They wasted no time and took their clothes off. Illuminated from behind by the dim light, she was an angel, a sexy angel wearing a necklace more befitting the occasion than could have been planned. The light highlighted the silver bird on the chain escaping its cage, gleaming in the low light. The monster kept her locked away, her own life like a cage. William freed her.

She held her head up, looking at him wordlessly. Eyeing his body up and down twice, she lingered on his midsection which is when she raised an eyebrow. She wasn't insecure with William. She was quite the opposite. He let her have wants of her own, to explore what she liked, and she wasn't judged. She was confident when she was with him.

They stood in front of each other with their emotions and bodies exposed and vulnerable and yet they felt none of that. They both felt loved, powerful, and comfortable like this, together.

Reaching out, she dragged her palm down his chest, winding her fingers through the light hair that adorned his skin and stopping at his belly button, twisting her wrist to where her fingers faced down and moved lower.

William's breathing picked up and she felt his heavy breath against own skin. He leaned forward and kissed her, his hands grabbed a hold of her hips, and he moved them to the bed. "Come here, baby."

Crawling onto the bed, she lay down next to him, his hands roaming her body as she closed her eyes. William watched her chest start to rise and fall as his fingers slid between her thighs. This was still so surreal to him that he got to be with her at all, much less touch her in such provocative and sexual ways.

She opened her eyes as his fingers found the place that sent shivers through her body.

Leaning down, he kissed her on the lips once then on her cheek, forehead, temple, then made his way down her neck and back up toward her ear. His warm breath made her skin pebble as he tugged her earlobe between his teeth. "William." She moaned as her hands found his skin hot to the touch and she gripped him to her. "You're teasing me."

He stilled his fingers and his mouth. "Oh, baby, I'm sorry," he whispered in her ear. "I want all of you at once, but still want to savor every part of you, starting here." Increasing the pressure beneath his fingers tips, he also nipped harder.

She became of puddle of goo beneath his hands and lips, beneath his words.

He smiled against her neck, a chuckle followed closely after. They had made love many times since the first time and he was happy to give her what she wanted and what she needed. William reached over into the drawer of the little table beside the bed and pulled a condom out. He slipped it on and touched her at the apex of her thighs. As he rubbed little pressure-pointed circles, he moved into position between her legs.

William stopped touching her, holding himself above her and looking down into her eyes. He could tell she felt safe and trusted him. He could also see how much she wanted him and hoped she could see the same reflected from him. He positioned himself while taking her hands, bringing one at a time to his lips to kiss then placing above her head. As he held on tight to her wrists, he pushed into her.

Her head pressed back into the pillow beneath her, and his dropped from the overwhelming sensation and they groaned each other's name in unison.

Opening his eyes, he watched her writhe below him in pleasure then let his eyes drift to where they were connected, feeling the intensity of their bond.

She wrapped her legs around him, encouraging him for more, her body moving of its own volition in tune with his every movement. Not long after starting, they finished together, cuddling and whispering words of love and devotion, the future, and forever.

The next day, Evie woke up bright and early, mainly due to the fact that the blinds were left open from the night before. She turned her head and saw William facing her with his eyes still closed, his face beautiful and rugged, content with a slight smile curled on his lips. She kissed him lightly so as not to disturb him before rolling out of bed.

William grabbed her by the elbow, and muttered, "No, stay. Bed. Me."

"I love you, but I've got to shower, honey."

A grunt of disappointment was all she got in return.

It was Monday morning and as they walked out of their building, her dad was waiting in front of his town car, which was parked at the curb. They stopped, somewhat surprised to see him, somewhat happy, and somewhat nervous. "Dad?"

"Good morning, Everleigh, William."

"Good morning, Richard," William replied, holding tight to Evie's hand. This was an odd time to visit, especially since they all saw each other last night. He was guarded and feeling very protective of Evie right then.

"There's been a strange discovery, and I need your opinion, Everleigh."

"Okay." She was cautious.

Richard glanced to William. He was well aware nothing was kept a secret between the two of them, so he didn't request privacy. He also got straight to the point. "Mr. Whitney put some of his assets in your name. They were hidden in a side account. His company, now my company, has no rights over them since his name is not listed as the primary holder. I need to know how you would like to proceed with these accounts."

She stepped forward. "I'm confused. Why would there be anything in my name?"

"I don't have the answers. I only know what we've found. I'd advise you to come by this afternoon and look the papers over. I can have my accountants and lawyer there if you have questions. It's several large sums of money. You should act quickly," Richard said, closing the gap and embracing his daughter. "How are you?"

She smiled as she hugged him back. "I just saw you last night, Daddy."

"I know, but I missed you."

She felt such happiness in her father's arms, realizing the name 'Daddy' slipped out.

"Evie," William started to say as he stepped forward, "you don't work today. I think you should go after class and settle this sooner than later."

She turned around, and asked, "Will you come with me?"

"I'm out at three today. I can go with you then. Are you sure you want me there? I know this is a personal matter."

She smiled at him, turning and taking his hand in hers. "I want you there. I have no secrets. We have no secrets."

He nodded.

Turning back to her father, she said, "We'll be there at three-thirty."

"I'll see you then." Richard leaned forward and shook William's hand. "Good to see you as well, William."

"Did you miss me too, Sir?"

They laughed. "Yes, well, I guess I did." They continued laughing.

William met Evie outside the English building just after three. She was sitting on the nearest bench and was stunning in the autumn afternoon. The sun was golden and bright, revealing the different colors highlighted by the waves she now wore, shades that were hidden when she lived in darkness all the time.

They took a cab to the financial district and walked through the lobby of the high-rise. William felt underdressed and tried to straighten some of the wrinkles out of his shirt as they entered the elevator.

Evie walked with confidence past the three gatekeepers and straight into her father's office without knocking.

After a quick greeting, two of his accountants and his legal advisor joined them and they set up at the large table by the window. They went through and explained how they thought Tom was scamming by trying to hide the money from the government in some way. The silver lining is the auditors had been contacted, and if Evie pays the due taxes on the new accounts, she could have full claim to the remaining dollars.

As they walked back out the building an hour later, William asked, "Hey, for old time sake, you want to go for a ferry ride?"

"I'd love to."

They caught the next ferry, but remained in a bit of a daze from the meeting.

"Evie?"

She turned to William and just seeing his face made her relax. She cuddled into his side, the wind blowing around them as they stood on the deck of the ferry and the sun started to set. "How are you?" she asked, tilting her head up to see the truth in his expression.

"I'm fine. How are you?"

"Believe it or not, I'm great. He set those accounts up to dupe the government and used me to take the fall. My dad said he'll help me pay the taxes to make the accounts legal if it means Tom will never see a penny again."

William didn't fear Tom. William feared him having any part in their lives, including his money. "What are you going to do with it?"

She looked back down, resting her cheek on his chest. "I don't know."

That would have to suffice for now for both of them.

"Is it silly to feel this good?" Evie asked William once they made it home and climbed into bed later that night.

"No, not silly. Not silly at all. I feel the same." He rolled onto his side and wrapped his around her.

She rubbed her hand up and down his arm, feeling his muscles as they flexed under the skin.

William sat up, easing his brow with his fingers. "I don't want us to change or for his money to come between us." Looking down at his bent knees, he sat there quiet in thought.

A minute passed, and Evie was anxious from the silence, so she said, "It won't. On the ferry tonight, I realized I want the money to mean something and make a difference to someone. It means nothing to me. It's a bad reminder of him, so I'm giving it to the women's shelter that I helped to raise money for at the fundraiser."

William lay back down next to her. "I think that's a great idea."

"I'm going to have my father make the transfer in the morning, an anonymous donation. I don't want the glory. I just want it to be used for something good."

"Evie, you don't know what that means to hear you say that. I know four million is a lot of money, but it's blood money—"

"I have no problem ridding him from of our lives. I want no part of anything to do with him ever again."

"He's out of our lives for good now. Our future can now begin."

Chapter 36

In early November, William surprised Evie by meeting her after class. He talked her into taking another ferry ride despite the chilly weather. She thought they were going to visit his family, but they got on a different ferry—the ferry that took passengers around Manhattan.

William wrapped his arms around her, her back to his chest and they watched the cityscape before them. As they rounded the curve of the river, when they were just about to be shaded by the skyscrapers, he got down on one knee, held her hand in his, and asked her to be his forever.

After wiping her tears away, she pulled him to his feet before grabbing him around the neck and saying, "Yes. Yes. A thousand yeses." As he slid a delicate gold band with a small inset diamond on her finger, she gasped. Her sentimental side recognized the ring and she was overcome with pure joy. Evie kissed him again. "Is this my great-grandmother's ring?"

"Yes, your mother gave it to me in case I was planning something like this."

"My mother has fallen in love with you. She's been trying to get you into the family since she met you . . . well, since you came to dinner that first time."

"She made it easy for me. She said you would like the ring. I hope you do."

"I love it. My great-grandfather came from a fortune, but he hadn't inherited it when he married my great-grandmother. This ring was all they could afford. It cost him twenty-eight dollars in 1926, which was his entire savings. They were our age when they married."

William smiled at his soon-to-be bride. "I was hoping we could marry right after your graduation. Is that too soon?"

"It's never too soon to start forever with you, my love."

When they docked, they took a cab straight to her parent's home to share the news with her family. He called his family on speakerphone to join in the celebration. The moms started in on their elaborate plans, but this time Evie would have her fairytale wedding. It wouldn't be conventional for her family's expectations, but instead be everything she wanted and nothing she didn't.

In mid-December, both of their families gathered at her graduation. They stood and cheered as she walked across the stage to accept her degree. William and Evie had a private celebration just the two of them at the apartment over Mexican food and tequila.

She decided tonight was the night to reveal the only secret she had been keeping from him for his own sake and sanity. So, after two shots and a full stomach, she tried for casual, and said, "We need to talk about money, but I'm afraid you'll get upset."

"Why would I get upset?"

"Sometimes you seem to have issues talking about money."

"I don't have issues talking about money. I have issues wi—"

"Just let me get this off my chest, okay?" She turned to face him, crisscrossing her legs in front of her. "I have a trust fund. My grandparents set up a trust on my behalf." He could see how nervous she was, so he took her hand and held it in his lap as she spoke. "Audrey has one, too. We both do."

"All right, so you have money you'll get one day."

"Exactly. When I'm twenty-five, I'll inherit it. But, I thought you should know it might be a lot."

"Have you always known about it?"

"Uh-huh."

"Okay, one day we'll get a few thousand. It's rightfully yours to do with as you please. Do you want me to sign a pre-nup?"

"No, no. That's not why I'm bringing it up. The money is ours. I don't want a pre-nup and it might be more than a few thousand." The last few words rushed from her mouth.

"Do you know how much it is?"

"No, it's supposed to remain sealed until received so my life path wasn't altered by it, but they were wealthy."

"Okay, a hundred thousand or so." He had a great idea. "That will help with our retirement fund then." William leaned over and kissed her.

Evie didn't have the heart to tell him it would be in

the millions because she didn't want to overwhelm him. She had three more years before she had to deal with it anyway.

A few days before Christmas, William and Evie exchanged vows in an intimate ceremony inside the New York Public Library Genealogy Room. Once married, the doors opened and they ran out hand-in–hand, and were greeted by their families, including Dallas and Audrey, who had become attached at the hip, Bobby, Tracy, Professor Lang, and Walter. Flower petals rained down on them as they jumped into a waiting taxi and headed to their favorite park wanting to spend a few minutes together there alone. On the ride over, she picked a lone pink petal off of his hair and smiled. The petal reminded her of how much her life had changed from that first defiant act of visiting the park last spring. Remembering the blooms she saw that day in the park to the flower petal she held in her hand, she felt her life had come full circle. Her happily ever after was as real as the rose petal she now cherished. She tucked it inside her small clutch, planning on saving it forever.

Evie leaned against her husband and kissed him over and over on his lips and chin and jaw and cheeks. William used the large tree, their tree, as support, holding his bride in his arms and enjoying her mouth on him and affections.

He stopped her before she pulled away. "Please don't ever stop kissing me, Mrs. Ryder."

After placing one last quick peck on his lips, she said, "I will kiss you forever, my dear husband. You have made me the happiest woman in the world."

"Words can't describe the happiness I feel. I love you, my beautiful wife." He smiled, cocking one eyebrow up, and added, "I really like this wife business. You are officially my wife."

"Yes, I am."

A few minutes after they strolled through the park, they caught another cab and headed to Pizzeria La Cucina for their small reception. Everyone cheered as they entered and greeted them with hugs and kisses. Champagne was served and then William dragged his new wife over to the cake, but Evie started tearing up as soon as she saw there was no cake. Instead, there was a table full of blueberry muffin tops and no bottoms. "I made the decision that you should have all the best things in life on this day and that means just the tops for you, my love."

"You are the most wonderful man." Evie stroked his cheek then joked with him. "Did it hurt to know that all those bottoms went to waste?"

"I couldn't bear it." With his hand over his heart, he pointed with the other to the miniature cake boxes at each place setting. "Everyone is going home with a muffin bottom as their favor." They both laughed then kissed, which would have been inappropriate if she had invited her high society acquaintances, but she didn't and their guests, family and real friends, enjoyed seeing the display of love and cheered some more.

After dinner and the toasts, the minister approached. "We need to make it official before you go running off on your honeymoon." He flattened their marriage certificate on the table and held out a blue ink fountain pen.

William was quick to correct the situation as Evie looked on in horror. "Don't worry, I've got this." He pulled a black-inked pen from his suit pocket and her face softened into a smile. They each signed their names and sealed the deal with a kiss.

By the end of the festive afternoon, a car awaited the newlyweds in front of the restaurant. They hugged everyone good-bye, grabbed their suitcases, and hopped in. Richard Wright handed William an envelope as they shook hands once more and patted him on the back. "I know you'll take care of her and I'm proud to call you son."

William thanked him and slid closer to Evie. As the driver pulled into rush hour traffic, William turned to his wife, feeling all the love they had ever shared. "You've made me the happiest man alive. Thank you for marrying me."

She couldn't resist him. She pulled his face toward her and kissed him deeply, letting him know exactly how she felt.

A few hours and a lot of snuggling and making out later, the couple pulled up to the Wrights' Hamptons beach home. William carried his bride over the threshold and they rushed to the kitchen, starved from their day's festivities. They found a mini buffet set up by her family, and each made a plate. Sitting at the bar together, still in their wedding attire, they didn't want to be apart from the other even for a second.

After eating, Evie put a CD on as William poured the whiskey. He handed her a glass to toast. "Bottoms up, Mrs. Ryder."

"Figuratively or literally?"

"Both."

"Whiskey, though?"

"Yeah, whiskey," he replied with a sexy smirk.

Another shot later they made it half way up the stairs before their clothes went flying. Evie tripped in the high heels, landing on her bottom on the top step.

William climbed up, stalking, until he was hovering over her. "This will work."

The newlyweds spent a blissful weekend together making love, teasing, and loving each other completely.

On Sunday morning, they discovered a fruit tray left in the fridge for them. Picking out a strawberry and biting into it, Evie saw the envelope from her father on the island. "What's this?"

William eyed it before remembering Richard giving it to him on Friday. "Your dad gave it to me when we were leaving. I forgot about it." She handed it to him figuring if it was given to him, he should be the one to open it.

William slipped the flap open and pulled what appeared to be a large contract out. Confused and curious, he looked it over for clues to what it was exactly. His eyes settled on his address, but he didn't understand why his address was listed.

He flipped to the title of the document again then back to his address. In a whisper, still not fully comprehending, he said, "I think your parents bought our apartment and gave it to us as a wedding gift."

Evie jumped up, grabbing the document from his hands, and exclaimed, "What?" She skimmed the main parts of the front page and gulped. "No, William. I don't think so—"

He pointed to the line where it listed the building's address. "Yeah, I think so. It says something about 'titles to said listed properties' right here."

"No, I mean, I think they bought the whole building."

His jaw dropped open just as Evie rushed him, almost knocking him off the barstool. "They bought the building! Your parents bought us the building?"

She smiled, rubbing soothing circles on his back as she held him. "Yes, they did, babe."

They spend a good portion of the ride back to the city going over the document in full, line by line and making sure they understood it.

When it finally sunk in, they realized they were now the proud owners of a four story worn-down pre-war building in a relatively safe part of Manhattan.

When the newly married couple returned to their apartment, they found a pile of mail stuffed in their mailbox. "Wait here," he said, dashing up the stairs with their bags and dumping them outside the apartment door. He ran back down stairs, kissed her on the forehead and they continued up the stairs together, this time William insisting he carry his bride up to the second floor. As he acted strong and brave, she could feel his arms starting to shake a little below her and hoped he could make it to the landing before dropping her.

Holding her while she worked the keys and unlocked the door, he ran in, setting her down in the middle of the room. "There," he announced, proudly. "Welcome home, Mrs. Ryder."

"Who's my big strong husband?" Her words were laced with sarcasm, but it didn't shrink his ego. He turned back and grabbed their suitcases out from the hall. When he re-entered, Evie was holding an envelope between her fingers "What's this? It's from Pepperdine. That's in California."

He rushed toward her, almost knocking her over while grabbing it out of her hand. "Um, I don't—"

"Um . . . hmm. You must really want it if you're tackling me for it. Well, open it." She started unpacking her bag leaving him alone with his precious envelope.

After he read over the letter for the third time, he stood up. "I got in." He looked at her and said, "I got a job, too, babe."

She reached out and took the letter from him, reading what it said. Her eyes darted up, meeting his eyes in astonishment. "You got into Pepperdine in California?"

He nodded. "Lang wrote a letter on my behalf recommending me for the job after I told him I wanted to get away and do my Master's degree there. I kind of forgot about applying there last summer with all we were going through." Excitement brightened his eyes. "What do you think?"

She read over the letter before giving her opinion. "I think it's an offer we shouldn't refuse. I mean it's a Teaching Assistant position with a stipend and you've put it off long enough. I've graduated now, so there's no reason not to follow your dream."

"You'd move to California? What about your family?" William looked around his apartment feeling a bit emotional. "What about the apartment and building? We now own them."

She held her hand up, flashing her wedding ring, and said, "This says I go where you go. I can get a job in publishing out in California. There are some great companies there and you can't pass up this opportunity. My family can visit us. We can visit them." She sighed, feeling a little nostalgic over the tiny apartment. "We can keep the building, rent it out."

"We only have three weeks. So, California, huh?"

"California, here we come."

Chapter 37

Within two weeks of ownership, they changed the building to be rent-controlled and Dallas moved into their studio apartment. Their families got together and threw a huge going away barbeque at his parent's house on Staten Island and they didn't let winter dampen their party.

Four days later, William and Evie walked into their new home, a small one bedroom bungalow on the beach in Malibu. Her parents offered to pay the rent while he finished school to give them one less worry, and they accepted.

He started school the next day. At five o'clock, he walked through the front door to find Evie making the bed. She stopped and turned, jumping up on him and wrapping her legs around his middle while covering his face with kisses.

Slamming the door shut behind him, he flopped with her still attached, onto the bed.

They made out for a few minutes before he caught a breath of air. "I see the bed was delivered, but why is it in the middle of the living room, baby?"

She straddled him, grabbing him by the lapels, and said, "We'll get to that. First, welcome home, Mr. Ryder. How was your day?"

He took the strap of his messenger bag, a survivor from the move from New York, from over his head and let it land on the floor next to the bed.

"That's sexy."

"The mister part or me?"

"You calling me that."

He pulled her down on top of him then rolled over on top of her, settling between her boy-short-clad legs. They kissed passionately and laughed hard.

"I thought we could christen the new bed before dinner." She sat up, stripping his shirt off and working on his pants.

"Sometimes, I think you only have a one track mind, Mrs. Ryder, and I like it. Actually, I love it."

They made love, making a mess of the newly made bed. Afterward, they were lying together looking at the ocean through the huge sliding glass doors a few feet in front of them. He kissed her on the head and nodded, smiling. "Now, I understand why the bed is in the middle of the living room."

She kissed him on the shoulder where she was tucked, his arm secure around her. "I loved our apartment and wanted to create the same cozy feeling here; just one main living space. So the bedroom is now a walk-in closet. I brought way too much stuff from my bedroom at my parents' home. Oh and it's here because of how amazing it will be to wake up to that view every morning."

William could never tell her no. "Sounds like a

brilliant idea, although it might get awkward when we have friends over."

She laughed. "Eh, we'll figure that out. Anyways, the weather is perfect here. We can entertain on the deck."

He never minded giving into her. He loved all her sides and moods, and wanted to support her being her, which at this moment meant making a living room into a bedroom and a bedroom into a closet to store her massive amount of clothes.

Within a month of their arrival in California, Evie found an entry-level job at a local publishing house. She loved it. It paid almost nothing, but she still loved it. William had settled into his job and used his time between classes and some evenings to work on a book he began writing because he still had goals of being published one day. By July, he typed 'The End' on his manuscript.

Lying next to his wife at sunset, William lifted her shirt and kissed the bump. "How are you in there, sweet baby? Can you hear daddy?" He kissed her belly one more time and rubbed soothing circles with his hand flat against her skin as she looked down at her adoring husband. "I love you and your mommy with all my heart, baby."

Evie ruffled his hair and smiled at her beautiful husband. Falling back onto the pillows next to him, they spent the remainder of the day in bed, loving their life.

* * *

A year and a half later, Evie rushed into the bookstore in Century City grasping a tiny hand in hers. She didn't expect all the challenging tantrums she had to deal with that morning. When she entered, she saw William at the podium reading an excerpt from his book. Picking her son up, she whispered, "Look, there's daddy."

"Daddy!" the child screamed, causing William to look up, temporarily making him lose his place. He saw the two of them at the back of the bookstore, and smiled. After a few glances from customers who were sitting in the audience waiting for him to continue, he looked back down at the overly highlighted text and continued reading where he left off. The night before, Evie teased him about his highlighter habit and jokingly suggested he seek professional help once again for his addiction. The memory made him chuckle and stumble over his words. She still didn't realize that she was his only true addiction. Well, she and their son to be more accurate.

After the reading, Evie and her son reached the front of the line and she set her purchased book down on the table, and asked, "Will you make it out to Max please?"

William laughed. "I have ten copies at home. You didn't need to buy one, baby." He stood up, walking around the table, and kissed his wife then rubbed the top of his son's head. He was tempted to pick him up, but he knew he needed to get back to his book signing.

"I wanted to buy one and I want it personalized to 'my handsome son' from his 'daddy.'"

William sat back down, opened the jacket of the hard bound book, and wrote:

To my son, Max. You are the light of my life and your mother is the guiding path I travel. I love you always, Daddy.

P.S. Don't forget to floss and brush your teeth every night.

P.P.S. Hey look, your mom will be so proud, I used black ink.

Evie smirked at William then turned to Max. "Your

daddy is a very smart man, baby boy." She nuzzled him quickly, and took the book. "So, you're going to the book party after you finish here?"

"We have a babysitter, right?"

"Yes, I'm taking Max home now. The sitter will be there in half an hour and then I can join you."

"I have a better idea. There's this restaurant I've been wanting to try with an inn located right next store. What do you say we skip the party and try those out instead tonight?" William used his most charming smile as he asked his wife out on a date.

She shook her head, and laughed. "You are going to miss a party being thrown in your honor to hang out with me?"

"I'm hoping to do more than just hang out, baby. Anyway, I'm here now. I can only handle so many accolades before they start going straight to my head, feeding my ego," he teased.

She laughed again. No one made her laugh or as happy as her husband did. "Okay, Mr. Ryder, but we still have to be home by eleven."

"I think I can handle that."

"We'll see how much you can handle later." She winked at him.

They sealed their plans with a kiss before she took their son and left the bookstore.

Almost two hours later, Evie and William sat across from each other at a very intimate bistro. She smiled as she handed him a letter. "This came for you today."

He quickly examined the return address and glanced

back up. "Our alma mater, huh?"

As William read the letter, Evie watched him carefully. She could see the happy glint in his eyes and had a gut feeling what the letter might say, but waited for him to share.

"Professor Lang is looking for someone to take over his position when he moves into the Director role in the fall. He wants me to be a part of the British Literature program. The program is small and would be a good challenge, but do you want to move back to New York, baby?" he asked, placing his hand over hers.

"It would be nice to be near both our families again. I miss them, but I love the sun and the life we've built here. As I've always said, home for me is with you no matter where we are."

"This is a good opportunity and I miss our families." He took a sip of wine and then offered his glass to her.

She smiled, and shook her head. "No, neither baby nor I want any wine, but thanks for asking."

"If we move back to Manhattan, you might have to go back to work. Or, we could live out on Staten Island near my folks and I could commute. That way we could afford for you to continue to stay home with the kids."

"I love being home with Max and I want to be at home for this baby, too," Evie said, rubbing her stomach. "By the way, have you come up with a name for this little one yet?"

"I'm thinking Elizabeth?"

Evie's eyes lit up, and she repeated the name in her head. "Elizabeth is perfect! Elizabeth Ryder. It's beautiful. It was also my great-grandmother's name."

"It made sense since it was her wedding ring." William continued as Evie twirled the gold ring around on her finger. "I hoped you'd like that name."

They spent so much time at the bistro talking about their future and all the options and possibilities of being back in the New York area that they didn't have time for the rendezvous at the inn next door.

After arriving home and checking on their sleeping baby, William joined Evie on their deck overlooking the ocean. He wrapped his arms around her, and she whispered, "We can live in Manhattan if you want."

"I'm sorry, honey, but the job pays decent, but not for a family of four in Manhattan, and I don't want you to feel like you have to work if you don't want."

She turned in his arms, her large belly pressing into his toned one, face to face. "My birthday is next month."

"Did you think of something you'd like as a gift, something I can buy you? I know last week you said you didn't need anything, but birthdays aren't about needs, they're about wants."

"I inherit my trust fund from my grandparents next month." She just said it. She stood there, resting her hands on his chest and silently let him digest the information.

"I'd forgotten about that. The extra money would probably be enough to supplement for you to stay home. But we should probably consider one of the boroughs or Staten Island. Manhattan real estate is crazy expensive."

"William, we can live close to your parents if you really want. I think they're great and Max loves them to death. I think it's a healthy place for kids to grow up. I mean, look how great you turned out." She paused. "I don't want you to freak out or anything though, okay?" William gulped and looked concerned, but nodded in agreement anyway. "I received the paperwork necessary to receive the fund and it's a lot of money, more than we thought." She rubbed his chest lightly as if to comfort and calm him.

"How much more?"

She could hear the nervous strain in his tone. "Don't freak out, all right?"

"Evie, just tell me."

"Ten million dollars." She said it carefully and cautiously.

"Ten million dollars!"

"Remember, it's just money, honey. Money is not evil. We can use it or not use it however we want. William? William?"

By this point, William went into a mild form of shock.

Evie backed him up until the back of his knees bumped into the chair, forcing him to sit. Holding his shoulders, she asked, "Are you alright, babe?"

"I uh... uh, I, uh... I." He shook his head in disbelief.

"Babe, it's there if we need or want it. It's security for a life that's already perfect. It's money that will help us to not have to struggle so hard sometimes. Please say something."

William's eyes trailed down her body until he came across her belly. He leaned forward and kissed it, then whispered, "Your mommy is a very rich lady, baby Elizabeth."

Evie tilted his chin up to look at her and corrected

him, "We're rich together. Always together, remember? And, if you take that job, I want to live in Manhattan. I want to be able to have lunch together and I don't want you wasting time riding the ferry back and forth when you could be home with us already. We'll have this money and if you want, we can sell the building."

"I don't think we'll need to sell the building. It's solid income." He smiled and stood, not able to deny her. "I'll do anything for you, my love. Manhattan, here we come." He punctuated his words with a kiss on the nose.

* * *

A year later, Evie left her favorite little park pushing her stroller with baby Elizabeth inside and Max in tow. They caught a cab and waited on a bench outside the Literature building where William now taught. When he walked out, Max ran to him, almost knocking him over. William swiftly swung him into the air then carried him over to greet his wife and daughter.

"You get more beautiful every day, baby," he said before kissing Evie entirely inappropriately for a teacher on school property, but neither of them cared.

She laughed as he leaned down and kissed the baby. She said, "We should go. My parents hate when we're late."

"They had nannies to prepare the kids. We don't, by choice, of course, baby, but they don't remember the challenges of having youngsters." He took Max's hand and they walked the few blocks to Pizzeria La Cucina.

When the family arrived, the hostess escorted them to the private room in the back. William immediately set Max down who began to run around the table after greeting his grandparents.

Richard and Kitty Wright got lost in baby babble as

Kitty took Elizabeth right out of Evie's arms, and Richard chased Max. "I thought they loved us, too," William joked.

"No, we're just the people who brought them their grandkids to play with." Evie laughed out loud, enjoying the togetherness.

After they finished off the second bottle of wine, Kitty leaned closer as if she was going to share a secret. "We wanted to talk to you kids about something important."

'Something important' always meant money. *Evie knew this.* William did not.

Kitty sat back in her chair, taking her husband's hand with pride as Richard said, "We're leaving you almost everything when we pass. Well, Audrey gets half, but we don't want to burden her with talk of this at this stage in her life."

William's head turned toward Evie who placed her hand on his thigh. "It's all right," she whispered. Then she directed her attention back to her parents. "Dad, that's very kind, but you know you don't have to talk about it if you don't want, and we have our grandparent's money from the trust still."

Richard raised a hand in the air to silence her. "I know, but we're adults and should be able to talk about this. We're leaving some of the money, well a lot of the money, to charity, the same women's charity that you work with. I was always impressed by your generosity, time, and energy, Evie. We'll also be using some to cover retirement expenses. We set aside a portion for Audrey as well. We thought you should know that we don't want you to worry about money. We love you, all four of you so much, and we're proud of the woman you've become and the choices you've made." Evie teared up as Richard directed his attention toward William. "You've also made us proud and you've become a fine man, William. This way we can make sure you're taken care of, so please don't argue and accept the money when we pass."

William leaned across the table, and shook his hand. "Thank you, sir. Thank you for thinking of us."

Kitty cheerfully chimed in, adding, "I hope you use some of the twenty million to travel. I know you kids have always wanted to travel."

William's jaw dropped open and once again, he slipped into a mild form of shock. Evie took his face in her hands, and reminded him, "It's just money. Money is not evil. We can use it or not use it however we want."

"Twenty million dollars!"

"Remember, you and me together always."

He looked her in the eyes and saw them alight with love and happiness. "Yes, you're right. You and me together always."

The End.

About the Author

S.L. Scott has a degree in Journalism and is the author of the novel, *Naturally, Charlie, Good Vibrations*, and several novellas, including *Sleeping with Mr. Sexy* and *Morning Glory—all currently* available on Amazon. Pursuing her passion for telling stories, she spends her days escaping into her characters, letting them lead her on their adventures. She is a Contributor to Huffington Post as well as writes for her own blog along with several other popular sites.

Travelling, music festivals, and surfing are a few of her hobbies she loves, but she doesn't get to enjoy on a regular basis. She has an obsession with movies, a varied taste in books, and collects Fitz & Floyd teapots. With a memory full of useless trivia facts, and a Keurig addiction, she loves a fun night in with her family as much as a loud night out with her friends.

Scott lives in the lively city of Austin with her husband, two young sons, and two Papillons, enjoying life in the beautiful hill country of Texas.

www.slscottauthor.com

If you or anyone you know is experiencing abuse and need and/or want help, please contact the

National Domestic Violence Hotline at

www.thehotline.org

or call 1–800–799–SAFE (7233)

www.ingramcontent.com/pod-product-compliance
Lightning Source LLC
Chambersburg PA
CBHW020506260626
47156CB00006B/1893